Out and Proud

Lisa Young

Yellow Rose Books

ISBN 978-1-61929-392-2

First Edition 2018

9 8 7 6 5 4 3 2 1

Cover design by AcornGraphics

Published by:

Regal Crest Enterprises

Find us on the World Wide Web at
http://www.regalcrest.biz

Published in the United States of America

Acknowledgments

I would like to offer my heartfelt thanks to Cathy Bryerose of Regal Crest Enterprises. Thank you for believing in me and allowing me the opportunity to fulfill my childhood dream of becoming a published writer.

To Sheena Billett, my first editor, thank you for your enduring support and patience throughout the initial editing process of the manuscript. You are truly talented and your advice and guidance helped me to grow as a new writer. I now consider you a lifelong friend.

My gratitude to Ann McMan, the talented graphic designer responsible for my book cover, and to the inspirational Nat Burns, my book editor, for your words of wisdom and kind praise during the final editing process.

Thanks, and love, to my friends who endured endless discussions about my characters and the plot of this book, especially Victoria Burrows. Your faith and encouragement have helped me more than you will ever know. Special thanks to Emma Allcock, my greatest supporter and to Marie Bower for the inspirational wedding speech.

My love and respect goes to Sam Jenkins, a great friend and the talented designer of my website lisayoungauthor.com.

Special thanks goes to my sons, Oliver and Sam. You have, and continue to be, a daily inspiration to me both in my writing and as I watch you develop into the phenomenal men you are becoming. You both live in my heart daily.

Lastly, but most importantly, I would like to give a special mention to my amazing wife, Lucy. This journey began when you finally pushed me out of my comfort zone, in front of my computer and with the promise of an endless supply of whiskey while we holidayed in that sweet cottage in Pennan. You believed I could do this long before I did and you were right. We completed this journey together. You held me steady and pushed me past the inevitable writer's block. You are the inspiration for this book and I am so honoured to have created this story with you. This book, quite simply, could not have happened without you. I love you always.

Dedication

I dedicate this book to all those women who have found the courage to become their true selves, and to all of those who are embarking upon their journey.

Part One

New Experiences

POISED ABOVE HER girlfriend and trembling with anticipation, a single bead of sweat trickled down Lottie's flushed face. Trying to look confident and hoping to exude an air of sexual dominance, she leaned forward and immediately became aware of the elastic waistband of the strap-on cutting uncomfortably into her sides. Pausing for a moment, she wriggled and adjusted the strap slightly, her discomfort only serving as a reminder of the newness of this experience. She inadvertently held her breath.

My first strap-on lesbian sex ever. Here goes!

Her girlfriend, Alice, appeared to be swept up in the moment as she parted her legs slightly and looked towards Lottie, her eyes hooded with lust. Encouraged, Lottie gently lowered herself until their breasts brushed. A delicious thrill of anticipation tingled up her spine.

With a committed thrust, Lottie aimed blindly with the strap-on until she felt the plastic protrusion make contact with Alice's body.

"Ouch!" exclaimed Alice.

Oblivious to her partner's protestations, Lottie's brow furrowed with concentration as she lunged forward once again, confident she was now inside the object of her desire. Below her Alice had frozen, causing Lottie to pause as she belatedly registered Alice's cry of pain. Lottie hadn't expected that reaction. Too rough maybe?

Unsure of what might have provoked the pained squeal, she decided to try and cover her inexperience with a confident smile. Once again, she thrust blindly forward, her smile widening with the expectation of the pleasure she was undoubtedly delivering to the delicious Alice. Gaining some momentum, she inwardly high-fived herself, she hadn't thought it would be so easy! Alice writhed beneath her in what, Lottie concluded, could only be spasms of ecstasy.

EARLIER THAT DAY, Lottie had sought advice from an online website, dearpru.com. She had joined the lesbian site some months previously, looking for support on the journey to release her inner lesbian at the grand age of thirty-nine.

Through the awkward, early months of dating women, Lottie had gained some invaluable advice from an online guru, who claimed to have vast experience in affairs of the lesbian heart. Prudence had strongly advised Lottie that there was no need to confess to Alice that she had limited experience with lesbian sex, or that she had never used sex toys. Lottie had felt this was somewhat dishonest, but Prudence had reminded her of the importance of presenting a front of sexual confidence, particularly in lesbian relationships, where aloofness was considered attractive. Lottie had to agree that showing her sexual inexperience was likely to be off-putting for Alice, who, no doubt had a lifetime of steamy lesbian encounters.

Prudence had been somewhat disparaging about Lottie's late coming out, and she had commented that she now needed to embrace wholeheartedly her true self. Lottie was still discovering who her true self was, but she had appreciated the sentiment. With no gay friends, other than Virginia, a recently acquired work acquaintance, and little in the way of sympathetic confidantes, Lottie had relied heavily on the advice of Prudence.

Pru, as she liked to be called by her clients, prided herself on her mature years and claimed to have a number of professional qualifications in counselling and holistic therapies. She plied her services through her website where visitors could receive help and advice. She also ran a group for those who wished to meet up, but Lottie had avoided this so far. Having finally been able to accept her inner lesbian, Lottie had regularly accessed the site to request advice on the variety of dating dilemmas she encountered during her coming out process. As a mother of two children and previously married, coming out in later life had proved to be an embarrassing and difficult experience for her.

"STOP! STOP! *STOP*, Lottie!" Alice frantically wriggled away from the protrusion and pounded wildly on Lottie's back.

Lottie could not help but feel a smattering of irritation at being halted in her stride, convinced she had been developing a steady rhythm.

Alice continued to struggle in a bid to get Lottie to stop. "You're heading to the wrong hole, Lots, *wrong hole!*"

Hearing those words, Lottie was horrified and froze mid-stroke. Oh my God, wrong hole? Surely not!

Hastily pulling away the tool of intended pleasure, she made eye contact with Alice who was clawing her way up the bed to a sitting position. Lottie realised that the way Alice was looking at her was less than lustful. Reaching down to her delicate area, Alice tentatively checked herself to ensure her perineum had remained intact. Establishing that all was well, she slumped forward onto a pillow and burst into an uncontrollable bout of laughter.

Large tears rolled down both of her cheeks as she tried, and failed, to find her words. Instead she pointed at Lottie shaking her finger towards the now ludicrously wobbling plastic penis, which was still attached to the shamed Lottie. "Christ, Lottie, you've turned it into a weapon of mass destruction. Go steady with that thing, will you?"

Lottie glanced past Alice and noted a shiny wet nose and two soft brown eyes peering hopefully at the side of the bed. Odie, Alice's dachshund, was attempting to indicate his interest in getting onto the bed, oblivious to the disaster unfolding in his mistress's boudoir. His stubby legs provided insufficient jumping power to assist him in his desire to nuzzle down into the comfort of the thick duvet, which was his only self-interested aim.

Following Lottie's gaze, Alice spotted the interloper and swatted at him with her free hand. "Go away, Odie. Go and find your bone!"

Odie reluctantly took the hint and loped back to his bed in the corner.

Lottie had to admit she felt more than a little shocked by her shoddy aim, which was clearly hindering her virgin attempt to master the strap-on. She felt a pang of regret that she hadn't been more honest with Alice about her lack of experience with sex toys when they'd been discussing them earlier that evening. Somewhere, between the first bottle of intoxicating Pinot and the second, she had felt that she could handle pretty much anything new that was thrown at her, so strong was her sexual chemistry with Alice. Although it was only their second date, the intimate setting of Alice's plush pad and the casual nature of their conversation had inevitably set the scene for a sexually charged encounter. Alice, who clearly wasn't a heavy drinker, was more than a little giddy as she had introduced the subject of Lottie's sexual experiences with other women. Lottie, as she discovered Alice's interest in all things plastic and vibrating, had given a vastly inflated account of her knowledge of lesbian sex toys.

As the evening had progressed, with much assistance from alcohol, both Alice and Lottie knew they had a mutual interest in one another. Lottie felt that this was an interest not solely reliant on their obvious sexual chemistry. She was overwhelmed with excitement, and marvelled at how strongly connected she felt to Alice. Alice was a confident, always been out lesbian, who had a few serious relationships under her belt. From their discussions, Lottie knew that Alice wasn't desperate for a relationship and was simply relishing her position in the small rural community as the local veterinarian.

Lottie's observations to date found Alice to be intelligent, with an easy sophistication, and a slender boyish figure. Her hair was the traditional lesbian spike, dark with delicate flecks of ginger, betraying her Highland heritage. Lottie, by contrast, was two years older and had the more squishy body type one would expect after two pregnancies, but she was still proud of her pert bosom. She lacked Alice's confidence, partly due to her previous thirty-nine years as a closeted lesbian. What they both shared however, was a phenomenal sense of humour for all things inappropriate. In the many phone calls preceding this second date they had spent hours sharing their stories and dreams. Both Alice and Lottie had a strong desire for a stable and honest relationship and this was the foundation on which they had met for their second date.

When the effect of the wine wore off, Lottie acquired a sober perspective of her failed sexual prowess. She had so desperately wished that this would be a night that Alice would not forget, but for reasons of passion rather than possible anal penetration. Although she'd made a hash of her first attempt, she remained stoically undeterred.

She moved forward towards Alice for a second time. In her head, Lottie was trying to stem the flow of self-doubt, but she couldn't help noticing that Alice's expression was one of sheepish distrust—not the lustful look that Lottie had hoped to inspire. Lottie breathed deeply in an attempt to steady her nerve and tried to recreate the moment. Anxious to make a better job of it this time, Lottie wisely used her hand to locate the correct hole. Please God, don't let me make that mistake again, she silently begged. Tentatively, she aimed the tool and entered Alice.

It felt right. Was it the right target?

She noticed that Alice was groaning and was giving her a look of encouragement as her head lolled backward.

Lottie steadied herself in readiness. *I'm in. Let's do this!*

She ground her hips with renewed vigour as she tried to anticipate the direction of the cold hard plastic piece that was a newly acquired limb of her body. How on earth do people know how to control this thing? If she had to describe it to a stranger she would say that it reminded her of lying on her own arm for too long and then trying to tie her shoelaces. Virtually impossible.

With a renewed mental effort, she brought her mind back to the job at hand. It's all about the rhythm, she counselled herself as she gradually gained confidence and built up to a faster pace. Alice lay motionless beneath her, but it was difficult for Lottie to gauge her performance while trying to manage her exertion, as she became increasingly breathless. She had hoped for a more enthusiastic reaction but was glad of the stillness while she worked hard to establish a regular motion.

Several moments had passed before Lottie realised she'd been holding her breath. Suddenly, desperate for air, she let out a loud gasp. Aware that her panting was less than sexy she attempted to stifle her desperation to suck air into her lungs. At the same time, she realised that a heavy sheen of sweat was collecting on her forehead, running down her face and gathering between her pert breasts. Determined not to show Alice the huge effort she was making, Lottie tried to steady her breathing, but to no avail as the sheen of sweat quickly became a stream flowing freely between her breasts and down the crevice of her back as she continued to pound away.

After a few more moments, she could no longer contain her desperate need to breathe. Alice, meanwhile, was eying her with undisguised curiosity. Lottie smiled with what she hoped was reassurance, but she was also becoming aware that her heart was pounding and her breath was rasping. She finally collapsed in an undignified heap over the naked body of Alice, who had once again been overtaken by a fit of uncontrollable giggling.

With spittle flying out of her mouth, Alice cried with undisguised amusement. "Oh, Lottie, why didn't you tell me you're a strap-on virgin?"

A gentle shiver of horror crept across Lottie's mortified face, as she debated continuing her ruse of a sexually experienced woman. Alice grinned at her with fondness and amusement, and Lottie realised the game was up. Shrugging, she signalled defeat. Alice smiled back at Lottie as she took off the plastic weapon of mass destruction, which she threw to the floor with a sigh of resignation. Lottie caught a glimpse of herself in the mirrored wardrobe door and realised with horror that she looked as if she had run a marathon. Her face was tomato red and her short blonde hair shot out wildly in all directions, as if she'd had a thousand volts coursing through her body. She couldn't help but smile as she looked at the caricature of her once-dignified self.

Meanwhile, hearing the dull thud of plastic hitting the laminate floor, Odie skittered excitedly back to the edge of the bed and eyed them with a considerable degree of undisguised suspicion, before he settled himself down next to the strap-on which he started to chew.

"No, Odie!" they both shouted in unison, as Alice leapt from the bed to remove the offending article before gently chastising the dog.

Looking more than a little put out, Odie emitted a disgruntled yelp, before exiting the room to a round of fresh laughter from the now hysterical pair.

Man Predator

THE NEXT DAY at work, Lottie was finding it hard to concentrate as she waited impatiently for her break. She worked as a call centre operative for the local newspaper, the Fraserburgh Guardian in Aberdeenshire, Scotland, and the day was turning out to be particularly busy with a flurry of calls, as the public celebrated or commiserated their life events in various advertising columns. Lottie was glad that the events of the preceding evening remained firmly in the private domain, but she was finding it impossibly hard to concentrate on her work as she was bombarded with embarrassing flashbacks.

After getting home in the early hours, Lottie had sought counsel from Dear Pru. She had posted a question asking whether she should be instigating a discussion with Alice about her disastrous attempt with the strap-on, or whether she should try to ignore it and hope that things would move on naturally. Given Pru's advanced years, Lottie felt a certain sense of reluctance in asking about her technique with sex toys, feeling that it was somehow disrespectful. But then again, Pru was a self-proclaimed expert in all areas of relationships, or so she loudly and proudly stated on her website. She also reminded her readers, frequently, that she was an experienced counsellor, and so Lottie consoled herself with the thought it was probably something Pru would have heard on many occasions. Between calls, Lottie impatiently checked her phone, and noted that there were no responses to date.

While she waited for the clock to hit the golden hour and the arrival of her break, she was flooded with renewed anxiety. She comforted herself with the knowledge that, aside from the past night's humiliation, she had tried hard to embrace her inner lesbian since she finally came out a year ago. Lottie had wholeheartedly thrown herself into the dating pool. With the encouragement of her friend Mel, she had registered on several gay dating websites and had familiarised herself with the gay club scene in Aberdeen. There had been varying degrees of embarrassment, which Lottie preferred not to recall, as she had experimented with a procession of casual partners. However, she took some reassurance at her progress since the earlier days of inexperienced fumbling, as she had expanded her knowledge and technique as a lover of women. Lottie had lost her lesbian virginity to a kind and generous, but nameless, sexual partner in whom she had been able to confide her inexperience. Nevertheless, this latest debacle with Alice felt like a significant setback and it served as a reminder to her that she was very much a late comer to this party.

Satisfied that she had mastered the basics of oral, fingering, and frottage, Lottie had yet to encounter the infamous strap-on until Alice had produced it from the naughty drawer the previous night.

"Bugger," Lottie mumbled aloud.

She was wracked with pangs of regret that her fear of being judged by others had led her to delay her coming out. She was painfully aware that her lack of sexual experience with women was a direct result of these fears, and she worried that this would handicap her relationship with Alice, where she was desperate to be seen as a sexual equal. Checking her phone for the hundredth time that morning she noted no message from Alice. Fuck, she thought, I've blown it. Although they'd parted on good terms, she had a lingering doubt that her less than fabulous bedroom performance may have put Alice off.

Her finger hovered above the accept new call button on her workstation but she fell short of pushing it as her thoughts wandered, and she inwardly cringed as her mind flooded with memories of her inexperienced sexual encounters during the past months. The wrong hole epic had definitely ranked at the top of her most cringeworthy experiences to date.

Lottie sighed and her finger traced Alice's name on the desk. She was devastated to think that the past night could have slowed such a promising start for her and for Alice. Shaking her head in an attempt to regain her focus, she chastised herself, and reasoned — well, two holes, it's so confusing and they are so bloody close together. She wondered whether she was always going to feel like a born again lesbian virgin forever.

One thing Lottie knew for sure was that she had seriously underestimated the differences between sex with men and sex with women. Despite her dislike of the penis, hairy chests and sperm, she had children and so knew what was required of a woman in pleasuring a man. In all things heterosexual, Lottie knew that generally men were pretty simple to please and usually took the lead. Sleeping with a woman, however, required her to be more proactive and there did not seem to be a particular role she could adopt. She had assumed that following her more innate and natural sexual desire to be with a woman would inevitably make her first experiences with women more spontaneous. After all, this was what she really wanted.

Lottie had always known, deep down, that she was attracted to women, but she had so desperately wanted children that she had tried to bury her fleeting attraction to other females. With a wry smile she acknowledged that it was inevitable that her true self would eventually surface, and she knew for sure that she did not regret it. After having her two sons, she felt less need to masquerade as something she was not, and the process of becoming her real self had released a reservoir of energy and enthusiasm for her new life which had previously been banked, while managing her continued deception as a heterosexual woman.

She glanced idly around her sparse workspace, noting the lack of photographic evidence of her outside life. Colleagues had commented on her blank pin board, fishing for details of her world, but Lottie had decided that when she started her new job she wouldn't be as out and proud as she had previously been. After several failed promotion attempts in her previous job, including a run-in with a lecherous supervisor who wanted to watch, she had decided that being out at work was probably more trouble than it was worth. Nevertheless, the difficulties in maintaining a conversation while referring to a sexless partner had not been lost on her.

Virginia, a gay colleague and, increasingly, a close friend, seemed to manage this with ease, and could often talk for up to an hour without revealing that her partner was a female. Lottie, on the other hand, had always found this an incredibly difficult task, with conversations quickly becoming disjointed while Lottie stumbled out her sentences in an attempt to keep the conversation in a neutral sexless zone.

Lost in her own thoughts, Lottie failed to notice the triangular lights on the wall illuminating in unison, indicating an increase in the call volumes coming through.

An authoritative shriek from her supervisor about forty calls waiting shook Lottie back to the present and she hurriedly fake-typed to buy herself a few more precious minutes of thinking time before she returned to the monotonous world of classified advertising.

To her left sat Linda Lovely, a talkative and slightly scatter-brained colleague who was difficult to ignore. Lottie could feel Linda's curious eyes boring into the back of her head, hoping for some eye contact that would be her cue to chatter. Lottie had deliberately turned her chair to prevent any accidental eye contact with Linda.

Lottie found Linda an odd, yet endearing soul. At the age of twenty-eight, Linda was fully ripened for marriage and babies. Lottie accepted that most women of that age were preparing to step into the next stage of life, but she couldn't help but think that Linda's lack of success so far was partly, or almost completely, due to the air of desperation she exuded. It was not lost on Lottie, or any of the call centre crew for that matter, that Linda was a full-fledged man predator. Lottie determined that Linda must have a built-in new man radar which efficiently detected a fresh testosterone presence within fifty feet of her regular seat in their workplace. Her unusually long neck allowed her to give a good impression of a meerkat in heat if a male specimen appeared in her sights.

When Linda was appraising, or rather stalking, her potential prey, she would begin in a relatively subtle way, starting with the odd surreptitious glance. However, as the testosterone filled her nostrils and the subject got closer in proximity, her self-restraint rapidly became severely compromised. Without fail, she became increasingly excitable, glancing nervously around as she monitored the competition of other singletons in the office who might also have eyes on her prize. If she was able to establish that she was a lone hunter, her arousal levels hit the roof. Her waist length hair, dyed black and frazzled by over drying, resembled the fine strands of candy floss, and a once-natural curl had been reduced to a wild frizz. Unfortunately, she viewed her hair as one of her seduction tools and she would wildly toss her mane in an attempt to gain attention. Sadly, oblivious to her own ever more excited state, she would begin to giggle nervously but with a pitch almost too high for the human ear to process. The volume of this high-pitched giggle would inevitably increase, resulting in a simultaneous snort as she frantically calculated how she could fake an encounter with the unfortunate target. Linda also had another distinguishing feature, a pronounced limp from a childhood injury. When in a state of heightened excitement this limp would become more obvious and she would become clumsy, often walking with a lurching gait as she headed towards the male object of her affections.

This time, the arrival of Jonno, the son of the local sandwich shop owner, kindly delivering a lunch order, was the trigger. Grabbing a copy of her *Sponsored Slim* form, Linda waved in an

attempt to attract his attention. Hoping to halt his progress
through the office, she leapt to her feet and lurched towards him
snorting and giggling simultaneously. Lottie had observed this
dance of the hunted prey on a number of previous occasions, her
own amusement overridden by mortal embarrassment on Linda's
behalf, as she registered the panic of the selected target. In an
attempt to maintain an appropriate boundary, Jonno gave a stiff
nod, hastily placing his basket of wares as a physical barrier
between himself and the mad one. Lottie noticed that he smiled
politely, without making eye contact while he skilfully side-
stepped Linda as she stumbled forward. She caught her foot on a
bin and landed in an undignified heap in the space which he had
occupied only seconds before.

Without looking back, he moved swiftly towards the exit,
expertly depositing sandwiches on desks without stopping to
chat, while continuing his journey away from Linda's desperate
clutches. With an inevitable look of utter defeat and rejection,
Linda lurched back to her desk next to Lottie and consoled herself
by leafing furiously through the latest edition of *Bride* magazine,
her constant companion at work. Lottie risked a small concerned
smile. Attempting to demonstrate her solidarity while avoiding
any committed eye contact, she focused instead on Linda's pin
board which proudly displayed a variety of elaborate wedding
gown cut outs, ideas for table decorations, and the latest in glitzy
Aberdeen wedding venues, which were numbered in order of
preference.

Feeling sorry for Linda but nevertheless glad of the
distraction from her own misery, Lottie cringed as she took an
appraising look at Linda's choice of workwear for that day. Linda
was a firm fan of the motto T-shirt. Lottie was pretty sure it was
virtually impossible to buy T-shirts with marriage quotes from
the local shopping centre and she feared that Linda had mail-
ordered her custom-made attire, which appropriately reflected
her dedication to the quest for marriage. Today's T-shirt
contained a quote she recognised from Jane Austen's *Pride and
Prejudice*.

```
It is a truth universally acknowledged, that a
single man in possession of a good fortune, must
be in want of a wife.
```

Lottie inwardly shook her head as she dragged her attention
back to her workstation. Glancing at the clock, her thoughts

returned to her own sexual exploits, and she desperately wanted to discuss her feelings in more detail with her new friend and colleague, Virginia.

Lottie and Virginia had met some months earlier when they had both auditioned for parts in a local amateur production of *Tipping the Velvet*. Even after being chosen by the *New York Times* as their book of the year in 1998, it seemed that the locals of the village of Pennan, where Lottie lived, had not been ready for the lesbian-themed voyage of self-discovery and first love. Once the local village council had caught wind of the intended lesbian-themed subject matter, a meeting had been hastily convened. The members had voted unanimously that the church hall should not be available for such a pornographic depiction of first love. The self-appointed director, a local bohemian female sculptress with an undisclosed sexual history, was quickly dispatched and a newly appointed director, who also happened to be the longest standing member of the primary school Parent Teacher Association, was ceremoniously appointed. After a short discussion, it was agreed that they would opt instead for a safe production of *Gregory's Girl*, a wholesome heterosexual tale of coming of age and love in a small town. Much to their disappointment, both Lottie and Virginia had secured minor non-speaking roles as part of the crowd in the girl meets boy scene.

Unsatisfied with their acting debuts, they had bonded over their disappointment and shortly thereafter took similar positions in the call centre offices of the local newspaper, as telesales operatives in the classifieds advertising section. The happier outcome was that they had quickly developed a satisfying and mutually supportive friendship. It helped that Virginia was forgiving of Lottie's late coming out, and was happy to provide advice and support to Lottie as she blundered from one dating disaster to the next. Virginia showered Lottie with love and support as she battled to establish herself as the newly-birthed lesbian of the village of Pennan.

A loud siren screech again jolted Lottie back to her telesales reality, as her frazzled supervisor swept through the office waving with near hysteria at the flashing lights on the wall. The siren heralded an unacceptable level of forty-three calls which were patiently awaiting an answer. The office descended into a flurry of activity, and Lottie reluctantly clicked her accept new call button, aware that an encounter with a grieving widow calling to place an *In Memoriam* advert for the anniversary of the death of her dearly-departed spouse would considerably jeopardise the possibility that she could coincide with Virginia in the canteen for break.

However, she was in luck, and after quickly dispatching a call from a poodle breeder, she left the office to the relative sanctuary of the canteen, where Virginia beamed a greeting. She waved her towards their usual table, on which was a latte grande and a substantial slab of deliciously heavy lemon cake. Lottie plonked herself down unceremoniously and sighed. Virginia smiled in anticipation and raised an inquisitive eyebrow as she waited for a blow-by-blow account of the past night's date with Alice.

Aware her back was becoming increasingly painful, Lottie adjusted her position on the cheap plastic chair and tried to reach around to soothe it. Clearly, strap-on sex worked muscles she had previously been unaware of, and she inwardly smiled at the unplanned aerobic benefits of her workout.

Virginia rubbed her hands together and leaned forward in anticipation of the latest instalment in the saga of Lottie's love life.

Suddenly shy, Lottie reminded herself that Virginia had briefly had a fling with Alice before she had settled down with her long-term partner, the lovely Jess. Although Virginia had dismissed her knowledge of Alice as a drunken fumble, Lottie knew they'd dated for a few months. She couldn't help but feel a strange sense of disloyalty towards Alice as she contemplated discussing the details of the past night with her friend. Nevertheless, she was desperate to unburden herself to someone, and Virginia was a solid and reliable source of common sense. She seemed genuinely delighted about the blossoming relationship between the two and had expressed a fondness for Alice, who she thought was a thoroughly good catch. She also knew that Lottie had strong feelings for Alice, despite the newness of the relationship, and she had already revealed her opinion that they were very well matched.

Both women were animal crazy and as Alice was the local vet, it had been Virginia who had introduced them, as she struggled to get Lottie to understand that her cat had serious mental health issues and posed an imminent threat to the life and limb of any visitor who passed through the doors of Lottie's chaotic nest. It was an ongoing bone of contention between herself and Virginia, as Lottie continued to assert that her cat had anger management issues rather than a full-blown psychosis. She felt this was easily manageable if she kept Boots at a safe enough distance from any form of human contact. Of course, this had not been a fool proof plan and, after a particularly nasty incident involving a trip to accident and emergency with her youngest son's best friend who had come for tea, she had agreed to seek medical assistance for her personality-disordered pet and Virginia had recommended Alice.

While Alice had been compassionate about the difficulties of Boots the cat, after several return visits, she finally realised that Lottie had an ulterior motive for her appointments, and so she made the first move, asking Lottie out for coffee.

Lottie finished recounting her sorry tale of woe. Virginia mopped up the last of Lottie's untouched lemon cake and smiled a kind, wry grin. "Practice makes perfect?" she offered lamely.

Lottie sighed. "Oh, V, when will I ever make it in the world of lesbian sex?"

Virginia chuckled. "You already have, silly girl. It's all about the connection. Alice really likes you, and the rest will come with time."

As if to affirm the words of wise Virginia, Lottie's phone pinged with an incoming message from Alice which contained a variety of emojis including a heart and a picture of a flower.

Lottie smiled. She knew for a fact that Alice was worth it, and she was going to conquer her fear of the strap-on if it was the last thing she ever did.

Coming Out

THANKFULLY, THE WEEKEND soon arrived, and as Lottie skipped out of work on Friday evening she did the weekend dance. She drove home a little faster than usual, keen to deal with the wishes and wants of her two boys, Archie and Robbie, before she headed to Aberdeen for a well-deserved night out with her best friend, Mel.

As she slowed to negotiate the difficult descent to the small seaside village of Pennan, Lottie tried to do a mental inventory of the contents of the fridge. She was only too aware that as a parent of a teenager and a tween, she needed a well-stocked fridge and a plentiful supply of patience to deal with the day-to-day dramas of teenage living. Being a dating parent, she was concerned that, in recent months, her parental duties had suffered and so she was determined to rectify this before she headed out for a carefree night on the mojitos.

Expertly parking her little MINI adjacent to her cottage, she was careful to leave enough room for other cars to pass and access to the harbour ramp, which must always be kept clear. The small and picturesque village of Pennan was home to only a handful of residents, who all lived in a row of small cottages nestled into the rock at the bottom of the cliff side. Access to Pennan was via a single-lane road winding tightly around the cliff, with a sheer drop on one side, and stunning countryside with seasonal bright yellow gorse and purple heather on the other.

Lottie paused for a moment to breathe in the strong, salty air of the north-east Scottish coast, as the resident seagulls bickered between themselves about the abandoned scraps of a picnic. Lottie surveyed the small street and marvelled that she never grew tired of the dramatic coastal beauty of her home. At the bottom of the road was a small stony beach area where the occasional tourist, who had wandered off the coastal path, would uncover the hidden gem at the bottom of the steep and treacherous clifftops. Those lucky enough to discover the village would inevitably stay a while to enjoy a wee dram at the village pub. Lottie glanced across the familiar beach area to where the gulls had made homes in the crevices in the cliff side. In the early evening, they could be seen roosting, their unified squalls guiding in the final stragglers to settle as they saw out the darkness of the night. Mingled with the crash of the waves against the fallen rocks which formed a barrier to the edge of the cliff, the cacophony of sound was a soothing seaside lullaby to Lottie.

Sighing with deep satisfaction, she lifted the stiff latch on the cottage door and was greeted by all the signs of the teenage life form dwelling within. The monotone of rap music droned relentlessly down the stairs competing with the noise of the Disney channel coming from the TV in the living room. Assured that both boys were home and engaged in their various interests, she shouted a quick greeting.

Not expecting a reply, Lottie headed straight for the kitchen, where she hastily unpacked her purchases from the local supermarket, which included a packet of ready-made salad and an oven-ready pizza.

Setting the oven timer, she ran for the shower, only to find that the bathroom window was wide open, allowing in an icy blast which stopped her dead in her tracks. Leaning out to reach for the catch she paused to admire the spectacular view of the Pennan harbour, a view she could only truly appreciate from this vantage point. The sea rumbled endlessly on to meet the barely visible horizon, which was transforming before her eyes into a delicious pink hue with marshmallow-white puffs of cloud floating alongside the cliff tops. She smiled in appreciation and inhaled the distinctive smell of the sea, never failing to appreciate the beauty of her surroundings. Amongst the rocks she saw a regular visitor to the rock pools, a heron, who was systematically investigating the cool puddles hunting for a juicy morsel. The seagulls watched on, as the more daring members of their clan swooped and dived into the waves, successfully plucking out fish and returning to their cliff side homes.

Reluctantly, she leaned forward to shut the window, but as she did so, she spotted a pile of cigarette ends in the guttering of the kitchenette below.

Disappointed that Robbie was still smoking despite the extensive terrifying literature she had strategically strewn around the cottage, she bellowed for him. "Robbie!"

A hooded figure appeared from the nearby bedroom, trousers barely covering his boxer shorts and one hand tucked snuggly into his crotch, "Uh?" he grunted in reply.

Breathing deeply, Lottie spoke. "I've asked you to smoke outside. I would like you to collect the cigarette ends out of the gutter and put them in the bin where they should be. Stop bloody smoking!"

Pulling out his earphones, he glared at her with barely disguised contempt. "For God's sake, Mum, it wasn't me!"

Raising her eyebrows in disbelief she retorted quickly. "And who else might it have been then?"

Tutting loudly, Robbie leaned precariously out of the window to scoop up the evidence of his just-legal addiction. "Seagulls nesting or summat?" he offered unhelpfully.

Robbie threw the cigarette ends out of the window in the general direction of the bin. He tutted loudly once again, abandoned his unwelcome task, and returned to the darkened pit of his man cave.

Just then the cooker buzzer sounded, and saved Lottie from the inevitably pointless confrontation. She headed downstairs to plate up that evening's slightly crisped offerings, not forgetting to eat herself, as she needed to line her stomach.

Passing cautiously through the utility room, home to Boots, the emotionally-challenged tomcat, she gingerly reached out, intending to rub the top of his head. Snatching her hand back in panic, she recalled in the nick of time that he only liked to be approached from the front. Surprising him with affection was not an option, despite the rigorous medical interventions Alice had made, to address his stress issues. Making a mental note to ask Alice if male cats could experience the menopause, Lottie returned to the kitchen and divided the pizza onto three plates.

She entered the living room, precariously balancing two plates of pizza and salad with a can of fizzy orange, and approached the oblivious Archie, who was engrossed in the much-repeated *Wizards of Waverly Place*. Lottie gave an involuntary shudder and cringed as the American canned laughter bounced uncomfortably around the room.

Her youngest son, Archie, looked up with his almond-shaped hazel eyes. She smiled as he rose to greet her, marvelling at his ability to grow almost two inches overnight. She noted that he was now in desperate need of new trousers, as they flapped around his ankles, hitched up at the waist in a Simon Cowell-type fashion. She noticed he was clutching an envelope, which he offered to her with one hand, as the other gratefully received the singed pizza. Smiling, she settled down to read the latest in what was a steady stream of written affirmations her youngest son had been keen to bestow upon her after she'd shared with her children that she was gay.

As she sank into the worn sofa, she briefly recalled the differing reactions of her two children as she'd attempted to explain to them that she was now dating women. Robbie had been mildly disgusted, but had been able to explain that he had a very fit maths teacher and that he would be happy to put a good word in for her at the next parents' evening. Much to her amusement, some hours later he'd returned to seek her out, and the two of them had sat together, sides touching on the outside bench.

Robbie had offered his acceptance. "I don't care if you're gay, Mum, as long as you're not going to fancy my girlfriends!" Coyly, he'd placed his arm briefly around her shoulder, giving her a playful pat before his hood was once again pulled up and he returned to furious typing on his phone. She smiled at the memory, rare though they were these days. A close moment with her eldest son left her with a sense of pride and awe at the man he was becoming.

Archie had demonstrated his ever-present sensitivity and had stopped mid-prance in the living room as he practised dancing in her high heeled shoes. Practising for what, she didn't quite know. Flinging his arms around her with complete abandon, he told her that he loved her, no matter what. This, although no surprise to Lottie, was nevertheless a heart-warming reminder of the kindness of this wee man.

While opening the creased envelope, she noted the title of the page, *Best Mum Ever!* Reading on, she noted that Archie had catalogued her various positive attributes including the fact that she could play chess and always won. He noted that she also burned food, but that it always tasted good anyway. After listing her various friends and noting the difference between girls who were friends and girlfriends, he declared that being gay was okay and that no one was allowed to be mean to gay people, especially his own mum. Attempting to scoop him into her arms and failing, she instead chose to plant a kiss firmly on his lips, thanking him for the letter and promising to save it with the others. She hurriedly ate her pizza and headed for the delayed shower.

As she came down the stairs, both boys tore their eyes away from their electronic babysitters to give her the once-over.

She stepped into the room. "You look nice, Mum, but a bit gay," Robbie said.

Wondering briefly what gay actually looked like, and feeling ridiculously self-conscious, she tugged on her leather jacket and looked at Archie who beamed at her.

"Wow!"

After reminding Robbie of his babysitting responsibilities, she glanced guiltily around the sitting room, as the ironing pile called to her from the corner, reminding her of the jobs that never seemed to get done around the house. Never mind. Life's too short, she thought, as she firmly shut the front door behind her.

ARRIVING IN ABERDEEN an hour later, after paying the taxi driver, Lottie reluctantly entered the trendy city bar alone and perched uncomfortably on a stool while she waited for Mel. Aware of her friend's poor time management, she anticipated more than a bit of a wait so she ordered herself an iced, mint-laden delight, her old friend, the mojito. She self-consciously pulled down her top, avoiding the stares of the curious men around her, silently cursing her friend for being so determinedly straight. At least if you're going to make me hang out with the male species be on time to be my wing woman, she inwardly admonished Mel.

Following her confession to Mel about her attraction to women, Lottie recalled Mel's initial shock. Though she was pleasantly surprised at how quickly this had passed, she felt that as time had gone on, Mel had lived a new life of exploring relationships with the female sex somewhat vicariously through Lottie. Not that Mel wanted to be gay, but the difference of it appealed to her adventurous nature. This had included a day at an *Adopt a Cat* event run by the local RSPCA. All lesbians have cats, she'd assured Lottie after she had spent nearly an entire Saturday in her pyjamas using search engines to learn the facts of lesbian life. That particular adventure had led to Lottie's rash acquisition of Boots, who had seemed a beguiling tomcat, showing no signs of any mental disturbance.

As Lottie sipped her mojito and checked her phone for the inevitable running late text, she was reminded of the unforgettable night that she'd had with Mel, which had turned out to be coming out day for Lottie, in a rather unconventional way.

Having known one another since their school days, Mel and Lottie shared a friendship that had survived both their marriages. The various perils and pitfalls of post-divorce dating had cemented their bond, the only difference being that Mel was determinedly straight, and that Lottie had started to acknowledge one of the major contributing factors to her divorce was her own sexuality. Since Mel had been one of the few friends privy to Lottie's secret, she had taken this responsibility very seriously and had taken it upon herself to support Lottie in entering into the gay world. This being, of course, a world that Mel knew absolutely nothing about. With the enthusiasm of an untrained puppy, she catapulted Lottie into an uncomfortable but amusing rollercoaster ride of internet dating sites, pubs, and events she found on search engines during her lunch break at the mobile phone shop where she worked.

Smiling fondly, Lottie allowed herself to remember their first visit to the gay club scene of the granite-gray city of Aberdeen, where they had a mojito-fuelled night of dancing and exploration. In addition to discovering the delights of the mojito, the various highlights of that night—of which there were many—as Lottie recalled, was the kiss. In the dark and comforting environment of the dubiously named nightclub *Laydee,* and while severely intoxicated, Lottie had kissed a woman for the first time.

The memory of that kiss was etched indelibly in Lottie's memory, despite having had various experiences since then, and not negating the most perfect of kisses with Alice on their first date. Lottie remembered a slow motion walk across the crowded dance floor, as feeling brave and alive, she had walked towards the smiling invitation of the woman in the white dress. As the stranger took her hand, she had placed a finger under Lottie's chin and tilted it slightly before gently touching her lips to Lottie's. Lottie had shuddered with a ripple of excitement as she remembered the electricity that had passed through her in that brief encounter before they'd smiled and parted ways.

Her first lesbian kiss!

She remembered Mel's look of pure ecstasy, as she clearly felt entirely responsible for successful mission of meet woman, kiss woman. Lottie later described it to Virginia as a moment where, in the world of the club, completely accepted for who she was, the kiss had somehow determined her future.

The evening had progressed and she had made a somewhat drunken but determined resolution to share her news with people, and she recalled an alcohol-fuelled haze of happiness. They had resolved to celebrate with a few more cocktails, which had been on special offer, at five for ten.

Arriving home later that night with Mel, Lottie had begrudgingly paid the second taxi fare of the evening. Although she loved the remote location of her home, it certainly had its disadvantages when she wanted to spend some time in the city.

Cackling hysterically, between them they had somehow made it to Lottie's back door and after several efforts to locate the keyhole, Mel had confidently clambered up the steps and through the door, tripping and entering the kitchen in a not dissimilar way to the taxi exit performed by Lottie.

"Fuuuuck!" she screeched as she'd fallen head-first into the used cat litter tray at the far side of the kitchen.

Lottie had left it there in the hope that Robbie would clean it out.

Concerned for her friend, Lottie had dashed unsteadily forward as Mel lifted her head with some effort and grinned inanely in her direction. Collapsing against the fridge, Mel had hiccupped loudly. "What a fucking amazing night!"

LOTTIE SMILED AT the memory as she ordered a second drink. She cradled it, turning towards the door to look for her friend. She gave way to an involuntary shudder as she relived what had followed next. While the consequences remained emblazoned on her memory, the details of the actual events that transpired were thankfully little more than sketchy.

What she did recall was that she and Mel had logged onto her Facebook account, as they had both had a burning urge to share with their community the pictorial evidence of their most fabulous night out. Downloading pictures of the various drinks and locations of their rampage through the city, Lottie seemed to remember that pictures were almost always more interesting when they had a caption so she typed:

I kissed a girl and I liked it—as in the song!

Late morning of that same day, she had made her way gingerly along the landing, side-stepping the trail of dried cat litter while trying to breathe through her mouth so as not to tempt her delicate gag reflex. Deep in the recesses of her brain she was aware of a steady throb indicating the oncoming hangover and a vague recollection of Facebook antics. She peered into the spare room but saw only a mound of empty duvet. She headed downstairs to the computer.

Logging on with trepidation, her worst fears were confirmed as she scrolled down and read the forty-three comments on her captioned photo. She recalled with increasing horror, that the photograph she had posted had been her and Mel giving their best pout to the camera while at an undisclosed location.

Those less hungover had logged on to the news, and assumed that the woman Lottie had kissed was, in fact, Mel. Not unreasonable she thought, given the picture and the caption.

Reading down, her dread increased as she saw other comments.

    Bob, friend-of-a-friend: Can I watch?

    Virginia: I like kissing girls, too!

With undisguised horror Lottie found comments from her family members, clearly unimpressed with her revelation.

    Tony, her brother-in-law: Really Lottie! Did you
    actually kiss a girl for real?

    Amanda, her sister: Does this mean I have to
    embrace diversity?

"Oh shit!" Lottie had cringed.

Lastly, but by no means least, Mel, at some time—during which Lottie had clearly lost consciousness—had logged on and posted.

    The girl in the white dress, God, Lottie, she
    was well fit and what a kiss! Amazing night,
    welcome to the world of gay!

"Triple fuck!" Lottie had groaned aloud.
No going back now. Thanks, Mel.

She had decided to ignore the ramifications of that night, and was brought back to the present by the ping of her phone, and a welcome text from Alice.

    Have an amazing time, but stay away from girls
    in white dresses!

Smiling, Lottie popped her phone back in her bag as Mel arrived, planting a smacker on her cheek, and gulping down the waiting mojito.

"Let's get this party started!" she said.

Pru's Group

THE NEXT MORNING, Lottie woke to the repetitive patter of rain on her bedroom window. She stole a glance at the clock and groaned inwardly as she realised that a considerable part of her Saturday had been lost to a post-hangover lie-in.

Remembering that Mel had made it as far as the living room carpet, she rose unsteadily and peeled the pillowcase from her face. Heading downstairs, she remembered, thankfully, that the boys had texted her during the previous evening saying they were headed for an impromptu sleepover at their father's house. The peace of her cosy living space helped to soothe her aching brain.

On the kitchen worktop she discovered a note:

```
Amazing night. Lunch in the week? Mel xx
```

Feeling slightly relieved that she didn't have to face any chatter, or autopsy their night out, Lottie robotically went through the motions of making a cup of coffee that she didn't have the stomach to drink, before she logged on to check her e-mails.

In the anticipation of a weekend night out with her friend, Lottie had managed to temporarily banish all thoughts of her ongoing dilemma regarding the strap-on incident. She remembered the earlier message she had posted to Pru's noticeboard asking for advice and noticed a new mail message in the corner of her screen, indicating a response. Logging into her e-mail account, Lottie was pleased to see that it was Pru herself who had responded to her personal e-mail, and she imagined *Dear Pru's* distaste at her message containing such personal information on a public forum.

```
Dear Charlotte.
```

This wasn't actually her name but Pru had apparently assumed that Lottie was a crudely shortened version of Charlotte, and Lottie hadn't bothered to correct her.

```
I really am feeling a little frustrated with
```

you at this point. I did tell you in my previous
correspondence that lesbians do not appreciate
new lesbians being so upfront about their lack
of experience. Being a long-term lesbian, <u>I feel
you need to hear this.</u> All this does, my dear,
is remind us that you were once in the
heterosexual world. Really, why would you want
us to remember this? I do urge caution in your
constant quest for honesty. Let sleeping dogs
lie! I am a real lesbian and I find it somewhat
incredulous that you younger lot feel the need
to enter one another with a plastic implement,
it just seems so heterosexual. But, whatever the
case, my dear, I really do feel you may need
some more specific support during this seemingly
difficult period of your life.

As you know I'm a counsellor of many years
and I practise Reiki healing, amongst other
specialist therapies. In case you didn't read my
home page, you should be aware that I work with
spiritual guides to take people through their
issues and help them to heal with the benefit of
nature. It's very powerful, dear, very powerful!
People simply rave about my tambourine
techniques which I've been told is something
unique to experience. Anyway, I'm inviting you
to pop along to my support group. It's on
Thursdays in Longbottom Row Village Hall,
Fraserburgh, seven p.m. sharp! Please bring a
contribution to the refreshments. We do ask
people bring food that doesn't compromise anyone
who may be wheat, meat, nut, or sugar
intolerant. Oh, I should say that every week we
have an expression-through-therapy theme and
this week we're all going to bring a piece of
writing or a poem that we've written. It's
always jolly good fun! Look forward to seeing
you there!

Go Well,
Prudence
Director of Healing, Inside Out Organisation.
BSHHiT, PhD in Healing Therapies

Abruptly closing the computer screen, Lottie fought a sinking
feeling, as dread gathered in the pit of her already fragile
stomach.

"Crap!" she muttered, knowing full well that she wasn't

going to be able to refuse a direct instruction to attend.

Apart from the fact that anything Pru said sounded more like an instruction than an invitation, one of Lottie's character flaws was her complete inability to think on her feet and escape dreaded social situations. She also couldn't lie convincingly. On the odd occasion that she had braved a lie and gone for a sick cat or a dying aunt she had felt an overwhelming burden of guilt, and, after being caught out, she had vowed that if her brain wouldn't give her an excuse in the moment she would simply have to bear it.

Lottie felt that Pru was a powerful force, and she always found her instructions hard to refuse. Oh well, she thought, there were no plans for Thursday as Alice was away for work and she could probably get Mel to come along for moral support. She resigned herself to the inevitable, mentally noting she needed to call at Sainsbury's on the way home from work to pick up a suitable food contribution. Although, what she could get without offending the delicate constitutions of those attending, she couldn't quite decide.

A BUSY WEEK followed, including a dinner date with Alice where, thankfully, sex was not in the cards as she had an early call at Grant's Farm the following morning. Keen to avoid any exploration of her own sexual history, Lottie had embarked upon a mission to keep the conversation firmly based on Alice's life. Although, try as she might, Alice had remained frustratingly tight-lipped about her own relationship history. Lottie considered herself skilled at eliciting personal information from virtual strangers, after all, she was grade three in her sales skills training, and yet she could not seem to get a coherent account from Alice about her previous partners. Lottie was left with the sense that Alice was being evasive, and she felt herself becoming frustrated and all the more curious about Alice's experiences. In a desperate attempt to obtain some context to Alice, Lottie had made the mistake of requesting Alice's *number*. Lottie realised that this was a risky strategy, as she might be asked to provide her own, and so she had abandoned her feeble attempt when Alice had waved both hands in her direction indicating a vague ten. Lottie was keenly aware her own number would easily fit on one hand.

LOTTIE GAVE PRU'S group little more thought until

Thursday teatime, when she called into Sainsbury's after leaving work early. She felt somewhat dismayed that Alice had come home a day earlier than expected from the female vet's conference. Lottie had not confessed her use of the internet advice site, as she felt that Alice would think her rather foolish. So she had been forced to claim a work overload and promised to see her the following day, meaning that she now had a small white lie to remember. Lottie was not looking forward to meeting Pru. A night of re-bonding with Alice was a far more tantalising prospect.

She strolled through the gaping jaws of the local Sainsbury's, and, thirty minutes later, she was still pacing the aisles reading and rereading the ingredients of the various biscuits and cakes. Heading for the gluten free section, she pounced on a packet of uninviting almond slices. They were gluten free and had no meat in them. She recalled these being the main criteria. Glancing at her watch, she congratulated herself on finding a suitable contribution, despite the time delay. She hurried home for a quick shower and bite to eat before Mel arrived.

Opening the front door, Lottie could barely contain her delight as she laid eyes on her friend. "Oh, Mel!" she shrieked. She felt it was quite possibly the most amusing sight of Mel since the cat litter debacle.

Taking her time to fully appreciate Mel's butched-up outfit, she chuckled.

Slightly bemused by her friend's reaction, Mel looked a bit aggrieved before mumbling a reply. "I've got to have some bloody cover if I'm gonna fit in with a bunch of lezzers. Am I getting a cuppa before we go or what?"

Lottie had not anticipated that Mel would need a gay disguise, but quite clearly she was intending to bluff it. Slowly looking her up and down, she noted a pair of stonewashed denim dungarees, a pair of Converse trainers, and a trilby hat, set at a jaunty angle, all of which clearly made her feel somewhat camouflaged in readiness for Pru's group. It was also the first time Lottie had seen Mel make-up free. Her hair, free of cat litter on this occasion, was scraped into a sideways ponytail that reminded Lottie of Kylie Minogue in the eighties.

Lottie moved to let her pass, still chuckling, and noted her red talon nails, fully acrylic, not the usual nail etiquette of a fully-butch lesbian, but she didn't want to criticise her friend's obvious effort. Humouring her friend, Lottie fished out her own black Converse trainers to an approving nod from Mel, before they set off into the night and headed for the local village hall

They had rounded the corner and began the descent into the village, when Lottie was startled by the bright lights of a car approaching from the rear at an alarming pace. Lottie worked to the rule that these country roads were strictly thirty-mile-an-hour zones, especially after dark. The blind bends and the treacherous descents into the villages from the cliff tops meant that most local drivers preferred to get to their destination alive, if a little late. Tempted to move aside to let the maniac pass, she looked at the car clock and realised she needed to keep moving or else she risked being late.

As she looked in the rear-view mirror again she felt her heart hit an irregular beat as the lunatic appeared a mere inch from her bumper flashing their headlights frantically and hooting in a repetitive motion on the horn. Touching her brakes momentarily in a reflex reaction of panic, Lottie broke out into a mild sweat. She was blinded by the full-on headlights of the stranger's car and felt she was being pushed farther towards the blind bend ahead. In response the driver swerved wide of her car attempting to pass.

"Bloody maniac!" Mel shouted as they rounded the blind corner, and the driver, seemingly oblivious to the complete lack of vision ahead, passed them making frantic gestures of a rude and unpleasant nature.

Shocked as she realised the driver was a woman, Lottie pulled into the nearest passing point as the tail lights of the angry red car disappeared into the distance. The driver had found a way to open her sunroof and was making continued wild gestures with her two fingers, leaving Lottie under no illusion that she was considered incompetent to drive. Despite her aggressive behaviour, Lottie had heard the unmistakeable tones of Vivaldi's *Four Seasons* drifting from the open sunroof. Shaken and unnerved by the driver's erratic behaviour, she slowed to a snail's pace as she rounded the corner and into the village, where she pulled into the village hall car park and pulled hard on the handbrake.

After a moment in the car to regain their composure, Lottie and Mel clambered out, Lottie clutching her packet of slightly squashed almond slices. When they approached the hall entrance, there, parked in the disabled spot, was the red Citroen 2CV.

The maniac driver, who turned out to be rather portly, was attempting to manipulate her body to make an ungainly exit from the small car while she mumbled under her breath. "Bloody cars, built for skinny French men!"

She was followed by a scrappy and dishevelled passenger who was barely visible above the towering pile of tins and boxes she was balancing precariously in her spindly, liver-spotted, arms.

"How the hell did someone else fit in the car with that mountain of woman?" Mel mumbled.

Lottie returned her attention to the driver, reminded of Archie's well-used copy of *Matilda* and the indomitable headmistress, Ms. Trunchball.

Seemingly unaware that Lottie was the victim of her earlier outburst, she grinned through thin lips announcing with gusto. "Well then, you must be Charlotte. I'm Pru, and this is my assistant, Miriam."

Miriam's wizened face peered meekly from behind the tins as she reluctantly parted with a timid smile.

Lottie's jaw dropped as she approached Pru, noting her home-knitted cardigan and her linen smock-dress. However, she smiled meekly and managed to reply. "Nice to meet you and so looking forward to the meeting."

With a stern glance, Prudence gave Mel a swift appraisal and turned sharply, raising an enquiring eyebrow at Lottie.

"This is my friend, Melanie. She'd like to come to group, too."

"Invitation only, my dear!" Prudence snapped, but quickly recovering, she smiled in a half-drawn sneer. "One more won't hurt, I suppose. I hope you've brought your piece of creative writing."

Without waiting for a reply, she turned with remarkable grace for someone of her size and headed for the door into the hall. Following closely at her heel was Miriam, who turned to throw them a nervous smile as she held the door open for Prudence with her free hand. Lottie threw Mel an apologetic grimace, and together they followed the odd couple through the door and into the hall.

Poetry in Motion

LOTTIE LOOKED CURIOUSLY around the hall at the odd assortment of females in Pru's exclusive clan. Pru was nowhere to be seen, and so Lottie concentrated on observing her anxious assistant, Miriam, who was busying herself at the front of the long hall with an assortment of tins and chairs. Suddenly, Mel nudged her sharply in the ribs, causing Lottie to turn towards the noise coming from behind them. A loud guttural groaning bounced around the room and Mel grasped Lottie's hand anxiously as they all turned to look towards the back of the hall.

Pru appeared in a cloak that seemed to be constructed of feathers. Her head held high towards the sky, she groaned again, her eyes rolling upward towards an invisible source. She lifted her arms and breathed heavily. Lottie noticed her bosom heave with the physical and mental effort.

The room fell silent.

Slowly, Pru made her way towards the front of the group, sweeping her cloak across the heads of the women who were sitting in the circle. Some ducked away instinctively. Others breathed deeply and also lifted their eyes upward. Lottie noticed the faint smell of incense as the cloak passed above her, and she saw what she thought were blackbird feathers in amongst the grander eagle-like ones.

Eventually, Pru rounded to face the group. Her eyes still closed, the groan became a keening wail, and as her lips pursed and gradually disappeared into her face, she uttered a welcome. "The Spirits are amongst us, ladies. Let them speak to us!"

The room remained silent.

Mel shot Lottie a worried glance and Lottie shrugged her shoulders in apology. At the front of the room, Miriam dutifully shook a maraca which had appeared from one of the unlabelled tins. At this signal, Pru made her way regally towards her chair, where she shot a frosty glare at Miriam, who hastily prepared Pru's seat with a brightly coloured cushion. Pru unceremoniously plonked her ample behind down onto the hard plastic chair and rearranged her cushions with a sigh. Pru glared once again at Miriam, who avoided her gaze by studying the floor and nervously plucking at an invisible thread on her cardigan.

Lottie glanced around the room, and noted that there were a

variety of reactions from the women. Some clasped their hands in their laps and looked avidly in the direction of Pru, waiting for guidance from the spirits. Lottie noticed two younger women, seemingly oblivious to the ongoing drama, as they shot furtive glances at one another, clearly sizing up their options. Mel had not moved from her chair but Lottie was painfully aware of the acrylic finger nails digging into the side of her leg.

"The spirits support us, friends, on our voyage of self-discovery and improvement. They wish us well. Now, *be gone* spirits!" Pru shouted, sweeping her cape off dramatically and shaking her head slowly, while regaining her composure.

The room remained silent.

Everyone looked to Pru.

Suddenly, and without warning, she snapped her head up and pointed with a gnarly wooden stick to the whiteboard which had appeared at the front of the room.

"Ladies!" she shrilled. "Welcome to *Pru's Group*. Let's start with some group ground rules, shall we?"

Gradually the room returned to some form of normality and a hushed chatter could be heard. Pru looked enquiringly around the room, apparently awaiting a response, and suggestions for the group rules. At the edge of the group, a slightly built woman with unruly wild hair stood up. Lottie hadn't noticed her before now.

She looked around the room nervously before announcing proudly, to no one in particular. "Hi, my name is Ella and I'm an alcoholic. I've been clean for twenty-eight days!"

The room fell silent once again.

Without warning, Pru leapt to her feet and in one swift and incredibly nimble movement firmly gripped the woman's arm. "Wrong night!" Pru spluttered. "This is not a group for *alcoholics*!"

There were nervous titters around the room.

Clearly agitated with the impostor who had taken centre stage, Pru pulled her towards the door muttering under her breath about people breaking her connection with the spirit world. Lottie noted, with interest, that the two younger women who appeared to be locked into some weird mating ritual had taken the opportunity to close the gap between them, as they moved their chairs closer together. As she looked around the room, she caught the eye of a member of the group who looked relatively normal. In fact, Lottie was convinced she'd seen her before but she couldn't place where. Her train of thought was disturbed by Mel who was squeezing her leg frantically in an attempt to get her attention without incurring the wrath of Pru.

"What?" Lottie hissed.

"You didn't tell me I needed to bring a piece of writing! What am I supposed to be writing about?" Mel responded, ignoring Lottie's eyes pleading with her not to draw attention to them.

Lottie whispered. "I don't know. I think it's supposed to be a type of therapy, so anything about coming out or a problem in your life?"

Mel shot her a look that said she was treading on very thin ice. "Lottie, I've not come out because I'm not a bloody dyke! I can't believe you've roped me into this looney show. Gimmie some paper!"

Lottie passed along a notepad, which had magically appeared from one of Miriam's tins. She had taken advantage of the lull in proceedings to hurriedly rectify the fact that it was becoming apparent that several members had not come prepared with suitable written contributions. Lottie hastily removed a sheet for herself, and they both scribbled frantically before returning their attention to Pru.

Re-entering the room with a dramatic flourish, Pru muttered aloud. "Next we'll have the bloody *bisexuals* trying to get in on the act. Honestly, that lot are bloody gays in denial. Get a grip!"

Realising she was overheard, she smiled charmingly in the general direction of the group and returned to her place on the raised stage at the front. Lottie couldn't help thinking that Pru seemed to revel in being the centre of attention in this small gathering, and she hoped that it wasn't the sort of group where she picked volunteers to contribute.

"Group rules people!" Pru said, scanning the hall with her beady eyes, and Lottie felt as if she was assessing them all for their weaknesses. "I should say of course that *Pru's Group* is a working title for the group. We've been running for just more than a year now and have debated various titles for the group but we don't seem to have come up with anything suitable. So anyway, I'll just say that we'll give it a mention again at the end of the group, and of course any suggestions are always welcome. It's your group after all, not mine!" Pru chuckled and shook her head. Her jowls jiggled unattractively in unison with each shake, as she looked to Miriam for approval.

Miriam anxiously made eye contact. "Suggestions, welcome, yes, welcome," she muttered, before focusing back on her invisible thread. Lottie wondered briefly whether Miriam had mental health issues.

She was also beginning to very much doubt that anything would happen in this group without Pru's explicit instruction, but she made a mental note to offer a suggestion at the end, to show willingness. She mulled the *Bisexual and Lesbian Society*. It sounded very serious and inclusive, which she somehow hoped would challenge Pru's views.

Pru had begun to scribble furiously on the whiteboard, clearly forgetting that she'd asked the group to come up with the rules.

```
NO mobile phones, switch them off please!

RESPECT other people's right to speak, everyone
has a turn!

FOLLOW the agenda, we need to keep to time!

LISTEN! We all still have things to learn and
every contribution has a value.

BREATHE, ground yourself and be in the moment.

SPIRIT! Remember the spirits are amongst us. Let
them channel through you.

Last, but by no means least, CONFIDENTIALITY!
```

Obviously happy with her rules, and not bothering to run them past the group, Pru turned her attention to the theme of the evening, expressive poetry. She pulled out her own contribution before turning to the group and asking them to pass their poem or writing to the person on their right. Lottie reluctantly swapped contributions with Mel, who seemed confident with her last-minute efforts.

"Okay. New people go first, a little tradition of ours," Pru smirked as she pointed a disproportionately large finger towards Mel, who instantly turned puce with embarrassment.

Nervously she cleared her throat and read Lottie's hastily scribbled ditty:

```
The fat cat sat on the wall.
He said "meow" and that was all.
```

Silence.
The eyes of the room fell to Pru who looked quizzically at

Lottie, squirming uncomfortably in her chair and refusing to make any eye contact.

"I see. Clearly some people have chosen not to respect the group, or take this seriously, which is a great shame as it shows a lack of consideration for our fellow group members, who have put in considerably more effort."

She paused, and rubbing her hands together violently she continued. "Well, clearly, I don't want to make a big issue out of this, although I would say at this point that the use of inappropriate humour tells us a lot about a person's state of mind and stability, *or lack of it*." She mumbled the final part.

Lottie continued to squirm, painfully aware that what she had considered to be a witty attempt at humour and light-heartedness was not something that Pru was going to run with.

"Perhaps, dear, you'd care to share your friend's contribution. Hopefully it's something written with a little more care."

Glad of the change of direction, Lottie glanced down at Mel's paper. She concentrated on assuming an appropriately serious tone of voice, and clearing her throat, read words that had a strange rhythm and sounded vaguely familiar. Confused by the lack of grammar, Lottie stole a glance at Mel, who grinned encouragingly at her. She focused her efforts back to the poem but as she continued to read, Lottie swallowed hard as the stark realisation hit her, Oh mother of fuck, please! She can't possibly have stolen the words from the infamous Katy Perry song, "I Kissed a Girl".

She glanced up briefly, and noted that the two younger baby-dykes had stopped their mating ritual and were rocking in unison, mouthing the words to the song. Shaking her head to clear it, she looked back at the page, but was unable to continue. Heat raged up her neck and through her cheeks as she coughed nervously. Her mouth had become bone-dry and there was a ringing noise in her ears. After the response that her tongue-in-cheek ditty had provoked, her stomach somersaulted in panic at the inevitable wrath that this offering would provoke from Pru.

The silence following her reading was deafening.

With some reluctance, she cautiously looked up.

To her utter amazement, Pru was standing in the middle of the room in some sort of rapture. Transfixed, she stared at Mel, who continued to grin inanely, clearly feeling she was fulfilling her fake dyke role. Pru's disproportionately large and manly hands were clasped dramatically to her ample bra-less bosom, and a tear slipped across her cheekbone towards her wobbling jowl. With Pru's apparent blessing, the group erupted into rapturous applause. Mel's beam reached the corners of her face and some of the others started to hum the tune, clearly recognising the reference that had, thankfully, escaped Pru.

Pru strode towards Mel, arms outstretched, and as Mel rose to the embrace, the room clapped once again.

"My dear! Simply splendid! So heartfelt, it truly captures the difficulties of coming out in later life, doesn't it? Well it must have taken you ages to phrase it in such superb and delicate prose, my heart sang with joy! Simply beautiful and *well done!*"

Mel sank back onto her chair. She turned to smile smugly at Lottie, who was speechless.

"You see, group, our expression through creative means has such a momentous impact on us all. I think we have time for one more and I'd like to share my own contribution if I may." Without waiting for a response from the group, Pru read aloud in a deep and gritty voice.

```
The garden bench...
The garden bench looks forlorn and alone
Uncared for, callously discarded
Like me
Like me
Summer beckoned but the bench remains cold
Not made for one, but two
Alone
Alone
Surrounded by lush green shrubbery
Framing its misery
Lost
Lost
You left me without a care
Moving onto a new life
Disregard for my misery
Abandoned
Abandoned
Happiness has left me
I am alone now
Only my bench for company
A bench made for two
Misery
Misery
```

She bowed her head, and then looked up to be met with silence.

Eager to redeem herself, Lottie clapped enthusiastically, hoping the others would join her. None did. Pru, composed herself before shooting Lottie a steely glare.

Taking a deep breath, she clapped her hands briskly and announced a fifteen-minute coffee break.

"Prompt return please, my dears!"

Taking the opportunity to escape Pru's steely gaze, Lottie jumped from her chair, ignoring Mel, who she felt had acquired a Teflon-coated pair of dungarees, making her immune from the wrath of Pru. She made up her mind to mingle with the rest of the group and intended to ask the two baby-dykes whether Pru would be likely to revisit Mel's poem, and realise the cultural reference, but she shelved that idea as she noted they were not in the room.

Instead, she approached the woman who had been sitting opposite her. Still feeling that she was vaguely familiar, she went up to her with the intention of striking up a conversation. She doubted that *Pru's Group* was something that people were easily able to leave, and she intended to find out whether anyone else in the group found the experience rather disconcerting. However, her good intentions were short-lived, as she heard a high-pitched shriek, followed by a loud thud as plastic chairs scraped and scattered along the parquet flooring.

Pru was in an ungainly heap, and with her dignity exposed, she clutched her chest dramatically and screamed. "Mim, my EpiPen! Now! *Nuts*, oh, dear spirits above! *Nuts!*"

Miriam, abandoning her collections of tins, was galvanised into action by the cries of her mistress, and surged forward with purpose. Lottie noted with horror the glint of a metal needle which Miriam held, warrior like, above her head. With her wild gray hair streaming behind her, she became a blur as she streaked past the frozen, assembled group and raced towards the motionless form of Pru, who had closed her eyes and was looking somewhat peculiar. The needle plunged through the thick material of the smock directly into the thigh of Pru, who gasped before collapsing once again, crushing the unwitting volunteer who had cushioned her fall. On the floor, Lottie noticed a half-consumed almond slice staring accusingly at her.

"Gluten free *almond* slice" she repeated silently to herself, dread dawning on her with a horrible wave. "Oh shit! *Nuts!*"

AS PRU WAS rolled, with some effort, onto a waiting

stretcher, Lottie noted the rolled eyes and glances exchanged by the ambulance personnel who clearly wished they'd brought their special heavy person chair. Grimacing at the curious passersby, they moved towards the waiting ambulance.

Lottie dashed towards Pru, determined to rectify her bad impression.

She clasped Pru's hand. "I know it's probably not the time, Pru, but I did have an idea about a name for the group."

Receiving no response, she moved forward boldly. "How about the Bisexual and Lesbian Society?"

Pru raised her head from the stretcher and cast a look of sheer disgust at Lottie. "BALS?" she spluttered, before she was hoisted, with considerable effort on the part of the heroic medical staff, into the waiting ambulance.

Lottie noticed the baby-dykes emerge from the toilets, hand in hand and waving enthusiastically at the passing ambulance, before leaving for a destination unknown. There would almost certainly be a swift moving-in, followed by a trip to Dykea.

As Lottie and Mel hurried to the car park, eager to escape the drama, the familiar stranger tugged on Lottie's sleeve. Turning around, she gasped in dismay as she finally remembered why she looked so familiar, it was Ms. Bentley, the teaching assistant from Archie's class at school.

"Hey," Ms. Bentley greeted her. "Small world."

Lottie nodded, looking at Mel who shrugged in return.

"Ms. Bentley, how nice to see you."

Ms. Bentley leaned uncomfortably close to Lottie, who was trapped between her heaving bosom and the car door. "Call me Janet."

Lottie felt Ms. Bentley's breath on her cheek, and turning her head to the side, she muttered quickly. "Sorry must go. Archie's waiting."

Grasping the car door handle, she hastily climbed in and started the car for the journey home. The radio leapt to life and the words of "I Kissed a Girl" bounced loudly around the small space. Lottie and Mel looked at one another, grinning at the irony of the situation, before they burst into raucous laughter.

Lesbianage

ODIE LOOKED UP from his basket with interest as Lottie entered Alice's chic, beachfront apartment. Lottie joked with Alice that she loved to visit her holiday home by the sea, even though she lived by the very same sea. What the flat did provide though, was an escape for Lottie from the responsibilities of family life and it was somewhere she would always treasure, as the place where they had started their relationship. Despite their relative newness to one another, both Lottie and Alice had agreed that this was the beginning of something serious. In the same spirit, they had happily exchanged keys to one another's homes, although Lottie secretly liked coming to Alice's plush pad the best.

Lottie slipped off her shoes and marvelled at the soft carpeting, minus any food scraps or cat hair. She looked forward to a weekend of indulgence, determined that Alice's homecoming would be special.

During the few days that Alice had been away visiting some friends, Lottie had plenty of opportunity to reflect on their emerging relationship. She was especially pleased that she felt she could totally be herself, well, with the exception of an exaggerated history of her use of sex toys, of course. In the grand scheme of things, Alice didn't seem to be concerned with Lottie's experience or lack of it. The earlier small white lie about sexual experience had emerged from Lottie's subconscious as she struggled to develop her new identity as an out and proud gay woman. In other relationships, Lottie had felt some pressure to present herself as more immersed in lesbian life than she had actually been. With Alice, things were different. With Alice, she felt fully accepted for the person she was and the person she was becoming. In return, she offered Alice love, as this was pretty much all she felt she had to give.

Lottie perceived that Alice was more of a loner. She was happy in the company of Odie, and seemed to love the sense of peaceful isolation she had managed to create in her home. Yet Lottie liked to make a fuss over Alice wherever possible and within the limited constraints of her single-parent budget. Alice was far from materialistic, but Lottie was able to demonstrate her affection for Alice through small but meaningful gestures.

Only a few weeks ago she had driven the short distance to Portsoy, on a mission to collect the most delicious Cullen skink soup in the whole of the north of Scotland. Alice had split it into three portions, intent on savouring it during the course of a week rather than devouring it in one sitting. She had expressed much warm appreciation of Lottie's thoughtfulness.

Lottie had a kind and generous nature, and gestures of this sort were second nature to her, hence her wide circle of loyal and well-established friendships.

As Lottie wandered from room to room, she touched the pieces that Alice had carefully selected, and which added to the classy ambience of her home. Alice had an eagle eye for a bargain as well as an avid interest in local artists who plied their trade at crafts fairs, creating home furnishings from natural products such as driftwood and wool. Lottie's taste was less eclectic and she strictly adhered to shabby chic born of Marks and Spencer's online catalogue.

One of the things that Lottie admired about Alice was her ability to put a room together with seemingly little effort. By contrast, Lottie's home very much depicted the lives of the family members within. Archie and his collections had spilled from his bedroom to the rest of the house. These consisted mainly of largely, fiddly, Lego constructions which he studiously arranged on any available surface. Robbie contributed an assortment of used dishes, which he assumed would somehow find their way to the kitchen to be cleaned by the washing-up fairy. Lottie herself had a large collection of novels and hobby equipment, most of it unused. In a quest to develop herself, she would start a new hobby on a bi-weekly basis, only for it to be usurped by a new and burgeoning desire to undertake a more creative craft a month later.

Passing through into the kitchen, Lottie struggled to manage her packages. A small, perfectly bundled posy of white lilies, a bottle of chilled prosecco, along with the ingredients for a delicious home-cooked meal. She hoped Alice wouldn't return having eaten, or worse still, too tired to explore another lesson with the strap-on. A sigh escaped her as she acknowledged that she still felt embarrassed about the strap-on debacle, and she'd been left feeling somewhat shy about the use of sex toys in general. In fact, she would go as far as to say she was suffering from a version of lesbian erectile dysfunction. Even her own faithful friend the Rampant Rabbit had stared at her accusingly within recent weeks, and as a consequence had been relegated to the bottom dresser drawer.

"I love you, Alice," she muttered to no one in particular. Alice had remained determinedly patient about the introduction of moulded-plastic assisted sex, and Lottie recalled the advice she'd given about the slow and steady thrust.

"Less is more," Alice had counselled her. "You're not a bloke, Lottie, so you don't need to fuck me like one!"

Smiling, Lottie imagined herself, sweat dripping from her forehead as she pumped away. She recalled the magnificent sight of Alice who had later taken control. Alice, kneeling confidently above her as she used one hand to guide the strap on gently into Lottie. Aside from her ability to navigate the plastic implement with ease, she had maintained delicious eye contact with Lottie throughout. With seeming ease, she worked the strap-on until Lottie's pleasure was apparent. Whether it was the strap-on, or, more likely, the complete ease in which Alice had made love to her, she felt strangely connected to her lover in a way that had helped her to understand what the strap-on brought to the bedroom.

Hastened by the memory, she finished her cooking and patted Odie on the head as he stared intensely at the closing fridge door, silently willing her to produce a tasty tidbit. Dissatisfied, he gave a rumble of displeasure and returned to his basket to await the return of his favoured mistress.

The pasta bake was in the oven. Set the bloody timer, Lottie, she silently chastised herself as she headed upstairs for a quick shower and change and a liberal squirt of Alice's cologne. She didn't know why she ever thought it was too butch to wear aftershave instead of perfume.

Better give *it* a quick wash, she thought referring to the formidable strap-on. Leaning across the bed she felt around to locate the naughty drawer, and fumbled around until she was able to pull out the strap-on. What on earth was all this stuff? She struggled to shut the drawer and unknown gadgets spilled out onto the carpet.

Rummaging to try to return the alien items to their rightful hiding place, she came across a soft plastic bulb. Curious as to what it was, she was driven to investigate further. She pulled the unfamiliar object out of the drawer and onto the bed. Chuckling with delight, she realised she'd discovered a new toy of pleasure!

Alice, your collection of sex toys is seriously impressive. I have absolutely no bloody idea what this is. As she turned it again and again in her hand, she observed that running from the soft plastic bulb, akin to an old-fashioned blood pressure pump, ran a soft purple piece of what looked like hosing. Attached to the end of the hosing was a bullet-shaped device, and when she located and pressed the start button it vibrated invitingly in her hand. Her eyes followed the hose down and she noted there was an oval-shaped end in which there was a soft sponge like surface that gently caressed the end of her exploring finger.

Lottie wriggled as an involuntary shiver ran through her. Smiling to herself, she made a spur-of-the moment decision. A quick try of this before her shower and at least if it appeared later on, she might be able to appear a bit savvier about how it bloody worked. Silently, she chastised herself for being so silly. She knew it was only in her head, the humiliation she was subjecting herself to about the strap incident. Yet despite Alice's assurances, she was still stubbornly determined to show sexual savvy.

Before she could talk herself out of it, she whipped down her pants and attached herself to the bullet-shaped end which was dully vibrating. Sinking down into Alice's duvet she vigorously pumped on the soft purple bulb, which immediately responded with appropriate pressure to her clitoris. Squirming with pleasure, Lottie experimented with different speeds and activated the vibrating spongy pad. Yay for Alice's drawer of pleasure! She was momentarily lost in the immediate pleasure it gave her.

A soft breath against her arm alerted her to the fact that she was not alone. Opening one eye, she noted that Odie had sidled up to the bed and was observing her with the look of disdain he clearly reserved for visitors who didn't have the courtesy to provide him with tidbits from the fridge.

Feeling somewhat unnerved by his judgemental gaze, she mumbled towards him. "Bloody hell, dog!" she said, while swatting at him with her free hand.

Despite her persistence, Odie remained resolutely unmoved. Suddenly, he lunged in a concerted attempt to get onto the bed. His long sausage-shaped body gave him extra height as he attempted to negotiate a full-on dive, assisted by the low bed frame. He seemed extremely confident that, with enough lunging, he could propel himself onto the coveted duvet. Several dog-lunges later and put off by his inappropriate interest in her bedroom activities, Lottie struggled to a sitting position, intending to put the toy away.

As she used one hand to swat the dog, the other became accidentally entangled in the purple hosing. The more she struggled the more her free hand became entangled in the hosing, which was cutting into her wrist.

"Fuck!" she mumbled feeling an edge of panic caused by her sudden lack of control of the implement which remained clamped to her privates.

In an attempt to free herself, she tugged frantically at the hosing, which she could barely reach. Adrenalin coursed through her as she realised with increasing panic that she could no longer control the speed button which was pressing painfully against her inner wrist.

"Oh fuck!" she gasped, more loudly this time, as she realised that Odie had made a successful leap onto the bed and was playfully pouncing on the purple bulb. This increased the pressure against her clitoris to a near unbearable level.

"It's not a bloody ball, Odie!" she squealed as he pounced again and again, oblivious to anything but the tempting prospect of popping the mysterious ball. Odie was obsessed with the squeak he knew was contained within any ball shaped object. Lottie had watched him on numerous other occasions engage in just such a frenzied chase until he obtained his prize. As she predicted, Odie mercilessly followed the ball as it moved into the crease of the duvet, and in hot pursuit was Lottie's free hand as she desperately attempted to recapture it.

Suddenly, Lottie heard a door slam downstairs. "Hey babe, I'm back! Something smells amazing, and not burned!"

Lottie froze.

Alice? Oh, dear God above. *Alice is home!"*

Her face flamed with embarrassment. Galvanised into action, she attempted to slither to the edge of the bed. The ball moved in sync, and Odie followed hot in pursuit, until Lottie lost her balance and they all tumbled from the bed and onto the laminated floor with a loud thud.

"Ah, baby you're upstairs. Coming up," Alice shouted.

Lottie managed to get to her feet, while frantically shaking her wrist in a lame attempt to free the controller.

Alice appeared at the top of the stairs and peered around the bedroom door, a large grin appearing from ear to ear upon seeing Lottie.

When Alice entered the room, a dishevelled and embarrassed Lottie greeted her, painfully aware of the destruction of her girlfriend's bedroom. Lottie was literally frozen to the spot, mortified by unfolding events. Her work pants were around her ankles and the sex toy, dangling from between her legs, was still tethered to her wrist. She gave a feeble smile of apology.

Despite the return of his mistress, Odie was oblivious and remained fixated on capturing the plastic ball. Sensing his time was limited, he made one final and determined leap towards the dangling bulb, untying the hosing and pulling the entire toy loose. As Odie achieved contact with his intended target, the unsuspecting Lottie was also driven downward towards the floor by the weight of the focused sausage dog, and she landed in an ungainly fashion at the feet of the bemused Alice.

Some moments later, after wiping tears of laughter from her face, Alice took the mortified Lottie into her arms to a warm embrace.

"Baby, what a homecoming!" she chuckled. "The pasta bake smells amazing but the sight of you performing a weird sex act with the assistance of my dog will be something that I'm pretty sure I should report to someone."

Lottie slithered farther into Alice's arms, hiding her face in the soft folds of Alice's beautifully laundered cashmere top. Not able to hide her smile at the sheer ludicrousness of the situation, she chuckled. "That's not the half of it, I haven't told you about last night yet!"

Realising that her pants remained around her ankles, she hurriedly pulled them up before putting the toy up high out of Odie's reach. She led Alice through into the living room and served up the pasta bake, charred of course, but edible. After three welcome glasses of prosecco, Lottie had mustered the courage to recount the events of the group meeting and her near assassination of the group's formidable leader.

"Lottie, I'm trying to keep up," Alice mused. "But what I'm really struggling to know is why you felt the need to turn to some internet wacko for advice about our sex life?" She leaned forward and kissed Lottie full on the mouth, leaving her a little breathless. "Bloody hell, woman, you're full of surprises! Tell me who exactly is this group leader? She sounds like an unpleasant character."

Lottie explained to Alice how she had discovered the Dear Pru advice site some time ago while searching for support groups, following a particularly difficult early encounter with a stammering vegan psychologist.

"Oh God, Lots, baby. I really do understand you were having a difficult time but I know *that* Prudence of old. She's a wily old badger with only one interest in life, that's herself!"

Lottie raised her eyebrows quizzically. "How on earth would you know her?"

With a sigh, Alice repositioned herself and circled her arms protectively around Lottie. "You really are green sometimes, Lottie. There's a whole world of lesbianage out there, you know."

"Lesbianage? What the hell does that mean?" asked Lottie.

Alice sighed and got comfortable for a long explanation.

"So, the first thing you need to know, Lottie, is that lesbianage is rife. Everyone knows everything about everybody. Make no mistake, lesbianage, my lovely girl, is how you would describe the more unpleasant and insidious underbelly and goings-on of the lesbian community. At the heart of that community, for a long time now, has been Pru and her hangers-on. Pru is well known for being a meddling and self-serving egomaniac with a desperate need for the admiration of others and a burning desire for power. She's set herself up as a type of self-help guru and claims to have mysterious powers, or some such nonsense. Lesbianage is my way of saying she likes to meddle in the relationships of those who are happier than she is, and she's the absolute master of this. It helps her feel needed but it's rarely helpful to those on the receiving end. This is such a small community, Lots, and everyone knows everyone. People are interlinked, usually because at one time or another they've slept together. Pru is a master of exploiting this for her own ends. She loves to manipulate the relationships of others and she'll often be found as a third wheel in these relationships, sneakily targeting the weakest partner and making sure the stronger partner of the two is aware of her partner's flaws. I used to think she did this because she fancied one of the parties. I quickly realised the reason she actually does this is that she's alone, and she can't bear the thought that other people are happily monogamous, so she sabotages happy relationships at any opportunity she gets. Simply put, Lottie, she is a dangerous person with no good intentions."

Lottie absorbed this information with some curiosity, and a healthy degree of scepticism. She hadn't had many dealings with Pru and her crew yet, but she didn't seem exactly dangerous. Misguided, yes, Egotistical, yes, but dangerous? She just wasn't sure that she could class Pru in the same category as Ian Brady or Rose West. Nevertheless, she was glad that Alice had taken the time to explain the concept of lesbianage.

Alice, obviously seeing that Lottie was unconvinced, decided to shelve the discussion about Pru for a more a general introduction about lesbianage. Several glasses of prosecco, and a couple of hours later, Lottie felt she had a greater understanding of the sometimes-incestuous world of lesbian dating.

Lottie had always been an avid viewer of *The L Word* and thought she knew all about the supposed links between every dyke and their exes. However, Alice's florid account of the local community liaisons had brought this vividly to life. In the Scottish villages there was a limited choice of potential new partners, and recycling was very much the fashion. Most of these people, had at one time or another, ventured onto the internet in search of a date, or to expand their circle of gay friends.

Alice had explained that during one such phase she had encountered the one-and-only Prudence, who had been posing on a dating website as a deeply spiritual woman with healing powers, who also had a keen interest in animals and nature. Alice, keen to meet a fellow animal lover, had arranged to meet Pru in a local coffee shop. Lottie knew Alice to be a polite and kind person, so was not surprised to discover that she had stayed much longer that she wanted to, despite knowing instantly that there was zero attraction. Lottie chuckled to herself as Alice recounted that Pru had been a master of superficial charm and charisma. Shrewdly, Alice had quickly deduced that her companion had no integrity and was a determined social climber with a ruthless streak of ambition where her career was concerned.

"So how did you end the date?" asked Lottie, fully aware that Pru was not someone who would be easily dismissed. Alice said she had eventually established that Pru's sole aim had been to capitalise on her vet client base, in order to try and expand *her* services to include pet healing and a cross-over service for pet owners struggling to cope with the grief after the loss of a pet loved one. Alice giggled with near hysteria, as she described how Pru had inhaled three slices of carrot cake, gluten free, nut free, organic, and extortionately priced, and two extra-large chai teas. By this point, she recalled feeling professionally violated, as she had shared far too much information about her client base under skilful interrogation by Pru.

She had finally managed to make her excuses — early cow birthing, she recalled — before beating a not-hasty-enough retreat. Reflecting on her dating experience, Alice felt she'd had a lucky escape from a ruthless psychopath and had immediately cancelled her membership to the website. But not before sending a tactfully worded e-mail to the website organiser to suggest she may wish to carefully vet the profiles of the users.

Alice had later heard through her social network, that Pru

had started her own website, which she had been somewhat worried about, but ultimately decided to let sleeping psychopaths lie. Literally lie, as it turned out, when she had a quick look and discovered that Pru's claim to be a qualified counsellor with numerous academic accolades was questionable to say the least.

After listening to Alice's story, Lottie settled down to watch a film with Odie, newly forgiven, on her lap and Alice wrapped snugly behind her, dozing lightly.

Lesbianage, she mused, was not as new a concept to her as she'd thought, although the term was unfamiliar. Thinking back, she revisited her earlier grim internet dating days before she'd met the fabulously alluring Alice. On several occasions, when she had been chatting with women on the websites she'd felt like she was an extra in an episode of *The L Word*. She wasn't sure which part she had been playing, probably some gay version of the hapless Bridget Jones, but she had quickly established that in the pool of thirty women in her local area, most had dated one another.

Some were less discreet than others, which meant that she had been subjected to confessions of unrequited love, bordering on stalking, depending on how you chose to view it, or more frequently it seemed, warnings from those who were keen to describe their horrific experiences with women with issues.

Lottie had taken this view with a pinch of salt at first, after all, *all* women had issues in her limited experience, look at Linda Lovely. However, after a sobering encounter with a roadside-eatery worker by the name of Alison, she saw why she should have heeded the warnings of some of the other women on the site. Alison, it seemed, had been rather too captivated by Lottie's Scottish accent during three long phone calls, while Lottie, indecisive at the best of times, struggled to formulate a plan to explain that there wasn't any chemistry.

"It's you, not me, or rather it's definitely you, not me!" Lottie felt she wanted to scream down the phone.

After enduring three two-hour phone calls, Lottie was galvanised into action as she acknowledged that she was probably in serious danger of encouraging an actual real-life stalker. She came to this conclusion after Alison revealed that she had searched the web for Lottie. Bugger the internet, bugger the fact that she hadn't been bothered to create a username that wasn't her actual name. Lottie was startled to discover that Alison had uncovered her home and work addresses as well as her Facebook profile, including her mobile number, to which she began sending hourly text messages. Most concerning of all, was the fact that Alison had discovered from Lottie's Facebook profile that she was the owner of an angry cat, and had taken the liberty of creating a blogging site on behalf of her grumpy pet, to ask for advice from the internet community about possible cures/pet-therapy sessions.

A result of this experience, was that Lottie found herself along a similarly undignified path of warning all the people she was in contact with about the crazy table-clearer. Initially, she had remained on the site and tried to ignore the ever more persistent, and passive aggressive, messages she was receiving from Alison. However, after a homemade compilation CD—three of them actually—over the period of a week, all titled *Love, Relaxation, and Soulmates* arrived in the post at her workplace, much to the amusement of Virginia, who had warned her against internet dating in such a small community, she withdrew her profile and temporarily disabled her Facebook account.

She later discovered from another woman with whom she'd kept in touch, that herself, and four others were in various stages of the application process for non-molestation orders in connection with Alison, the egg-flipping lunatic. Lottie had taken a back seat from internet dating after that, but had met and embarked upon a short fling with a stuttering psychologist called Imogen, from Birmingham, with whom she shared rather better communication in the e-mail realm than she had accomplished in the face-to-face meetings they'd had at a local gastro pub.

Lottie smiled as she recalled her ultimate desperation to try to make a connection with Imogen in person, who struggled significantly with communication in real life. Imogen had explained in her e-mails that it was important for her to finish her own sentences otherwise it added to her psychological barriers when talking. Lottie had struggled to be inventive enough with her facial expressions to continue to convey, one, an interest in whatever the mystery end to the sentence might be, two, support for Imogen's right to complete her own sentences, and three, hiding the pain she was experiencing through her usually frozen facial muscles as she nodded and smiled with what she hoped was not a desperate, slightly insane grin as she waited for Imogen to speak.

The brief affair came to a brisk end when Lottie forgot the sentence rule and committed the ultimate faux pas of finishing Imogen's sentence. Forgetting she wasn't playing charades, and guessing the name of the film that Imogen was attempting to say she had seen, was not going to get her a prize. With a sudden surprising fluidity of speech, Imogen conveyed how upsetting she had found this and red-faced and shamed, Lottie had beaten a hasty exit.

Many months later, after returning to the dating site, Lottie understood that Imogen had met and entered into a civil partnership with a stand-up comedian whose finishing-off of her sentences also contained a humorous edge and this, apparently, would circumvent the rule of no sentence finishing.

Swigging the dregs of her prosecco, Lottie rolled to face Alice, whose sleepy eyes opened to meet hers as they moulded into a kiss that would finish at some time in the early hours of the morning.

The Gay Curriculum

"MUM!" ARCHIE SHOOK Lottie from her duvet cocoon. She awoke with a start, panicking that the alarm hadn't sounded and that they were late for school.

This transpired to be the truth, and after simultaneously tackling the latest offering from Boots, an expertly butchered rabbit, or what was left of it, a fluffy rear end and an eyeball, and cremating two waffles which Archie subtly binned, they hurriedly left for the twenty-minute drive to Archie's school.

On the way, Lottie noticed that Archie was not his usual chatty self.

"Anything up, sweetheart?" she asked as she slowed down to let a harassed yummy mummy out of the village side road.

Archie shot her a worried look and quickly shook his head in the negative, although his face told a different story. Noticing the abandoned waffles, she had registered his lack of breakfast and so, ignoring the time, she decided to detour through a fast-food drive-thru and make time for a mum chat.

While they consumed a calorific egg muffin apiece, Archie recounted his tale of woe. "Mum, it's just not nice, people always say things are sooo gay! It's just mean to gay people like you."

Lottie nodded absent-mindedly, as she made a mental list of all the things she urgently needed to do if she ever got to work this morning.

Archie repeated more slowly. "So gay, Mum, means they're using the word gay to describe things that are bad or not nice."

Lottie swallowed the final bits of her muffin while she considered his dilemma. "Archie, sweetie, they're just kids and they don't mean anything by it. They aren't meaning anything horrible about me, it's just something that people say. I really wouldn't worry about it."

Archie leaned forward and spoke earnestly. "Mum, I don't think you can just say that, because they shouldn't do it and it's not right, and anyway, people will think bad things, and it upsets me."

Hearing that Archie was telling her he was upset, Lottie's parenting radar spun as she considered how she could show Archie that his feelings mattered, even though she did consider them somewhat misguided.

Archie looked at her expectantly, and Lottie felt the pressure to provide an answer to his dilemma.

However, glancing at her watch she realised she was now horribly late for work. "Can't win them all, kiddo!" she weakly offered, patting him on the head.

When she was rewarded by a frustrated sigh from Archie, Lottie lamely attempted to change the subject, while she facilitated a speedy departure from the restaurant.

They soon arrived at Archie's school. Guiltily, she double-parked in the housing estate near to the school, silently willing the owner of the driveway she had blocked not to notice her transgression. Holding onto one another, they carefully shuffled through the slippery layer of autumn leaves and slid down the predictably un-cleared pathway, which led them to the school. Mentally she counted at least two broken bones of children attending the school the past year and yet still no bloody caretaker out before school. Joined by a few other stragglers, Lottie slip-walked determinedly towards the open gate.

A child walked alongside her chatting to his friend. "So like, I said like, you can't do that, it's like sooo gay!"

With a sense of foreboding doom, she glanced at Archie who was already staring at her with a look of disapproval. "See?" he mouthed.

At the gate she planted a firm kiss on his cheek but he scowled back. "Well?"

"Well, what?" she asked slightly confused, glancing once again at her watch which accused her of now being unforgivably late for work.

"Well, aren't you going to come in and speak to my teacher?"

Looking around, she felt panic and dread creeping in as she mentally pictured the forbidding Mrs. Goodwin smiling through gritted teeth, as she edged towards her. Her eyes darted around for an escape route but nothing materialised.

With a resigned sigh, she humoured Archie. "But of course, sweetie."

The overbearing heat of the classroom smothered her as she opened the door and she immediately felt a steady flush rising up her neck towards her cheeks, which were soon flaming red.

Unaware of her discomfort, Archie strode confidently ahead, exuding an air of superiority due to the moral high ground he was about to establish. He nodded at her in encouragement and took his place at his table with a ringside view of both his teacher and her ever-eager teaching assistant,

Ms. Bentley.

With some trepidation Lottie proceeded. Inwardly, she acknowledged the fact that she was not a regular parent at the classroom door, so she was not surprised to be largely ignored by the teaching staff as they dealt with the regular parents, who were eagerly confirming the details of the arrangements for the upcoming visit to Loch Ness, where they were going to be parent-helpers.

There followed a painstaking wait of approximately three-and-a-half minutes — Lottie could state this as a fact because she had fixed her glare on the clock moving with sloth timing mounted above the interactive whiteboard. Sensing an ominous presence, Lottie looked sideways to witness Mrs. Goodwin approaching her. Gulping nervously, she glanced across at Archie who smiled broadly at her in anticipation of her superhero status as a social do-gooder. Squaring her shoulders and forcing a smile to her face, she moved to meet Mrs. Goodwin half way and was greeted with a quizzical but not unfriendly smile in return.

"Hello, Mrs. Goodwin. I'm Archie's mum."

"Oh yes, of course, dear. How can I help?" she replied. "Nice of you to pop in."

"I just wanted to have a quick word on Archie's behalf, as he mentioned to me that he's been a bit upset about something that some of the children have been saying." She paused as she built up to what she feared would be the grand finale.

Mrs. Goodwin's attention wandered to the handsome dad who had just escorted his daughter in.

Flustered by her distracted audience, Lottie blustered on. "Apparently, he's overheard a lot of children describing things as so gay which he doesn't like, as he feels it's offensive to gay people."

Mrs. Goodwin's brow furrowed, clearly struggling, as Lottie herself had, with the difficulty of this.

"I see dear, well, of course it's just something that children tend to say, isn't it? But, yes, I suppose he does have a point, although, it is just a saying, dear." She smiled patronisingly.

Lottie could feel that she was rapidly losing her audience and that Mrs. Goodwin was already turning to make a beeline for the yummy daddy.

Trying to assume an air of authority, Lottie drew a deep breath and spoke loudly. "Well, yes, I understand that, and I did try to explain to him, but he's struggling with it, and so I just wanted to, well, just to make you aware I suppose…" She trailed off, rapidly losing conviction and avoiding eye contact with Archie, who was watching avidly.

"It does seem a bit odd, dear, that he seems so bothered about this," Mrs. Goodwin said.

Lottie could feel herself going through the various stages of pink to puce for the second time that day. "Well, you see, the thing is, well, it's a bit awkward, but *I'm* gay," she said, drawing in a deep breath.

Silence.

Lottie was vaguely aware of the noise level in the classroom dropping substantially. Having been focused on trying to keep Mrs. Goodwin's attention, she hadn't been aware that her voice had been gradually increasing in volume.

Mrs. Goodwin appeared to be lost for words. Her mouth flapped soundlessly as she struggled to process this impromptu personal disclosure.

Lottie became increasingly aware of the loud silence that had now engulfed the entire classroom and, as she cast a quick glance around, she was horrified to discover that the ever-eager teaching assistant was frozen mid dinner-money count. Lottie frantically avoided the gaze of the curious parents, becoming increasingly aware of the intense gaze of Ms. Bentley, who gave her an exaggerated wink. Lottie, froze, surely the bloody teaching assistant wasn't coming on to her.

Several parents waiting to speak with the teacher had apparently been eavesdropping and were rather less obvious about this after Lottie's revelation.

Lottie was literally at a loss for words, and swore inwardly at the situation she had found herself in.

Turning back to Mrs. Goodwin, she noticed that she too was struggling to regain her composure spluttering out words. "Well, that's most unexpected. I would never have known!"

The clutch of parents pressed closer as they nodded to one another in silent agreement. "Although, of course though you *are* a Ms." she seemed somewhat relieved to have identified this retrospectively significant sign.

Behind her she overheard a mother whispering to her co-conspirator. "But she's so pretty, how can she be gay?"

Enjoying the unfolding drama, Archie gave Lottie a wink. She managed a weak smile in return. Well, at least her humiliation had served to prove to her sensitive son that it was okay to be out and proud.

Mrs. Goodwin, now aware of her growing audience, was

keen to achieve a green tick for diversity and reached out to Lottie to rub her arm in a consoling manner, before suddenly recoiling and snatching her hand back in horror, presumably thinking this may be construed as her making a sexual advance.

Keen now for the slow-motion car crash to conclude, Lottie smiled apologetically at Mrs. Goodwin before thanking her for her time and beating a hasty retreat to her car.

Now horribly late for work, she mentally berated Archie for being such a social activist and vowed to encourage him to watch more of the Disney channel, which was bound to increase his sense of self-preservation and selfishness. Coming out at nine to her son's teacher had not been in her plan for the day. What next?

Ripping up her freshly completed application for the parent governor position, she gratefully headed for work and the oblivion of classified advertising.

Pet Rescue

DESPITE ALICE'S WARNING about Pru and her crew, Lottie decided she would give *Pru's Group* another go. She was curious to see Pru again in her own environment, where she was sure that she would be able to establish whether lesbianage was high on Pru's agenda. Aside from that, Lottie had something of an ulterior motive. In her most recent e-mail, Pru was launching her latest service as a specialist in pet massage. Despite pharmacological interventions by Alice, Boots continued to exhibit somewhat psychotic behaviour, but Lottie hadn't given up and wanted to try something different. Pru had offered her service, at a not-so-discounted rate, to anyone who wanted to bring an animal to that night's group.

Pru had told Lottie that she strongly believed pet massage brought great health benefits to animals and that she also felt having animals present at the group would bring her closer to her spirit guides. Lottie figured that anything was worth a shot for Boots, who had now caused serious injury to three people and counting. Fearing that he may end up on some type of cat death row, she intended to embrace Pru's recommendation of a more unorthodox treatment with as much of an open mind as she could. There was also a small part of her that secretly hoped she might finally gain Pru's approval if Boots achieved a new-found sense of calm. Becoming one of her success stories would give Pru a chance of self-promotion which Lottie knew would stroke Pru's ego. After exploring *Dear Pru*, Lottie had discovered a number of proclaimed success stories littered with claims of Pru's miraculous talents and detailing her success with human—and now animal—misfits. Lottie marvelled at how self-serving Pru was, and she started to form the unqualified opinion that Pru exhibited significant traits of narcissism.

After a swift visit to Sainsbury's, Lottie emerged with some dried fruit, her contribution to tonight's food table. The evening before, she had received a somewhat abrupt e-mail from Pru strongly suggesting she should bring this, and mentioning that she would be very pleased to see Mel again as she felt they had a connection. Lottie shuddered at the thought of Mel in the clutches of Pru, but, determined to please Pru, she embarked upon several desperate attempts to persuade Mel.

Mel had been unmoved by the promise of post-group wine and had firmly declined to attend. "I'll end up a bloody dyke if you keep dragging me into this world, and if I'm going down that route I'm not gonna lose my lesbian virginity to that old crazy!"

Taking this as a fairly firm no, Lottie had consoled herself with the thought that she could redeem herself in Pru's favour by taking the suggested offering of dried fruit, and by providing Pru with the ultimate pet challenge, Boots. However, keen to mitigate any serious or life-threatening injury to Pru, she had persuaded Alice to give him a mild sedative, and felt reassured that he would remain placid for his therapy session.

She wrestled with the broken clasp on the side of the carrier, mentally noting that she needed to get a new one soon if the pet therapy sessions were to become a regular event. She confidently patted the top of the box containing the sedated cat as she drove down the winding road towards the group venue.

As she pulled into the car park, she could just about make out the wild hair of the meek accomplice, Miriam, who appeared to be hiding around the corner of the ramshackle hall. Curious to see what she was doing, Lottie followed a plume of cigarette smoke which grew more herbal in its smell as she got closer. Not being particularly street when it came to recreational drugs, Lottie wasn't sure at first if this was of the legal or illegal kind. After accidentally inhaling a lungful she tentatively ascertained that this was a herbal smoke of the illegal variety. This was soon confirmed by the startled expression on Miriam's face as she was discovered.

She hastily extinguished her guilty pleasure. "Purely medicinal, Lottie. By the way, my friends call me Mim."

Lottie chuckled to herself and gave the mellow Mim a reassuring rub of the shoulder before she returned to the car to collect the pleasantly catatonic Boots.

Well, that explains how she's able to spend so much time with Pru then, Lottie silently concluded. As Lottie gingerly lifted the cat carrier from the passenger seat, she noticed Boots lazily open one eye to survey his new surroundings with some disdain. Nevertheless, he seemed mostly nonplussed by his extraction from the utility room and quickly returned to his drug-induced slumber.

Entering the hall, Lottie smiled and nodded as she joined an assorted group of women in the vestibule. She momentarily wondered why the group numbers had significantly increased since she had attended. Maybe Pru had advertised the event, and she couldn't help but be secretly impressed by Pru's success in marketing her dubious talents. However she had done it, word had clearly spread throughout the disparate lesbian community in the deep heart of the Scottish Highlands. Lottie murmured with delight when she saw that Pru was also carrying a cat basket, containing a beautiful, pouting, pure-white Persian.

Excellent, she thought, something we have in common, both cat lovers!

Despite the nagging doubt created by Alice's disapproval of her continuing attendance at the group and her warning about Pru, Lottie had a good feeling. She felt that Alice was being somewhat disingenuous considering her own failure in performing the required miracle on Boots, despite her medical qualifications.

A smiled played around her lips as she fondly recalled their first meeting after an introduction from Virginia. Always attractive in her professional environment, Alice had conveyed the appropriate amount of concern and authority in her crisp, white veterinarian's coat. Lottie had struggled to explain the severity of Boots' mental health issues, due to her instant attraction to Alice. However, his issues soon became apparent when Alice received the first of several warning bites from Boots who was not impressed at being brought into such a sanitised medical environment.

Lottie recalled several subsequent visits to the surgery, arguably more as a reason to see Alice than for any tangible benefits obtained for Boots. Alice had recommended several products to dampen down Boots' mania but none had the required effect. Lottie had begun to have sleepless nights about the limitations of her pet insurance policy after several excess policy payments, and the lack of success of the products recommended by Alice. Despite this, on her fifth visit and at the limit of her pet insurance, Alice had finally figured out the reason for Lottie's frequent visits and had asked her out on a date.

Thereafter, Boots had been banished to live in the comfort and solitude of the utility room where his wrath need only be braved for access to the washer and dryer. The warmth and relative solitude seemed to have its own calming effect on Boots, and he could tolerate visitors to his room as long as they didn't linger, or worse still, attempt to pet him without him explicitly requesting this by approaching them. The solution hadn't been fool-proof though, and not even Lottie was immune from a corrective swipe from Boots if the mood took him.

Hurrying into the inner sanctum of the cold hall, Lottie clasped the carrier closer as her anxiety ramped up a notch. A variety of pets had been produced for Pru's attention and Lottie felt concern for the safety of anything smaller than a Rottweiler in the same room as Boots. He had a well-established reputation for regular massacres of the local wildlife. More than a few greedy seagulls eating the final morsels of a picnicker's feast, had lost their life to his SAS-type stalking skills. Most memorable, was an incident involving the neighbour's Pekinese, who required a mechanical limb thereafter. Shaking the guilt of that bloody memory from her mind, Lottie took her seat as Pru repeated her strange and clearly well-practised entrance. Once again, using her feathered cloak to sweep across the heads of those seated close enough.

She introduced herself and welcomed those present to *Pru's Group*, before casting a challenge to her audience that dared them to suggest an alternative name for the group. No one, including Lottie, took the bait.

Proudly surveying the full room, Pru began. "Welcome especially, this week to our animal companions. Please note I *strongly* object to the use of the word pets as it is demeaning to our fur-or-feathered companions. I would like to say that the presence of animal spirits has strengthened my connections to the spirit world and I intend to channel this through to our very own companions in an attempt to bring love and harmony to our gathering."

Pru rose from the chair and invited her first subject to join her on the staged area. Adopting a shrill voice that could, quite probably only distinctly be heard by dogs anyway, Pru laid her hands firmly upon a frisky collie dog. Looking at her with mild interest, the dog easily tolerated her vigorous and frenetic rubbing and eventually submitted to a sitting position where he took the opportunity to sniff the feathers on Pru's cloak. Taking his seated position as a sign of submission, Pru repeated her hand-waving ritual across the coat of the collie who looked on with an expression which definitely showed traces of amusement.

"As you can see, friends, Alec the collie is in fact now connected to his spirit ancestors, hence his submissive position. In my world, I am aware that he is communing now with his spirit leader and so I intend to return to finish his massage later in the evening. Please could I ask for another volunteer?"

Lottie saw her opportunity and she took it. Beating a heavily groomed pedigree poodle to the front of the queue, she eagerly thrust the cat carrier into the waiting arms of Pru.

Still not having quite forgiven her for the evening she'd spent in accident and emergency, Pru forced a smile through her thin lips to greet Lottie. "Well, dear, let's pop him out. He's no good in there is he?"

Lottie's smile slipped. "Take him out? Holy fuck, no way!"

She inwardly panicked and looked up in horror as Pru reached into the inner recesses of the carrier, oblivious to the danger inside. Her huge hands firmly clasped Boots's rear end, the only part on offer to her in that particular moment. Lottie felt her life was suddenly running in slow motion as she lunged towards Pru, determined to take the inevitable injury that would follow once Boots felt the contact of a human hand. Thankfully, Pru moved swiftly, and with uninformed confidence she lifted Boots free of his jail and clasped him closely to her ample bosom.

Lottie felt a cold sweat prickle her breasts as she reached out to retrieve the evil offender, but was unsuccessful, as Pru held him aloft to proclaim his magnificence to the audience.

To Lottie's utter amazement, Boots nuzzled his bristly chin against that of Pru's and she chuckled with delight. "So, dear, what is the problem with this friendly wee fellow?" she enquired, while tickling the upturned chin of Boots, who had his eyes closed and was purring with pleasure at the touch of the spirited one.

Lottie was completed bemused by his behaviour, the remnants of the anaesthetic surely? Taken aback by his sudden mood change, Lottie hastily revised her prepared speech about the issues Boots had, and instead offered a more feeble account. "A bit temperamental, Pru, but really he's a pussy cat."

Pru chuckled again. "Clearly," she said as she carefully placed him onto the wooden bench in front of her, confidently moving her hands through his fur, still failing to provoke the angry reaction Lottie had anticipated from Boots. After performing various undisclosed ritualistic spells above him, Pru settled down to provide him with a robust rub down which he seemed to positively enjoy.

Once he was safely back in his basket, Lottie revelled in an unusual sense of pride towards Boots, who for once had exceeded her expectations in a positive way. Deciding not to tempt fate or a feline mood swing she popped him into the passageway, where she noticed Pru had also put her Persian darling. She then returned to the group to enjoy the rest of Pru's performance, and made a mental note to let Alice know that Pru did in fact appear to have a talent for handling animals which superseded her poor people skills.

During the break, Lottie successfully mingled with a number of people whom she hadn't had the opportunity to chat with, due to the nut debacle, at the past month's gathering. Thankfully, those she met didn't appear to be aware that she had provided the offending almond slices and she wisely chose not to share this information, instead enjoying the light-hearted chatter of her female companions.

Lottie was approached by the baby-dykes, who she now knew to be Davina and Trina. To no one's surprise they'd engaged in an impulsive fumble in the ladies room during the break at the past group. They were happy to share that they had quickly and fully consummated their relationship that very evening, and a week later they had moved into a flat together and were now happily cohabiting with their house-dwelling rabbits. They had come to group that evening in the hope of getting Pru's guidance about the next step in their relationship, which was apparently to adopt a jointly owned pet. Lottie and her companions warmly congratulated the pair. Lottie noticed Ms. Bentley sitting in the front row, clasping a cage containing a well-cared for parakeet. Keen to avoid another encounter, Lottie moved out of her view and turned her attention back to Davina and Trina.

Although not fully conversant in the ways of the lesbian world, one thing Lottie did happen to know was that baby-dykes, or young lesbians to be more politically correct, were known for their impulsive unions. They were usually quick to move in together and, sadly, sometimes even quicker to move out again. They stood side by side and sharing their enthusiasm for the home furnishings section of Ikea and their mission to create a love nest. Lottie observed that they seemed well suited, despite the obvious impulsivity of their cohabitation. They looked remarkably similar with their willowy athletic builds, as they stood side by side their bodies mirrored one another in expression and matching vibrant and eclectic clothing. Drawn by the happy chatter, others joined the group and Lottie's attention wandered.

Turning to talk to someone else she was vaguely aware that both Davina and Trina were attempting to get her attention, and were pointing in unison to the corridor where Boots was housed. The chatter drowned out their words but she could make out that they were both chuckling and clearly sharing a joke. Lottie gave them a quizzical look, and decided that she probably ought to check on Boots in case the sedative was fully wearing off, in which case she planned a quick getaway.

She shivered at the notable drop in temperature and the dim light as she entered the passageway. Lottie fleetingly considered that maybe Boots had somehow dimmed the light in order to avoid detection by any passing prey, but quickly dismissed her paranoia. She took a moment as her eyes readjusted to the dim lighting before she registered the open cage door of Pru's Persian pussy. For a moment she was confused. She was sure that Pru hadn't yet produced her prize pet for the crowd. As she stepped with trepidation into the depths of the darkened corridor, she noticed a peculiar low rumbling noise which appeared to be coming from behind the heavily-lined tartan door curtain. She hurried towards the noise and swept back the curtain and as she did so, stifled a horrified gasp at the sight before her.

Boots, obviously having taken advantage of the faulty clasp on his carrier, was fully mounted above the Persian who laid submissively below him with her bottom raised high in the air. It transpired that the nameless Persian was the source of the low rumbling noise as she appeared to be conveying her pleasure at his attentions. Boots ploughed determinedly on oblivious to his audience before skilfully dismounting to lay casually by the side of his sated mate.

Lottie spluttered with outrage as she attempted to shoo Boots away from his elicit union. Lottie was sure that her horror would only be surpassed by that of Pru if she had discovered the pair. Lottie couldn't help but think that Boots would not look amiss if he struck up a cigarette and shared it with his new-found love.

"Fuck!" she mumbled glancing furtively around for signs of any other witnesses. The corridor remained clear, and she hurriedly swept Boots up, for once oblivious to the danger of physical harm he posed and rammed him unceremoniously back into his sprung jail. The Persian did not require the same treatment as she happily ambled back to her waiting unlatched fur-lined basket.

Horrified by the potential and unthinkable implications of this illicit liaison, Lottie hurried to make her excuses and left the group. Once in the privacy of her car she loudly berated Boots for his lose morals for the duration of the journey home. Boots maintained a dignified silence. Lottie saw evidence that the sedative was quickly wearing off and he was most definitely showing signs of his old self, steadily eyeing Lottie from the dark recesses of his cage.

Once she was safely indoors she took no chances, as she unhooked the carrier door only once he was within the safe confines of his utility room home. Not waiting for him to emerge she swiftly shut the inner door and retreated to call Mel who she knew would be devastated to miss such a giggle-fest.

Lottie kicked off her shoes and retrieved the final unopened bottle of prosecco from the wine rack. Mel had not picked up the phone but sent her a stealth text to explain she was playing drinking games with a man she was pretty sure was alcohol dependent.

Lottie chuckled to herself, no doubt Mel would emerge late tomorrow afternoon with a tale of woe about why she found it so hard to find herself a decent bloke. Pouring the fizzy good stuff into the waiting glass, she remembered some of the men who Mel had presented to her during the years.

The best by far was the bigamist who had been discovered to be leading an alternative life with his wife and four children. Mel had struggled to understand why he stayed with her in her flat for only two out of the four weeks in any month, but it all made so much more sense when she discovered his second phone with the broken English text messages demanding he collect full fat milk and Calpol from the local Co-op in Fraserburgh. Not being the most multicultural district of the Highlands, it had not been too difficult for her to locate Poi, who had tried to explain that her husband was more than man enough for the both of them. Mel declined the offer and promptly returned to the flat to dismember his Armani collection of clothes, before posting a letter to his mother explaining that she had four new grandchildren.

Scrolling through her phone she discovered a virgin voice-mail from earlier in the day. "Ms. Grant, I need to talk to you urgently about Robbie. He's in rather a lot of trouble. Please could you call the school's main office to make an appointment?"

"Robbie!" she shrieked, spilling her prosecco as she headed for the darkened man cave on the second floor to search for signs of life.

Drugs, Sex and The Ex

THE NEXT MORNING, after a sleepless night, and as she drove rather recklessly, Lottie was ashamed to remember the evening before, when she had resorted to a tactic she didn't usually employ. Snooping. Robbie had left his mobile phone on the kitchen table, and as it was normally glued to his hand, its unguarded state was very suspicious. She had resisted checking his phone until nearly ten when desperation and curiosity had got the better of her. Having no luck in cracking the passcode, she had gotten no farther than the front screen, which had depicting an unsavoury picture of four female bottoms. She had resolved to confront Robbie about this and demand the passcode. However, Robbie had left the house early, and gone with him was the digital evidence she felt sure would inform her understanding of what was to come at school.

Lottie pulled into the school car park, and leaving her car haphazardly in the empty disabled spot, reluctantly made her way towards the entrance. She was still none the wiser about the reason for her summons to attend the school and Robbie had been silent on the subject, although she noticed he was showing an emotion unusual for him. Fear. This only served to compound her own anxiety and she was left with an inevitable feeling of foreboding. Not a stranger to a summons from the school regarding Robbie, she knew this was more than just a remonstration for his continuing failure to hand in homework. Nervously, she tugged at her suit jacket as she idly wondered whether she should tell her manager that she'd simply made a detour to pick up donuts for the team. She knew that whatever she did, her poor timekeeping would certainly be noticed this morning.

After several attempts to gain the attention of the school receptionist, who ignored her, Lottie sensed there was an air of disapproval. After what seemed like an eternity, Lottie was finally instructed to sit in the desolate reception area. She felt an overbearing sense of shame as she concluded that the receptionist clearly knew more about this mysterious situation that she did. Eyes cast down, she sat opting for an inconspicuous seat at the back of the area as a small act of rebellion against the receptionist who had instructed her to a different area of the room. Finally seated, she glanced around and was dismayed to see that she had missed the recent appearance of the biological father of her offspring, now filling an orange plastic chair with his hefty frame.

Donald was a heavily built man with a dark mop of ginger hair which flopped somewhat foppishly over his left eye. He had an irritating habit of flicking his head in an overly-feminine gesture to remove it, and Lottie had always been annoyed by his resistance to having it permanently removed by the barber. There were many other things about Donald that Lottie had found infernally irritating, but ultimately, she had concluded that this probably stemmed from the fact he was simply a man. The divorce had not been an amicable one, with various disputes about financial matters and child custody.

Since the resolution of those issues, the contact between them had remained strained but functional, in order to accommodate changes to the arrangements for the children, but little else. Now Robbie was older and in sixth form it was much easier to manage the situation with her ex. Nevertheless, a pang of guilt filled her as she realised it hadn't even occurred to her to call him about the mysterious summons to school. It seemed however, that the school had fulfilled that duty, which only filled her with concern about the severity of the situation.

Donald made brief eye contact with Lottie but made no attempt to move to a seat closer, opting instead for a formal nod in her general direction.

I wonder if he knows what this is all about, she thought. She wasn't aware that Robbie was in the habit of confiding in his dad, but then again, there was clearly a lot she wasn't aware of. He avoided all eye contact and continued to tug at invisible lint on his cheap suit. Lottie noticed with disdain that it was made of cheap shiny fabric and was clearly several sizes too small, with the buttons of his equally cheap shirt straining around his midriff. With his free hand he subconsciously ran his pudgy fingers nervously through his overgrown fringe, a tell-tale sign that he was equally nervous, which gave her some comfort. While she observed him from a safe distance, she battled an unpleasant metallic taste in her mouth. Lottie had finally ended her marriage to Donald after spending her twenties and early thirties battling with her own truth. She briefly marvelled at how she had managed to create two children with him and more importantly, how she had managed to maintain the façade of heterosexuality throughout their fourteen-year marriage.

Lottie nervously glanced at the clock, and tried to recall a time when she had ever felt attracted to the man she saw before her, but not one memory came to mind. Instead, she remembered the birth of Robbie at the Aberdeen maternity unit. After arriving at the hospital, Donald had resumed his deep slumber in the hospital chair and her irritation had increased as she recalled how he had quickly returned to sleep in the midst of her labouring through to birth with their first child. Ignoring the slumbering giant beside her, she had attempted to get into the bath to soothe the early stages of her labour. Twenty minutes later, she had realised this may have been an ill-thought-out plan as her contractions had increased dramatically, and she had soon realised that she was not going to be able to get out of the bath unassisted. Luckily, a midwife came to her rescue and chastised Donald for not keeping a better eye on her.

Disgruntled, he had moved his chair closer to the television and tuned into an episode of a popular soap opera. As her labour had progressed to the final stages, the midwife, clearly unimpressed by his lack of involvement, had firmly turned off the television and instructed him to come and assist with the birth. Lottie would never forget the loudly distinguishable tut that had escaped his lips. Angrily, the midwife had announced the imminent birth of their first child.

After that experience, Lottie had taken an easier option for the birth of Archie. Drafting in her mother and sister, she had sent Donald packing to the golf course until Archie had made an appearance. Her disappointment with his lack of enthusiasm surrounding the births of both of his boys was further compounded by his subsequent lack of involvement in their daily lives. One of the driving reasons behind her heterosexual marriage had been the desire for a family life in the traditional sense. But after a series of astounding disappointments she realised that she was essentially bound to be a single parent, albeit a married one. She decided to make the arrangement official and shortly thereafter she had filed for a divorce.

Despite their history she had a feeling that presenting a united front to the school today would be a more effective way to manage whatever it was they were going to have to deal with, and so she made a silent pledge to behave in a mature and adult way while they were forced together, for the sake of their firstborn. A shadowy female figure appeared and waved them both through into the staff area. Lottie passed through the metal detector, a sign of the times she thought. A loud bleep signalled the presence of something unauthorised and the security guard summoned her to him and gave a cursory glance into her handbag before waving her on. Donald dutifully passed through without incident. Fumbling with her handbag to compact the contents and attempt to secure the clasp, her hand felt a miniature vibrator, a joke present Alice had given to her earlier in the week. Alice had thought the miniature device was hilarious and she had called it a starter pack for Lottie which they had laughed about. Realising she had forgotten to take it out of her bag she rammed it firmly towards the bottom giving silent thanks that the security guard appeared not to have seen it.

Lottie and Donald stood a comfortable distance apart, having knocked on the closed staffroom door. Lottie was feeling increasingly impatient and could not shake the feeling that she was being treated like a naughty child. With great gusto, Lottie knocked very loudly once again on the closed door. A young, girlish member of staff immediately appeared and gave her a look of barely disguised disgust.

She sucked on the end of her pen. "Ms. Grant I presume?" she muttered. Ignoring Donald, she scuttled back into the depths of the room, her scarlet nail summoning them to follow her.

A bustle of activity from a faraway door broke the awkward silence, as the head teacher and his ever-present assistant, who Lottie knew was his second and much younger wife, swept authoritatively into the room. Lottie couldn't help but notice that he almost glided across the floor, and although she peered hard she still couldn't identify any movement in his feet. She concluded that he had a Voldemort-like quality, although clearly his tartan socks rather ruined this image.

He leaned forward in his chair in a definite attempt to emphasise his authority. "Your son is expelled permanently from this school with immediate effect!" he barked.

Both Lottie and Donald were frozen and continued to sit without response, while the stunned silence pervaded the entire room. Lottie cast a surreptitious glance at her ex-husband who remained quiet although his face was ashen.

Lottie clasped her arms around her waist. "I beg your pardon, I don't quite understand!" she stuttered.

The Headmaster looked on with a semblance of pity before slowly repeating himself. "Expelled, permanently."

Lottie inhaled sharply. She felt as if she had been kicked in the gut. "Robbie's *expelled*?" She recovered herself with remarkable speed as anger surged through her replacing the anxiety. Her lioness hackles rose as she defended her cub.

"Is he, fuck!" she spat venomously in the direction of the scandalised headmaster.

The tables were turned and now it was the headmaster's turn to look shocked. He exchanged a knowing look with his assistant/second wife which Lottie later recalled was a look that said *no wonder.*

"For *what*?" she asked.

"Dealing drugs, on school premises," the head teacher stated emphatically and with complete righteous satisfaction.

"This is just ridiculous. Ri-dic-u-lous!" she shouted back at him.

Donald remained silent as Lottie eyed the headmaster, exuding rage and defiance. Donald was frozen in his chair, failing to join in the remonstration, his head hanging as he took his typical avoidance approach to anything involving his emotional presence for their children. Irritated by his lack of involvement, Lottie knew she was close to a full-on meltdown.

Clearing her throat and forcing herself into an upright position, showing what she hoped was equal authority, she asked aloud. "Robbie was dealing what? How? I just don't understand!" She shot a glance at her ex who remained quiet and withdrawn. Suddenly, the realisation dawned on her and she hissed at him. "You idiot! You knew!"

Looking sheepish, and ignoring the others, he stuttered an explanation. "Well, not exactly, no. I mean I knew he was getting money, but he told me he was selling cola. I mean coke, well obviously not *that* type of coke. Shit! Well, you know what I'm saying."

Not trusting herself to respond, she remained silent and this time it was Donald's turn to receive the frosty stare of the others.

Lottie was seething with rage and her hands were shaking with a sudden desire to choke the life out of him, and not for the first time. "No, I fucking do not know what you are saying, you half-wit!"

As she strangled the strap of her handbag as an inadequate substitute, Lottie reminded herself that they were on school premises, undoubtedly now being judged for a thousand parental indiscretions. She returned her attention to the headmaster who was silently observing the exchange between the two dysfunctional parents of Robbie, and shaking his head to convey his disapproval of their manner of communication.

Undeterred by the judgement pouring down upon her she

persisted with her questioning. "Well, *how* do you know?"

"Forty witnesses, Ms. Grant, all of whom have provided a statement for the police."

Lottie swallowed hard. "Forty? The police?"

The headmaster fought a smirk. "Yes Ms. Grant, forty students have all testified to the fact that they bought cannabis from your son, on school premises."

Suddenly Lottie felt the world spinning and bile rose in her throat. Her son was the local bloody drug dealer! She desperately needed air and clawed at the tight neck of her jumper, and suddenly there was only a welcome blackness.

A SHORT WHILE later, she came around. Her legs were raised on a stool and the floor provided a pleasant cooling effect. Blinking, she gradually regained her bearings and found herself staring at the petite mule-clad feet of the headmaster's wife. In her hand she helpfully clutched Lottie's bag. Lottie looked to the side to avoid the view up the woman's skirt — which she observed was far too short to be considered decent in a school environment — and she was horrified to notice that the pink end of the vibrator was protruding through the opened zipper at the top of the bag.

"Ms. Grant, are you feeling better now? I can appreciate this must have just been such a shock! Your ex-husband has gone and the head had to leave for an important meeting about the budget. He's printed your son's exclusion letter, and a copy will also be sent to the local authority. Would you like me to call you a taxi home?"

Recovering herself, Lottie shook her head in the negative and fought back tears as she beat a hasty retreat from the school to the sanctuary of her car. As she sat for a moment she fumbled for the mobile phone inside her jacket pocket, and angrily hammered out a text message to Robbie.

Meet me at home, now! We need to talk!

On the short drive home, Lottie didn't even attempt to hold back the river of hot tears. She was devastated. Smoking cigarettes was one thing, but Robbie had taken his teenage rebellion to another level. She racked her brain for clues that she may have missed, and she was overwhelmed with guilt that she had been so wrapped up with her new relationship that she had surely neglected Robbie. He must have been so unhappy. Chewing on her fingernail, she vowed to punish him and then love him more, to try to get to the bottom of this.

For the remainder of the journey, she consoled herself with fantasies about the many ways that Donald could possibly meet a painful and grizzly end.

"Fat twat!" she mumbled venomously. He had obviously known that Robbie was in trouble, but how? Had Robbie gone to him to confess? Had Donald brushed it off? "It'll be all right, mate," as he was so fond of referring to his son.

"Fucking idiot," she seethed. "You're his fucking dad, not his mate!"

Angrily screeching to a halt outside the house, she abandoned the car, blocking both the harbour and anyone else who might be parked farther down the lane. Grabbing her keys, she rushed to the door.

In the living room, Lottie was met by a surly and defensive Robbie, who was sitting in the dark clutching his phone. He glared at her from the protection of his hooded top which partially shielded his face. His hoodie slipped and the glint in his eyes clearly conveyed defiance but behind that she sensed he was like a cornered wild animal.

When she arrived home, she had intended to read him the riot act. However, suddenly she felt unsure of how to proceed. Casting her mind back to her own teenage years, she remembered the fear she had felt when she had been in trouble which had required her mother's intervention. Confrontation had inevitably led to more anger, and she had remained fiercely determined not to show her mum how she felt, it was her only power. Determined not to fall into that trap, she sat down and placed her hands calmly into her lap.

Robbie continued to challenge her with a mean glare. He remained seated and she felt a glimmer of hope that this indicated she had a chance of being able to get through his steely demeanour. Lottie realised in that very moment that this test was something that she needed to pass if she had any hope of reaching her troubled teenager.

"Can you put the kettle on? That is unless you need to bag up some more spliffs before you lose the light."

Robbie looked at her in disbelief, sure he was being mocked. He hitched up his trousers and headed for the kitchen.

Sometime later, Robbie and Lottie sat in the living room. Dusk had overtaken them, but both were reluctant to break the newfound connection they had established during the past two hours. Robbie turned his head and tried to sniff inconspicuously. Despite the fading light, it had not escaped Lottie that Robbie was crying. Of course, there were going to have to be consequences for his actions, serious ones, but more importantly, Lottie had been desperate to know how Robbie had ended up on such a destructive path. As they talked, she had been horrified to discover that Robbie had been befriended by some local youths who had recently been released from the young offender's institute at HMP Inverness. Former pupils of the school, Robbie had vaguely known them and clearly felt some sense of community in their company as he struggled to stay in education after entering the sixth form. He told her that these boys had treated him as one of them and, having few friends of his own, he had found himself drawn into bunking off school and smoking weed with them at the local park.

After a while he said they had started to put pressure on him to earn his free cannabis by dealing it. They had told him that the school's students were an untapped source of cash and they wanted him to provide a conduit for the cannabis trade at his comprehensive school. He tearfully told his mum that he had increasingly felt out of his depth, and fearing the consequences, one of which, he said, was that they'd threatened to tell his mum that he was smoking weed, he quickly became trapped in a revolving door of sale and supply.

It transpired that his new associates considered him a gifted salesman, increasing the pressure on him to continue to ply his trade despite the increasing likelihood that he would be caught. Robbie knew that the person leading the sales operations was known as M but he had never encountered him, dealing only with the tattooed youths from the local prison. Eventually, an unanticipated locker search at his school had revealed him to be in the possession of a roll of sandwich bags and his mum's baking scales, with his locker providing a makeshift hideaway for his illegal trade.

With a long road ahead of them, Lottie realised that she would need to refocus on her parenting if she wanted to try to help him resolve this situation. She decided to give him some space while she had a much-needed drink and took time to reflect on the way forward from here. Robbie disappeared rapidly to his room.

The Coming-Out Party

YAWNING, LOTTIE PULLED back the bedroom curtains and perched on the end of the bed. With her spare hand she absently stroked Alice's foot which was peeking out from beneath the duvet. Her eyes scanned the horizon as she searched for signs of the winter sun through the hazy sea-mist which lingered on the horizon. Careful to avoid disturbing the slumbering Alice, she reached forward and opened the window. Closing her eyes, she was greeted by a sudden rush of frost-laced air, pregnant with the salty smell of the grey sea. What an amazing day to turn forty! She smiled in anticipation of the day ahead.

Grabbing her journal, she turned to a fresh page, writing in big letters:

```
40!!

So far:
Two gorgeous boys
Maintained my sanity through divorce (just!)
Finally out (except for work—must sort this by
41)
Spectacularly sexy girlfriend (keep her!)
Own house
Own teeth
Fabulous sense of humour

Needed:
URGENT—New school for Robbie
New job (with living wage, possibly even career
path!)
Playground street-cred
Housekeeper
Lottery win
Learn to sing (think about lessons)

Looking forward to the next 40!
```

She slammed the journal shut, noticing a sudden movement from the bottom end of the duvet. Odie appeared with his hound nose twitching frantically, sniffing for any possible threat from the chilly salt-laden breeze filling the room. Detecting nothing, he licked his mistress's protruding big toe before disappearing back underneath the covers. Leaning backward, Lottie tucked the duvet around the slender form of Alice and gently replaced an escaping strand of hair behind her ear. Alice broke a smile before burying her face in the pillow.

Pulling on her slipper socks Lottie felt a toasty warm hand creep up the back of her pyjama top. "Where are you off to so early, birthday girl?" Alice murmured as her hand gently caressed the small of Lottie's back. "Don't go without opening your presents!"

Lottie paused mid slipper-sock and was persuaded back beneath the duvet. Alice produced an envelope and a small red, ribbon-wrapped box. Lottie opened the envelope first, recognising the logo of a local travel agent. Squealing with delight, she hugged Alice as she read the details of a weekend for two in Paris. Alice was well aware that Lottie had longed to go to France and that she considered her schoolgirl French to be above average. She often told Alice she felt she must have been French in a previous life, much to Alice's amusement. She frequently reminded Lottie that her love of a baguette smothered in cream cheese did not constitute evidence of her French genetic heritage.

"*Merci beaucoup,*" Lottie drawled in what she hoped was a seductive French accent.

Alice shook her head in despair before drawing Lottie's attention to a smaller envelope which had fallen out. Picking it up, Lottie raised an eyebrow before opening it, and saw that inside was a small handwritten note. Reading the message her eyes filled with tears.

```
Lottie,
I love you. I think I knew after our second date
that I was going to love you and now I know I
do.
You make my heart sing,
Alice xxx
```

Looking up their eyes met and Lottie noted the anxious frown which was etched on Alice's delicate features. Reaching across she cupped Alice's cheeks and pulled her forward planting a tender kiss on her lips. The tension left Alice's face as Lottie replied. "I love you, too!"

Beaming broadly, Alice chuckled. "I knew you'd make me say it first though!" she said, before she pushed the box towards Lottie. She carefully unwrapped her second gift, squealing in delight for a second time as she discovered the contents. The rabbit-ears only version of the Ann Summers acclaimed Rabbit vibrator.

"Good job I didn't open that in front the kids!" she giggled.

Sometime later, Lottie emerged from the bedroom with an afterglow. Alice continued to expand her knowledge of the sex-toy industry and she was a willing pupil. Lottie flicked the kettle on to boil as she turned her attention to her mobile phone which had been buzzing insistently with multiple text messages and several missed calls during the past hour.

Scanning her messages, she noticed a text from Virginia.

Mate, can't wait to come to the party, it's going to be cracking, I'll bring bubbly, Love ya. V xx

Just then the phone rang and it was Mel. "Hey, sweet cheeks! No cocktails for you tonight, the family is coming remember? Anyway, can't stop. I promised your mum I'd pick up some booze. I'm guessing prosecco is the preferred tipple. I think it's gonna be a right laugh, but your mum has no idea who's coming! Happy Birthday! Laterz!"

Lottie groaned inwardly.

A couple of weeks earlier her mother had begun to harass her about her birthday plans. Not being big on event planning, Lottie had happily abdicated responsibility for organising anything, having given her mother permission to arrange a small gathering. Only three hours later, she had been horrified to discover that she had opened a Facebook invitation — *Lottie's 40th* — which was open to all and sundry. She had decided in the end that her mum's intentions were well meant and left it in the hands of her family to create a guest list.

Mel hung up and Lottie was nearly knocked off her feet by Odie who was hoping for his morning chicken. Behind him, hoodie up and his free hand unpleasantly lodged down his trousers, stood Robbie. In his other hand, thrust forward was what looked suspiciously like a birthday card. Lottie's heart was immediately filled with love. Her surly teenager had managed to muster up a card! This was going to be an amazing day. She thanked him rather too profusely, leaving him embarrassed. He hastily retreated from the unwelcome attention, back to his man cave.

Lottie flung open the back door and gulped in two large

breaths of fresh air. The familiar gurgling of her irritable bowel reminded her that she needed to remain steady and calm in order to avoid an unwelcome flare-up of her condition. However, thoughts of the day invaded her peace, and she wished she had paid more attention to the guest list.

What she knew for sure was that the family was coming, her brother and sister along with their various offspring and unsuitable spouses. Also her mum, Elspeth, who had until recently lived abroad in France, was making a guest appearance.

Pre-Alice, Lottie had a determined approach of complete denial to the stealthy progression of years leading her forward towards this significant milestone. But now she felt a renewed sense of optimism for the second act of her life, and she intended to embrace her new-found prospects by immersing herself in the celebrations, vowing to put the struggles she'd had to get to this point behind her.

As she poured hot water from the kettle, she contemplated the upcoming family-bonding time with little enthusiasm. Suffice to say, her family was not close. Her elder brother, John, however, had been a source of support in her coming out days. He maintained a determined approached to support her no matter what her life choices were, as she did with him. A prime example of this was his choice of spouse. Lesley, his wife, was not a favourite on Lottie's list of in-laws. Adding to this was Lesley's determined scepticism about Lottie's sexual orientation. She continued to struggle with the concept of Lottie's newfound sexual proclivity.

"But Lottie, you're not a *real* lesbian, you've had cock!" she had announced at one family occasion.

Lottie had chosen to humour her sister-in-law, and the conversations she wasn't able to avoid usually ended with Lottie biting down hard on her lip while nodding and smiling. At a previous gathering of the clan, Lesley had been faced with the wrath of Archie who was a firm supporter of his mum's choices, and was a flag-waving rainbow-wearing member of the Mum's out and proud support club. Archie had come in on the back of yet another awkward conversation between Lottie and Lesley, where Lesley had been enquiring as to whether Lottie had considered herself perhaps as bisexual as opposed to gay. Without uttering a word Archie had purposefully marched forward towards his aunt and skilfully pushed a pickled gherkin into her flapping mouth. Aunt Lesley recoiled in horror at the offending pickled object, and pushed Archie's hand firmly away trying to eject the unwelcome condiment.

"Archie! For goodness sake, what are you doing? Get off, you know I *hate* gherkins!" Suddenly Archie stopped and a broad smile broke out across his juvenile features. With resignation he sat back on his ankles and proceeded to dip into the jar he'd been carrying as he munched on a gherkin.

Shocked by his physical assault, even Lottie was rendered speechless, and both had stared at Archie with something akin to fear.

Archie, oblivious to the fuss he had caused, had paused in his munching to declare through a full mouth. "*You* don't like gherkins and Mum doesn't like boys!"

Point made. Lottie smiled broadly remembering the pride she had felt at her child's simplistic, yet ingenious, explanation of his point. When it came to worldly understanding and loyalty, Archie was her favourite person for grounding her back to what was important.

Lottie folded napkins around her meagre collection of battered cutlery, while her mind wandered as she recalled her past encounter with her sister's husband, Tony, the previous year. Lottie had made a dutiful visit to her sister, Amanda's, home, despite her reservations about their lifestyle and the New Age church organisation they had immersed themselves in. Lottie was not religious but nor was she anti-religion. Nevertheless, after some difficult discussions with her sister on the topic of the Bible's supposed view of homosexuality — she hated that word — she wasn't a frequent visitor to her sister's home.

However, during this particular stay, the church was holding a fellowship gathering which had required Lottie's participation. To her relief the gathering was very informal, and food and non-alcoholic beverages were in plentiful supply. Mingling as little as possible, Lottie had made several skilful circuits of the downstairs rooms, avoiding in-depth conversation with any of the guests. Tony was a self-proclaimed preacher who had partially completed a course in theology before opting out to make his own interpretation of the ancient religious scripts. Lottie could not deny that their home was impressive. Generally filled with a large collection of social misfits, the occasion exuded acceptance.

On previous visits she had encountered a number of unusual individuals who carried with them stories of their past lives before they found Tony, and ultimately repented their sins before the Lord. During one such stay Lottie had met an armed robber who was on the run from the police. Initially, Tony and Amanda had chosen to respect his choice to follow his own path, which happened to lead him away from the area where he had committed his crimes. However, on waking to prepare for the Easter service they had discovered a number of missing valuables, including their handcrafted crucifix, which had caused a considerable amount of upset. Being a professional, Tony had concluded the service and fellowship obligations before forming a posse of willing volunteers to find the culprit—including a basset hound not so inspirationally called Fred. She was surprised to see the number of—possibly illegal—weapons carried by some members of the group, including an elaborately decorated Samurai sword, and several knuckle dusters. They tracked the offender for a number of miles—from the scent taken from his bed sheets—and found him in an inelegant embrace with a local barmaid who had a fancy for a rogue.

The offender was quickly dispatched to the waiting arms of the local constabulary with only minor cuts and bruises, and Tony and Amanda had subsequently added a polite question to their welcome pack asking potential group members to *please* disclose their previous convictions.

On her most recent visit however, Lottie's luck had run out when she was collared by a buxom middle-aged woman who was keen to engage her in conversation about her new and improved shortbread recipe. Lottie had endured a polite exchange, but was casting her eyes around the kitchen looking for an excuse to exit. In the dimly lit corner of the kitchen she spied a pantry and managed to continue her conversation about shortbread while making stealthy steps towards that general direction hoping for a darkened sanctuary. Still nodding vigorously at the stranger who was debating the importance of salt in her shortbread, she spotted Tony in the darker recesses of the storage cupboard. Peering into the gloom, it was apparent that he was in the company of another male whom Lottie recognised as the local stable boy who provided livery for Tony's three prize-winning stallions. Turning to fully face the entry of the pantry she was sure she had glimpsed Tony run his hand along the crotch of the stable lad. After she'd politely read the revised recipe for Highland Shortbread which the woman thrust into her hands, both had disappeared from view and Lottie had felt it was not her business to make any further enquiries. Keen to avoid any family friction, she decided she must have been mistaken and made a decision not to have that conversation with her sister, instead beating a fast retreat for home at the first opportunity.

Her mind returned to the present task of gathering any crockery remotely useful for presenting food, as she considered her other major problem of the day. Her mother had only recently entered the world of social media, settling on Facebook for her experimentation. She was less than savvy in the etiquette required for social networking, and Lottie noticed that she had proceeded to add Lottie's entire list of contacts to her own, as she had shamelessly canvassed for attendees for the birthday gathering. She knew that many of her friends and associates, being too polite to decline, now had her mother as a Facebook friend. Elspeth had quickly become remarkably techno savvy for her advanced years, and Lottie had to admire how she had embraced social media to make Lottie's day special.

She was less hopeful about responses to the *Lottie's 40th* invitation from her Facebook friends, some of whom were work colleagues that she hadn't appraised of the details of her personal life. Virginia had drawn her attention to this earlier in the week, and she had an uneasy feeling that she may inadvertently have been outed by her over-exuberant parent. Through the course of the week Lottie had received several confusing messages from her colleagues in the advertising department, including her very own boss, all confirming their attendance to her birthday soirée, clearly oblivious to the details of her personal situation. Ultimately, this had left Lottie with little choice but to embrace the process and hope for the best.

Lottie made a mental damage-limitation list of the likely candidates that would no doubt be attending that evening out of sheer curiosity. There were quite a few. She knew that the biggest issue during her earlier days had been to accept she was gay, but this was also equalled by the sure and certain knowledge that acknowledging this would involve readdressing her heterosexual identity to her friends and family. Following her divorce, Lottie had chosen not to share the details of the subsequent exploration of her attraction to the fairer sex, telling only a few close friends and family. As a teenager, she had explored her sexuality, but had then chosen the path of safety and family life, attempting to catalogue her earlier experiences as experimentation.

A failed marriage and two children later, Lottie had accepted the inevitable and embarked upon her dating career with women. She had never looked back. When starting her position at the newspaper she had hoped to be more open about her sexuality. However, following a startling encounter with a frisky Marketing

Director by the name of Colin in the lift to the car park, she soon understood that the world of advertising sales was misogynistic and testosterone driven. She was also scarred by her previous attempts to be out at a previous workplace and so had opted for the safety of the closet in her new job, but always intended to be more open with those who she could trust.

Making her way to the utility room, Lottie retrieved the wine glasses, and as she piled them haphazardly onto the work surface she was grateful to notice that Alice had tidied and organised the night before. She felt a spontaneous rush of love and impulsively decided to be out and proud at the party and be damned. Alice didn't deserve to be a dirty secret and the most important people in her life had already accepted her choices, so why should she care what her workmates thought?

Her thoughts were interrupted by the loud and assertive ringing of her doorbell.

"What on earth...?" she mumbled as she made her way towards the hallway.

"Superb daarling!" The front door swung open and the gravelly tones of her mother greeting Mel on the doorstep were unmistakeable.

After a hearty embrace, the pair tripped through the doorway, and grinning happily, Elspeth deposited Mel on an uncluttered sofa with a corkscrew and a bottle of wine. Lottie was warmed by the genuine affection between Mel and her mother, who fluttered around plumping cushions before she excused herself.

"Early start, my darling, early start! Those *vol-au-vents* won't make themselves you know!"

Grasping her firmly with her burly arms, she pulled Lottie into a warm embrace planting two wet kisses firmly on either cheek as she passed. Lottie dodged the bulging carrier bags she'd collected from her car, one of which she noticed seemed to contain something that looked like a collapsed flag pole. Lottie returned her mother's warm embrace, taking in the faint smell of lavender before she was swept towards the kitchen where her mother determinedly rolled up her sleeves.

Sometime later, and after a couple of hefty ports, Elspeth and Lottie had prepared a feast fit for kings and possibly also screaming queens. Forgetting her anxiety at the arrival of people unknown, her mum was techno savvy, but her memory let her down and she couldn't quite remember exactly who she had invited, Lottie disappeared upstairs to make sure there was an ample supply of toilet roll, and to see what top she could pillage from Alice's new staying over drawer. The arrival of a few of Alice's belongings in an allocated drawer had excited Lottie beyond what she thought was possible, and she still liked to look in the drawer to remind herself how serious her relationship with Alice was. Through her dating years following her divorce from the fat ginger one she had never imagined she would be in such a healthy and satisfying relationship, let alone that a drawer in her home would be dedicated to a new partner. Pilfering through the Alice drawer she grabbed a crisp white T-shirt and a pair of low rise jeans. She fingered the material, revelling in Alice's good taste in clothes — excellent and stylish, but understated.

Remembering Elspeth, who was clattering around and mumbling about ramekin dishes, she hurried downstairs again. Entering the living room, Lottie paused in shock at the cacophony of colourful balloons which were suddenly attached to every available piece of furniture.

From behind a rainbow-coloured bunch appeared Alice, who was waving at her frantically and mouthing dramatically. "The garden, the garden!"

Lottie smiled at her, attempting reassurance. The garden was a little overgrown, granted, but Lottie had been forewarned of her mother's birthday plan, and so she had spent three hours the previous evening battling the cold weather to ensure the grass was a reasonable length and that the fence panels wouldn't fall and kill an innocent reveller — anyway the chill would surely draw people inside. She smiled again at Alice and shrugged before re-entering the kitchen to arrange the prawn *vol-au-vents* her mother had spontaneously knocked up.

Elspeth was clearly stuck in an eighties time warp, thought Lottie, as she battled her way through balloons of all colours. Outside she heard Robbie giggling. Bemused, as she hadn't heard that noise come from her surly teen in a long time, she was about to go and investigate, when she heard a shriek from the utility room.

"Shit. Boots!" She broke into a sprint entering the lair of Boots to discover her mother was backed into a corner, shielding her body with a silver tray which she was wafting wildly in the direction of Boots who had risen from his own corner and stood eyeing her with interest. "Still got that, interesting cat then, dear?" she asked, as Lottie used her own body to shield Elspeth so that she could beat a hasty exit.

Shutting the door firmly, she bumped into Archie who

approached the door with determination and a wad of blu-tack. He posted a colourful note on the door:

```
BEWARE, do not enter. My cat is very angry and
he will bite you! From Archie Grant. Age 11
```

What a pretty rainbow he had drawn above his name. So artistic! A loud crash from the kitchen galvanised her back into action, just in time to note her mum disappearing outside with another bunch of balloons. Passing Archie, she tugged on his shirt and ruffled his hair, making a mental note not to drink too much prosecco until her son was safely tucked up in bed.

At the next trill of the doorbell, Lottie headed for the door, interested to see who her mum had managed to summon up for her surprise guest list. She swatted at Alice who was making feeble attempts to stop her from answering the door, still muttering about the garden. Lottie started to feel a little peeved. After all, Alice could surely have made a bit of time to assist her with the last-minute tidy-up if she'd been so worried about the outside of the house! Lottie couldn't help but feel that this was rather ironic given that earlier in the day Alice had been more interested in de-gaying the house in an attempt to avoid any awkward questions from Lottie's work colleagues.

The under-stairs cupboard now contained mounds of back copies of *Diva* magazine and the over-mantle picture of two women kissing had been replaced with a more conservative Highland scene. Likewise, the Banksy *Kissing Policemen* fridge magnet had disappeared into the depths of the cutlery drawer. She hoped that things would go without a hitch and that her two worlds could bob along beside one another for the duration of her 40th birthday celebration.

The doorbell rang out three sharp and angry jabs and she planted a kiss on Alice's cheek before firmly moving her to the side to get to the door.

"Surprise!" Lottie took a horrified step backward as Pru surged forward clutching a large Tupperware container. Behind her Mim hovered nervously.

Lottie recovered herself swiftly. "Prudence, Mim, what a lovely surprise! Do come in. Let me take your coats." Lottie turned for assistance from Alice, but she had vanished through the back door. Smiling in what she hoped was a sincere fashion, she put aside her sudden feeling of vulnerability as she welcomed the indomitable Prudence into her home.

Pru's beady eyes expertly swept the room, quickly taking in the pile of un-ironed school shirts which Lottie had not quite managed to hide properly behind the threadbare sofa.

Casting a knowing look at Mim, Pru muttered ominously. "Lovely home dear, simple and homely. Now where is your mother, who was kind enough to include me in her invitations? I have a little contribution."

As if sensing a presence, and much to the relief of Lottie, Elspeth appeared, smiling sweetly. "Well, of course you must be Prudence! Please come through, dearie."

Pru leaned forward to peck Elspeth on the cheek with her thin mealy lips before pressing the Tupperware container into her waiting hands and mumbling conspiratorially something which Lottie couldn't quite hear.

At the sound of the doorbell once again, her mother reappeared giving Lottie a quick squeeze on her way past. Lottie was filled with love for her mum in spite of her over-tanned skin and her colourful collection of neck scarves — today she was sporting two of her current favourites. It was so great to have her back in the country again, after spending many years communicating via Skype.

Her parents had separated when she was very young and her father — or Graham, as she referred to him — had not been a positive role model during her formative years, having a strong attachment to the Highland nectar, or whisky as it was called in the supermarket. Their contact was limited to the odd postcard, as he continued his tour of the distilleries of Scotland. She knew for a fact that it was highly unlikely that Graham would be making a guest appearance at the party given that her parents' divorce had rivalled the Charles and Diana saga. Glad not to be a referee, she was reassured by this thought, and fixed her smile before heading towards the living room once more, as a steady procession of guests arrived, all clutching various parcels and bottles of fizz.

Amongst them was the ever-eager Linda Lovely who Lottie was fairly certain had *not* been her Facebook friend! Eyeing her suspiciously, she could only assume that she had caught wind of the party from the others and had bagged herself an invite. However, Lottie did feel excited by the number of work colleagues who had made the effort to travel to the village for her birthday, and she greeted them warmly. She decided to introduce them to Alice, if she could track her down.

Standing with a group of work colleagues, Lottie noted that

Linda Lovely had abandoned her usual motif T-shirt in favour of an odd, but striking, rainbow-coloured dress. Lottie was amused and wondered if Linda was going to do a complete U-turn and come out as gay. Catching Lottie in the act of staring, Linda laughed loudly and emitted a loud snort which caused her boss, Ann, to drop her glass of prosecco. Oblivious, Linda waved frantically at Lottie pointing dramatically to her outrageous attire and giving Lottie an exaggerated thumbs-up signal. Ann bent down to ineffectively dab at the spilt wine and grimaced as she accidentally brushed against the corner of Lottie's comfortably worn leather chair.

Vegan, Lottie mentally noted. One of Ann's many extreme lifestyle choices. Lottie made a mental note to introduce her to Pru later, and hoped that her mother had remembered that prawn *vol-au-vents* did not constitute a vegetarian option.

Linda was still frantically trying to attract her attention, but Lottie was keen to avoid unnecessary communication with Linda, and so she smiled while scanning the room for a preferable chatting companion.

Out of the corner of her eye she noticed Odie pulling his long sausage body awkwardly up the stairs, no doubt intending to hide in the bedroom until the noise levels had receded. The house sprang to life as an unknown person reconnected her stereo speakers, and the dulcet tones of Boy George filled the room.

Still scanning the crowd, she noticed that Robbie appeared to be staring hard at Mim. She didn't have time to give him the standard manners warning about staring being rude, as she suddenly noticed the reappearance of Odie waddling awkwardly towards Alice, his small tail wagging frantically. Lottie saw that he had a white object in his mouth which he was dragging along the ground. She leaned forward for a closer look, discovering to her horror that it was her newly acquired ears only rabbit from Ann Summers. Alice skilfully swooped forward to retrieve the item from his mouth, as she swatted him playfully on his bottom. Leaning over the shoulder of her brother and bemused sister-in-law, the baby-dykes from *Pru's Group* chuckled in synchronicity while giving Lottie and Alice the thumbs-up. Lottie blushed furiously, and inwardly cursed the ever-curious Odie. That damn dog had a twisted fascination with sex toys which was bordering on the obsessive. At least Boots' anger management issues didn't flaunt her bedroom activities to the world.

Sometime later, as she tried to locate Robbie again, she was sure she saw him mouth M? Her brain was firing, and she felt sure that she was missing something. Then, suddenly, she made the connection. Surely not M, the kingpin of cannabis supply in the Highlands? She looked for Mim, and following Robbie's gaze from the front garden, she saw her climbing up towards the house from the harbour. She also noticed two dubious-looking youths climbing back into a battered VW Golf and making a hasty getaway, heading back up the hill away from the village at a speed which suggested they were leaving the scene of a bank robbery. When Mim realised that she was the object of Lottie's attention, she had the decency to look slightly embarrassed, but Lottie couldn't help but notice that she appeared to be struggling with the weight of an oversized rucksack that had an unidentified leafy plant pushing its way out through a partially closed zip. Bemused, Lottie couldn't help but think that the meeting with the two youths had been a drug deal.

Feeling shocked, Lottie forcefully challenged Mim. "Miriam, are you M?"

Smiling with undisguised pride, Mim leaned forward and whispered conspiratorially. "Pensions aren't what they once were, Lottie, I like to think of myself as The Gardener."

"The bloody *Gardener*!" Lottie shrieked.

Robbie appeared breathless at her side. "Mum, don't, not now!" he pleaded grasping her arm tightly in an attempt to stop Lottie from closing the gap between herself and M.

Lottie spluttered, unable to find the words she wanted to say but managing a feeble accusation. "You stupid woman! You've ruined his life!"

Mim looked away, seemingly ashamed.

Robbie tightened his grasp on Lottie's arm, turning her away from Mim and back towards himself. "Mum, listen! *She* didn't ruin my life, I did that all by myself! I'm a fucking idiot, I asked her to let me in on it. She said I shouldn't. She's not all bad. I'm so sorry, Mum, just so sorry!"

Lottie felt herself relax slightly, and gave her son a hug, choosing to ignore M for the time being.

Wondering if the day could get any more surreal, she spotted Pru making a beeline for Mel, who was oblivious to her approaching admirer, as she happily chatted to Virginia. However, sensing a presence, Mel turned at the last minute only to be grasped firmly by the elbow as Pru blocked any chance of her escaping. Mel looked around in wild eyed terror as Virginia abandoned her, melting seamlessly into the crowd. Even from her position of safety, Lottie could make out Pru's cackling laughter as she ran a hand through her short, thinning hair while stroking Mel seductively on her arm. Lottie laughed nervously as Mel locked eyes with her, as frantically, she tried to convey her utter terror at being targeted by a butch dyke, old enough to be her grandmother. Much as she found it funny, Lottie felt a strong sense of obligation to rescue her. However, before she could reach the increasingly desperate Mel, Alice appeared beside them. She leaned in towards Mel's ear whispering something while using her free hand to uncouple Pru's death grip on Mel's elbow. Mel stumbled backward in an ungainly fashion, before making a beeline for the alcohol-laden table at the back of the garden. Holding onto Pru's elbow, Alice steered her firmly towards Lottie, who then had her own moment of horror before regaining her composure. Pru allowed herself to be led, but occasionally glanced backward towards the disappearing Mel.

Alice planted Pru firmly in front of Lottie. "I was just explaining to Mel, that her fiancé was looking for her. I think he went towards the bottom of the garden."

Quickly picking up on Alice's attempt to resurrect Mel's heterosexual status, Lottie countered. "Really? I thought I'd seen him in the living room. Hopefully they'll track one another down."

Pru smiled knowingly, and leaning towards Lottie she spoke with enough conviction to lightly shower her with spittle. "Really dear, that lovely girl just needs to be herself. She's clearly *confused!* I thought we'd made some progress when she came to group with her poem, but she seems to have regressed. Well, everyone has their own journey, I suppose, but I fully intend to offer her my support because I can feel her frustration about her situation, and I want to offer her a lifeline. Try and encourage her to group on Thursday, dear. Ask her to come a little earlier, and I'll give her some personal time." She stumbled off determinedly, in search of Mel once again.

Alice hissed at her. "Lottie! You've properly put poor Mel in a predicament. She's positively in danger, and you need to sort it."

Lottie, smiled apologetically, but soon found the situation just too funny and chuckled. Before long Alice couldn't help but join in.

A cheer came from the back garden, and Lottie was heading out to see what was going on when an ear-piercing screech halted her dead in her tracks.

"What on earth?" she muttered. A loud tapping sound was

followed by a round of applause and her mother's voice boomed loudly across her own, and several other neighbours', gardens.

"It sounds like she's on a bloody microphone!" Lottie mused as she rushed forward into the dimly lit garden, which was shrouded in the pink glow of the early sunset. She turned the corner of the kitchen extension and was flabbergasted to note that there seemed to be even more balloons tied to the fence posts. Her mum must have bought a job lot—it looked like a bloody gay pride event! When her eyes adjusted to the dim light, Lottie was horrified to see that a makeshift stage had been constructed from old crates. She caught site of her mother standing proudly in the centre of the stage clutching a microphone. Above the staged area, was a rainbow display that had been constructed from helium balloons. To the side of the stage she noticed a large rainbow flag standing high enough to be seen from the next village.

The majority of the guests had now found their way out into the garden. The crowd of people parted as she passed, and she was greeted with pats of encouragement on her back. Making her way towards her mother with the intention of finding out what the hell was going on—she headed towards the staged area, where she noticed a banner was tacked up against the shed. Not able to make out what it said from her current position, she noticed her mother, whose arms were now outstretched, beckoning for her to come closer. Archie rushed forward, placing his chubby warm hand in hers, and he assisted her in moving through the crowd propelling her forward. Pru loomed into view thrusting her Tupperware container under Lottie's nose. Glancing downward, while still being propelled forward, she glimpsed a rainbow shaped cake covered with thick and colourful icing declaring out and proud. Confused, Lottie threw Pru a look that she hoped conveyed gratitude.

People clapped and wolf whistled and Lottie cringed to be centre of attention. She couldn't fathom how many people appeared to be squeezed into her small garden. Out of the corner of her eye she noticed Alice flapping her hands frantically towards the banner. Pleased to see her partner-in-crime, she followed Alice's indications and refocused on the banner:

Lottie Grant, age 40, Out and proud!

Lottie stood frozen to the spot. A horrific realisation slowly dawned on her. Multi-coloured balloons, rainbow decorations—

this wasn't just a birthday party. This was a full-blown coming out party! Desperately glancing back, she made brief eye contact with Alice, who shrugged apologetically before breaking into a semi-hysterical chuckle. Unable to avoid the invisible hands that propelled her forward, she managed to snatch a glass of fizz from a smiling stranger as she found herself beside her mother on the stage area. Her mother's tapping of the microphone meant that there was a persistent squealing noise, which hampered Lottie's ability to think.

The rest of the evening was something of a blur to Lottie, and which resulted in something she later thought of as being akin to post-traumatic stress disorder. She remembered a long speech by Elspeth, delivered with complete sincerity, in which she told the avid audience about her initial shock, as Lottie had announced her sexuality to her while peeling potatoes for a shepherd's pie. She informed the crowd that she had found her daughter's transition to an openly gay woman something of a challenge in the early days. Although initially concerned about the moral corruption of her grandsons, she had eventually accepted, and fully supported her daughter's lifestyle choices. She had noted that since becoming more open about her dating choices, Lottie and she had shared much hilarity about her dating disasters before she met the lovely Alice. Lottie vaguely remembered her mother becoming somewhat tearful before reading out a postcard from Lottie's father, which clearly signalled that there had been a temporary cessation in the thirty-five years of hostilities, to allow her father to make a contribution to the event. After struggling to compose herself, Archie had stepped in to assist his grandmother. He read aloud.

```
Dearest Lottie,
So sorry to miss your coming out party!
Your mother informed me you are celebrating your
40th with a wee bash for your close friends so I
won't embarrass you with any stories of your
early years!
```

Forgetting she was still holding the microphone Elspeth was heard to snort loudly before mumbling "Couldn't bloody remember any, more like!"

```
Anyway, sweetheart I'll just say that I'm
delighted to hear you are happy and well, and I
support you no matter what you choose to do with
```

```
your life, even if it is just a phase.
Love Pops x
```

A raucous round of applause saved Lottie from responding to defend her phase, and she felt the swoop of arms around her waist to discover that Alice had appeared by her side. Turning to one another, momentarily the party noise dulled as they kissed, only causing more cheers.

Robbie sidled up to the stage and grinned at his mum. "A coming out party, Mum, how cool!"

He giggled again, before shoving his hands deeply into his pockets and disappearing into the crowd.

A Child-Free Zone

GINGERLY, LOTTIE LIFTED her head from the pillow and squinted at the daylight as the slow and familiar throb of the inevitable hangover resonated with purpose, bouncing around inside her skull. Peeling her short hair back from her forehead, she leaned forward to take the cup of steaming coffee being offered to her by a smiling Alice. Alice pried open her hand and placed a pink ibuprofen tablet in it. Gratefully, Lottie forced it down with a generous swig of hot coffee, and smiled sheepishly at Alice.

"Well, that was certainly a different party, wasn't it?" she said.

Alice laughed. "Different would be one way to describe it, baby, but everyone seemed to enjoy it. Even Pru. She seemed to hit it off with your window cleaner! Why do you have your window cleaner on Facebook anyway?" she teased. "On second thought, there's probably a story attached to that, and I'm thinking that we probably haven't got time for it at the moment. I'm off to the gym, sweetie, to burn off some of the prosecco, but I'm so glad it went better than expected with your boss and work gang. Maybe now we're out we could think about moving in together?"

Lottie spluttered across her coffee. "Moving in?"

That was a bolt from the blue.

Although they'd discussed future cohabitation, they had only been seeing one another for a matter of months, and Lottie had assumed that, although this would be something certain to happen, it was definitely for the future. Nevertheless, she was surprised to find she didn't have any adverse feelings towards the idea.

Alice leaned forward and pecked her on the forehead. "Sorry, baby, you're probably not in a fit state to have this chat. Tell you what, I'll be back with lunch, so stay in bed and I'll be back to service you later. I've never been with an *older woman*!" With a cheeky pat of Lottie's not-so-pert bottom she skipped off to work her *very* pert bottom at the hellhole known as The Oasis, in Fraserburgh.

How on earth Alice had the energy to go to the gym after the amount of alcohol they'd consumed was beyond Lottie. Alice was a regular attendee at the gym, and Lottie had also been persuaded to join, although the number of times she'd actually gone, she could probably count on one hand. She was usually found working up a sweat in the sauna, although she did like to venture into the gym area to watch Alice pound the treadmill—she found it incredibly sexy to be with such a physically fit woman.

Alice bounded down the stairs to gather up her gym kit. Lottie carefully propped herself up on the pillow. "Moving in?" she repeated slowly to herself, savouring the sound. She was unable to quite believe that Alice would seriously consider living with her in the chaotic child-filled house she called home. Up until now, as a single mum, Lottie was somewhat smug that she had achieved and sustained a new relationship while simultaneously servicing the needs of two children—almost— and keeping down a job. She needed to give some serious thought to the significant hurdles which would have to be overcome in merging their two households, before being able to make the necessary progression towards achieving a cohabitation arrangement.

Alice was amazing with the kids, but visiting and living together were two completely different things. Lottie was loath to admit it, but she lived in a daily whirlwind of chaos. Chasing children out of the house for school, precariously balanced washing-up that was sometimes there for days, and more importantly she still hadn't mastered the art of pooing in front of Alice, except for the irritable bowel explosions that were too difficult to contain.

Despite all of her reservations, she did feel excited and hopeful about how things were going with Alice. Pulling the duvet over her head, she allowed herself a small squeal of excitement as she basked in the now-certain knowledge that Alice wanted to take things to the next level.

Alice's head unexpectedly reappeared around the door. "Oh baby, just one thing. It would be nice to have a little adult-only zone. Something to think about, maybe the dining room?" Without waiting for a reply, she was gone.

Lottie watched her metaphoric bubble shrivel and wither away.

And there it was.

She knew it was too good to be true. Although not entirely unexpected, a request for a child-free room within their proposed new nest of domestic bliss did not fit with Lottie's vision of them all playing *Monopoly* around the log burner. A log burner she didn't yet have of course, but she was sure this would come with a dual income household. A deep sigh escaped her as she retreated back beneath the covers to consider the request. Desperate to rationalise Alice's thinking, she tried to compare it to someone making a reasonable request for a non-smoking room in a hotel or maybe a ground-floor room with a view. She just couldn't get the image of her children knocking gingerly on the dining room door, hoping for a pass to enter, and she was flooded with misery.

She sighed again.

It was as if she'd been given a glimpse of what could have been, combining her current life with her dream life, with rails full of Alice's crisp business-like shirts. Lottie shook her head as other images crowded in: her delightful boys knocking politely on the firmly closed door of the child-free room, before a barked *enter*. Poor Archie stepping in with trepidation to request a game of *Cluedo*.

Lottie recognised that there was some history behind her extremely negative reaction. She couldn't help but feel that her tragic pattern of disastrous relationships was rearing its ugly head again. She pulled out her journal and aimlessly roamed through the previous year, remembering that a similar scenario had been suggested in a previous relationship, but in that case, it had been a summer house at the bottom of the garden. To Lottie, such a room represented a locked place where the cohabitee could assume a retreat position from family life as required. At the rebuttal of the summer house request, other suggestions had followed which included the purchase of adjoining properties where an internal door could be a portal between family life and a promising silence and sanctuary on the opposing side. Lottie slung her journal under the bed and swung her legs around to a sitting position, her enthusiasm to escape her own thoughts helping her to temporarily forget her banging head. She desperately tried to see things from Alice's perspective. She was no stranger to these conversations having therefore chosen to date non-parents in the main. Was this, in fact, a perfectly reasonable request from Lottie's procession of seemingly un-family-friendly partners? After all, she was well aware of the chaos that was her daily pattern. She felt she wasn't being fair to Alice, who she observed, had made strenuous efforts to engage in family life.

Only the past week, Alice had taken Archie to the vet's surgery for a shadowing day. Although, this didn't turn out so well she recalled, as Archie had turned out to be rather militant about what he mistakenly believed was a trapped rat in a cage in the recovery area. After letting the rat free, he had stubbornly refused to disclose its whereabouts, until a near hysterical receptionist had located it in the filing cabinet next to her desk.

Despite all of this, Lottie couldn't fight her disappointment that Alice had appeared to adopt the position of a non-parent cohabitant, and she thought she should probably look carefully for the tell-tale 666 markings on her children's perfectly-formed heads. After all, it seemed to be a pattern. Later that day, after a rummage through Archie's overgrown hair, she was satisfied that there were no such markings that she could detect anyway, although she did contemplate filling the bath with holy water just to double check.

Casting her mind back into the murky memories of her distant child-free times, she had a vague recollection of avoiding booking holidays abroad during the summer months and studiously avoiding the swimming pool during half term, reminding her of a once pre-children mind set. But since the arrival and ensuing encampment of the darling ones, her primary concern had been less about the spa facilities of a hotel and more about the credentials of the kid's club facilities. She had also learned a valuable lesson, that a post sardine-packed swimming pool trip can always be soothed with a large vanilla latte. These little things had assisted her in making a successful transition to parenthood, so why then did the presence of her children seem to be a recurring blockage to the progression of her post-divorce relationships?

Revisiting her recent choices of partners, it occurred to her that they had little in common apart from one fact, they were all, through choice, childless. Until this light-bulb moment, this fact had seemed to be something of a plus point in all of these relationships making it seemingly easier to manage only prioritising the needs of her own children rather than someone else's. It had seemed clever and well thought out—less so now though it seemed! So, if a child-free zone within the house was agreed, then it would surely seem only right that Lottie could counter-request her own bedroom complete with a sealed window which would never be opened to expose her to the icy cold blasts of a winter's night, or the incessant and irritating too-early-in-the-morning birdsong? Or, it may be more realistic to consider counter-requesting a room in which her phone calls could be made and received without the rolling of eyes as Alice expressed her dissatisfaction with length of time she spent on the phone. Not that Alice actually did this, but Lottie had experienced a surprising venture into pure melodrama by the time she had found her lost pyjama bottoms and stubbed her toe on the bed-end.

Feeling something akin to existential dread, she wrung her hands. So why then did she find herself, on more than one occasion, facing the knowledge that while she appeared to have been sufficiently beguiling for someone to want to make a home with her, she was firm in the knowledge that they did not want to share the same space with her biological descendants? The reason she concluded, was a simple one. Those who chose not to be parents were even less likely to choose the role of live-in step-parent. Concluding that she had reached an epiphany of understanding, she stomped down the stairs in search of toast and a soothing episode of *Home and Away*.

By the time Alice was due to return, Lottie had worked herself up into a self-righteous position of indignation. She decided to tackle this issue head on, and so she dragged herself into the shower, intending to banish the children to Grandma's for the afternoon, while she and Alice thrashed out the issue. She was determined that she wasn't going to compromise the well-being of her children for the sake of her own happiness.

MANY HOURS LATER, and after a lot of thrashing that didn't involve much talking, they emerged from the bedroom to rescue the roast beef and deliciously fluffy roast potatoes that Lottie had miraculously created. It seemed her cooking was much improved when she was in a traumatised state.

"Lottie, you are a twit sometimes," Alice murmured, rubbing her hand into the curve of Lottie's back while Lottie wriggled as she wrestled with the pan of tantalising meat.

"Well, bloody hell! I hadn't even thought about moving in together, and then you throw that curveball. Child-free bloody room indeed!"

Alice shrugged. "I didn't see it as such a biggie! I was just asking for a small office space to do my invoicing, but I might have phrased it a bit better, I suppose. What I meant was, a space to work in, not a room to avoid your kids — who I really like, by the way. I can't believe you worked yourself up into a frenzy, you lunatic. I'm all for family life, especially if this is what I can expect for Sunday lunch."

Lottie put down the hot pan and swirled around towards

Alice, shamefaced and feeling vulnerable at her unintended attempt to sabotage the relationship.

Sensing her fear, Alice firmly gripped her hands and looked into her eyes. "Drop the baggage, Lottie. I'm not like the others. This relationship is amazing and I want you, family and all. I know a good thing when I'm onto it and I know we'll be happy. We're perfect for one another! I'm asking you to consider letting me move in, and Odie too, of course!"

Lottie smiled coyly and they kissed deeply. Lottie felt breathless with the passion conveyed in the kiss and drew a deep brave breath before replying. "Sorry, I know, I know! It's just been a struggle, Alice. My kids are, well deliciously unusual and I know it's a big thing to take this whole family on. But I won't, I simply *won't* ban them from any room, although I understand some quiet space for work is needed."

Alice beamed. "It only makes me love you more. Now, get my bloody dinner out. I'm starving!"

Chuckling, Lottie waved the carving knife in her direction. "Watch it! I haven't made the Yorkshire puddings yet. There's still room for a cooking disaster."

Alice swatted her with the oven glove. "You're under cooking supervision. It's a team effort my gorgeous girl, a team effort!"

Lottie's joy was interrupted by the shrill ring of the telephone and she hurried to answer it. From the handset a loud piercing shriek chilled her. Lottie resorted to holding the phone away from her ear, finding the noise difficult to tolerate.

Eventually, through considerable gasping and crying, she made out the unmistakeable tones of Pru. "P-Pregnant, my beautiful darling princess has been *defiled*! *Raped*! *Deflowered*!"

Lottie gulped. "Really?" she asked, her voice slightly too highly-pitched. "Shocking, Pru! What on earth could have happened? That's simply awful!"

Pru swallowed back mucus noisily. "Oh Charlotte, I knew you would understand, being a cat lover. It's as if my child has been mistreated!"

Crossing her fingers and everything else that would bend, Lottie replied cautiously. "Pru, it's simply unbelievable and I'm sure that the culprit will come forward, they've surely got to!"

Clearing her throat, Pru consoled herself. "Well I suppose that Jasper, the Siamese terror from next door, and my darling Sappho will inevitably make a handsome brood. I can't think how they could have been alone in an intimate sense but it's something we're going to have to get past, I suppose!" Pru ended the call abruptly.

Lottie was still shaken by the revelation that her son had been a drug dealer, and now a phone call declaring her a grandparent in waiting. "Only one thing for it!" she thought, and she retrieved the bottle of Glenfiddich she kept in the utility room for medicinal purposes.

Clicking the light switch she reached to the higher shelf, leaning precariously above the empty cat basket. Startled by a loud bang, Lottie turned as Boots leapt from the open window onto the worktop below. Prowling backward and forward, he purred loudly before doubling his body to firmly lick his balls.

"Boots! You are shameless!" Lottie shrieked before grabbing him firmly and ejecting him through the open window.

Out of Office

BUOYED BY THE prospect of impending cohabitation, Monday morning was looking rosy and Lottie silently resolved to embrace her new out status with her boss and work colleagues. She had to admit that she had been somewhat perturbed by her mother's clumsy efforts to celebrate her diversity but she did feel a sense of relief that it was finally out in the open with everyone. If she was honest with herself, she knew that she would never have found the right time to redress her assumed heterosexuality with her colleagues, and the longer she had been in the closet the harder it had become to even contemplate it. As a token of her appreciation for their acceptance of her, Lottie had brought the remainder of the rainbow cake for colleagues who had not been able to make it to the party. She hoped that it would not be too long until she stopped being the subject of office gossip. She had never liked being the centre of attention.

Lottie pulled into her usual space in the car park, and spotted Dan-from-accounts who gave her a sheepish smile before disappearing into the building. Shaking her head in dismay, thoughts of her own notoriety left her as she remembered her recent encounter with Dan late one evening.

In short, Dan had revealed himself as the secret bottom-photocopying maniac that had posted numerous copies of his ample and clearly hairy posterior on desks around the call centre. The pictures had been the talk of the office for many weeks preceding her discovery, and there had been a number of potential suspects in the frame. Lottie was a kind soul, and she had loyally kept his secret for a number of months now, despite her developing phobia about the bacteria content on the buttons of the photocopier. She had feared that revealing his identity would inevitably lead to his dismissal, something she did not want on her conscience.

During their late-night encounter, she had discovered a number of things about Dan-from-accounts, including his apparent fetish for wearing female underwear. She had discovered this stomach-churning fact when she had gone to the photocopier to copy her timesheet ahead of her supervision session, in order to avoid the weekly lecture on poor time management from her boss, Ann. Ann was the queen of micromanagement — born of her exceptionally high anxiety levels about her own tenuous position in the management of the company.

On that fateful evening, Lottie had struggled to open the door to the photocopying room and used her shoulder to give it a sharp shove. Momentarily unbalanced, she had stumbled forward into the darkened room, and as she did so, she tripped on a pair of men's shoes. Grabbing the edge of a nearby filing cabinet to steady herself, she dragged her battered body to a standing position and had been met with a frightful sight. Sitting astride the photocopying machine, with his legs spread wide and his trousers dangling around one ankle, had been Dan-from-accounts. As startled by her sudden appearance as she was by his clearly semi-naked self, he had leapt from the machine clasping his genitalia, wildly hitting out at the cancel button.

Lottie had stood frozen in horror, and without a word passing between them Dan, sweeping up his clothes, had fled the room towards the nearby fire-exit stairwell. Taking a moment to recover, Lottie had hurriedly retrieved the offending photocopies from the print tray. She had noted that he was experimenting with his artistic style — the latest pictures boasting a legs-akimbo pose, which exposed his back, sac and most awful of all, a no-holds-barred view of his crack. Shuddering, she had avoided any direct contact with the sullied glass and ripped the copies firmly into two before stuffing them into the depths of the recycling bin. As she did so, a florescent pink item caught her eye, and bending, she gingerly retrieved a pink lace thong with a cluster of dark, wiry, male pubic hair still attached. Still reeling from the shock of discovering the identity of the office pervert, she had hastily stuffed the thong into the recycle bin before photocopying her timesheet, which she held with the corner of her sleeve as she had exited the building by the public entrance.

Coming out into the brightly lit car park, she had vowed that the next time she saw Dan she would be sure to make her disapproval obvious. However, after a few sheepish encounters by the water fountain during the following weeks, it had become apparent to Lottie that Dan was a somewhat pitiful character. She was pretty sure that the first time she saw him he had mumbled an apology, and she had not felt able to confront him after all. Nor, she decided, would she report him to the management.

After their untimely encounter she had been relieved that no more pictures had appeared and she was left feeling sorry for him, after hearing through the office grapevine, that his wife had left him for another woman some years previously. She had felt rather smug that she had been able to adopt a mature and forgiving approach to the situation and had largely forgotten about it, although she still, through force of habit, used anti-bacterial spray on the copier before she used it. Sighting Dan had, however made her remember she had something to offer to the gossip hotbed if she remained in the spotlight herself for too long.

Taking a deep breath, she pulled hard on the double fire-doors and was greeted with the usual cacophony of ringing telephones and a steely glare from Ann as she looked pointedly at the large clock in the centre of the office.

After ringing the speaking clock out of curiosity during a recent break, Lottie was well aware that the office clock was intentionally set ten minutes early. After sharing this information with her colleagues, no one had been brave enough to challenge the managers, and so the timekeeping in the office meant that they all arrived ten minutes early. But the bonus was, of course, that they finished ten minutes early, so no one was overly bothered. Lottie still felt she had the moral high ground as she settled in to her familiar desk and assured herself that she was not technically late. Adjusting her seat, she guided it neatly under her desk into her semi-private work booth and noted a few stray birthday cards and a couple of promising gift bags, which she concluded were from colleagues who were not on Facebook, and therefore excluded from her mother's global invitation. The usual faces lifted to greet her, all smiles, and she noted that no one appeared to be bursting to question her about the party, and so she relaxed and concentrated on her work.

Her peace was soon interrupted.

"All right?" asked Leonard, otherwise known as Shaggy — not due to his sexual prowess but due to his uncanny likeness to the Scooby Doo buffoon — who had appeared at her shoulder making her jump. Recovering herself, she smiled. Lottie tried to avoid any conversation with Leonard, as she found him rather irritating, and more than a little sleazy. Aged thirty-two and with a long-suffering wife, Lottie's kindest description of him would have been nice but dim. He would frequently monopolise the work environment with his marital difficulties, keen to obtain a female opinion on his latest wedded predicament.

The past week, Leonard had informed his nearby colleagues that he and his wife, or partner as he insisted on calling her, had been experiencing some difficulties following the birth of their son, Leo. Having traits of extreme narcissism, Leonard was keen to emphasise his sexual prowess in capturing a younger wife, and he always seemed to manage to crowbar this into any conversation about his unfortunate spouse. Lottie often wondered what had drawn her to the obnoxious Leonard, but seemingly, the relationship persisted. His only son and heir had been born a few months earlier and Lottie had struggled to comprehend how such a selfish man was going to be capable of parenting successfully.

Sure enough, only a few weeks after the birth of Leo, Leonard had announced that he was struggling with the demands of a small child, and that he had decided to resolve this by moving himself into the spare room, abandoning his long-suffering wife to deal with the colicky infant alone. Leonard had considered this a suitable solution given he was required to go to work while his partner was sitting around at home. Needless to say, this had resulted in some marital discord which was compounded by Leonard explaining to his wife that she was not going to successfully lose her baby weight if she continued to eat chocolate bars.

"I told her," he proudly announced to the group. "I said, you need to lay off the chocolate and have some grapes."

Lottie shuddered at the memory, but had no interest in engaging Leonard in conversation to find out if his wife had left him yet.

"Good birthday, mate?" Alicia from directly opposite enquired, as she handed Lottie a steaming cup of freshly-brewed Earl Grey tea.

Lottie, always pleased to chat with the decidedly normal Alicia, smiled. "It certainly was, shame you couldn't make it, but I expect you've heard about it?"

Alicia grinned back at her. "Heard about it, oh yes, I certainly did, about ten minutes before you arrived! That'll teach me to go and book a holiday without checking the diversity-events calendar, won't it! Seriously though, no issues here with this lot, everyone is pleased you've found someone. A vet too, I hear, perhaps Boots will finally get a diagnosis!"

Lottie smiled back gratefully, loving Alicia for her frankness, and in the knowledge that she would have been the first person to leap to her defence if there had been any office gossip.

She took this as a good sign, and attempted to return to her work.

Irritated to be ignored in favour of Alicia, Leonard leaned

closer, thoughtlessly invading Lottie's personal space. He had clearly caught the gist of the conversation. Lottie could not avoid the stench of garlic, no doubt due to the fact he had not cleaned his teeth that morning.

"A fella, eh, Lottie? About bloody time. I thought you must have healed up." He nodded purposefully towards her vagina.

Subconsciously, she crossed her legs and colour instantly flooded her face.

Dirty pig, she thought as she shot him an angry look. Alicia looked up briefly to give a sympathetic shake of her head. Lottie determinedly straightened her shoulders and looked Leonard square in the face. "Actually Leonard, *he* is a *she*, I've met a woman."

The minute she spoke, she instantly regretted it.

Chuckling, Leonard was about to respond when Ann bore down on them hissing. "Switch on your phone points, you lot, we've got forty bloody calls waiting!"

Glad to be saved from further discussion with Leonard about her love life, Lottie flicked her accept switch and found a local letting agent keen to place his weekly advert—this time for a seedy bedsit in the heart of Fraserburgh, in the cheapest, basic advert style— no spaces, no highlighted title, and sadly, no commission for Lottie.

Encountering Alicia in the toilets sometime later, she found that, although Leonard had not pressed her for more information, he had, in his usual sneaky fashion, pumped poor Alicia for details of the party and Lottie's new love interest.

"He thought it was a wind-up, Lots."

Lottie gave Alicia a reassuring rub on the shoulder. "Don't worry, just tell him what he wants to know. I think I'm actually out and proud finally, so just tell him, and then I'm sure things will settle down."

Happy to have an official sanction for the conversation, Alicia returned to her desk and Lottie whipped down to the cafeteria to meet Virginia for her lunch break.

Arriving back at her desk a short while later, Lottie was dismayed to discover that Leonard was lying in wait like a predatory misogynist, oblivious to her obvious dislike of him. She resigned herself to question time which would, no doubt, include sleazy jokes and innuendo.

Taking a deep and steadying breath, she turned her chair towards Leonard. "So, Leonard," she said and paused, taking in his boyish, underdeveloped body as she struggled to manage her revulsion. "I understand Alicia told you I was gay, but that you thought it was a wind-up?"

Leonard almost choked on his half-consumed Panini, clearly not expecting such a direct approach from Lottie. "Well yeah, it's got to be a wind-up."

"Really. Why?" Lottie responded.

"Because you're not gay! You've shagged blokes and you've got kids." Leonard stated the last part triumphantly, and looked around to see if he could muster any support, but those nearby studiously ignored him, keen to avoid being aligned to this dinosaur.

"How do you know that I'm not gay, Leonard? How do you know my kids aren't adopted? How do you know I've ever slept with a man?" Lottie tried, and failed, to veil her frustration. She had expected some questions, but clearly Leonard felt entitled to be very direct with his opinions, which was rather shocking to Lottie who hadn't experienced such direct homophobia anywhere before.

"I just do," he shrugged, unsure why his factual analysis of the situation was proving so difficult for her to grasp.

"Well I am...gay," Lottie shot at him venomously.

"Seriously?" For a moment he appeared shaken but could not quite marry this with his obviously superior intellect.

"Seriously!" Lottie stated emphatically.

"Oh, okay then." Leonard retreated to the safety of his cubicle where he furiously started to type, before he asked over his shoulder. "So, do you feel like a big weight has been lifted from your shoulders?"

"Not really. No." Lottie refused to humour his slightly more empathetic approach.

"Oh, right," Leonard was once again confused. More typing ensued.

"So how do you *know* you're actually gay?"

Lottie sighed. "Because I fancy girls."

A sanctimonious grin spread slowly across his face. "Oh right," followed by an exaggerated wink.

After a pause, he stated with utter delight. "So do I!"

He looked vacantly into space, and Lottie concluded that he was clearly revisiting what she knew would be his limited knowledge of lesbian relationships based on his home porn collection.

Slyly, he leaned in towards Lottie and once more he repeated it. "So do I! So, can we compare notes and stuff?"

"Probably not, Leonard," Lottie replied, seeing Alicia shaking her head in complete despair.

The smile slipped from his face. "Oh, okay! Bummer! Oh sorry, that's the male lot, isn't it?" he replied, clearly still not understanding the offensive nature of his comments. Cackling at his comedic brilliance, he was satisfied with the exchange and returned to staring at his screen.

Rolling her eyes at Alicia, Lottie took another incoming call, keen to dispel the increasing awkwardness she was feeling at the cheek of Leonard, and the apparent salacious view he took of her relationship with Alice. Typing in an advert for a child minder she made a mental note not to open avenues of conversation with her colleagues which might mean that she had to explain, or justify, her sexuality.

Shortly afterward she received a welcome text from Alice:

```
Hey baby, hope it's going okay, just wanted you
to know I'm thinking about you. By the way I've
got some prosecco for later, so don't worry. No
matter how bad it is, it'll soon be wine
o'clock! Love ya, sexy bum xx
```

Smiling, Lottie decided to stretch her legs before her supervision session with Ann. She made her way down the office and was greeted by various colleagues whom she had seen at the party, and received grateful thanks from many for remembering to bring in Pru's leftover cake, which she had heard was surprisingly tasty.

Finally, she could avoid it no longer and headed in the direction of Ann's office for what she knew would be an interminably long supervision session. Lottie was dubious about the benefits of supervision, bearing in mind that Ann often took it as an opportunity to bemoan her relationship issues, before telling her that her sales targets were going up.

When Lottie first started in the newspaper's telesales department, she had realised there was as much of an art to feeding your sales figures to your manager as there was to selling anything in the first place. As a telesales operative, it was Lottie's job to upsell incoming calls to adverts with white space around them or bold titles. On the odd occasion when she had managed to get customers to buy an actual box of space, having regaled them with the many benefits of highlighting their item in amongst the millions of classified adverts, she had remained unconvinced about the actual benefits in real terms. She considered herself a reluctant sales woman, often skipping the sales pitch to the bereaved, or the poor — those burying Grandma or selling her antique possessions. However, this had to be done carefully, as the eagle-eyed Ann had a remote monitoring facility in the corner of the office, meaning that she could tap in at any point to a sales call made by one of her team.

Knowing full well the split personality of her manager, Lottie was surprised that Ann had made the effort to attend her party, and she could only attribute this to her own mother's sales skills. Entering Ann's lair she glanced around, noticing that, as with her own area, no family photographs hung from the walls. A wall of fame board hung squarely adjacent on the facing wall, which currently sported Leonard's mugshot with the title, *Top sales person of the month*. Leonard had written a speech bubble alongside. "You know it, baby!"

Lottie could not understand why Leonard had such prestige with their manager although she couldn't fail to notice the flirtatious banter between the two. Both consistently failed to meet their core hours in the building, and of course, their car-share to the office had almost certainly helped him to achieve a sympathetic ear. She was always suspicious that there was more to their relationship than they revealed, but she seldom allowed those unsavoury images to cloud her thoughts for more than a moment.

Ann looked up, her glasses perched on the very tip of her hooked nose. Lottie tried hard to look Ann straight in the eye but this wasn't without its problems, as Ann had a pronounced squint, meaning you were never quite sure in which direction she was looking. This had caused Lottie, and other colleagues, many difficulties in the past, as Ann felt ignored if they failed to notice that she was talking to them. This only served to increase Ann's paranoia about lack of respect in her workforce, all culminating in a horrible overbearing and micromanaging boss. Lottie had endured hours of delicate discussions about Ann's emotionally abusive husband and delinquent children, in her own feeble attempts to win favour with her.

Waving her hand in irritation, Ann signalled for her to close the door, therefore sealing Lottie's fate of a minimum of forty-five minutes of being supervised before home time and the enticing prospect of wine o'clock.

As soon as she was seated, Ann swivelled in her orthopaedic chair to face Lottie. Smiling nervously, Lottie had often wondered about the protruding hump on Ann's shoulder and sometimes found it hard not to stare directly at it during the morning sales meeting.

Waving paperwork dramatically at Lottie, Ann sighed as she recited Lottie's failings in her monthly figures. Lottie attempted to feign interest, but her attention was lost as she squinted to get a better look at Ann's screen which she was sure was displaying the log-on page of a well-known dating site. Intrigued that Ann might be venturing away from her controlling husband, she accidentally gave herself away, as Ann raised her line of sight momentarily from the paperwork mountain and locked onto to Lottie's point of interest. Flushing, Lottie attempted to pretend she'd been peering curiously at the Venus flytrap, but Ann was quick to note Lottie's discovery.

"You see, Lottie, I think he may be having an affair. *With a man!*" she said, coughing awkwardly.

Lottie inwardly cringed. Bloody hell! Was there no end to this man's vileness? When in God's name was she going to leave him? Framing her audible question more tactfully, Lottie gently enquired as to how Ann had discovered this new fact about Greg.

HALF AN HOUR later, and after Ann had confessed to having purchased illegal surveillance equipment to install on her husband's computer, Lottie learned that Ann had identified a number of gay dating websites, which sported the profile of the not-so-delightful Greg, including a very unattractive picture of his Neanderthal thatched chest as it escaped from the unbuttoned Armani shirt he was wearing for the purpose of the photograph.

As Ann clicked through the site's pages, giving a pained explanation of her husband's suspected activities, Lottie was distracted by a familiar image.

"OMG! Tony!" she exclaimed, leaning forward.

Ann stopped scrolling, as Lottie appraised an undeniable image of her very own brother-in-law! With a deft click of the mouse, Ann enlarged the screen to reveal a picture of Tony with his shirt fully unbuttoned to reveal his own version of the gay-man chest-thatch. Next to him, stood her sister, who was busy dutifully serving iced buns, at what she presumed was their Sunday fellowship meeting. Lottie commandeered the mouse, quickly scanning his profile and was shocked to discover that Tony was portraying himself as a single man about town, or about Aberdeen, to be precise. His intentions were no strings encounters with like minded males, and that he wanted his intended partners to have a strong faith base.

"Bloody hell!" Lottie muttered murderously, but Ann, oblivious to Lottie's trauma, soon lost interest and steered the meeting back to finish the monthly supervision session.

Ann appeared slightly peeved that Lottie was less than focused on her own personal trauma. However, as she drew the meeting to a close, she thanked Lottie for the indirect invitation to the party. Lottie recovered herself and made pleasant small talk about how lovely it had been to see so many colleagues there, to celebrate with her.

Simultaneously her mind whirled with the implications of her discovery, and she was filled with dread about the inevitable conversation she was going to have to have with her sister.

She brought her mind back to the meeting, as Ann leaned towards Lottie in a conspiratorial fashion. "On the subject, I wanted to say I've had a thought relating to you and your situation."

Lottie supressed a grimace. "Really?" She had to admit she had felt relieved to know that there weren't going to be ongoing issues in her workplace.

"Yes, Lottie. I was thinking that you possibly ought to consider a dating site yourself."

Lottie paused in anticipation of where this may be going, remembering that she had not been able to introduce Ann to Alice.

"Yes, well, quite honestly I don't know why I didn't think of this before. It was staring me in the face. I know how much you like to travel, Lottie, and it occurred to me you should get on one of these websites for people in uniform. A man in the army or navy would be simply perfect for you. You'd get to go around the world!"

Lottie fumed. *A bloody man! What was wrong with these people?* She managed to stifle a less than gracious response, and retreated to the safety of her booth and the lecherous glances of Leonard.

This is crap! she thought, and what on earth was she going to tell her sister? Desperate for the wisdom and comfort of Alice, and the prospect of wine o'clock, she headed for the car park, and home.

Part Two

The Miracle of Life

CHRISTMAS CAME AND went, and spring in all its glory finally arrived in Pennan. The gorse peppering the cliff side with its majestic yellow bloom provided a stark contrast to the chocolate brown of the peat-rich soil. There was still a chill in the air and the odd early morning frost, but the winter sun had grown stronger and the coastline was coming to life with the sounds and smells of spring.

Alice was busily refilling the dressing's drawer at her surgery as she pondered the events of the past few months, and the rollercoaster ride that life with Lottie could be. She couldn't believe she'd found Lottie, after having had a few unsuccessful long-term relationships. Despite her numerous idiosyncrasies, she was learning that Lottie was a kind and funny woman. What she lacked in coordination she made up for with her boundless enthusiasm for her life and her loyalty to all the people she had in it. Alice hadn't been sure how she felt about the prospect of joining a ready-made family at first, but now that she had gotten to know Robbie and Archie, she was pleased about her developing relationships with them. She chuckled as she recalled the disaster of taking Archie to work with her, on what was now known as Rat Liberation Day, but his fierce desire to protect the vulnerable was such an endearing quality.

As she pushed her hip against a cupboard bursting with paperwork which desperately needed filing, she basked in the final success of her chat with Lottie about moving in to the house with them. It had eventually gone a lot better than she had anticipated, given Lottie's woeful tales of failed cohabitation attempts in previous relationships. She knew she would meet resistance from some of her friends who would think that it was too early, but she didn't care. She was aware that they would tease her and remind her of one of the well know clichés of lesbian life, U-Haul dykes. Alice had had a few encounters with U-Haul dykes herself, where she would date a woman and as soon as they had sex and breakfast there was a sudden expectation they would move in together and get on with ordering a U-Haul/Pickford's van.

"Scary!" she said aloud. Yet despite this, the speed at which her relationship with Lottie was developing had been cause for her friends to urge caution, but it just felt so right.

In her pre-Lottie days. Alice had feared the judgement of others and realised that she had probably relied too heavily on the opinions of her friends, largely because she felt she had made poor relationship decisions in the past.

Her previous partner had left her for a man, more than two years ago. Alice had no experience with male relationships and she struggled to process the situation, realising with hindsight that this relationship had affected her far more than she'd cared to admit at the time. The pain of the break-up was only matched by the pangs of angst she'd felt throughout that relationship, when she'd realised that the woman only brought out her worst qualities—jealousy and paranoia.

Looking back—which she generally avoided doing—that period of her life had definitely been a low point for her, as she'd struggled with the aftermath of being abandoned. One of the things she so greatly admired about Lottie was that she was generally a good judge of character, and this was one of the many attractive qualities which had resulted in the speedy development of a strong and trusting relationship between the two.

She was well aware that Lottie was, first and foremost, a fierce mother lion. Another of the things that she adored about her. Alice couldn't help but draw parallels between how Lottie was with her boys and the natural mothering instincts she saw in some of the animals she treated. Lottie wouldn't have any of that though, admitting that she was constantly seeking a parenting score, or success, as Alice corrected her.

She felt that Lottie's insecurities about her parenting were, in part, a result of her heterosexual masquerade in earlier years which had led her to constantly compare herself to the yummy mummies in the playground. Alice laughed as she recalled Lottie's description of her attempts to develop coffee buddies amongst this group, only to discover that the inner sanctum of the yummy mummies consisted of core individuals who bonded in their marital misery. Lottie had told her how she had tried to offer support and advice to this group only to find that she actually had no affinity with their issues, which led to her having little of substance to offer them. Failing to discover a gay alternative to the yummy mummies, Lottie had had a brief friendship with the one-and-only gay playground dad, but this had ended abruptly after Archie had revealed that his son had a predilection for dissecting pets, including a hamster and three gerbils.

She had wondered whether moving in so quickly was a good idea but it just felt right, and that was all the analysis she was prepared to give to the situation. Granted, Lottie was a bit of a clumsy clod at times. In fact, she would probably go as far as to say that Lottie probably suffered from some form of mild dyspraxia, and yet, somehow, it all added to her charm. Sometimes, when Lottie was busy burning food in the kitchen, or when she was studiously doubled over her son's homework, her face creased and perplexed by the subject, Alice had the chance to observe the essence of Lottie. Her kindness and patience towards others knew no bounds, but while she had an outer air of confidence, she was insecure about her decisions around the children, and worried about the impact on them of her coming out later in life.

Alice felt proud to the core, sometimes on a daily basis, as she watched Lottie walk tall, or sometimes stumble clumsily, through the various situations that life threw at her. No matter how others treated her, Lottie would smile and reach out to those around her, and Alice sensed that simply being around Lottie made her feel that she was becoming a better person.

Alice believed that she'd made a place in Lottie's family, although she was well aware that this was a constantly evolving situation. She had secretly shared a roll-up with Robbie on the odd occasion, when he surfaced from his man den. In fact, Robbie had sought her out after the school debacle to ask how he could get his mum to trust him again. His ulterior motive had of course been to get Alice to negotiate on his behalf. So, Alice, being all too aware of this, had simply patted him reassuringly on the shoulder and advised him that time was a great healer. Robbie had not seemed overly impressed with this advice, however, her overall non-judgemental approach to his predicament had apparently not been lost on him, and he would sometimes seek her out when she was in the house to share a companionable silence which she took to be a sign of acceptance.

Archie was a longer project, Alice felt. While he happily accepted her version of a Harry Potter butter beer — Irn-Bru with an ice cream floater — and allowed her to partake in an episode or two of the Disney channel's finest offering, *Dog with a Blog*, he wasn't so invested in her presence in the house. As time passed, Alice had learned not to be overly affectionate towards Lottie in Archie's presence, as it tended to prompt a rush of babyish behaviour as he fought to win back the attention of his mum. She had, however, learned that Archie swam like a fish and so she had taken to collecting him from his child minder one evening a week for a quick swim at the local baths. She knew that Lottie was glad that she was making this effort with Archie. Keen to exploit the situation, Archie had discovered that Alice had a stash of fifty-pence coins in her car which happened to be the required amount for the sweet-dispensing machine in the reception area of the baths.

Alice chuckled to herself as she decided to abandon her drawer tidying. Archie had become a staunch vegetarian after accidentally discovering a documentary on television called *Vegacated* which consisted of a brief discussion on the benefits of a vegan diet, followed by a graphic portrayal of the slaughter methods used on a variety of farm produce. While Alice was not immune to the suffering of animals in their final moments, she demonstrated her love for animals by buying only organically farmed meat, which was readily available from the Highland farming industry. She had learned though, to expect a fairly dramatic reaction if Archie arrived home early to catch her in the act of making a bacon sandwich, which would involve opening all the windows in the house and making vomiting noises. She had taken to purchasing her guilty pleasure from the food van on the Aberdeen road, on the days she was required to head to the city.

Thinking about Archie reminded her of the comedy sketch she had been party to in the house that morning. The animal-loving mother and son had been horrified to discover yet another headless rabbit on the floor of the utility room. For many months now, since spring had arrived, Boots had pursued a campaign of merciless terror against the local breeding rabbit population. Now in full swing, the baby bunny numbers were soaring, and it was certainly a sight to behold on the hills around Pennan, often reminding Alice of a scene from *Watership Down*. On a daily basis Boots returned home at breakfast time with an offering of his own. Sometimes, if he was alone for a while he would dismember the helpless bunny into various tasty morsels as an offering to his family, an eyeball here and an ear there, gruesomely displayed on the utility room floor.

Lottie wasn't the most alert person in the morning, and inevitably this led to her treading in unspeakable matter as she went to retrieve the milk from the fridge. This usually resulted in a mild form of hysteria which drew Archie away from his TV programmes to join in the melodrama. Alice had given up trying to explain to them that this was a high form of praise in the cat world, and that Boots was simply contributing to the household in his own way.

Sometimes the unfortunate furries would be balanced between a state of life and death, which would galvanise Lottie and Archie into action, as they administered bunny first aid. There was now a specially dedicated triage unit in the corner of the kitchen, complete with a shoe box lined with tissue, otherwise known as the recovery unit. After much discussion about ways to reduce the slaughter, Lottie had decided to attempt to put a collar and bell on Boots to provide an early warning system for the rabbits as Boots stalked them. Unfortunately, Boots was more or less a feral beast and did not take kindly to the offensive collar. Eventually, they achieved the collaring, but not without a significant injury to Lottie, which Alice was sure should have been stitched. Boots sat sulkily in the corner of the room constantly shaking his head and glaring at Archie, no doubt plotting a bloody form of revenge. Convinced he would attempt suicide by hanging, Lottie had insisted that Alice take him to work to keep an eye on him while he got used to the offending article.

Reluctantly, Alice had managed to trick him into the cat carrier which was now shaking ominously in the corner of the surgery. Giving into her animal-loving instincts she gingerly lifted the cage into the only available recovery pen and released the perturbed Boots, who paced the side of the cage like one of his larger cat relatives. Shutting the door and clipping the latch firmly into place she hastily made her way to the front-of-house where morning surgery was due to begin.

Hearing raised voices in reception as she approached the waiting area, Alice turned the corner and came face-to-face with Pru who was arguing loudly with Elsie, her elderly receptionist. Spotting Alice, Pru abandoned her verbal tirade against Elsie and made a beeline for her. Smiling personably, she moved to meet Pru in the middle of the reception area, hoping to avoid bringing her into the treatment room, from where she would be more difficult to evict.

Shaking her finger in agitation at Alice, Pru seemed to have acquired a high-pitched squeak to her voice which betrayed her highly emotional state.

"You must *immediately* clear your diary, Sappho is in labour!"

Looking down, Alice spotted Pru's fluffy pride and joy who was yowling mournfully as she crouched low into her sheepskin mini-rug in the depths of her cat carrier. Immediately recognising from the pitiful noise that there may be a problem with the birth,

Alice relented and whisked the basket and its contents through to the surgery.

In spite of the noise Pru was making, Alice managed to lean in and get a better look at the precious Persian pussy. She noted that Sappho fitted nicely into the obese category, despite her heavily pregnant state. Obesity was known to complicate birth both in humans and animals, and although Alice determined that the birth was not imminent, she decided that the best thing for Sappho would be a restful environment minus her semi-hysterical owner.

Looking around, she eyed the holding cage containing Boots. She had not banked on such a full house at the surgery and she didn't think that Sappho would be happy to share with a feline enemy in her vulnerable state. Fortunately, there was one adjoining cage free. Hoping that Pru hadn't noticed that Sappho was going to be in the same vicinity as Boots, she hastily removed Pru back to the reception area with a promise that she would be called when the time came. Pru settled reluctantly into a plastic chair and retrieved a snack box which she had abandoned temporarily while on her emergency mission to get Sappho to a medical professional.

Happy that Pru was safely out of the way Alice fired a quick text to Lottie.

Baby, you're not going to believe who is at the surgery! Only Pru and Sappho and you're soon to have grand pussy babies! Xx

Waiting for a response, she glanced towards Boots who appeared to have forgotten his post-collaring rage as he strutted backward and forward, flicking his tail and yowling a greeting to Sappho. It appeared that the two had remembered one another despite their brief one-night stand and Sappho rose to meow a greeting in response.

Her phone beeped loudly and she read Lottie's response.

LOL, oh God, Alice, make sure she doesn't clap eyes on Boots, she's bound to finger him as the dad! Xxx.

Her train of thought was interrupted as once again the reception area appeared to burst into a cacophony of noise and Alice once more headed out to the front to investigate. When she rounded the corner she was greeted by a cackle of older ladies all wearing long, shapeless garments and carrying a variety of homemade instruments. In the middle of the group she noticed Pru, who was busily uncloaking a bright orange tambourine, while passing out an assortment of drums to her friends. Pru glanced up briefly and confirmed to Alice that the group belonged to her.

"My spiritual coven, dearie, here to help me with the birthing ritual."

"Birthing ritual?" Alice had a sinking feeling as she started to anticipate her quiet workplace descending into a Stonehenge-like gathering. Without waiting for an invitation, Pru rounded up her troupe and headed into the treatment room. Alice watched with increasing trepidation as the group, galvanised into action, banged furiously on their collection of drums, while Pru shimmied her tambourine. She produced a hazel branch which was now being brandished ceremoniously around poor Sappho's cat carrier, which they had not noticed was now empty.

"Come ladies, come! Birthing represents one of the most auspicious and earthly experiences of the female. Sappho needs us now to draw upon our spirit guides to provide her with the optimum birthing environment."

The other residents of the holding cages raised their own objections to the ensuing chaos, with a variety of barks, growls and groans, in whatever way they were able to muster. Alice couldn't help but notice that Boots seemed remarkably unfazed by the spectacle, eyeing the group with something akin to amusement from the corner of his pen.

As Sappho progressed farther into her birthing experience, the noise steadied to a communal humming and a low rumbling undertone of drumming, with the occasional untimely tambourine shimmer, which left Alice a little more able to regain her composure before she quietly extracted Sappho from the holding cage and onto the table, assisting in the safe delivery of five striped delights of a decidedly un-pedigree origin.

Licking her new brood clean, she was sure that she saw Sappho glance across to Boots for his approval. However he, it appeared, was engrossed in firmly licking his balls in a silent acknowledgement of his own fertility.

Alice couldn't help but be amused by his sheer arrogance, but she felt she should probably be talking to Lottie about a little corrective op for Boots to remove the offending body parts. She also thought this would stem his bloodthirsty slaughter of the hapless rabbits of Pennan.

Brought back to the present moment by the delighted squeals of Pru, she couldn't help but soften towards her as she showed clear and genuine delight as she headed towards the table for a closer look. Alice headed her off at the table corner, a light sheen of perspiration, the only give away to the stress she felt.

"Sorry Pru, they just need twenty minutes or so. She needs to feed and groom them, and to bond. Then you can come back through for a look."

Pru smiled, and thanking Alice profusely, she headed back to the reception pulling from her backpack a second snack pack.

Alice manoeuvred Sappho and her brood from the table and back to a free holding cage. She could not help but feel amused as she observed the kittens with their unmistakeable stripy backs and unusually large bush-baby eyes, all belying their genetic heritage.

"Bloody hell, Boots," she muttered to no one in particular as she bashed out a hasty text to Lottie.

```
Babe, help! How am I going to stop Pru getting a
look at these kittens? She's like a preening
proud parent!
```

She clutched her phone anxiously waiting for a reply:

```
LOL! Rather you than me, Alice, probably better
done in public anyway, then she won't make a
connection with Boots, so we'll be fine! Love
ya! Xx
```

Alice grimaced.

Won't make a connection as long as I can get Boots into a different—

Pru burst through the treatment room doors before Alice could finish her thought.

"Right, let the fox see the rabbit!" she said and headed with speed towards the holding cage.

Alice clutched the edge of the worktop tightly to steady herself. "Prudence, we probably ought to—"

Again, Alice was cut off in mid-flow.

"Dear Gods above! Isn't this Lottie's cat? Oh, dear Lord! These little runts look exactly like him. But I don't understand! Oh wait, I *do* understand. The group. He must have got to my poor Sappho at the group!"

Alice was galvanised into action as Pru collapsed in a faint and slumped unceremoniously at the side of the holding cage.

Without warning, Boots shot a stripy paw forward, accompanied by a deep and ominous growl. Claws extended, he swiped with a direct hit at Pru, leaving her with a bloodied cheek and an expression of unadulterated indignation, as she regained consciousness.

Alice was horrified at the sheer audacity of Boots, but inwardly chuckled in spite herself, as Pru threw herself forward squealing in misery,

"It's bloody feral! What on earth am I to do?"

Pussy Parenthood

PRU AWOKE TO take in the surroundings of her snug wood-cladded bedroom. Her bag-laden eyes betrayed the difficult night she'd had as a new parent to five demanding kittens. Pru had always prided herself on her ability to connect with all things feline, but, at four thirty in the morning, she had wept in despair as Sappho continued to provide inadequate parental supervision, apparently considering parenthood something of a bore. Sappho was nothing, if not discerning and Pru felt that the inferior genetic heritage of her offspring may be something Sappho was inherently unwilling to accept.

Struggling to get into an upright position, Pru remained in bed and reached across to pull her curtain open, revealing the beach view at the top end of the small village of Pennan. Despite her difficult night, she smiled with pleasure as she drank in the exclusive view, which had been a deciding factor in her purchase of the cottage, despite the more exclusive postcodes available in Fraserburgh. These were the views which inspired her abstract art creations.

As well as having a true appreciation of the natural beauty of her surroundings, Pru was always focused on new business opportunities, and had readily been able to sell her eclectic artwork to passing tourists. After an astrological star-chart consultation, Pru had been assured that she was innately creative, and despite not gaining local acclaim for her work, she was positive that people from farther afield had a greater appreciation of her artistic talents. She would often sit on a small stool outside her property, plying her trade to passers-by. Annoyingly, the few locals with whom she had become acquainted tended to studiously avoid eye contact when they passed her. The tourists, however were less wary. Often, she would engage them in conversation about the location, considering herself a local historian, she would charm them with anecdotes about the village before moving on to a fairly hard-core sales technique, which frequently left her victims feeling obliged to make a purchase.

Willing herself to get up, she slowly hoisted her leg over the well-worn bed and it returned her efforts with an involuntarily groan as it dipped to receive the additional weight of Pru's hefty frame. She rose to complete her morning t'ai chi routine. She wasn't quite sure how the routine was officially done, but she had developed her own sitting version of the ancient practice in order to reduce the amount of balancing and straining required, as her cumbersome frame wasn't built for prolonged stretching.

After a couple of minutes of stretching and humming, Pru was satisfied. She ducked to avoid the homemade, dust-laden, crystal chandelier which blocked the exit to her bedroom. She tutted loudly as she stubbed her toe on a pile of books, which were balanced precariously to stop the door from swinging shut in the night. Pru believed in the circulation of air through all the small rooms of the cottage. She had explained this to guests, as being necessary to ensure the passage of the spirits, who she believed lived with her in the house. She would often leave the landing window open to allow them easy exit. After all, her house was the oldest on the street, and undoubtedly held some spiritual companions from the days of poor souls lost to the sea, when the harbour had been more active.

Stooping with some difficulty, she grabbed a couple of books from the top of the pile and moved them to the edge of the large pine chest containing her tambourine. This reminded her that she had yet to plan a theme for this week's group activity. She had begun to feel that the new starters, Lottie in particular, were taking control, and she felt disgruntled by this, being the founding member and natural leader of the group. Once again, she tutted loudly to no one in particular, as she descended to the living room via the steep staircase.

Pru's furrowed brow displayed her distaste as she recalled the events of the previous day. She was extremely disappointed to discover that Sappho's offspring had a mixed biological heritage, and she considered Boots to be from poor stock.

Pru had written in her gratitude diary that she felt she had accidentally purchased a jar of instant coffee instead of her usual superior blend of imported beans, direct from Puerto Rico, fair trade. Pru had written that she was not accustomed to having possessions of inferior provenance. It was well known amongst her associates that she had made it her business to collect low cost, good quality belongings. In fact, her home was bursting at the seams as she struggled to part with anything she had acquired. She chose, instead, to erect cumbersome display cabinets which housed the majority of her curiosities, most of which were covered with an unhealthy layer of dust.

Pru tucked into her hearty, full English breakfast. She glanced around her living area, reflecting that some of her braver friends had told her the room was oppressive. Every wall was clad in dark mahogany and heavily stencilled with a fleur-de-lys pattern, which distinguished the darker lower stain from the lighter stain above. There were few available surfaces, as each bookcase, fireplace mantel and occasional table, groaned with a shocking display of Pru's crafting activities.

The display of half-completed projects did not provide the onlooker with much reassurance that Pru had any natural talent for her chosen crafts, but this did not deter her. Her small home was literally overflowing with an unimpressive collection of unfinished curiosities.

In the corner of the living room, stood a strange oval-shaped, woven basket from which spilled forth a variety of colourful yarns, and its accompanying, dusty spinning wheel stood proud, but unused. Along the walls an impressive collection of eclectic local art was hung clumsily from the cladding, some of which bore the flourish of Pru's own signature. Creating her own impressionist versions of local scenery was something Pru was currently pursuing, because she saw it as a potential source of new income. It was a well-known fact amongst the local community that Pru considered herself something of an entrepreneur, and she was always keen to exploit what she saw as her extensive creative talents, in order to improve her impoverished bank balance.

In her mid-life years, following the end of a long-term relationship, Pru had lived somewhat extravagantly in an attempt to fill the vacuum of loneliness she had experienced. Unfortunately, this had left her in difficult financial circumstances, but unwilling to cut her cloth to tackle her debts, Pru had embarked upon a series of, mostly unsuccessful and expensive crafting courses, with the intention of opening a craft shop on the beach.

In theory this had been a good idea, as the village lacked any outlet for tourist spending, other than the box of hand painted postcards by another local artist, which sat with an honesty box on the corner of the street. Prudence considered these postcards to be rather substandard in comparison to her own selection, although it was hard not to notice the similarities between the two, and Marion's efforts had been acknowledged in a local travel brochure, much to Pru's disgust.

While she demolished the final bits of her eggs, Pru leafed absent-mindedly through the books on the nearest shelf. She ran her fingers along the spine of *Inuit Women Artists* before settling on a copy of *Adventures in Knitting*. Perusing the pages, she folded corners with the intention of revisiting the potential ideas for quick production of the garments at a later date. Shoving the books back between a volume of *Artist's Houses,* and *Seaside Interiors,* she cleared her plate away to the miniscule kitchenette in the corner

Pru's thoughts were interrupted by a timid tapping on the front door. Pulling her nightgown down to cover her modesty, she shuffled to the door, mumbling to herself about the annoying tippy-tapping, and wishing that people would knock with a little more gusto.

As she swung the heavy door open, she was met with the sight of a highly anxious Lottie, who appeared to be unable to keep still. Lottie's fear was palpable as Pru eyed her with suspicion. Pru did not hide her irritation at being disturbed, which Lottie seemed to detect, rendering her temporarily mute. Pru eventually ended the doorstep stand-off, swinging the door wide open, and barking to Lottie. "Enter!"

Lottie stumbled forward, but it was not lost on Pru that she cast a desperate backward glance towards the outside world, as if she was worried she wouldn't make it back.

"Morning, Pru," Lottie muttered, taking a deep breath. "Lovely day, don't you think? Look, I thought it would be worth popping up to have a quick chat about the cat situation. After all, it's hardly ideal but there's not a lot to be done at this stage, is there?"

At the end of her rambling torrent of words, Lottie literally gasped for air, and Pru stood by silently, eyeing her accusingly, with her arms planted across her chest, and her wide legs akimbo.

While the pregnant pause continued, she wondered why Lottie was always so interminably nervous, although Pru was vaguely aware that she tended to have this effect on a lot of the people she encountered.

Breaking the awkward silence, Sappho mewed mournfully as she entered the room in search of her organic premium-cuts cat food.

Lottie reached down to pet Sappho who rubbed herself vigorously against Lottie, weaving between her legs in a confident dance.

"Poor little dear, I bet you've had a difficult night. The little ones will have been keeping you up no doubt?" she asked the speechless feline.

Sappho settled next to her empty bowl, nudging it pointedly, as Pru struggled to her feet muttering to no one in particular.

"Huh! Privileges of the pampered!"

Lottie didn't have to wait long to see her surrogate grandchildren, as Sappho quickly consumed her organic offerings and headed back to the basket in the dark recess of the room, from where a loud high-pitched, group mewling began. Pru watched with some malicious satisfaction as Lottie nervously edged her way towards the basket, and confirmed very quickly, that the striking markings of the five were undoubtedly those of the indomitable Boots.

A small squeak of excitement escaped her as she scooped up the nearest furry offering and nuzzled it to her chin. Seeming to forget for a moment that she was in Pru's home, she slid to a sitting position, kicked off her trainers and appeared lost in the wonder of nature, and the product of her cat and his opportunistic encounter.

Pru had never been one to miss an opportunity, and the aching of her old bones and her need to disappear back to bed told her she wasn't in this step-grandparenting situation for the long haul. Observing Lottie busily spreading her love equally between the five offspring, while tickling Sappho absent-mindedly with her naked big toe, which she noted needed an urgent pedicure. She purposefully determined to help herself out of a temporary situation, which after all, she reasoned, was not of her own creation. She could never understand why people and circumstances constantly let her down.

"So," she drawled as she sidled closer, proffering a cushion for Lottie to sit more comfortably. "This really is a most unfortunate situation and could not have come at a worse time for me. I'm sure you're aware, Charlotte, that I am locally renowned for my rather unique artworks and I have been invited to a small fringe festival in Edinburgh next week as it happens."

Pru observed Lottie glancing up at her art works. "Very few artists have been as innovative as myself in integrating mediums, that is, using watercolour and oil in the same piece. I am aware that you are no art expert, Charlotte, but rest assured, those at the cutting edge of the art world are beginning to notice my work. It's only a matter of time."

"I could take them for a few weeks, Pru, while you went to your show and Sappho could stay as well," said Lottie.

Pru didn't hesitate to seize the opportunity which she hadn't expected to present itself so easily and hurried to collect all the pet accoutrements she could find, before Lottie could change her mind.

"Good, good, let's get them packed up then, no sense in dillydallying, eh?"

Lottie rolled to avoid the oncoming Pru, who deftly swiped the kittens up in both hands and firmly deposited them into the carriers. Sappho, sensing an upcoming move, dodged between Pru's planted legs, but Pru, obviously used to catching her, leant precariously backward to catch her as she emerged. Going limp with displeasure, Sappho allowed herself to be unceremoniously deposited into the second basket. A few moments later, a carrier bag bulging with cat food and grooming equipment found its way into Lottie's free hand.

"Well, dear, so nice of you to pop in, I'll let you know when I'm back and settled."

She propelled Lottie unceremoniously to the front door, a carrier in each of Lottie's hands, and the bag of goodies tucked under an arm.

"Well, yes, I mean ideally, Pru, it would be good to have an idea of when that might be."

Pru, mumbled something incoherent before speaking aloud. "Yes, absolutely, dear, absolutely! I'll see you soon then, regards to Melanie!"

Pru shut the door firmly and heaved a sigh of relief at the thought of heading back to bed with a cup of tea.

STRUGGLING UNDER THE weight of the new family additions she was carrying, Lottie shuffled back along the short distance to her own home, where Alice was waiting in anticipation of the outcome of the grandparent summit talks. Lottie leaned down to release the catches of the carriers while a cacophony of noise and fur spilled forth into the living room and Alice raised an eyebrow suspiciously.

"Exactly what has happened now?" she asked as Lottie sank down into the well-worn sofa.

"Well, I think I've been stitched up. That's a fact! I've never seen a family of cats dispatched so quickly into carriers. And I've no idea how I'm going to look after this lot as well as everything else. It's all a bit shit," Lottie said.

Following Alice's look of displeasure, she noted, with horror, that one of the kittens was depositing a long stream of sticky tar-like poo on the carpet.

"Shit is about right!" said Alice as she shuffled closer to Lottie to avoid the aroma she was expecting to hit her nostrils at any moment.

"Bloody hell!" groaned Lottie as she reacted, involuntarily moving the kitten away from the mess, whereupon it encountered the unsuspecting Odie who had pottered in for a closer inspection of the new visitors. Eyes wide, Odie darted for the door, standing in the sticky mess and managing to spread it through the living room and into the kitchen.

"Oh, shit!" shouted Alice and Lottie in unison.

Inner Calm

LOTTIE RELUCTANTLY PULLED on a loose top and a pair of old jogging bottoms. She'd been trying to contact Pru for the past few days and she was convinced she must now have returned from her art exhibition. In fact, she was sure she'd been overtaken by Pru's Citroen 2CV on the narrow Highland lanes, although she couldn't make a positive identification because of the speed of the passing vehicle which had forced her to pull aside for safety. After some early evening spying, Lottie discovered that Pru's bedroom light had gone on at seven twenty-four the previous evening, confirming that someone was in the house. Despite her reservations about Pru's integrity, Lottie remained hopeful that it wasn't Pru's intention to have dumped the feline hellcats on her permanently. Alice, however, was more sceptical and urged Lottie to stop spying and go and hammer on Pru's door.

Lottie's home now reeked of the unmistakeable odour of cat urine, and the sofas sported dubious luminescent stains. Adorable though the kittens were, both Lottie and Alice had struggled to cope with the never-ending chaos that the furries caused. They each had their own personalities, and Lottie was disturbed to discover that the genetic influence of Boots and his feral heritage seemed to be showing itself in his offspring, who were adorable one minute and then a ball of teeth and claws the next. Alice had tried to reassure Lottie that kittens were very much split personalities as they explored their sharpened tool kits, but Lottie wasn't so sure. A few times the kittens had mysteriously found their way into the utility room, home to the virile Boots, who seemed to be revelling in his new-found family. If Lottie hadn't known better, she would swear that Boots had perfected a half smirk. More concerning was that, after retrieving the kittens from his lair, their behaviour would temporarily worsen as if the mere presence of Boots had taken them to a new level of rebellion.

Only Archie and his boundless love of animals had provided some respite for the sleep-deprived adults. In his room he had created a kitten-friendly pen area, which usually successfully contained them for short periods, before they found new and innovative ways to escape. The ever-patient Archie had spent hours entertaining them with various homemade contraptions which he had invented for their amusement. His latest invention was made from a swinging baby chair that he had bought in a charity shop in Fraserburgh. Archie had used various dissected clothing items which included Lottie's brand-new bra, to form cradles in which he placed the protesting pussies. Ingeniously, once he activated the vibration and rocking settings, the kittens would temporarily calm with various furry limbs hanging limply until they felt the urge to swipe idly at anything passing in close proximity.

Lottie knew that, much like toddlers, the kittens would eventually grow out of their destructive ways. Nevertheless, the constant soiling meant her love for Boots' offspring was wearing thinner on a daily basis. She was also worried about the prospect of finding a cat-sitter for their upcoming trip to Paris, and she remained determined to track Pru down and get her to resume her grandparenting responsibilities. After several failed attempts to get Pru to answer her door, Lottie realised that her last resort would be to go to the mindfulness class that Pru was running that evening. She was working on the presumption that Pru would never miss her own group, still known as *Pru's Group*.

Lottie marvelled at Pru's ability to avoid an alternative name for the group, even though she went through the pretence of canvassing the opinion of the attendees at every meeting. When she had mentioned this to Alice recently, she had been met with some playful scorn,

"Oh Lots, you really are naïve sometimes! Of course it's still called *Pru's Group*, she's never going to relinquish her control of the group. It's a dictatorship! I understand you've made some great friends there but meet them outside the group and save yourself the trauma."

Lottie sighed, and aware that this meeting was likely to involve a lot of lying around and breathing on the draughty village hall floor, she grabbed a tatty tartan blanket on her way out.

She arrived in the car park where she spotted Pru's Citroen 2CV and felt smug that her determination had been rewarded.

"Gotcha!" she said, as she strode purposefully through the main doors.

She encountered Mim in the main entrance and they exchanged brief eye contact. The Gardener, now unveiled as the link between her son and an international drug smuggling syndicate, smiled weakly before giving an apologetic shrug.

As Lottie passed her, she fought to contain her parental rage at the cheek of the woman. She had had a long heart-to-heart conversation with Robbie after the party, and he had convinced her that he was extremely remorseful about his brief foray into organised crime. After a few unannounced room searches, Lottie felt reassured that Robbie was now on the straight and narrow.

During her rummaging she had discovered a few well-read copies of *Nuts* magazine, a girl's hair brush and some moisturiser. Shortly, thereafter the owner of the hair brush and moisturiser had made herself known in the form of Annabel, a young woman who was the epitome of geek chic, and no doubt a contributing factor in Robbie's return to a law-abiding life.

Lottie had been somewhat surprised at her son's choice of girlfriend, who did not resemble his *Nuts* idols, and she had mistakenly mentioned it briefly at breakfast one morning. For her trouble she had received the most scathing of looks from Robbie as he corrected her information.

"She's a friend that's a girl, not a *girlfriend*, duh!"

Lottie smiled at the memory recounting the blush of crimson that had crept up from the base of his neck into his newly-bearded face. Aware that her boy was now a becoming a man, she didn't press for further information, trusting that he would come to her for any advice he needed.

Alice seemed slightly more disturbed by the presence of a girl in the man cave and insisted on a step-parenting intervention to ascertain her age and whether her parents knew of the friendship that was developing. Pleased that Alice had chosen to involve herself, Lottie willingly stepped back and Robbie had reacted in a far less hostile way to the step-parent intervention. After some discussion, an agreement was brokered between Alice and Robbie. Annabel was verified as being seventeen, and provided the door of the man cave remained open during her visits, they were free to come and go as they pleased.

AS LOTTIE MADE her way into the main hall, she was greeted with the sight of Pru's large and saggy derrière, as she bent awkwardly, unrolling yoga mats into a circular formation. Lottie noticed a large inflatable mattress in the middle of the circle, which she could only assume was Pru's mindfulness throne for the evening. Balanced on top of the mattress was her feathered cape, several orthopaedic pillows and an assortment of tambourines and other unidentified musical equipment.

Pru rose and Lottie quickly averted her eyes. Pru turned to face her giving her a mealy-mouthed grin which didn't quite reach her eyes.

"Well, Charlotte, my dear, what a lovely surprise. I was going to pop in after group to let you know I was back and check on the furry dears. I expect they are quite the picture now." Without waiting for a reply she went on. "The show was a huge success, *huge*! I had a lot of interest in my work, and do you know, dearie? I don't know if it's because they are more cultured in Edinburgh, but I did sense a real appreciation for the uniqueness of my pieces."

Lottie struggled to hide her cynicism. "How lovely, Pru, and how many pieces did you sell? Did you have enough with you, as you left in such a hurry?"

Pru's eyes narrowed as if assessing whether Lottie was mocking her. "Oh dear, you obviously don't know much about the art world do you? People view work at shows, they don't come with their cheque books. But I am expecting a lot of follow-up business and so I imagine I'll be busy for the rest of the season. I'll probably be away quite a lot, so I'll have to ask you to hang on to the furry dears for a while longer. Their primary bond will now be with you of course, and attachment is very important."

Lottie was determined not to get side-tracked by Pru's constant slur on her artistic understanding and the simultaneous shirking of her parental responsibilities. Yet there was a part of Lottie that couldn't help but admire the stealthy way in which Pru managed to get her own way.

Unable to think of an immediate retort, Lottie managed to stutter. "Well, we wouldn't see• them homeless obviously, although I think their primary attachment is with Sappho, their mother, so wherever she goes is probably where they ought to be."

Pru blinked and raised an eyebrow. Leaning forward, she grabbed Lottie's forearm just a little too tightly, and hissed at her. "You're certainly persistent, aren't you? Attachment theory, girl. Attachment theory! The primary bond is crucial, and you and I both know that Sappho is not a natural mother. If you break the bond formed by those kittens, you'll cause them emotional trauma. E-M-O-T-I-O-N-A-L T-R-A-U-M-A!" she spelled it out.

Turning her back on Lottie in dismissal. "Attachment Theory. Bowlby, dear, Bowlby, Look him up!" Covering the length of the village hall with remarkable speed, she cast one final look of despair at the forlorn Lottie, before barking orders at Mim, who jumped to attention to complete the remaining preparations for the session.

Resigned to her fate as a permanent foster carer, Lottie sank onto the nearest mat and swathed herself in the blanket, which she noticed also had a faint smell of cat urine. Pru took her place on her mattress where she assumed an awkward cross-legged position giving Lottie an unpleasant glimpse of her underwear, which looked both gray and unappealing. Trying to shake the image from her mind, she looked away as Pru hastily adjusted herself before commencing on a speech to the group about the principles of mindfulness techniques.

Despite her initial disinterest, Lottie learned that mindfulness was based on Buddhist principles, a spiritual view she had always admired, which promoted selflessness and awareness of both your own state and that of the world and people around you. Lottie had some experience of meditation, having gone on a day course in her early twenties to learn the art. It had been run by shaven-headed Buddhist monks, both male and female, who wore colourful orange gowns. What had intrigued her was their perpetual state of happiness—all were grinning from ear to ear for the entire day, leaving Lottie to conclude that they had obviously cracked the code to inner happiness and were laughing at those who had not. Despite their cold and slightly drab surroundings, the monks had walked her and the others through the ritual and meaning of meditation, and Lottie was pretty sure she had reached something of a serene state by the end of the day, although her bottom ached for a week afterward thanks to the unforgiving hard wooden chairs. She had declared the meditation day a success—something akin to a mental spa day, and she had vowed to follow the practice to help her through the marital strife she was experiencing at the time. This good intention had quickly gone by the wayside, however, following the arrival of Robbie and the sleepless nights he brought with him. But she was looking forward to revisiting this in the group, and hoped to take something useful from the evening, even if she had not achieved her primary goal of returning the kittens.

She squeezed her eyes shut and attempted to concentrate, as Pru persistently banged the gong, much to Lottie's rising irritation. How did she manage to turn a supposedly soothing gong into such an unpleasant din? Seemingly oblivious to Lottie's annoyance, Pru barked out instructions for the group to get comfortable on the thin mats, while she sat resplendent on her luxurious version.

Lottie carefully lowered herself into a semi-reclining position, trying to train her line of sight on Pru, keen to observe the technical processes as closely as possible, in the hope that she could replicate them at home. Pru was rocking rhythmically while gently stroking the edge of her feathery cape with one hand and striking the gong with the other. Lottie fought her irritation and tried to allow the noise to wash across her as she leaned back to a horizontal position. Conscious of the scratching noise of the mat which adjusted under her weight, she desperately attempted to remain serene as she shuffled her bottom cautiously. Suddenly there was a noisy clattering of coins as they slid from her unzipped pocket and hit the polished wooden floor. She grabbed at the open pocket, but only in time to save the remaining few coins from hitting the floor. The others rolled bravely in the direction of Pru.

Lottie felt a prickle of heat and embarrassment making her cheeks pink as she reluctantly cast her gaze in the direction of Pru, whose beady eyes glared accusingly back at her. Several titters came from the surrounding mats, and she fumbled clumsily to grab the coins closest to her before shoving them quickly back into her pocket, where she secured the zip firmly. Fighting the humiliation, she tried to refocus on Pru's resumed commentary.

"So, we've explored and become aware of the parts of our body, focusing on our breathing. Now feel the breath come naturally through your body, slowly, peacefully..."

Lottie breathed deeply, feeling the rise and fall of her chest and the gentle warmth of the air as it escaped through her nostrils.

In and out.

The breath left her body. Her mind wandered but, as instructed, she carefully brought it back to sound of her own breathing. The soothing rhythm of the act of breathing as it left and returned to her body left her in awe of the natural ability of the human mind.

Pru once again reminded the group not be distracted or anxious about the wandering mind.

"Just bring it gently back to your breathing. Acknowledge the thoughts and then let them pass calmly from your mind. Notice how each breath you exhale, leaves your body and enters into the world, carrying your problems and worries with it."

Lottie inhaled sharply, her rhythm disturbed. She hadn't

been thinking about her medley of worries, but now that Pru had mentioned it, her mind became distracted and started racing as issues surfaced — her cat-sitter problem, Robbie's new relationship, whether Alice would remember not to leave the hair straighteners on. Alice didn't have many faults, but this was one of the few.

"Come on, Lottie, focus, focus!" she counselled herself, but to no avail. Pictures of her parents flashed before her, the divorce, the custody issues, and the mountain of unopened e-mails which crowded her inbox at work.

She sighed loudly, again attracting a disapproving glare from the exasperated Pru.

Unsettling Times

THE FOLLOWING SUNDAY, cruising idly through her e-mails, Lottie picked through the endless list of junk mail until an e-mail from a tutor she had contacted to help Archie with his English classes caught her eye. Clicking it open, she quickly scanned the details confirming an appointment with the tutor, Maddie, for the next day, offering an initial meeting to discuss her proposed curriculum.

"Babe, the tutor got back to me. She's happy to help with Archie's English and she's coming tomorrow teatime."

"Uh huh," responded a distracted Alice who was studiously basting a delicious roast.

Convinced that Archie's dyslexia, which was becoming increasingly evident since he had started the last year of primary school, would not get the professional assistance he needed once he was at senior school, Lottie had decided that intervention was needed. She had pondered the inevitable battle to get him to accept help, before she belatedly wandered into the kitchen to offer help with dinner.

Alice considered the problem of engaging Archie in the plan.

"At the end of the day, babes, he's going to have to work with her. Where did you find her? Is she vetted?"

Lottie nodded in assent. Aware of the horror stories about home tutors, she had purposely picked a female tutor, and hoped that Archie would make the most of the opportunity to catch up before he was too far behind.

Odie waddled through the kitchen, following his nose towards the smell of the basted lamb, and looked expectantly at his owner.

"You'll be lucky!" Alice winked at him, before accidentally dropping a chunk of the delicious meat, which never reached the floor but was caught mid-air by the alert and ravenous hound.

Alice listened as Lottie thought aloud about the difficulty she was going to have convincing Archie that this was in his best interests.

"The trouble is, the school say he's already a year behind. If we don't get on top of it now it's only going to get worse."

Alice nodded in support, as she juggled a steaming hot pan of gravy with freshly-made mint sauce. The smell was making

Lottie salivate and she postponed the discussion, offering to be the taste tester before being sent to set the table.

"NO!" SAID ARCHIE through a mouthful of the tender meat. Alice sighed and busied herself with clearing the table, deferring to Lottie's parental status and silently hoping that she would assert her authority with Archie.

Lottie was fast losing her patience. Archie had evidently hit the pre-teen roadshow with some speed and had strong opinions which often didn't sit well with her.

"Look, this is what we'll do — let's get her here tomorrow and meet her, see what she's got to say and then we'll take it from there." Her voice, she noticed was a little too falsetto at the end of the sentence, reflecting her feeble attempt to cajole him into submission.

"Okay, right!" The emphasis on the *t* spat at her was a clear signal that the conversation was now finished.

Alice peered round the door to give Lottie a subtle thumbs-up before collecting the still salivating sausage dog for his evening walk.

Archie stomped up the stairs and the loud slam of his bedroom door confirmed that the battle was only postponed. Lottie hoped he would keep his cheekiness in check long enough for her to get Maddie to sign on the dotted line.

Making the most of the peace and quiet, she tapped in the number provided on the e-mail and a few short rings later, a voice purred down the line. "Hey, it's Maddie."

Lottie drew in her breath. "Christ!" she muttered, not realising she'd said it aloud.

The tutor's voice oozed sensuality and Lottie felt an involuntary shiver run up her spine. As she froze, she registered a confident chuckle with a hidden silky undertone. "Ha! Christ on a Sunday, well that's original. Not religious myself, but hey, if that's what does it for you!" Maddie purred.

Lottie spluttered, aware that she was making a complete fool of herself. She cleared her throat and announced herself as formally as she could manage. "Hi Maddie, this is Lottie, Archie's mum. We've e-mailed, and I was just ringing to confirm our appointment tomorrow."

Maddie sighed with satisfaction, and Lottie was having trouble keeping her mind on the conversation. This wasn't going to plan! Why was this stranger having such a profound effect on her?

Anxious not to make a complete fool of herself, she decided to concentrate on managing her breathing as Maddie easily took control of the conversation to finalise the arrangements.

She ended the call insistently. "It'll be a pleasure, sweetie. So looking forward to meeting you both." Without waiting for Lottie to get out her goodbye, she hung up.

Drawing a deep breath, Lottie was aware of the warmth which involuntarily flowed through her body, and absent-mindedly she stroked the phone. There was something deeply sexual about Maddie and she felt quite disturbed by it. She cleared her throat and hoped that at that same time it would help to clear the intrusive sexual thoughts she was having.

Recovering herself, Lottie chuckled at the irony of her reaction and imagined the likely reality that Maddie would be a middle-aged frump, as so many of the Highland teaching community were. Comforted by this thought she headed for the kitchen to clear up the dinner mayhem.

WHEN LOTTIE LEFT work for the short drive home the following afternoon, her thoughts returned to her impending meeting with the tutor. She thought she had successfully dispelled the thoughts of the previous day, but had suddenly become strangely nervous. Being affected in this way by a complete stranger had shaken Lottie, who prided herself on being intuitive when it came to people.

As a child she had been innately shy and socially awkward, and always highly anxious in social situations. She had honed her skills in reading people as a way of avoiding embarrassment in these circumstances, and she had learned how to present with false confidence. Through her early teens and into adulthood she had successfully masqueraded as a straight woman and these skills had become finely tuned, hiding in full sight of both her family and her friends for many years. Through the latter years of her marriage she had met a few women towards whom she had felt a strong physical and emotional attraction, but these were feelings she hadn't followed through because of a sense of loyalty to her family unit. Nevertheless, the strong physical attraction she experienced would, at times, literally leave her breathless. Much like the feelings she seemed to be experiencing now. There was no doubt in her mind that when she had met Alice she was attracted to her on many levels and that sense of strong physical connection was established even before they had begun to date.

Since she had been immersed in their blossoming relationship she had given little thought to any sort of attraction to other women. She was sure that she hadn't wanted it, or noticed it, until now.

Parking in the tight pull-in at the front of the cottage, Lottie noticed an unfamiliar vehicle parked some way up the road. Keen to get in and clear away the breakfast dishes before Maddie arrived, Lottie juggled her lunch bag and her keys to open the front door. A car door slammed and Lottie turned, key in lock, to observe a woman get out of the parked car and walk confidently the short distance down the street towards her. Lottie silently observed the tutor approaching her. Athletic in stature, she wore a figure-hugging gray pinstriped trouser suit, with crisp white shirt cuffs showing beneath the jacket. The tight fitted shirt skirted the outline of her small pert breasts and a small pendant necklace disappeared into the depths of the high collar. As she walked, the light caught her cufflinks which glinted, and Lottie noticed she had one hand casually tucked into her trouser pocket emphasising her slender hips.

Still frozen on the door step, Lottie checked herself for any form of gormless expression which might give away her thrill at seeing the woman she observed. She plastered a toothy smile onto her face and gave an over-eager wave in the direction of the stranger. In return, the Amazonian beauty gave a curt nod, a smile teased around her lips and her bright blue eyes sparkled as the light caught them. Lottie felt her mouth go dry, desperate for lubrication before she was expected to hold a conversation with the woman she was now sure must be Maddie. She swallowed, regretting it instantly as her cheeks stuck to her teeth.

Maddie was now at her side, and Lottie felt heady as the breeze brought the subtle scent of her perfume, teasing her heightened senses. Unable to muster any verbal welcome, she silently ushered Maddie into the living room. Instantly making herself at home, Maddie deposited her slender form onto the sofa and tucked a slim leg neatly underneath her.

Lottie dashed into kitchen, and dipping her head directly underneath the tap, she greedily glugged the cool tap water. "Tea?" she called. Without waiting for a reply, she hastily boiled the kettle.

Silently, she berated herself. Get a fucking grip! She sucked in two deep breaths and ran a hand though her hair before joining Maddie in the living room, carefully choosing the opposite chair to avoid the intoxicating allure of Maddie's musky scent. The same wry smile played around Maddie's lips as she eyed Lottie with a mixture of interest and amusement. Maddie ran a finger sensuously along the rim of the mug of tea and Lottie noticed how strong her hands looked, as she was entranced by the finger as it circled the mug. Catching herself, she hastily averted her eyes.

Maddie confidently surveyed her surroundings and her eyes stopped at the spilling-over bookcase beside her. Reaching in to pluck a paperback by Patricia Highsmith entitled *The Price of Salt*, she flicked through the pages with those same sensual fingers — she seemed to be reliving a memory and she closed her eyes for a moment with her hand resting lightly on the front of the book.

Seizing on the opportunity to break the pregnant silence, Lottie mumbled. "Oh, yes, really good book that. It was made into a film, you know." Without waiting for a response, she gabbled onward. "The film was called *Carol*, a good lesbian story, with a happy ending for once!" She drew a breath clumsily as Maddie peered at her with curious intensity.

Avoiding eye contact, Lottie nevertheless felt the scorching glare of Maddie's scrutiny and struggled to maintain her composure as she continued. "It's my partner's book actually. She loves it, she's got the film as well..." Her voice trailed lamely. Staring intensely at the coffee table between them, Lottie was aware of a movement on the other side of the room.

The presence of the musky scent alerted her to the close presence of Maddie. Swallowing noisily, she looked up and Maddie handed her the book, and as she silently took it their hands brushed briefly. Lottie felt an unwelcome shiver of anticipation.

"A great love of mine once had the same book. We said it was our story," Maddie offered, smiling, before returning to her seat.

Lottie nodded carefully, and feeling more assured, she ventured. "Did it have a happy ending?"

As soon as she had asked the question, a shadow crossed Maddie's face. "Sadly not. One of the few regrets of my life actually." For a fleeting moment, she looked vulnerable.

Lottie was mortally embarrassed, and silently berated herself for asking such an intrusive question. What right had she to ask such a personal question to a complete stranger?

Maddie reached for her bag and Lottie felt immediate panic and a sense of disappointment that she was going to leave.

"Shall we have a look at my plan for Archie and take it from there?" Maddie offered, resuming a cool professionalism.

Frustratingly, Lottie found she was keen to hear more of the sensuous tones of this woman, and so she nodded a silent assent as she allowed Maddie to outline a term's worth of lesson plans for her son. At the rhythmic intonation of the tutor's voice, Lottie became aware that her own hands were ever so slightly trembling and that there was a warmth through her entire body, despite the chill in the room. Clasping her clammy hands together she tried to concentrate on the teaching outline, vaguely catching snippets of the one-way conversation as she mentally battled with her instinctive reaction to the undeniably striking woman sitting before her.

Catching a look at the clock she noted forty-five minutes had elapsed, and there was still no sign of Archie. She tutted loudly, wondering where on earth he had got to. Clearly, he was avoiding meeting Maddie, but right now she could do with a grounded motherhood check. Maddie paused at the sound of the tutting and raised a perfectly manicured eyebrow in question. Anxious to reassure Maddie that it hadn't been the content of her sessions that had raised her disapproval, she explained that Archie was a little reluctant to engage, but that she hoped that when they had met he would become more enthused.

"Don't worry, I'm sure he'll warm to me. They usually do," she stated before winking at Lottie as she packed away her paperwork. "Why don't I swing by again tomorrow, and we'll get started. Is that okay?"

Lottie nodded, although a cold misery had crept into her mind. She waved goodbye to Maddie before purposely closing the door, determined not to watch her walk up the street. She sank onto the nearest available seat, feeling horribly conflicted about her disloyalty to Alice. Dear, sweet Alice. She felt as if she had virtually cheated! She mentally shook herself, this was all because she was in a settled relationship.

"Relationship jitters, that's all it is," she said aloud as she tried to convince herself. A smile broke out as she realised the irony of the tutor's surname, Jitters. Feeling slightly reassured that she had identified the source of her unsettled feelings, she decided that she needed to do her own version of grounding and picked up the phone to check in with Alice, determined to cook her favourite pasta bake for tea as her own form of penance.

Crushed

ALICE LEFT FOR work early the next morning. Conscious that she was about to take some time off for the Paris trip, she was attempting to get ahead of the few things she could forward-plan at her practice. Today was a mass vaccination day and she anticipated a surgery full of mewling kittens and rambunctious puppies.

Lottie had been out of sorts the previous night she concluded, after having a very strained conversation about the tutor. She didn't feel any the wiser about how they were going to tackle Archie's school issues. His resistance was palpable and she felt that Lottie was going to have a battle on her hands. She rarely interfered in any parenting issues, but she felt she needed to raise this with Lottie later, after Archie had collared her on the landing early that morning and pleaded for her assistance. She agreed with him that the final terms of primary school were just that, time for kids to unwind and get past that school year before embarking on the next level up. She accepted that Archie had issues which needed to be addressed, but she was convinced that these could easily wait until the next school year.

She felt that Lottie didn't always understand the impact of her decisions on the rest of the family. Once she got embroiled in a scheme, she became hell-bent on following her grand plan through to its conclusion. Alice felt irritated as she wondered whether the tutor was up to scratch. Lottie had been reluctant to give any details about her background, and this made Alice suspicious that Lottie may stubbornly be going forward with someone who she wasn't utterly convinced could do the job. She felt strongly that if Lottie was going to get Archie on board, she could at least make sure that Archie would like the tutor. Cautiously easing around the blind corners towards her surgery, she decided that the least she could do was support Archie. If she could get through the deluge of small creatures today, she determined she would be home to meet this tutor and help Archie out in negotiating terms with his mum.

LOTTIE LEFT WORK one hour early determined not to have another awkward doorstep encounter. Earlier in the day she had confided her crush to Virginia, who had dismissed her concerns as normal relationship jitters. Feeling reassured she decided she would assume a more professional approach with today's introduction to Archie, and that later she would discuss it properly with Alice — aware she had frozen out her interest the previous evening as she had wrestled with her guilt. Once home, while waiting for the kettle to boil, she quickly gathered an after-school snack together for Archie — the more he chewed the less opposition he would be able to express. Satisfied that she had covered all bases, she was nevertheless relieved when Archie made a noisy entry, meaning she wouldn't have to spend any time alone with Maddie. Settled on the sofa, Lottie made some last-minute adjustments to the bookcase moving the novel which had provoked the unexpected disclosure firmly to the lower shelf and out of sight.

Shortly afterward, Maddie arrived. Lottie was relieved to note that her seductive powers seemed to have abated somewhat, although she still wore the same rather lovely perfume. Maddie's attention seemed to be directed appropriately towards Archie who, despite himself, appeared to be enjoying being the centre of her undivided attention. Making no move following the inhalation of his snack, Maddie had capitalised on his attention and was introducing him to her dyslexia-friendly curriculum. Satisfied that things were progressing in the right direction, Lottie made herself absent, sitting in the kitchen and flicking through the holiday brochures that Alice had left for her.

An hour later, Archie rushed past her and headed for his bedroom. He mumbled quietly. "She's all right, Mum."

A begrudging admission that filled Lottie with some hope that she had won the battle to get Archie on board with her plan.

Returning to her brochures the now familiar musky smell alerted her to the presence of Maddie, who was stooping above her, peering with curiosity to see what Lottie was reading. With her unexpected presence, a familiar stirring of desire unnerved Lottie, who hastily shuffled along to the far chair which Maddie took as an unspoken invitation to sit, leaving Lottie trapped in the corner.

"Going on holiday?" she asked, idly thumbing the corner of the page Lottie had marked for Paris.

Distracted by her closeness, Lottie only managed to nod, her nostrils filled with the perfume and she felt a heady combination of excitement and fear. Her earlier resolve to be business-like was quickly dissipating and she felt a renewed physical attraction to

Maddie, who was chewing her bottom lip absent-mindedly.

Suddenly, she turned her full attention towards Lottie. As their eyes met Lottie felt a jolt of excitement and her body seemed to take on a mind of its own. A smile toyed around Maddie's lips, her finger casually caressed the edge of Lottie's hand. Unsure of whether this was accidental, but shocked nonetheless by her forwardness, Lottie awkwardly extracted her hand and sat firmly on it causing Maddie to break out into a grin.

"Coy little thing, aren't you?" she muttered, her voice having lowered to a husky tone.

Lottie couldn't speak. Undeniably attracted to Maddie, she felt ashamed. This was a total betrayal of Alice and she knew it. Flirting with someone in their own home was tantamount to an affair. She suddenly felt claustrophobic in the small space. She was hemmed in, and this woman was definitely coming on to her.

Relief flooded through her at the sound of the front door slamming shut, and a blast of cold air from outside gratefully grazed her warm cheeks.

"That must be Robbie already!" she said, relieved to be able to issue a reminder to the interloper that she was a respectable mother, and she jumped to her feet anticipating the introduction.

Maddie chose to ignore Lottie's attempt to break away from their moment and Lottie feebly sat down in her chair again, having no other choice as she was trapped in the corner.

"Hey!" a voice called from the living room, not Robbie, but Alice. Lottie still felt relieved not to be alone with Maddie.

Alice entered the kitchen, for a moment distracted by the depositing of her bags into the under-stairs cupboard. Lottie realised too late that she and Maddie were sitting far too close together to be viewed as anything but unusual to Alice. Anxious to avoid any awkwardness she cleared her throat noisily, as Alice looked up.

Lottie rushed to make the polite introductions, now fully pinned against the kitchen wall, in an effort to create the illusion of distance between her and Maddie.

Falsely bright, she chirped. "Alice, so glad you're back early. This is—"

Before she could finish her sentence, Alice, whose face was visibly shocked, finished the sentence for her.

"—Maddie!"

Maddie nodded her head in a slight gesture of acknowledgement as one of her perfectly manicured eyebrows lifted in a question. Confused, Lottie looked towards Alice for an explanation, but her eyes were trained on Maddie, who was looking at Alice with equal intensity.

Puzzled by their silent exchange, Lottie rushed to mask what seemed to be an awkward silence. "Maddie was just showing Archie some of the work she planned for them to do together, weren't you, Maddie?" Looking to Maddie for some acknowledgement, she noticed the same look of amusement etched into the tutor's features that she had noticed the previous day.

A flash of anger, or was it jealousy, registered clearly on Alice's face and Lottie felt a rush of self-consciousness. Before Lottie could ask her partner the obvious question, Alice had rushed past them both, failing to make any pleasantries and headed for the stairs.

Confused, and rushing to keep up, Lottie caught up with her in the upstairs corridor. "Babe?" she asked, reaching out to catch Alice's hand.

Roughly, Alice pushed her away. "What the fuck have you done, Lottie?" she muttered furiously, before hiding herself away in the bathroom, leaving Lottie alone and thoroughly confused.

Lottie was filled with panic.

Fuck!

She hadn't meant to allow herself to flirt with Maddie, it was a moment of ridiculous chemistry, and now Alice was furious with her. But how the hell did they know one another? Something unspoken had passed between them, and Lottie was utterly bewildered about what the connection could be.

Deciding to tackle Alice about her odd behaviour later, she rushed downstairs determined to cover Alice's social faux pas and keep the tutor on site. When she reached the living room the silence informed her that Maddie had left. Clearly aware of the tense atmosphere, she had understandably decided to make herself scarce.

Although embarrassed at her own behaviour, Lottie was furious with Alice for jeopardising the delicate relationship between Archie and his new tutor. Lottie distracted herself by busily clearing away the paperwork strewn on the carpet.

AN HOUR LATER, Lottie sat alone at the kitchen table. Above, she could hear Alice running a bath. Her embarrassment had given way to overwhelming confusion. Alice had clearly known Maddie, and it was obvious that Alice had not been pleased to see her again. But why was Alice so angry? Never before in their relationship had she seen Alice this angry, and now she was hiding away upstairs and refusing to speak to her!

Lottie felt an ache in the back of her throat, and tears pricked her eyes. Alice was behaving like a complete idiot! Anger flooded her again, and she skirted round Odie who was annoyingly clinging around her legs, to take the stairs two at a time, insistently rapping on the bathroom door. "Alice? Alice! Answer me!"

From inside the bathroom Lottie heard the slosh of water, and Alice appeared at the bathroom door looking small and frail.

Silently, they walked to the bedroom and Alice shut the door behind them. Lottie perched on the edge of the bed and waited expectantly for an explanation. Alice seated herself some distance away on the wicker chair and glowered at Lottie.

After a moment of painful silence, Lottie was overwhelmed with a desire to understand what was happening. "What's going on?" she questioned.

Alice continued to glower. "What the fuck have you done, Lottie?" she repeated loudly.

"I don't understand, Alice. What do you mean, 'What have I done'?"

Alice sighed angrily. "Don't pretend you don't know who that woman is. How could you let her into our home, and into our lives?"

Lottie remained silent, but inside, her mind was racing. She didn't know Maddie! She had found her on an internet site for private tutors. She hadn't recognised the name. What exactly was it she was supposed to know?

Leaning forward to remove the distance between them, Lottie tentatively placed her hand on Alice's knee, noting that she was shaking. Alice brushed her hand away, and pulled her towel closely around herself, shielding her body from Lottie's presence.

Lottie felt emotion well up inside her, she felt rejected and suddenly very alone. Her relationship seemed to be in a bad place and she sensed that Alice was furious at her, but she didn't know why.

"You were flirting, Lottie, I *saw* you, she may as well have been sat on your lap!" Alice's eyes clouded with tears but she was too angry to give way to them.

Lottie felt contrite.

Sobbing, she withdrew her hand and Alice leaned forward, lowering her voice to a venomous whisper. "It took me *years* to get her out of my head, Lottie, and then suddenly I come home and she's sat on your fucking lap? Was that some twisted joke?" Looking at Lottie for an explanation she withdrew back into the shroud of her towel.

Lottie couldn't speak, tears spilled down her cheeks and her chest throbbed with the effort of containing the hurt which seemed to want to burst from her chest. Breathing to try and stem the flow of tears she managed to speak. "Is she an ex?"

This seemed to enrage Alice further. "You know perfectly well she's a fucking ex, Lottie, she's *the* ex!"

Lottie struggled to search her memory of an early relationship discussion she and Alice had about their past loves. She did vaguely recall Alice talking about a particularly serious live-in relationship which had ended badly after Alice had discovered that her partner had cheated on her. From what she recalled of that discussion, Alice had been very reluctant to go into details, placing the story firmly in the past. All she remembered was that Alice had told her how she had learned from that relationship everything that she would never put up with in a new relationship.

Lottie felt devastating shame. She had been lusting after the very person who had hurt Alice so much, and now she had disrespected Alice by bringing Maddie right back into her present.

"For God's sake, Alice, I didn't even know her name! I didn't know that was her. How could I?"

Alice seemed unforgiving, although Lottie noticed there was hesitation in her voice. "I didn't want you to know her name because I don't want her name in my head, Lottie! Fuck! That woman nearly destroyed me. Have you got any idea what it was like to see her sitting in *our home*, her eyes crawling across you?"

Lottie rose to her feet with all the dignity she could muster. It was her turn to be angry now and she leaned towards Alice, "You lunatic! How could I know? How could I, when I didn't even know her bloody name! The way you're acting, it's beginning to make me think that your past isn't as *past* as you seem to have convinced yourself it is! You still fucking *love* her, Alice, and how do you think that makes *me* feel?"

Rushing for the door, Lottie felt dizzy and sick with horror. Her girlfriend was still in love with another woman. Someone that she had had a passing infatuation with had turned out to be the love of Alice's life!

"I feel like I don't know you at all. I feel like I've *never* known you!" she spat. Racing for the bathroom, she was barely able to lift the toilet seat before being violently sick, tears still falling silently as she retched continually into the bowl.

Sometime later, Lottie left the safety and darkness of the bathroom. Clutching a tissue, she felt so bereft, and it had taken more than an hour to stifle her sobbing.

Alice had left her alone, she hadn't come to comfort her or offer any explanation about the clear misunderstanding that had taken place.

In the kitchen, Lottie gravitated without thought towards the kettle. Clicking it on to boil, she noticed a hastily-written note on the back of a used envelope.

With trembling hands and a sickening sense of dread she picked it up.

I need some time to think. Gone to my flat.

No signature, and no kiss.

Renewed distress flooded her body and her stomach churned with this new information — Alice was gone!

Never had they spent a night apart since the early days of their relationship. Racing up the stairs and into their bedroom, she discovered Alice's drawers were open and clothes strewn across the bed as she had rushed to pack her bag and make a hasty escape.

Lottie groaned and desperately clutched at items of Alice's clothing, frantically trying to bring her back by inhaling her scent.

"Oh no, Alice, no, no, no! Don't please, I don't understand..." she shouted into the empty room, before the fight suddenly left her and she lay, spent, on the bed — her mind struggling to cope with the inevitable fact.

Alice was gone.

Stubbornness and Pride

LOTTIE STRETCHED OUT her arm from inside the quilt and felt the familiar shape of her mobile phone. Pulling it back into the dark depths of the duvet she checked her messages for the hundredth time, despondently noting that there was nothing.

On a whim, she hit new message and typed, but overcome by pride, she hit delete. Why should she be the first one to make contact? Alice was being completely illogical. There was no way she could have known that Maddie was her ex.

Hitting the play button on her music player, she selected her 1980s collection of music and the dulcet tones of The Bangles filled the room, as a self-pitying sniffle escaped her. Cautiously she looked into the mirror, and her worst fears were confirmed as her mournful face, swollen with puffy dark circled eyes looked pitifully back at her.

Clearing her throat, she checked the volume button on her phone before throwing it crossly across the unmade bed. Anger surged through her as she wondered why Alice was being so irrational. Getting out of bed, she threw on an old pair of jogging bottoms and a stained vest top and gingerly made her way downstairs, hoping as she went, that she would find Alice returned and asleep on the sofa.

The darkness of early morning confirmed that Alice was still absent and so she rallied herself with the business of making breakfast for the boys, exhaustion and anger sweeping through her body in equal measure. She tried to imagine how Alice would have felt seeing the woman who had broken her heart pinning her girlfriend into the corner of their kitchen. She inwardly sighed, as she slopped milk into the bowls overflowing with cereal, and a scattering of cornflakes spattered across the floor.

Tutting with annoyance, she opened her mouth to shout to the dog before realising that Alice had taken him with her. Consoling herself with a dry croissant, she impatiently shouted up the stairs to the boys until they responded and the chaos of bickering teenagers provided a momentary distraction from her misery.

Robbie paused mid-bicker and looked at Lottie quizzically. "Everything okay, Mum?"

Lottie bit back the rising lump in her throat, and smiling a little too brightly, she nodded — not trusting herself to speak.

Archie ever attuned to her feelings, turned to look at her with curiosity.

Realising she would have to provide some form of explanation for her dishevelled state, she swallowed hard.

"Alice and I have had a bit of a falling-out. Nothing serious, so don't worry. Just grown up stuff."

Lottie tried to ignore the dismay that she saw in Archie's delicate features. "You'll be off to your dad's tonight. Training day tomorrow, remember? So, we'll both see you when you're back after the weekend, okay...?" she trailed lamely.

Both boys nodded solemnly, and without being asked, grabbed their bags and headed for the car.

After dropping the boys at school, she found herself turning the car towards home. When she had left earlier, she had fully intended to go to work and lose herself in the mundane world of classified advertising, but she soon realised she couldn't face it.

Parking outside the cottage she sat for a moment, still clutching her phone, sure that Alice would make contact. Staring at the front door she felt physically sick at the thought of going inside to the empty rooms.

"Pull yourself together. You've been alone before and you can damn well do it again!" she chastised herself aloud and grabbing her bag she made her way inside. Suddenly her phone chimed indicating an incoming text message, her heart soared with hope as she leapfrogged the kitchen chair, dashing to the living room to swipe up her discarded phone from the sofa. Unlocking the screen hope instantly faded as she saw a text from Linda Lovely:

Babe, where are you?

Sighing, she tapped out a quick reply feigning illness and asking Linda to pass on the message to Ann. Slinging the phone back onto the sofa, she slowly climbed the stairs, seeking the sanctuary of the darkened bedroom and the oblivion of sleep.

ALICE PULLED HER Range Rover to a stop outside the cottage. Pausing with her key in the ignition, she noticed Lottie's car in their small parking space. Odie, oblivious to the unfolding drama clambered anxiously onto her knee eager to be lifted down and back into the warmth of the cottage. Alice swatted at him, forcing him back into the passenger seat.

Torn, she realised that Lottie was so upset she'd not been able to go to work, but she was still angry at the memory of her sitting in such close quarters to the toxic Maddie. Also angry with herself now, as she recalled the stab of pure jealousy she'd felt as she saw the flush of excitement on Lottie's face. She had seen that Lottie had been attracted to her ex and it invoked in her a fury she hadn't known she'd possessed. Spending the night in her heatless old flat, she had thought about how she felt after seeing Maddie after all those years and was relieved to note that the only feelings she could identify had been disgust and anger.

Alice felt distraught at the thought that Lottie believed she still had feelings for Maddie, but she had felt so furious when Lottie had been so blatantly flirting that she hadn't wanted to reassure her, and she hated herself now for wishing Lottie to feel hurt and insecure. Tapping the steering wheel anxiously, she was frozen. She wanted to get out and go and speak to Lottie, but she didn't know how to explain how she'd felt, and she was sure that although Lottie would listen, she may well have caused irreversible damage to their previously strong union.

Through the long sleepless night, she had revisited their previous discussions about exes and other less serious relationships. She had to admit she'd downplayed the story of Maddie, not wanting Lottie to know how desperately badly she'd allowed herself to be treated by someone. Lottie saw her as strong and wise and she certainly knew that she hadn't been when she had wasted so many years with Maddie who had constantly cheated on her. Much to her shame she had turned a blind eye to Maddie's selfish behaviour, so desperate was she to not be alone. Stubbornly, she had hung onto the relationship, determined to make it work. She had ignored the steady erosion of her self-esteem, as evidence of betrayal after betrayal surfaced in the form of Maddie's sudden absences from their home, and clandestine appointments with her mobile phone behind the locked bathroom door.

However, she had never felt more alone than she did at this moment and the physical pain she was experiencing was a stark reminder that this was what it felt like to truly miss someone you love.

When Maddie had finally left her for the male physical education teacher, Alice had realised that the primary feeling she had was one of relief. Relief that she did not have to summon up the courage to end something that was so clearly wrong. From that moment she had made herself a promise that she would stay single until she found her own strength of character, and until she had restored her deflated self-respect. But she was now filled with doubt.

How could Lottie forgive her behaviour?

Lottie had an inner fragility that was all too evident when it came to dealing with perceived rejection or conflict.

Alice tried to swallow the hard lump that was burning in her throat. She had hurt the one person she loved more than all others in the world, and if she was capable of such cruelty, Alice reasoned, she would only cause Lottie more hurt in the long run. Panicking, she slammed the car into reverse, causing Odie to skid back into the depths of the passenger seat, Alice drove precariously fast, away from the cottage.

LOTTIE PEERED THROUGH the closed curtains of the bedroom. She was sure she'd heard a car outside, and her heart had soared at the thought that Alice had also not gone to work and was coming around to sort things out. Straining to see up the small street she saw a vehicle in the distance turning the sharp corner marking the ascent to the top of the hill, and a squeal of wheels caused her to tut out loud.

"Bloody idiots!" she muttered, assuming it was one of the local youths in their souped-up car.

She had cried, on and off, for twenty-four hours and was aware she was becoming quite dehydrated. Though her stomach still churned, she decided she'd chance a glass of water. Running the tap to cool she cast a weary eye around the kitchen, noting the solidifying contents on the previous night's dinner plates, the smell of leftover fish and chips making her stomach churn anew. Filling her glass, she gingerly sipped on the cool liquid and almost jumped out of her skin in response to a sharp rap on the front door.

"Alice!" she whispered, rushing past the kittens who were fighting about a piece of dried fish that they had stolen from the tray on the stove.

Flinging the door open, Lottie was met with the sight of the inimitable Pru, complete with a dark woollen cape and dramatic sunglasses. Glancing furtively around her, she shooed Lottie aside as she barrelled past, slamming the door behind her.

Deflated, Lottie slumped onto the sofa nursing the still full glass of water. Pru seemed barely aware of the dishevelled Lottie, as she busied herself greeting her grandkittens while examining their furry coats for signs of pedigree. Disappointed by the lack of apparent evidence of their semi-superior heritage, she roughly discarded the two she was holding and turned her beady eye towards Lottie, eyeing her with suspicion.

Lottie would never have answered the door if she'd thought to look through the peep hole. Although somewhat intrigued by Pru's bizarre outfit, she was pretty sure she didn't have the energy for a full discussion with her about her current distressed state. Pru continued to stare at her, stroking her furry chin and raising an inquisitive eyebrow awaiting an explanation from Lottie about her ruffled appearance.

Lottie sighed deeply and summoned up enough energy to enquire why Pru was wearing sunglasses on such a cloudy day.

Sensing her disinterested audience, Pru plonked her ostentatious sunglasses on top of her thinning hair. "Have you and Alice fallen out, dear?"

Despite herself, Lottie found her eyes instantly filled with tears.

Pru joined her on the smaller sofa and patted her leg robustly, clearly impatient to find herself in the role of comforter when she had intended to be the topic of conversation.

Hastily, Lottie wiped her eyes, annoyed that she had been so transparent and vulnerable to Pru's enquiry.

"Now, now let's not have silly tears, shall we? A little upset was always to be expected when you are so utterly besotted with someone like Alice. I could have warned you that she's riddled with self-interest, but I thought you ought to find out for yourself, Charlotte!"

Lottie felt a surge of anger. How dare Pru presume to know Alice after one ridiculous date! Alice may have some flaws, but selfishness certainly wasn't one of her characteristics and despite her current ridiculous behaviour, what she knew about Alice was that she was full of kindness and integrity.

"I think it's time you left, Pru."

Pru, recognising that she had overstepped the mark, and struggling to backtrack from the forwardness of her opinion, adopted a placating tone. "Oh dear, perhaps I expressed that badly. I only meant to say that you two are very different."

Receiving a frosty glare from Lottie in return, she bumbled on. "I mean, dear, you're sure to work through any minor issues! Well, they are minor, aren't they?" Her face furrowed in concentration as she attempted to read the silent Lottie.

Lottie sighed again, all fight going out of her. Pru was supposed to be a therapist after all. Drawing in a sharp breath, she started to recount the mournful tale of the past twenty-four hours and ended dramatically with her current conundrum of whether to swallow her pride and contact Alice. "I just think she ought to make the first move, she's the one in the bloody wrong," she muttered mutinously.

Pru shook her head in disapproval and the sunglasses slipped from her head to be pounced upon by the ever-ready kitten army.

Oblivious to the loss of her disguise, Pru launched into a lecture about the dangers of attachment. "Very unhealthy dear, very unhealthy! You need to get a grip. You shouldn't expect others to provide you with happiness. It's unnatural. We are all individuals, we come to this world alone and we leave it in the same way." she concluded, seemingly confident that she had saved Lottie from future heartache.

Lottie silently berated the arrogance of Pru and wondered if this was the reason that Pru had been single for the past eight years following the end of her long-term relationship, when her partner had run off with her best friend.

Not feeling empowered by Pru's psychobabble, she decided to change the subject, "I do wonder if things would be a lot easier if I was with a man. I mean for God's sake, all they want to do is eat, sleep, fuck, and watch football. Women are so bloody deep!" she growled.

Pru raised an eyebrow in clear disapproval at the crudeness of Lottie's description, "Oh, my dear!" she muttered, and leaning in she whispered to her. "Once a vagitarian, *always* a vagitarian!" She snorted with laughter at her own wit.

Lottie chuckled despite herself. "A vagitarian" she clearly was. God, why was she being so bloody proud? She needed to contact Alice and sort this out.

With a renewed strength of urgency, she brusquely thanked Pru for her useful advice and dispatched her out through the front door.

Grasping her phone with resolve she went to select new message but noticed a waiting message instead, and clicking open her inbox she gasped with joy, Alice!

```
Hi Babe, I am so, so sorry. Please, can I come
home?
```

Furiously Lottie typed a reply.

```
Come home now, please. I love you. I want to
talk about this. We can sort it XXXXXX
```

FORTY-FIVE MINUTES later, the front door opened and Alice sheepishly grinned at Lottie who ran across the living room to embrace her. Reluctant to let her go, Alice pulled her gently towards the sofa and they sat, legs entwined, treating one another gently, both careful not to rock the boat.

Lottie waited expectantly as Alice struggled to make eye contact with her. The anger was gone but Lottie sensed something else. Fear? She reached to stroke Alice's cheek which was warm from the spring air.

Alice captured her hand and gently placed it back in her lap, Lottie felt the breath catch in her throat and a sudden feeling of dread started to grow. She had thought Alice had come to sort things out, but had she come to end it?

Removing herself to the other sofa, Alice absent-mindedly fingered the cover of the book that only a few days ago had drawn the attention of Maddie. Catching Lottie observing this, she pulled it from the bookcase and placed it on the coffee table between them.

"This book was given to me by Maddie, shortly after she had cheated on me for the first of what was to be many times. She said it was a 'sorry' present, but the only thing she was really sorry about was that she had been caught. I think she cheated on me a total of seven times, and each time she seemed to take it that little bit farther. One weekend she just didn't come home and when she did come back, she looked at me with so much scorn, I felt numb at her complete disregard of my feelings. I thought I had died. Lottie, and each time she did it, I made plans to leave. I spoke to friends who told me to leave, but I didn't. In the end she ended it when she finally moved in with a male teacher. I despised myself and the pitiful spineless idiot I had been, and I didn't know if there would ever be a time when I could get over giving myself so totally and utterly to someone who was so completely unworthy. I would see them sometimes around the village, and she would give me a look that told me what I already knew, that I'd been discarded. I wasn't interesting enough, funny enough, sexy enough to mean anything to her."

Alice's breath caught but she cleared her throat and

continued. "I hardened myself to love. I was determined that never again was I going to let myself be that vulnerable, and then I met you."

Alice looked up at Lottie who was staring at her intently, not wanting to speak for fear of breaking the spell, so Alice continued. "You made me feel like I was invincible. You made me feel like I was the funniest, sexiest woman alive and I was terrified. Terrified that you'd hurt me. Terrified that you'd cheat on me, or worse, leave me. Our life together has been magical, it's been full of love and kindness and lust, and I started to forget that fear. I started to trust you. Then I came home, one uneventful day, determined to convince you to give Archie a break concerning this tutor thing, and there she was. The spiteful creature that behaved so cruelly towards me, pinning you to a wall in the kitchen and you, *you*, with excitement in your eyes at the attention of a she-devil!"

Lottie mumbled an apology but Alice silenced her with a glance.

"I felt like a thousand knives had gone through my heart, Lottie. I felt murderous, I wanted to kill her. I wanted to kill you both!"

Lottie looked at her own hands in her lap and shame flooded through her. What was she to say? How could she explain her stupid flirtation? She looked up as Alice sat beside her once again, gently encircled her hands in her own. Lottie looked up into Alice's piercing eyes, clouded with pain, and her stomach churned with regret.

"But, Lottie, after I'd calmed down, I realised two things. I realised I never need to worry that you'd cheat on me, and that you hold my heart and I hold yours. Sure, flirting, that was apparent. I've had that type of attention from her before. I know how intense it feels, but unlike me, Lottie, you'd soon be able to see what's behind that, because you're the smartest person I know."

Lottie's mouth curled to form a coy smile and Alice gently touched her lips to Lottie's forehead.

"I'm stubborn, Lottie, always have been but I know when I'm onto a good thing and I'm so sorry I stormed out like that."

Breathing deeply, Lottie touched her fingers to Alice's lips.

"My turn now," she said. "I am smart sometimes, Alice, but I've been so incredibly stupid and I'm the one who should be sorry! I was flattered by the attention, but please know that I never would have acted on that. I have never thought of myself as attractive and I felt stunned and out of my depth with Maddie's persistence. I wanted to tell you what was happening. I fully intended to talk to you, but then my pride got in the way. I thought I could handle it myself. It was because of my own stupid lack of self-confidence, that when I got such intense attention from an attractive woman, I felt overwhelmed. I've never thought of myself as attractive, until I met you. You made me feel like the hottest woman on the planet. Before that, I'd hidden myself for years and then when I finally did come out I always ended up being the one who did the chasing. Then I met you. You noticed me and you let me know you liked me and I can't tell you how that made me feel. I suppose when Maddie showed me attention, my fragile pride was bolstered and I had a glimmer of myself as an attractive woman to someone other than you."

Alice shook her head. "I know she's attractive, Lottie, but she's not a nice person."

Lottie silenced her. "I know that, Alice. I know that! It wasn't ever anything other than a stupid fantasy starring myself as a woman of allure, capable of attracting the attention of a stranger. Never more than that..." she trailed off, unable to explain, fully conscious of the fact that Alice would not welcome her full disclosure of the physical attraction she had felt towards another woman.

In a moment of silence, Lottie and Alice looked at one another. Both felt vulnerable having revealed their inner thoughts.

"I love you," Alice whispered.

Lottie leaned in and nestled close into the warm nape of Alice's neck. "I love you, too. Let's not let anything come between us. Stubbornness..."

"...or pride," Alice finished.

AS THE DARKNESS of the spring evening descended, Lottie and Alice remained entwined on the sofa. Neither stirred to switch on the light, not wishing to break the peace that encased them. Lottie could feel the steady gentle breath of Alice in the nape of her neck where her head was resting, as Alice unconsciously stroked Lottie's forearm.

As the room became fully darkened Lottie's senses felt heightened to the warm presence of Alice's body. Tilting her head, she felt for the softness of Alice's lips and savoured her rapid breathing in response. Gently, Alice ran her hand along

Lottie's arm cupping her chin before lifting her chin until their lips fully met. Sensuously running her bottom lip against Lottie's, her tongue flicked into the warm cavern of Lottie's mouth carefully exploring her taste.

Leading, Lottie clasped Alice's hands in hers and pulled her to a horizontal position on top of her. She could feel the pounding of Alice's heart against her chest and she felt choked with love for her. Without speaking, she lifted Alice's top cupping her left breast and gently teasing her nipple until it was erect. A gasp of pleasure escaped Alice as she submitted.

Alice slipped her hand down the front opening of Lottie's trousers and eased herself gently into a comfortable position, unhurried she explored the warm folds of Lottie's most intimate place.

Lottie responded by kissing her with more certainty, and finding the opening of Alice's jeans, she pleasured her. Their lips remained locked in a tender kiss as they both mutually climaxed, the tenderness reaffirming their love for one another.

The Acceptance of Strangers

ROLLING ONTO HER side, Lottie awoke slowly, taking time to drink in the early morning light as it caressed the naked body of Alice who lay silently beside her. Tenderly, Lottie ran a finger along the outline of her shoulder, lingering in the nape of her neck. Alice stirred. She rolled to face Lottie with a lazy smile, squinting into the light before wordlessly reaching to pull Lottie towards her. Lottie did not resist and fell easily into Alice's embrace, taking in the traces of her aroma and the musky scent she always wore. Alice ran her hand through Lottie's unruly morning hair and gently brushed it to one side, before pulling her roughly towards her and crushing her with a kiss laced with lust and love. Lottie let out a small gasp and the two rolled until they were entwined with the cool sheets and their lust was quickly sated.

Work beckoned, and Alice showered quickly, throwing Lottie a trail of kisses over her shoulder as she left clutching her satchel and a croissant. Briefly, Lottie wondered why Alice was leaving so early, but she had little time before leaving for the school run herself and, after burning toast for Archie, she managed to rouse Robbie and stole a few moments for herself in the bathroom which was swathed in a sensual steam following Alice's shower. Lottie smiled as she remembered the sex of that morning and congratulated herself on the continued passion in their relationship since Alice had moved in, which, if anything, had intensified following the Maddie trauma of a few weeks ago.

Lottie had read about the phenomenon known as lesbian death bed which was, apparently, experienced by lesbians who were in long term relationships. Being a relative newcomer to lesbian sex, she sincerely hoped that this was a myth, as she would consider it a tragedy to lose what she had so recently found. Lottie had previous partners with whom the sex had inevitably dwindled, signalling the demise of those relationships. She had read that the lack of sex often ended relationships, but she thought that, in bad relationships, sex, or rather the lack of it, was merely a symptom of other more serious issues. Sex was definitely not an issue for Lottie and Alice, but she never intended to take this for granted because she knew that the absence of sex would surely impact on the closeness they felt.

As she peered into the steamy bathroom mirror to apply a light coat of mascara she grimaced as she noted yet another set of wrinkles appearing in the creases of her eyes. Alice teased her that they weren't wrinkles, but laughter lines, the sign of her enduring humour in the numerous ridiculous situations she seemed to get herself into. Lottie was determined to maintain an illusion of youth, however, due to an irrational fear that Alice would suddenly notice her imperfections and ditch her for a baby-dyke.

Wiping the mirror clear for closer inspection, Lottie leaned forward to apply some concealer, and idly wondered at the rollercoaster ride that had been her forty years on planet Earth. One heterosexual marriage and a lot of soul searching later, Lottie believed she had finally managed to emerge from her shell to become her true and authentic self. She fervently hoped that her children would come through their own journey with her, largely unscathed. What she had lost, though, were many friends who had failed to accept her new choice of female partners.

Lottie was painfully aware that she had made some unfortunate and hasty decisions in her quest to become sexually competent. She had proceeded with a quantity-over-quality methodology, hoping to catch up on lost learning.

Even now, Lottie still had some lingering insecurities in terms of her sexual confidence, which had been inevitably compounded by the strap-on debacle. She was able to laugh about this now, but in truth it was still her nemesis and she couldn't quite accept that her lack of rhythm meant it was unlikely this was ever going to be her tool of choice. After realising Lottie's insecurities, Alice had been exceptionally sweet in trying to tease out her natural rhythm, but after numerous failed attempts to master the implement, it had remained in the drawer now for some months, with a silent agreement between the two that it had entered its retirement years. Lottie was struggling to reconcile this with her strong sense of pride, and she was determined to take it with them on their weekend to Paris to give it one final hurrah before she finally threw in the towel.

After a quick inspection of the additional new frown wrinkles on her forehead — would Botox really be *so* awful? — she grabbed her toothbrush and cleaned her teeth quickly and efficiently. She noticed that Alice had left her assortment of jewellery on the side of the bath, in her haste to leave for work. Absent-mindedly, Lottie fiddled with a thumb ring which she coveted despite the fact that Alice had informed her it was a gift from a former lover. Putting it down, she picked up the two other rings, both of which were plain silver Tiffany pieces but classic and very much in tune with Alice's semi-butch but classy style.

Momentarily, she fantasised about the type of ring she would buy Alice if she were to propose. In the early days of their relationship, Alice had boldly stated that she had a five-year plan for them which included commitment, or more specifically, marriage. Lottie had internally baulked at the idea of another marital commitment after having struggled so hard to escape the past one. But having lived with Alice now for six months, and having jointly survived the trauma of Maddie's reappearance, she somehow now felt bolder about the idea of a marriage. Lottie could only attribute this to the feeling of completion and connection she felt with Alice, and she truly believed she'd found her soulmate.

Lottie felt that the recent upset and subsequent revelations had brought them closer and cemented their relationship. What would marriage to Alice look like? Slipping Alice's Tiffany ring onto her married finger she noticed it was a perfect fit, and she found herself turning it to look at the inscription inside which told her it was from Tiffany and was a size "T".

Her fantasy was rudely interrupted by the shrill ring of her mobile phone and she dashed back to the bedroom, tripping on Odie who was headed back to the warmth of his bed. She grabbed the phone to see a missed call from Virginia who she was supposed to be picking up this morning for a lift to work.

"Shit!" she muttered as she slung on the least-creased pair of black trousers and a chiffon top.

"Archie, we are *very* late. To the car please!"

On the ride to work, Lottie was feeling increasingly irritated by the smirk that seemed to be permanently etched on Virginia's face. Despite the close confines of the car, she had managed to turn her entire body to get the best view of Lottie who was struggling to contain her annoyance. Lottie was already regretting that she had spontaneously blurted out to Virginia her earlier marriage fantasies. These had been met by complete hysteria and Virginia appeared to think that this was the best news she could possibly get on a Wednesday morning. While her smugness was irritating, Lottie had to acknowledge that even as she'd been recounting her fantasy to Virginia, it appeared to be taking on a more solid and purposeful form.

"Sooo," Virginia drawled in an exaggerated way. "Is this going to be a Paris proposal then, or what?"

Lottie struggled to concentrate on the conversation, narrowly avoiding a stray hare as it bounded across the lane in front of them.

"Bloody hell, V, I don't know! I mean, wouldn't that be a bit too soon? We've only been living together for six months."

But even as she protested, Lottie smiled, as images of a romantic proposal at the foot of the Eiffel Tower crowded her mind. She imagined the look of delight on Alice's face, with the backdrop of a French landmark and a cloudless sky behind them, walking together hand in hand through the streets of Paris. Every now and then they would have to stop so that Alice could giggle and admire the sparkle of her perfectly fitting ring.

Sudden and terrifying clarity hit Lottie. She did want to get married!

She *did* want to get married to Alice.

It was true that the sum total of their relationship in months was less than a year. People were bound to think it was too soon, and there would be warnings from family members who were all too familiar with her impulsive disasters. She wondered if she could cope with the continued disapproval of her family when they had only just got used to her being gay. Only fleetingly did she consider the response of her children, being assured that Archie would quite simply be delighted to add some permanence to the new expansion of their family. She suspected that Robbie would be equally pleased but that this would be hard to detect as it just would not be *gangsta* to show demonstrable approval. Her mum on the other hand...oh, shit! Well at least any future parties hosted by her well-meaning parent would not involve her de-gaying their home, although she suspected a rainbow engagement cake would be an inevitable part of any celebrations.

"V, do you reckon she would say yes?"

Virginia spluttered into her latte. "You're bloody mad! Of course she'd say yes, you daft mare! You two are made for one another, anyone can see that. Peas in a pod," she stated with absolute certainty.

As if to offer a more solid confirmation of her approval, Virginia's manic grin softened and she patted Lottie reassuringly on the shoulder. "Lots, babes, you've had such a disastrous dating history, surely this can only help you to see how right this relationship is. Don't sabotage it or run away because you're feeling scared and out of your comfort zone. Easy is good, remember? That's how it's meant to be. Leave all the high drama behind."

Lottie smiled, now pleased to have Virginia as her confidante. With Virginia, you always had to be prepared for the painful truth, but to hear her talking now with such honesty only served to reaffirm to Lottie what an amazing opportunity she and Alice had to build a real future together.

Later that morning, Lottie managed to survive another supervision session with Ann. She had actually been a little concerned about Ann following their previous meeting. Following her complete despair, Ann had turned detective and had posed as a twenty-year-old gay architect in order to entrap her cheating spouse. Needless to say, this had not proved to be a positive experience for Ann, who had even gone to the lengths of arranging a fake date with her husband in order to confront him, in the style of those American *Cheaters* programmes. Ann had actually written to the *Cheaters* producers but had been rebuffed on the basis of her remote home location.

Much to her utter despair, Ann's husband had apparently told her how relieved he was to finally be caught, feeling that a great weight had been lifted from his shoulders. Ann had tearfully recounted to Lottie that he had then proceeded to buy her a large gin and tonic before telling her he was moving out of their marital home.

Since he had left, Lottie hadn't dared to broach the subject with Ann, who had become uncharacteristically introverted. However, she noted the absence of Ann's wedding ring, which could surely only mean it was finished. Someone else who also appeared to have noticed the missing wedding ring was creepy Leonard, who had upped his efforts to have one-on-one time with Ann, which Lottie determinedly disrupted as far as was possible. She wasn't Ann's biggest fan, but she wouldn't watch her be exploited in her current vulnerable state.

However, Ann had not been in a chatty mood today, so Lottie had made the most of the opportunity to have a more productive review of her work and was tantalised by the prospect of an actual lunch break where she could have a quick dash around the shops. Lottie remembered that she was still avoiding the conversation she knew she would have to have with her sister at some point. She pushed that to the back of her mind. After all, it was their relationship, and she did not feel she was in a position to sit in judgement of people who were still hiding in the closet.

Lottie exited the building giving a cheery wave to Linda, without stopping to be drawn into conversation. Linda was lurking with intent outside the main entrance, a menthol cigarette attached to her bottom lip with the help of some loud and adhesive red lipstick. Lottie knew for a fact that Linda was actively lurking. Earlier she had an unfortunate encounter with Linda in the ladies' loo, where she had revealed to Lottie that she had developed a huge crush on the new security guard who had recently started at the newspaper. Lottie pitied the unsuspecting male who was about to be lured into Linda's marital web. Lottie studiously avoided anything other than brief encounters with Linda, who had a voracious appetite for gossip and was particularly intent on uncovering what she thought would be the salacious details of Lottie's recently publicised attraction to women.

Turning to enter the shopping centre, Lottie caught a final sight of Linda as she bent to pick up the contents of her overflowing fake Gucci handbag, which she appeared to have dropped in an attempt to attract the attention of her victim, who had appeared at the exit of the building. Lottie felt as if she was watching a hawk circling its furry prey, as Linda squashed her uneven cleavage together to exacerbate its appearance as voluptuous, while she bent to gather her belongings up from the cobbles which included the latest copy of *Brides Monthly*. Lottie cast one final look of pity towards the unsuspecting security guard before refocusing on her task to scour the shops for last-minute Paris bits as well as a birthday present for Alice.

During their stay in Paris it would be Alice's birthday, and Lottie had decided that she was going to splash out following her recently earned bonus, to buy Alice a leather bracelet with an Eiffel Tower charm—a stroke of genius she smugly thought. Although they had a tacit agreement to not spend money on presents, Lottie wanted to show Alice how much she meant to her, especially as Alice had spent so much on the trip. Lottie wandered up and down the first floor of the department store convinced that she had previously seen a jewellery counter situated there somewhere.

"Can I help, madam?" A velvety voice halted her in her tracks. Embarrassed to have to explain her mission to a stranger, she averted her eyes, pretending to study the nearest case of jewellery which she noticed contained sparkly rings of varying styles.

In that moment, a lightning bolt of clarity hit Lottie for the second time in a matter of hours. Later, she would describe it as a decision based on pure impulse, but Alice would say that it was a moment preordained in the destiny of their relationship.

"Yes." Lottie found herself saying as her eyes rose to meet the piercing blue eyes of the interested shop assistant. She was awaiting further instruction, as her hands clasped the keys to her cabinet of jewels. Lottie took her time, looking down again to scan the sparkling array of love tokens.

"I want to buy a ring for my..." At this point she stumbled. Hell! Did she really want to have to come out in her local branch of Jenner's department store?

Taking a breath, she managed to speak again. "Well, yes. What I meant to say was, I want to buy a ring for a close friend of mine, and these look lovely. Can I have a look at these three?" She pointed to three mid-range rings, all containing the obligatory diamond, but all with a unique style.

Eager to oblige with a potential sale, the assistant replied quickly. "Certainly!" She simultaneously placed the rings out onto the shiny glass counter and twisted them expertly to display them to their best effect.

Lottie sighed. So much choice. She caressed the rings one by one as she tried to imagine them on Alice's engagement finger. A small thrill ran through her as she fantasised about seeing Alice wearing a ring which shouted to the world that they were betrothed, promised, and committed. Struggling to contain her excitement, Lottie pointed to a particularly beautiful ring with one solid diamond and then smaller diamonds inset to the sides in a classic white gold band.

"Would your friend like that one, do you think?"

Nodding, Lottie's voice became a little more high pitched. "Yes, I think so. Well, I don't know...it's only a gift for a friend, so it shouldn't take too much choosing, should it?" Without waiting for an answer, she slipped the ring onto her own engagement finger to explore the glint of the diamond and the sparkle in the brightly lit shop.

Lottie felt a flush rise through her cheeks as she struggled to maintain the ruse that she was buying for a friend, I mean what idiot would be buying her friend an engagement ring for goodness sake? Her own embarrassment at the hash she was making of her conversation with the shop assistant was distracting her from deciding.

"Do you know the size of your *girlfriend's* finger then, or is this a surprise?" The shop assistant leaned forward with a conspiratorial whisper. "After all, it is a big decision and the size isn't that important as we do offer an exchange."

Lottie felt an instant rush of relief and gratitude towards the shop assistant. She fought the urge to give her a hug of thanks as the pretence evaporated. Lottie beamed at the woman who returned her smile with equal warmth. Thereafter, she spent a pleasant twenty minutes of her lunch break discussing the pros and cons of the diamond carat versus the weight of the gold band and the inevitable conversation about insurance offered by the store. Totally overwhelmed by the acceptance of the shop assistant, Lottie purchased the insurance out of a sense of loyalty for the kindness she had been shown. Further reinforcing her view that this was meant to be, the shop also had the correct sized ring in stock, and she was able to take it away, tucking it securely into the zip pocket of her bag, along with the receipt and insurance certificate.

ARRIVING AT HOME before Alice, who was unusually late, Lottie decided that in the interests of family harmony, she would confide in Robbie and Archie her plan to propose at the Eiffel Tower. Both seemed remarkably unperturbed by her plans and, while feeling reassured about their support, she couldn't help noticing that they had exchanged a knowing glance, and that Robbie appeared to be supressing a smirk. Archie looked a little worried, but he covered it well and Lottie was sure that such a big announcement was bound to take a little time for Archie to digest.

Lottie grabbed her case from the loft and stashed the ring inside one of the many pockets on the inner lining, and smiling, she reached across to their, now shared, drawer of pleasure which had formerly been Alice's drawer of sex toys. She grabbed her nemesis, the strap-on, and shoved it in beside the ring box and zipped the pocket, padlocking it securely. Looking at the clock, she noted Alice was still missing in action, and dialled her number.

Alice answered her phone sounding breathless and a little guilty, "Hi babe, running late but won't be long. Mrs. Alcock is having some problems with her foal. I'm aiming to leave shortly."

Before Lottie could engage her in conversation, Alice hung up, but Lottie could have sworn she heard the noise of a loudspeaker announcement and supermarket-type music in the background.

"Where is she?" she wondered briefly, before her mind wandered again and she grabbed her phone to hammer out a quick text message to Virginia and Mel:

Bought a ring. Proposing in Paris! #meant to be!
Xx

Awaiting a reply, Lottie pondered on how she would propose, quickly deciding that going down on one knee would leave no opportunity for misinterpretation. She thought she would allow the words to flow naturally as she gave a small speech to Alice and the adoring crowd about how much she meant to her, and how she wanted to spend the rest of her life loving her and burning her dinner! Laughing to herself, Lottie threw on an old pair of jeans and T-shirt and made her way downstairs to contemplate the food situation before she would no doubt resort to her fall-back position of a Chinese takeaway.

While they were eating, Archie eyed Lottie and Alice with an equal measure of suspicion as he steadily munched his sweet and sour chicken. Alice had just delivered the news that his tuition was on hold for the time being, but he was obviously suspicious about this sudden change of plan. Lottie winked at Alice who grinned in return, oblivious for a moment to the suspicions of Archie. Feeding the remains of his food to the waiting Odie he retired to his bedroom, seemingly happy about a study-free summer.

Two go to Paris

IN ORDER TO combat Lottie's terror of flying, Alice was braving a phobia of her own, the inevitable queue at the coffee shop as she went to get Lottie her favourite vanilla latte. Meanwhile, Lottie paced anxiously outside the Aberdeen Airport departures gate. She knew her inevitable flying phobia would need to be dealt with, but this time she was also battling the nervous anticipation of proposing. Despite numerous reassurances from her friends that Lottie was onto a sure thing, that Alice would join her on her knees with love and gratitude when the big moment arrived, Lottie still had residual anxiety about possible rejection.

Their flight for Paris was leaving in two hours and, earlier in the day she'd waved off her two boys to their dad's house. Much to her surprise, both had made relatively little fuss about her disappearing for a few days with Alice, in fact Robbie had given her what could only be described as a lingering hug. She had noticed as they'd left, that the boys were both clutching a crisp twenty-pound note, which she could only assume had been given to them by Alice as a sweetener for being sent to their father's for a few days. She smiled. My future fiancée, child friendly and totally gorgeous as well!

Her smile turned quickly to a frown as she clutched at her case anxiously. She had debated and agonised long and hard about whether to keep the ring on her person or to hide it in the case, but as she knew that there would be the inevitable x-ray machines and she didn't want to risk being asked to empty her pockets in front of Alice.

Despite her trepidation, Lottie felt a fresh thrill of delicious excitement as she visualised, for the umpteenth time, her plan for the big proposal at the foot of the Eiffel Tower. The weather was set to be divine and she was sure that it would not be too busy because they were well out of the school holiday season. Before they left, she had triple checked with the tour company with whom they had booked the day trip to the Tower, who offered her assurances that she would have plenty of time at the site. Although her schoolgirl French had its limitations, she was pretty sure she understood that they would have a good hour at the Tower for lunch and so she planned to surprise Alice with the picnic she had pre-ordered. She was going to make her proposal underneath the Tower itself before they queued to go up to the viewing floors. Lottie had never been to Paris before but she imagined the Eiffel Tower site was quite large and so she hoped that she could find a quiet spot to propose to Alice and steal a romantic kiss with her new fiancée under the famous landmark.

Eager to get the journey underway, Lottie smiled gratefully at Alice, as she returned with her drink mumbling about franchised over-priced coffee and child labour. Lottie tickled her neck, playfully aware that Alice was ready for a break and also seemed stressed compared to her normally calm self.

"Come on, Ms. Stress Head, let's get this romantic mini-break underway!" She gulped her coffee quickly and immediately felt the beneficial effect of the caffeine.

Alice smiled gratefully as Lottie took charge. Hand in hand they made their way through to the baggage check-in with their luggage. Alice had been a little bemused by Lottie's insistence that she had her own luggage, after all, they were only going for two nights. After some discussion Lottie had convinced Alice that she needed her own bag as they might be bringing back some souvenirs and would need extra space.

"Let's get them on," Alice said, chivalrously lifting Lottie's hand luggage onto the conveyor belt, closely followed by her own. Alice and Lottie stood side by side as they watched their bags disappear into the black tunnel where they were studiously examined by the middle-aged, overweight customs officer, who looked like he needed a good wash and a few nights off the red wine.

Suddenly the conveyor belt ground to a noisy halt.

Lottie swallowed nervously. Bloody hell!

Alice looked bemused as the worker eyed them both suspiciously, and nodding towards them, he shouted loudly towards them. "Can you tell me which of you this case belongs to?"

Lottie cleared her throat nervously, painfully aware that Alice was standing at her shoulder and was peering at the frozen screen outlining the contents of Lottie's bag.

Lottie answered meekly, "Yes, that's my case," She hoped her pleading look would be understood by the odious little man whom she was loathing more and more by the second.

Lottie squirmed uncomfortably as she focused on the very obvious outline of the box containing the beautiful ring which she thought she had stashed cunningly into the zip pocket of her case.

The bright glare of the x-ray machine made the case look naked and the contents vulnerable. She anxiously waited, aware of the queue behind her which was rapidly becoming longer with disgruntled travellers. The elderly couple immediately behind tutted loudly and muttered about people over-packing their hand luggage.

Farther back in the queue, Lottie noticed a group of boisterous males, pushing and jostling one another clearly already worse for drink despite the fact they hadn't yet hit the duty-free shop. Unintentionally, she caught the eye of one of the men who was quick to wink salaciously at her, nodding at his mates and pointing at the screen where the magnified contents of her bag were still on display.

"Shit!" Lottie thought, "They can see the bloody ring, they're bound to say something. Alice will hear!"

Riddled with anxiety, she nervously cleared her throat hoping to cover the ever-increasing racket coming from the noisy group of men as they guffawed and pointed in the direction of her bag. Casually, she tried to follow the gaze of the airport worker, and quickly confirmed he was very definitely focused on the zip pocket area of the bag. His faced was furrowed in concentration as he hunched with difficulty due to his barrel-shaped belly, towards the keyboard where he thumped at a few more buttons with unnecessary ferocity. He glanced furtively around in an attempt to see who was witnessing his importance, and smirked with satisfaction at the lengthening queue, before looking back towards Lottie, silently shaking his head.

Eventually he succeeded in further magnifying the image to provide a clear view of the contents of the zip pocket and the very definitely identifiable ring that Lottie had worked so hard to conceal.

Fuck, fuck, fuck, fuck! Lottie was now frozen with fear. She felt that everything was happening in slow motion and she wished fervently that she had taken Alice up on her offer of something stronger than the swiftly consumed vanilla latte.

Suddenly, Alice gave an involuntary gasp as she dragged Lottie ferociously towards her and leaning in to Lottie's ear she whispered urgently. "Oh my God, babe. Is that what I think it is?"

Lottie swallowed hard, disappointment struck her like a thunderbolt. All that work, all that planning, and it was ruined before they had even left the country! Accepting defeat, she turned to Alice with barely contained disappointment, "Yup!"

she mumbled, "I thought it might make Paris a bit more exciting!"

Alice chuckled, and smiled knowingly at her. "Well, baby, you certainly know how to spring a surprise!"

Blind with panic, the moment now undoubtedly ruined in her mind, and without further thought, Lottie dropped to her knees in front of Alice. In her head the fog cleared. I need to do it now, it'll be okay. Go on, Lottie, speak. The thought pounded in her brain as she cleared her throat once again in preparation.

As she looked up, she discovered that Alice had already turned away from her, and back to the officious little man who had now zoomed in on triple magnification. Following Alice's gaze, to her utter horror, Lottie noticed that he was not looking at the engagement ring but rather the strap-on which she had also stowed away in the zipped pocket.

"Bloody hell!"

He wasn't looking at the ring. It was *worse*! The odious little man, and for that matter, the entire queue including the boisterous football crowd, the elderly couple, and her future fiancée were all staring at the stowaway sex toy! Through the volcanic heat surging through her cheeks and the peripheral view of tittering fellow travellers, Lottie was at a total loss for words and had momentarily forgotten she was still on her knees in the middle of the queue.

The next few moments passed in hideous slow motion as she heard Alice tell the airport official, "Look mate, it's a strap-on, I'm sure you've seen one before, there's no need to make such a meal of it, you've made your point!"

Lottie couldn't bring herself to look up.

"Lottie, what on earth are you doing?" Alice asked.

Fumbling at her trainers, Lottie replied quietly. "Tying my lace, Alice, tying my lace. Come on then, the plane won't wait for us!"

Moving hastily onward towards the passport queue, Lottie silently berated herself for packing the strap-on, but she couldn't help but see the funny side when Alice showed her the picture she'd taken of the enhanced x-ray image on her mobile phone.

"Put that on Facebook, I dare you!" she said, giggling and taking Lottie firmly by the hand and moving towards the passport booths.

Walking away, Lottie felt a tap on her shoulder, and thinking that she was about to be dragged back to the x-ray area, she blustered with protest. "Look, this is enough now, we've got a flight to catch..." Trailing at the end as she realised that the tapper was in fact one of the football fans who was getting nods and smiles from his group.

"How can you tell a lesbian is butch?" he whispered, leaning towards her, but still with half an eye on his gang of sniggering mates. Without waiting for a reply, he continued. "She can kick start her own vibrator and roll her own tampons!" Delivering his punchline with some gusto he could barely contain his mirth as his crew fell about laughing, oblivious to the stares of other more conservative passengers. The wide smirk covered the lower half of his face as he clutched his pot-belly which wobbled slightly with his deep throated chuckle.

Lottie was horrified.

Did this ignorant oaf actually think he'd said something funny?

Turning to Alice she saw, to her horror, that Alice was wearing a look of steely determination. She took an involuntary step backward as Alice menacingly leaned in to the lout and whispered in a low voice. "Are you always this stupid or is today an exception?"

Without waiting for a response, she took a startled step backward waving her arms around as if in panic but giving a subtle wink to the confused Lottie. Alice said with exaggerated terror in a loud and authoritative voice. "Did you say you were pleased to see me or is that a *gun in your pocket*?"

The thug laughed, not realising at first the gravity of Alice's words, but a few short seconds later he was face down on the ground surrounded by airport security. Alice took Lottie once again firmly by the hand, and they melted into the expanding crowd. The man gestured wildly in their direction, but his arms were restrained as he was handcuffed and led away.

A FEW HOURS later the girls toasted the unknown male bigot with a glass of complimentary fizzy nectar as they adjusted to being in the air. After the short flight, they successfully negotiated Charles De Gaulle airport and joined the waiting coach, which would take them to their hotel in the Montmartre region of Paris.

Neither Lottie nor Alice had been to Paris before, and the short ride from the airport gave them a taste of what they could expect during the next few days. The tour they had booked included a river cruise on the Seine, and the weather forecast was promising. Lottie wondered at the brightly lit streets of Paris and enjoyed watching Alice marvel at the spectacular sight of the Champs-Élysées as dusk fell and the sun set behind the Arc de Triomphe.

Alice slipped her arm around Lottie's neck and gently caressed her ear.

"Alice, this was such a great birthday present," Lottie murmured. "If I forget to tell you later, I'm loving it!" Leaning in to Alice, she kissed her, and felt a tingle of anticipation shoot down her spine.

"You're welcome, my beautiful girl," Alice responded huskily. "I hope it will be trip we remember for years to come."

Lottie smiled back. "So do I," An involuntary shudder went through her in anticipation of the next day's secret proposal. Looking upward, she silently pleaded with an unfamiliar God, *Please, please let it go according to plan, for once in my life.*

The coach driver was enjoying giving his riders a preview of the full Paris tour, and didn't hurry to reach their destination. Alice settled back in her window seat, soaking up the sights through the diminishing light. Lottie was becoming increasingly uncomfortable as the familiar dull ache in her stomach signalled the onset of the dreaded irritable bowel syndrome that plagued her. She cursed silently, knowing it would only be a matter of time before she had to empty her bowels, despite being careful about what she had eaten on the plane. She decided she would be glad when the stress of proposing was past, as anxiety always ended up in an unpleasant trip to the toilet.

Wishing she hadn't been quite so free and easy with the complimentary fizz, she excused herself and swayed down the narrow aisle of the coach towards the toilet at the rear. Holding onto the headrests, she tried to counterbalance without success and managed to bounce her bottom and her breasts alternately into the faces of her unsuspecting travel companions. Turning sideways, she swayed back and forth as the coach took the roundabouts of Paris as only an experienced Parisian lunatic driver could. She smiled apologetically at the other seated couples as she passed, aware that despite her frantic clenching, gas was beginning to escape her in readiness for the inevitable spasm of bowel action before she would need to evacuate her bowels. Families and older couples were the main passengers and she tried to distract herself by guessing how many of the younger loved up couples would be returning to the bus the following evening wearing engagement rings.

Eventually she made it to the toilet and struggled to hook the latch to secure the door. The faint aroma of urine hit her nostrils, and she tried to breathe through her mouth as she struggled to unzip her jeans in the confined space. Just as she'd managed to sit down, the bus took another roundabout violently slinging her sideways she noted the slopping sounds coming from underneath her in the sewerage outlet below her. Trying not to think about the contents of the tank she hurried to relive herself. Suddenly her stomach gave a large gurgle and the inevitable spasm hit her with force.

Bloody irritable bowel! She rubbed her stomach willing it not to give into a full-blown attack of the nuisance illness. Another spasm hit her. Oh hell, there was no holding this back! Leaning forward to ease the cramping, she faced the inevitable fact as the faecal matter left her bowels at lightning speed, and Lottie inwardly groaned at the inevitable smell and loud gas noises that escaped her to pebbledash the toilet bowl. Wiping vigorously, thankful for the plentiful supply of toilet roll, she leaned in to flush the disgusting contents away.

While she was still recovering her equilibrium, there was a rapping noise on the door, "Excuse me. Are you okay? There is a bit of a queue out here."

Emptying the contents of the soap dispenser onto her hands she rubbed herself vigorously with paper towels and flicked the catch to open the door. Unaware—having been trapped in the cubicle for some time—of the smell she had trapped with her, she noticed the rapping man took a step backward and wrinkled his nose in disgust. He allowed Lottie to pass, her face glowing red and she made no eye contact as she hastily made her way down the bus to resume her seat next to Alice.

On her return Alice gave her a curious glance. "You okay, sweetie? Irritable bowel?" Lottie could not speak, but nodded. To show her sympathy, Alice firmly grasped Lottie's hand.

Secrets and Proposals

THE NEXT MORNING, Lottie and Alice awoke to the bright sunshine of Paris. Rolling together lazily, they mirrored one another's smiles as they anticipated the day of exploring that lay ahead.

Alice had booked them onto an all-day coach tour which she had been assured would give them a taste of everything Parisian. Arriving at the breakfast room, Lottie noticed with amusement the nervous glances and anxious looks of the young male bucks in the party all of whom she had bet would be dropping to one knee at some point through the day. After her phenomenally botched proposal of the day before, Lottie had consoled herself with the certainty that any proposal made in the romantic city of Paris could not fail.

The passion she had shared with Alice the night before, despite the earlier onset of her irritable bowel symptoms — now settled, thanks to her ever-ready medication — had left her in little doubt that she was right to propose to her life-long lover and soul mate. They munched heartily on warmed croissants and freshly-made cream-topped hot chocolate. They chattered happily about their plans for the day and came up with a wish list of the top places they wanted to visit.

After they had eaten their fill, Alice excused herself, disappearing back to the room and mumbling something about needing a quick trip to the loo before the coach left. Lottie hastily took the opportunity to pop the ring out from inside her jacket pocket, smiling she gave it a final polish with her sleeve and hoped the size of the diamond would be acceptable to Alice, who had always remained understated in the jewellery department, preferring white gold to the more expensive metals.

Glancing at her phone, she chuckled as she scanned the many text messages from her well-wishing friends all offering last-minute advice. From Virginia, a simple message.

Lol, watch out for pickpockets and don't forget the ring, will ya? Good luck! Xx

Catching sight of Alice returning she hurriedly deposited her phone into the secure pocket in the backpack. Noticing that Alice was smiling broadly, Lottie gave her a quizzical look.

"You left the bloody strap-on in the middle of the bedroom floor. That would have given the cleaner more excitement than she bargained for!" Alice said.

Lottie chuckled, it seemed as though that particular piece of equipment was always going to be a source of never-ending embarrassment.

As they waited for the bus, she secretly revelled in the knowledge that Alice had no idea what lay ahead of her on this bright and beautiful day. A day to remember, that's for sure. She was literally bursting with anticipation and didn't know how she was possibly going to contain her excitement for the rest of the morning.

Boarding the coach, she followed Alice down the narrow aisle, mentally revisiting her hasty rush the day before. She fervently hoped the coach driver had cleaned toilet and emptied the tank in time for their full day on the bus. She didn't much fancy further trips to the smelly cubicle if it hadn't been cleaned and disinfected. Even more mortifying would be listening to the other passengers' whispered conversations, as they debated who might have been responsible for the mess.

She was interrupted from her train of thought as a red-faced, spotty young man dived in front of her, bringing her to an abrupt halt as he sank to his knees and rummaged around underneath the adjacent row of seats. Bobbing down beside him Lottie took in his breathless state, as he met her eyes briefly and apologetically, he was frantically mouthing something to her that she couldn't quite understand.

Desperate for help, he mouthed more clearly. "I've dropped my bloody ring!"

Leaning closer to catch what he said, she caught a whiff of his mint scented breath and the overpowering odour of his strong, cheap aftershave, which didn't quite mask the stale aroma of his manly sweat.

Feeling instant empathy for her fellow proposer and for their shared anxiety, she fell to her knees beside him and blindly groped underneath the nearest seat. Running her hand along the firm nylon bristle carpeting her hand glided across something which was a solid metal object. Wondering if this could be the lost item, she pulled it into the daylight for closer examination. What she held was a simple, yet elegant, silver band, as she turned it in her hand she noted the inner inscription, *will you marry me?*

Forgetting his manners, the anxious-faced youth grabbed greedily at the ring as visible relief flooded him. "That's my ring! Thank fuck! I really thought I'd lost it," he muttered to no one in particular.

Closing his eyes briefly, he gave a silent prayer of thanks, and then remembering his saviour, he opened his eyes and grinned broadly at Lottie. Their eyes locked for a moment as a mutual understanding of their individual missions passed between them.

Lottie took control of the situation, aware that his unsuspecting bride-to-be was oblivious to the drama, engrossed in taking selfies against the bus window while pointing at the hotel.

Dragging the traumatised youth to his feet while struggling to hide the tide of pity she felt for him, she leaned forward and whispered with what she hoped was reassurance and genuine warmth. "Bloody beautiful that is. She's a lucky girl. Now put it away safely!"

Lottie felt a rush of pride, as she realised it was likely that she had saved his day. She pushed away the rising smugness, as she silently acknowledged that it was inevitable that her advanced years and life experience would surely mean that she would make the much better and more proficient proposer of the two of them. Patting her own ring, she slipped into her seat beside Alice who also, surprisingly, appeared to be engrossed in taking a similar selfie.

Lottie hadn't failed to notice that Alice had become much more interested in her phone since they had landed on foreign soil. Knowing Alice well enough to know that she was not one for technology, Lottie could only assume she was being bothered by work matters. In fact, Lottie was a little irritated that Alice had disappeared yesterday evening to take, what she assumed was a work phone call, and she had vowed to tackle her about her inability to switch off on their precious few days alone, when they got home. Glancing towards the back as the coach lurched into life she caught the eye of the young lad, who it appeared, had belatedly remembered his manners as he shot her a grateful glance before hastily taking his seat beside his potential betrothed.

Their morning tour of Paris passed by in a whirl as the happy pair hopped on and off the bus, taking numerous photographs alongside the Arc de Triomphe, and later at Notre Dame. The sun shone ever brighter as it rose and burned off the early morning haze causing the temperature to increase. As they were whisked from location to location, every so often a glimpse of the Eiffel Tower could be seen in the distance, causing gasps of delight and squeals of excitement from the group of travellers. Alice beamed happily and squeezed Lottie's hand tightly.

Finally, the magnificent steel structure came into close view. The bus negotiated its way towards the parking area and the driver noisily announced they would shortly be making their lunch stop at the Tower. Lottie listened carefully as he instructed that all those who had ordered a picnic lunch should meet him at the rear of the coach for collection.

"Please enjoy your time at this beautiful attraction," his co-driver hastily added, grabbing the microphone. "We will all be meeting back at the coach at two sharp. Also, please be aware that pickpockets do unfortunately operate in this area and we would advise you to place all valuables to the front of your person. While you may feel a bit silly ladies and gentlemen, rucksacks should ideally be worn on your front."

Lottie immediately jumped up from her seat, then panicked as she was pulled back into her seat by Alice.

"What's the hurry, sweetie? Let the older lot get off first."

Lottie placated her with a smile, before ignoring her and pushing her way into the stream of fellow travellers anxious to get off the coach. Frantically, she clutched at her rucksack and wiggled it violently, until she had managed to reverse it onto her front.

"You're kidding, right?" said Alice. "You haven't got the crown bloody jewels in there have you?" Chuckling, she playfully pinched Lottie's bottom. "Come on then, miss. You promised me a picnic lunch!"

Patting the front pocket of her rucksack one final time, Lottie was happy that she could identify the outline of the ring box. Reassured, she followed Alice round to the rear of the coach where they collected their picnic basket and headed for the green, perfectly manicured lawns which encased the grounds of the magnificent tower.

Lottie took a moment to marvel at how impressive the grounds were before they headed in the direction of the tower. The midday sun beat down on them and the bright cloudless sky provided an impressive frame to the backdrop around the iconic structure. As they came close enough to get a proper view, Lottie wondered at the sunlight, as it danced rhythmically on the inner rungs like a tune of light, and the reflection provided a rainbow of colours shimmering outwards to meet the heat of the Parisian day. Edging forward, Lottie felt the structure was enticing her with the delicious anticipation of the proposal!

Alice chuckled at the sight of Lottie walking openmouthed and very tourist-like towards the tower. Excited to get nearer for photo opportunities, she began walking slightly ahead of Lottie, happily snapping away using a variety of angles and lenses to capture to the best effect of the glinting steel structure. Lottie saw that, lost in her photography, Alice was gradually becoming less aware of Lottie and her whereabouts. In the meantime, Lottie was trying to manage her rising anxiety levels as she glanced around, trying and failing, to identify a private spot to set up the picnic.

She was surprised by how crowded it was, and she had not anticipated such a public arena for her proposal. Around her, for as far as her eye could see, was a seamless wave of tightly packed bodies, all moving as one in the direction of the main area underneath the Tower. Approaching it, she saw that they filtered into two enormous snaking queues to purchase tickets to go up the tower itself.

Alice, seemingly oblivious to Lottie's dilemma, and lost in her photography, had wandered quite a distance ahead. Lottie spotted her, but she was alarmed to notice a small group of Eastern European women were beginning to surround Alice. The warning of the coach driver about pickpockets echoed in her ears as she feared that her distracted girlfriend was about to provide the pickpockets with easy pickings and so she hurried to catch up with the oblivious Alice.

"No, thank you!" she barked loudly and firmly and dispatched the unwanted women, who it transpired, were in fact touting their poorly produced plastic Eiffel Tower souvenirs. The women dissolved back into the faceless crowd, and Alice smiled at her gratefully for a moment, but undeterred by her brush with the Eiffel Tower underworld, she continued to scout for photographic opportunities.

Feeling rather protective of her soon to be fiancée, Lottie stood back and allowed Alice to finish her circuit of the base of the tower. Alice gave her a cheery wave and Lottie waved back blowing her a heartfelt air kiss. She idly watched Alice, glancing around at her surroundings, confirming that her hope of a quiet proposal was doubtful. The throng of people ebbed and flowed, moving as a single entity, and Lottie accepted that she was going to struggle to separate herself and Alice from the tourist madness that surrounded the world-famous attraction.

Momentarily blinded by the sun, Lottie blinked hard. She had lost sight of Alice. Reeling around in a slow circle, a rising panic gripped her. Where the bloody hell had she gone?

She spotted an opening in the crowd and headed into the stream of moving people, hoping the tide would draw them back together. Searching the faces in the crowd, she looked for Alice. Unexpectedly, Lottie's chest exploded with a sudden pain as she realised she had experienced a significant impact as she collided into a shadowy figure, and she briefly wondered why he was working his way in opposition to the natural flow of the people.

Winded by the ferocity of the unexpected collision, Lottie was glad she had turned her rucksack around as it had provided something of a cushion. Nevertheless, she had been badly winded and had momentarily lost her balance. She wobbled, attempting to regain her balance the man reached out and firmly grasped her by the arm.

Without making eye contact, he worked to steer her back into the flow, and as she was taken by the tide of the crowd he mumbled, "Pardon, madam," in a heavy French accent — his deep husky voice just what she would have expected from a Parisian — before he melted away, and the crowd drew her onward.

With no time to contemplate the unpleasant encounter, Lottie pushed onward and eventually located Alice, who was leaning nonchalantly against the outer leg of the Tower.

"About bloody time! I'm starving," Alice joked as she reached to take the picnic basket from the sweat-soaked Lottie.

As they moved away from the crowd, a light breeze broke through the heat of the afternoon. Lottie drank in the sight of Alice, lithe and willowy in her khaki cut-offs and her sport branded T-shirt. Suddenly, the moment seemed to take on a life of its own — as Alice squinted in the sunlight and beamed broadly at Lottie. Lottie seized the moment and dropped to one knee on the grass directly in front of her.

Reaching into the front of her rucksack Lottie rummaged for the ring, Shit, I should have had it in my hand ready, she thought with irritation.

"What on earth…?"

Frantically rummaging around, her face creased with concern as Lottie registered that the front pocket containing the ring was already wide open. Worse still, it appeared that the contents must have spilled out at an unknown location somewhere behind her on the concourse.

Looking around with terror, she could only see that the

immediate area around her was a sea of feet which showed remarkably little concern about the unfolding drama.

Suddenly, the cold hard realisation hit her like a stone in the pit of her stomach. It's gone, fuck, fuck, fuck! It's gone!

Inwardly she groaned.

That man, he must have been a pickpocket! "Pardon, madam" my arse! He had bloody robbed her!

Oblivious to the unfolding drama, Alice joined her on her knees and busied herself setting out the picnic.

Discovering the bottle of prosecco, she smiled gratefully at Lottie. "What a lovely picnic, and a great surprise with the wine, too. Romance is alive and well in Paris."

She leaned in to kiss Lottie, and a rumble of appreciation and acceptance emanated around them as onlookers fanned out to provide them with a small circle of space.

Lottie sank back onto her heels, reeling with disappointment, as she realised the ring was lost. She managed to muster a weak smile as she met Alice's eyes. "Well, romance is a must in Paris."

She picked up the bottle of uncorked alcohol and swigged greedily, her throat dry from the heat, the stress and the burning disappointment which rose up from the pit of her stomach.

Struggling to hide her misery, she managed a wry grin. "Paris is certainly full of surprises, isn't it?"

Alice smiled back knowingly before turning her attention to the selection of bread and cheese that were waiting at the bottom of the picnic basket.

Lottie barely touched a morsel.

She had failed.

As Alice finished the last of the cheese, they repacked the basket and Lottie felt as if her legs were filled with lead. She was devastated.

How could her well-laid plans have gone so wrong?

Luckily, her purse and other valuables had been inside the rucksack, so at least she wasn't missing anything else, but how on earth was she going to propose now?

Seemingly unaware of her girlfriend's trauma, Alice chattered happily at her side as they made their way back to the waiting bus. Lottie clambered aboard, and on the front row was the spotty youth who made immediate eye contact with Lottie. Grinning widely from ear to ear he grabbed his partner's hand.

"We're engaged, I've proposed!" he said, lifting it high with pride.

Beside him, the blushing young girl bloomed with love and

promise, as she allowed him to parade her ringed hand to the other passengers as they arrived back from their various adventures. An impromptu round of applause further encouraged him, and he stood up to take a bow, clearly struggling to believe that he'd actually pulled it off, after his earlier difficulties.

Lottie mumbled her half-hearted congratulations as she moved past him to find her seat. Alice was clapping, joining in with the round of applause, before leaning in to Lottie. "Lovely to be proposed to in Paris. But talk about tacky! Who would propose under the Eiffel Tower? A bit naff!"

Lottie was utterly lost for words. She swallowed loudly and managed to bluster. "Yes, bloody naff if you ask me!" She sank lower into her seat.

Dear God, what on earth am I going to do now? She silently pleaded for divine inspiration. The insurance certificate was in the UK and she knew she could get a replacement ring at a later date, but for the moment things lay in ruins, and now it seemed that Alice would have found it all thoroughly awful anyway.

What a bloody disaster!

The bus pulled away jolting Lottie back to reality. Slipping her hand into Lottie's, Alice turned and whispered in her ear. "Montmartre and the artist quarter next. Apparently, it's the most romantic part of Paris."

Lottie laid her head on Alice's shoulder and sighed loudly.

"I have a place I'd like to go for dinner later on, if you don't mind following me for a change," Alice said, patting her leg reassuringly.

Lottie nodded miserably. At this point she was quite sure that jumping from the Eiffel Tower was not an option, but if she could try to get through the rest of the trip, she was sure she could put things right at a later date. After all, there must be other places closer to home where she could propose, but oh, how embarrassing! She'd told so many people about the romantic proposal, and now she was going to have to tell them her sorry tale of woe, and everyone would be laughing at her. She hoped the boys wouldn't be too disappointed that she'd botched it up. She'd have to take advice now from Virginia and the gang to see if she could come up with an alternative proposal venue at home that would make the cut.

AS THE AFTERNOON sun idled high in the bluest of skies,

Lottie's spirits lifted. Away from the crowds, they meandered hand in hand through the cobbled streets of Montmartre. Colourful canopies sheltered the tourists who had stopped for refreshments on the pavement outside the cafés, as they made a lazy ascent to the Sacré-Cœur.

They passed through the artist's quarter and the small but busy square, inhabited by the portrait painters, admiring the concentration of talent in this one small part of Paris. Unknown smiling faces stared back at them from the display of finished canvasses that adorned the small stalls of the talented, who smiled at the couple as they passed through, hoping to entice them to a sitting.

They left the blue umbrellas which sheltered the artists, and moved onward, up the incline and towards the whitewashed basilica which sat proudly at the top of the hill, boasting the best views of the city. Moving between the shade of the canopies and the bright sunshine, the pair drank in the sights.

When their interest was piqued, they would disappear briefly through the open doors of small boutiques, and they would weave between the outdoor displays of tourist souvenirs picking up trinkets to remember their trip.

The afternoon ended and Alice pulled Lottie gently onward. She smiled patiently as she reminded Lottie they had until later that evening before they had to get back to the coach.

Happy to be led, and invested now in the romance of their trip, Lottie moved forward with Alice as she led them on a small detour to a small back street.

Aware that Alice had mentioned a place for dinner, Lottie was happy to be guided to a pleasant eatery, where she hoped to rest her throbbing feet for a while. As they descended into the quaint side street, she spotted a beautiful bistro called *Le Paname*, which sat snugly between a shabby chic furniture shop and a handmade silver jewellery emporium.

Smiling, Alice led her by the hand through the petite entranceway, and Lottie noticed that the shabby shutters were opened and fixed against the cool stone walls to expose the front of the eatery to the cobbled street outside. A waiter waved to Alice, who waved back, before coyly turning to Lottie. "It's almost as if they were expecting us!" she said as she drew Lottie in.

Lottie giggled. "You must have spent hours on travel sites finding this little gem. It's lovely!"

Alice didn't respond, instead she smiled broadly in greeting to the waiter, who graciously responded by treating them like long lost friends. Insisting on serving them himself, he irritably waved away the other servers and, with a grand flourish he produced his own menus.

Lottie mumbled about being full from the picnic, but despite the disappointment of the day, the quaint interior of the restaurant and the enticing smell of onion and garlic drifting through from the kitchen stimulated her lost appetite. She felt a small thrill of excitement run though her as Alice, being surprisingly fluent in the language, ordered confidently for them both. The waiter reappeared with two champagne flutes and a bottle of very expensive champagne, which Alice tasted briefly before confidently nodding at him to pour.

Greedily, Lottie glugged at the cold liquid, although the irony of drinking champagne after a failed marriage proposal was not lost on her. Reaching for her refilled glass, she relaxed as she soaked in the pleasant atmosphere, and a quiet rumble of unfamiliar language around her lulled her into a full state of contentment.

She returned her attention to Alice who grinned and reached forward, gently slipping her hand into Lottie's before circling her remaining hand with hers as she prevented Lottie from taking another glug of the effervescent liquid. Alice ran a finger lazily up inside Lottie's warm palm, and meeting her eyes, Lottie noticed that Alice's eyes were shining brightly.

"Before you drink that, sweetie, can I propose a toast?"

Nodding silently, Lottie released her hand and grasped the cool base of the long stemmed of her glass which she rose to meet the lip of Alice's untouched glass. With a gentle chink the glasses clipped and parted.

"This toast is for my amazing girlfriend, who is my soulmate and my lover. In this beautiful city, on this beautiful evening I would very much like to propose this toast to our future together. I would like to celebrate our lives as they unfold together, and I would like you to answer this question."

Leaning towards her, Alice's eyes misted with tears. "I would like to ask you, my funny, sexy girlfriend. Would you do me the huge honour of being my wife for the rest of our lives?" Alice sighed deeply and leaned back in her chair as she waited for Lottie to answer.

Lottie's glass was frozen in mid-toast, "Are you p-p-p-proposing?"

Alice chuckled before looking at her seriously. She nodded,

and meeting Lottie's confused gaze, she nodded in the direction of a small box slipped onto the table by the eager waiter. It lay unopened on the red, chequered tablecloth.

Lottie gasped, excitement and shock rushed through her. "Oh, my God!"

Grabbing the box, she firmly clicked it open to reveal a beautiful white gold band with a set of three diamonds glinting in the fading light.

"Yes, yes, bloody *yes!*" Lottie shrieked, as they both jumped up and fell into one another's arms, to a round of applause from their fellow diners and the beaming waiter.

"Oh, Alice, you are so full of surprises! You've no idea what my plan was for this trip and yet you'd obviously had your own plan all along. Hilarious, you are just bloody wonderful!"

Slipping the ring onto her finger, a perfect fit, Lottie stuttered through words to fill in the astounded Alice on her botched proposals one and two, leaving Alice initially stunned for words and dumbfounded at the catalogue of errors that had led to a non-proposal and a lost ring.

"Oh, Lottie, you really are an absolute gift, do you know that?"

Alice grabbed her phone. "Come on. Let's put the boys out of their misery. I'm getting ten texts a minute from Robbie!"

Lottie squealed with delight. "Those little sods! They knew all about this? But they knew I was going to propose to you too, so I bet they're laughing their heads off!"

Grabbing hold of Lottie, Alice laughed and firmly whirled her around, planting a round of kisses across her glowing cheeks. "Daylight robbers more like! They both had twenty pound notes off me to keep quiet!"

Lottie laughed. She was engaged!

Dirty Talk

SMILING TO HERSELF, Lottie carefully placed the miniature metal Eiffel Tower replica on the shelf above the TV, not that she really needed a physical reminder of how amazing the trip had turned out to be.

She glanced at the understated sparkling ring which sat proudly on her engagement finger, and sighing with contentment, she reluctantly returned to the task in hand.

While she and Alice had been inadvertently competing to propose in Paris, the kittens had been at home creating a far more sinister outcome. Largely left to their own devices apart from regular feeding and checks from their well-meaning neighbour, the kittens had managed to unleash untold havoc in the small cottage.

Keeping her promise to Alice, Lottie had managed to get Pru to collect Sappho well before their few days away. Despite her reported attachment to her cat, Pru had invented a multitude of excuses for prolonging Sappho's stay. However, Alice had reminded Lottie that the longer Sappho co-habited with Boots, the more likely a new brood of furry nightmares would be on the horizon. This had spurred Lottie on to stand firm, and dispatch Sappho back to her rightful owner.

When Alice and Lottie had arrived back in Pennan earlier that morning, they had been met at the door by their unusually sheepish neighbour, Lisa. Without the usual pleasantries about their holiday, Lisa had failed to make any eye contact and hurriedly handed back the spare key. Looking considerably shamefaced she had mumbled something largely indecipherable although Lottie had managed to make out the words "demonic" and "evil".

Keen to see her furry little bundles, Lottie had forged her way through the door in blissful ignorance, only to be instantly repelled by the overwhelming acrid stench of cat urine. Turning to Lisa for an explanation, she was met only by the swift closure of the front door.

Venturing inside with trepidation, Lottie gasped in horror. The living room was littered with small but pungent mounds of cat excrement which she felt would largely explain the meaty smell which had stuck in her throat. Her eyes burned and she noticed the curtains were now non-existent. She could only surmise the kittens had used them to clamber up to a higher viewing point or possibly, for no reason at all, other than that they might have fancied the journey.

As if on cue, Stripe, the largest of the brood, swaggered nonchalantly into the living room. Eyeballing Lottie with unashamed pleasure he casually glanced around, surveying the mayhem he had undoubtedly orchestrated. Joining Stripe in surveying the chaos, Lottie was aware that Alice was making a break for it. She disappeared upstairs, muttering about e-mails and drug company orders, leaving Lottie alone to tackle what would undoubtedly be a lengthy clear up.

Thankfully, she was saved by the sound of her mobile phone ringing, and she dashed into the kitchen avoiding for the moment, the presents the kittens had left on the floor.

She answered the call from Mel.

"Hey, stranger! How did it go? I saw the ring picture on Facebook, I thought you'd bought a different ring. Where did that one come from?"

Laughing, Lottie filled her in on the saga, but was interrupted as the front door slammed and the noise of the boys and an over-excited dachshund filled the front room. Anxious to avoid anybody stepping in the mess, she hurriedly ended the call, "Sorry, Mel, the boys are back. Pop round tomorrow and we'll have a glass of wine and a proper catch up."

Arrangements made, she headed for the front room where the kids were desperate to revel in the fact they had held both hers and Alice's secret proposal plans. Archie was beside himself with excitement when Lottie showed him her ring, but his moods soon dampened when he discovered that Lottie's proposal had not been such a success. Reassured though, that Alice would also have a ring after Lottie had rung the shop to claim another one on the insurance she had luckily taken out, he had disappeared upstairs to check on Lucky the hamster, whom he had sensibly barricaded into his bedroom cupboard for the duration of his stay away. An anti-demonic kitten tactical plan that Lottie now wished she had taken more notice of.

In order to avoid the cleaning for a little bit longer, Lottie decided to check her e-mails. An message from Pru, entitled *Urgent!* drew Lottie's attention.

Clicking to open it, she was pleased to note that it was a long and friendly message which concluded by reminding Lottie that it was group this Thursday. Commenting on the drop in numbers,

Pru had requested that Lottie should try to get anybody else to attend who she thought would benefit from the group. She promised that she would waive the subscription charges for this week only.

Lottie was astonished at Pru's assumption that it would be easy to bring along newcomers to her group. While Lottie had grown used to Pru's alternative methods, the group was really about gay women who wanted a sense of belonging within their own small Highland community. It wasn't exactly an inclusive group and Lottie was pretty sure that anyone not defining themselves as a lesbian would feel the wrath of Pru's scathing views on bi-sexuality.

Deciding not to dwell on the finer points of Pru's discriminatory philosophies, Lottie shut down the computer and sent a quick text to Mel.

```
Hi, forgot its bloody group tomorrow, we'll have
the wine early and you can come with me. I think
Pru's past her crush for you now so you'll be
safe, promise! xx
```

The smell of cat offerings brought her back to reality, and she reluctantly started on the task of restoring their home to some semblance of normality.

AFTER GOING TO work the next day, Lottie arrived home still glowing from the excitement of the day, where most of her colleagues had been overjoyed and congratulated her on her engagement.

She noted that Leonard had managed to make an inappropriate comment on his card.

```
To the happy couple, long may you suckle! LOL,
lots of love-and thinking about you always LOL
Leonard xx
```

She shuddered as she recalled the short conversation with him beside the water cooler after she had studiously avoided him all day.

"Lottie, whoa there! Congrats and all that, dude!"

Lottie smiled politely but didn't volunteer any small talk.

Undeterred, he blundered on. "I bet there were some long lie-ins after you popped the question, if you know what I mean, eh?" Without waiting for a reply, he continued. "Anyway. I thought marriage was off the cards for you ladies. Isn't it called something like civic partnership or something?"

Lottie stared frostily at him trying to convey her dissatisfaction, as he headed into dangerous territory. "Well, I won't tell the big G man if you don't," Leonard sniggered. "Don't forget my invite!"

Pushing in front of her he filled his paper cup before turning to give her a protracted and salacious wink. "Sly dog, eh? Sly old dog!"

Later, at home, Lottie gave an involuntary shudder at the memory of his comments, and briefly wondered how his wife tolerated such a complete and utter sleaze. Shaking her head to dispel the memory, she dashed upstairs for a quick change before Mel arrived.

Mel was clearly not happy about being pressured into attending group again. "The last bloody time I was in a room with that woman, she chased me down like a sick dog!"

Lottie giggled. "Oh Mel, I'm so sorry. It was just such a manic party. Alice did tell me I had done you a horrible disservice, but I promise I'll protect you with my life tonight, and if we don't get this wine finished, we'll sneak it in!"

Reassured by the promise of an alcohol-fuelled evening, Mel relaxed and enjoyed a full viewing of the Paris photographs and the accompanying commentary by Lottie, as she recounted her doomed proposal attempts followed by Alice's far more classy effort.

"Bloody good job one of you can pull something like that off!" Mel commented as she reluctantly pulled on her jacket and settled herself into Lottie's car for the journey to the village hall.

AS THEY ARRIVED at the hall, Lottie saw the familiar wisp of smoke coming from the back entrance. She bit back her disapproval and wondered again why Mim spent so much time with Pru, who treated her so badly. She was clearly enterprising in terms of her cannabis empire, and so Lottie wondered what drew her to Pru and her hokey-pokey antics.

Lottie shot Mel a reassuring smile, before firmly guiding her into the hall.

Upon entering, Lottie was struck by the large pieces of obscure artwork which adorned the walls.

Squinting to examine the welcome splash of colour on the otherwise drab walls, she noted that there was no obvious form to the pictures which appeared to be pink and red and resembling sugar puff cereal. Mel was also engrossed in trying to fathom out the content of the pictures, tilting her head sideways she walked the length of the hall squinting and peering, oblivious to the rapturous delight on Pru's face as she registered Mel's presence. Determined not to fail in her friend-protection duties Lottie hurried to intercept Pru as she homed in on the unprotected Mel.

"Hey there, Pru. Thanks for the e-mail!"

Pru glanced her way in irritation as she was forced to halt in her tracks. "Yes, yes, marvellous, dear. Glad you got it. Kittens okay? Good, good."

Without waiting for a reply, she deftly skirted Lottie, who was left openmouthed as Pru caught Mel by the shoulder, spinning her around before bringing her into a full embrace — leaving Mel to surrender helplessly as Pru gushed. "Lovely, simply lovely to see you, Melanie, and what a wonderful opportunity! We're doing vaginas today, my dear, yes, we all have one and they're simply marvellous!"

Pru let out a high-pitched cackle as she attempted to flirt, and Mel grimaced at the unpleasant noise, failing to hide her shock as she sought out Lottie with her eyes. Ashamed, Lottie was proceeding with stealth, backward, towards an empty seat. Mel shot her a look of pure hatred and Lottie shrivelled away to a sitting position, mouthing her apologies as Mel was helplessly swept towards a seat closer to the front of the room and next to Pru's throne of power.

Pru was unnaturally giddy as she brought the room to order. "Now, ladies, let's get started. By the time you leave our gathering tonight, you will have an intimate knowledge of yourself. Before we start I want to draw your attention to group rules, always important to show respect to one another, and no mobile phones!"

Lottie observed the inevitable rustling in bags, as people hurried to mute their phones in order to avoid the wrath of Pru. The baby-dykes, now regular attenders, were often phone offenders, but they still caught Lottie's eye giving her a simultaneous grin as she nodded in acknowledgement.

Pru coughed impatiently, before leaning towards an uncomfortable Mel to roll her eyes dramatically in an attempt to demonstrate her patience of the intolerable persons within the group. Mel was studiously examining a piece of thread which she was nervously working back and forth between her fingers, avoiding all unnecessary eye contact with the over-eager Pru.

"Okay," Prudence asserted with authority. "The usual chance for you to put forward any suitable names for the group. Although we're currently under a working title of Pru's Group we are all participants and this is a collective decision."

Pru paused to scan the room. A few hands rose hesitantly and the baby-dykes were waving to attract her attention. Appearing to scrutinise the attendees, she studiously avoided the owners of the raised hands before nodding with mock modesty and a forced laugh. "Oh, goodness. At this rate it'll become a permanent title!"

Lottie shook her head in irritation at the sheer arrogance of Pru. It was something she found increasingly difficult to tolerate. It was perfectly evident to all concerned that she positively revelled in the working title which blatantly demonstrated her ongoing ownership of the group. The regular façade of a mock survey for alternative names never failed to strike Lottie as an insult to the group. Scanning the room, she saw a few shaking heads and a ripple of tuts, suggesting she wasn't alone in her view.

She tuned out Pru's droning voice which she found quite monotonous and once again glanced around at the pictures which Pru had hung on the walls. What the bloody hell are those? She craned her neck to get a better look at the painting nearest to her.

A large woman sitting next to her, bearing a plunging cleavage, gave her a conspiratorial nudge. "Fannies, love!" she murmured.

Choosing to ignore her, convinced that she must have misheard, Lottie tried to create a non-existent space between them, but became horribly conscious of a bulging arm which was sticking to her own as it encroached into her own personal body space. "Excuse me?" she stuttered, forced to engage with her.

Smiling to reveal a large gap between her yellowed front teeth, she leaned into Lottie. "Minge, love, we've all got one!"

Lottie felt the heat of the woman's breath on her now glowing cheeks. Slowly she turned to re-examine the picture closest to her which suddenly seemed to come into focus with alarming speed to reveal an angry red vagina.

"*Vaginas!*" Pru shrieked, making Lottie jump out of her skin. The rest of the room let out a nervous giggle. "Let's all say it together...*vaginas!*" she bellowed with gusto.

With some reluctance, the voice of the group sent back a feeble echo of *vagina* and Pru harrumphed with displeasure. Lowering herself onto a stool, she spread her legs wide and pointed towards her own modesty. "Fannies, minge, vagina, lady garden, so many names for our most precious area. All of the names come from *men*, they have claimed our vaginas for their own, but we want them *back*!"

Mim jumped up and grabbed her crotch, making a grotesque grinding motion. "Back, back, back," she chanted, with alarming regularity.

Pru leapt down from the stage area and prowled around the group, some of whom sheepishly returned her stare, awaiting enlightenment about how they could redeem their privates. While Pru swept around the room updating the women on the disastrous journey their vaginas had undertaken since the emergence of pornography, Mel turned to give Lottie a stare that would shrivel grapes.

Lottie gave a half-hearted smile and an apologetic shrug. Grappling with her handbag, she retrieved the hip flask she had stashed there, and stealthily slung it through the gap underneath the seats towards Mel's eagerly awaiting hands. Lottie tried to remain calm and turned her attention back to Pru. She really was starting to worry about her mental health.

Where on earth had it said on the e-mail that she needed to reclaim her vagina tonight? A cold sweat pricked at the base of her neck as she contemplated the possible progression of the group to the inevitable circle of women with mirrors exploring their own lady gardens.

As it turned out and much to the group's relief, Pru wasn't intending on revealing her vagina or anyone else's for that matter, instead she offered the women a relatively comfortable space on the floor prepared with yoga matting and invited them to create their own artwork. Breathing a loud sigh of relief that her panties would remain in place, Lottie took the time to examine the hangings adorning the walls and concluded that every one of them was a representation of a variety of tuppences that she hoped didn't actual belong to anyone she knew.

Trying to shake that image from her mind, she determined that each picture displayed could easily be interpreted for something else, an exotic flower maybe or some more like a garden slug. On closer examination one of the more impressionist interpretations contained, what she was pretty sure was the face of the Dali Lama, grinning broadly out of the delicate folds. Lottie shook her head in disbelief, pretty sure that this was some type of religious defamation. Taking her place in the circle on the floor she passively accepted a piece of drawing paper and grabbed a charcoal pencil from the jar in from of her. She was fairly confident that her vagina would only want to be represented in black and white at this stage.

To her surprise, the majority of the group were bent intently above their creative masterpieces. On finishing, women would hand their work to Pru who would hold it aloft and chant, "Vagina, vagina, vagina!" The group would rouse to a cheer before returning to their own creations.

Egged on by Mel, who had greedily consumed the contents of the bribery hip flask, Lottie reluctantly held aloft her black and white depiction of her own delicate folds, minus the Dali Lama. Bracing herself as the group all cheered and the inevitable raucous shout of *Vagina!* echoed around the hall.

Slightly out of time, due to her inebriated state, Mel shrieked out. "Cunt!"

The group fell silent, all eyes on Pru, who rose slowly. Dramatically she made her way to Mel, who was chuckling uncontrollably at her own variation on the group chant. Oblivious to the approach of Pru, Mel leaned to Lottie who was studiously avoiding eye contact, as she attempted to disassociate herself from her pissed friend.

Oblivious, Mel leaned across saying loudly and speaking to no one in particular "C U next Thursday, *cunt!*" she pronounced proudly, as she fell back onto her heels.

Pru towered above her, and Mel suddenly became aware of her presence, shushing herself before disintegrating into hysteria once again.

Pru swooped down decisively and grasped Mel's wrist, dragging her to her feet. Lottie gasped in shock. Christ, she's going to throw her out, or hit her! Lottie jumped to her feet, ready to rescue Mel, who was grinning inanely in spite of Pru's intense gaze.

Mel stood unsteadily beside Pru, who spun her around and around in front of the group, who were silent and spellbound by the unexpected events that were unfolding before them.

Taking a deep tremulous breath, Pru slowly raised Mel's arm skyward, and bowing her head she breathed noisily and muttered something incoherent to herself, before she raised her head to follow the stretch of Mel's arm. "Women and spirits!" she commanded. "Behold the bravery of one woman amongst so many!"

Legs spread akimbo, she shook Mel's arm, causing it to wobble with some irregularity. Mel was grinning inanely at

Lottie. "The spirit has entered Melanie, and her grounded sense of self-assurance and kinship to womankind has allowed her to recognise the importance of reclaiming our essence!"

Lottie looked at Pru and noted a single tear slipping almost unnoticed down her furrowed cheek, "Cunts are ours! They do not belong to men! They should not be depicted on the top shelves of our newsagents or used by men who want to dominate and control us! No! I say *no* more shall we allow the use of our cunts by others. They are ours forever more! Join me as we claim our cunts!"

Rising noisily and somewhat uncomfortably to their feet, the group tentatively joined hands, simultaneously mumbling *cunt, cunt, cunt* in a rhythmic chant.

Lottie remained speechless staring at Mel who was nodding in inebriated approval at the chorus of profanity that she had instigated.

With her energy seeming to be suddenly depleted, Pru sank onto a chair that had appeared beneath her at that behest of Mim.

Looking towards the group, Pru smiled weakly. "The spirit is gone now, my dears, I am weary. Your homework for this evening is to go home and reclaim your moist cavities in whichever way you feel the need to. Claim the language as our own, speak the words aloud for all to hear and live in the knowledge that we are the masters of our own pleasure!"

Not waiting for further instruction, Lottie grabbed the tipsy Mel roughly by the arm and headed for the car park and escaped to the safety of her car and home.

LATER THAT NIGHT, Lottie woke up with a start and sat bolt upright in the bed. Undisturbed, Alice breathed softly at the side of her. As she had drifted to sleep, the memory of the earlier group had lingered, unwelcome in her mind and had infiltrated her dreams where, bizarrely, she had volunteered to do a chalk drawing of Prudence's vagina with Mim grinning like the proverbial Cheshire cat as she encouraged the group towards them for a closer look.

"Holy shit!" Lottie mumbled, shaking her head to try and dispel the unpleasant images that still crowded her mind. Bloody Pru and her crazy groups. Lottie tried to unpick what kept her going, when every time it seemed like the subject matter bordered on the insane.

Glancing at the clock, she registered two oh four. Groaning, she gently slipped from under the heavy duvet, tiptoed out of the room and headed downstairs to the dimly lit kitchen. Leaning her head under the tap, she slurped the cool water greedily as it trickled into her mouth and ran down her cheek. She was pretty sure that the original allure of group had been the thought of bonding with other gay women who she wouldn't ordinarily encounter in her daily life. She was certainly the only gay in the village at work, apart from Virginia, of course, although the make-up of her small home village of Pennan was slightly more gay-friendly. Lottie took pride in her ability to blend into largely heterosexual environments although this didn't lessen the craving for a life which held more gay friends. Despite this, she was rapidly reaching the conclusion that Pru's ensemble of spirit-friendly hippies was probably not going to be a source of long lasting friendships for her.

She made her way cautiously back upstairs, then decided to visit the bathroom. Sitting on the toilet she noted with a mild sense of irritation that Alice's expensive brand of body wash was out and proud on the bath side. Since Alice had moved in, a silent battle had ensued as Lottie tried to passively train Alice to put away her bathroom accessories.

Long ago, Lottie had learned that the various needs of her small household, in terms of an assortment of shower gels and shampoos, could not be easily housed on the bath edge. After some prompting, the boys had accepted the inevitable fact that all showering accessories would need to live in the drawers beneath the sink. However, since Alice had joined them, a somewhat rebellious bottle of shower gel had reappeared on the bath side despite Lottie's persistent attempts to put it out of sight. Wanting Alice to feel completely at home, Lottie hadn't quite been brave enough to tackle the matter head on, instead she had adopted a somewhat passive aggressive approach by removing the shower gel after each post-shower visitation to the bathroom. At some point later in the day, the shower gel usually would make a reappearance, and today was clearly no exception. Almost without thought, Lottie swiped it up from the bath side and popped it back into the drawer, before she made her way back to the bedroom where Alice was still sleeping soundly.

Burrowing back down underneath the duvet, she found herself thinking about Pru's rationale for shouting vulgar obscenities with her friends. It was true that Lottie did not approve any more than the next self-respecting lesbian about the continuing existence of page-three girls in newspapers or hard-core pornography solely designed to get men off on the use and abuse of women. Despite this, however, saying the words out loud felt less like reclaiming them and more like a crudity that invoked extreme discomfort.

Despite now feeling somewhat more confident in her own sexual prowess, Lottie had never conquered the art of dirty talk. Occasionally, in the midst of passion, Alice would murmur a few words of encouragement which always spurred Lottie on in a sexual capacity. Somehow though, despite her train of passionate thought Lottie had, thus far, been unable to verbalise this and reciprocate towards Alice in that way. She reached beneath the cover and slipped her arm underneath that of the sleeping Alice and pulled her gently towards her. Alice partially roused and caught Lottie's free hand with her own pulling it towards her breast. As Lottie touched the softness of Alice's skin she noted the small pinprick of goose bumps rise up her back as she felt the response of Alice's nipple as it hardened to meet the palm of her hand. Lottie gave an involuntary groan, and Alice turned towards her wearing a deeply sensual and sleepy half smile. Without speaking she raised an eyebrow at Lottie who smiled in return. She reached towards Lottie and pulled her into a deep kiss, probing her mouth lazily with her tongue. Lottie gave a louder groan as she shifted her body weight and moulded herself between Alice's parted legs. Pulling playfully at Alice's top, and with no resistance she tugged it up fully to expose her fiancée's full breasts. Reaching forward to nuzzle into Alice's inviting warmth, Pru's words echoed in her mind, *reclaim the words...*

Could she?

Tracing a pattern of delicate kisses upward towards Alice's neck she heard her breath catch. Teasing her ear lobe, she breathed heavily into her ear. "Baby?"

Alice paused, arching towards Lottie. "Uh huh?" she muttered huskily.

Lottie pulled back and breathed across Alice's mouth. "Can I touch your *cunt*?"

As she said the word *cunt* with slightly too much venom, a small amount of spittle flew out of her mouth and hit Alice in the eye.

Blinking rapidly, Alice rose up on her elbows. "*Excuse me?*" she bellowed.

Lottie's smile faltered. "Perhaps that was a little clumsy. What I was trying to say was, can I finger your vag?"

Satisfied that she'd explained herself more clearly, she

slipped her hand down towards Alice's parted legs.

Alice spluttered in complete surprise. "You've got to be fucking kidding me, Lots! What on earth has got into you? Have you been drinking?"

Lottie froze.

"Oh crap, I think that may have come out wrong, I was trying to reclaim my vagina, well, yours actually. Well, you know, reclaim the word. Pru said," she finished lamely.

Alice was now in a full sitting position and grabbing a pillow, she placed it between her and the eager Lottie. "Excuse me!" she repeated. "That crazy old bag told you to *reclaim my vagina?*"

Lottie felt stuck. She was sure that she'd used the right terminology and hoped it would have enhanced the moment rather than destroy it. She was confused. Should she have used the word cunt instead? Perhaps the word vagina was too clinical.

Deciding to give it one final go, she firmly grasped Alice's breast and shouted assertively. "Cunt!"

Alice snorted loudly and laughed from her very core. Tears rolled down her face as she bit into the duvet in an attempt to try and stem her hysterical mirth.

Lottie leaned back quietly against the headboard and was thankful for the darkness which masked her glowing red cheeks.

She chuckled, but with less conviction than Alice who was literally beside herself with the humour of the situation.

Fuck! Lottie acknowledged how clumsy her attempt at seductive talk had been.

"Oh Christ, Lottie. You really are totally priceless! Tell me you planned this. It's not possible to be this funny off the cuff!"

Smiling brightly at the unexpected compliment, in what was none other than a significant fail on the sexual expression front, she playfully slapped Alice's thigh.

"Cup of tea?" she asked.

This galvanised Alice into a renewed hysterical outburst and so, without waiting for a reply, she grabbed her robe and disappeared back down into the kitchen, hoping to redeem herself with the delivery of a steaming brew.

"Bloody Pru!" she muttered murderously.

Part Three

Pondweed Archie

AS THE SUMMER drew to a lazy close, Alice was aware that Lottie was preparing herself for an inevitable but terrifying fact of life. Archie was about to go to senior school. Much to Alice's amusement, Lottie had studiously avoided any discussion of this, despite the imminent start date of the following Monday.

Alice had decided to play down the progression of Archie from Lottie's little darling into a tween with occasional mood swings and more than a passing interest in the female of the species. She was well aware that Lottie viewed Archie as a reflection of her youth and that the loss of the annual school nativity play, and that the constant need for boxes for abstract art projects, was going to inevitably take its toll on Lottie. Alice had a great fondness for the boys, but she was cautious in adopting a full hands-on parenting role, knowing that Lottie had prided herself on doing a half-decent job of single-parenting them through to their teenage years.

Not having a biological connection with the children, however, did not detract from Alice's desire to facilitate a harmonious transition for Archie, who she felt was going to need a lot of support in becoming a young man from his currently entrenched position as the baby of the family. Alice couldn't help but feel some frustration towards Lottie's inability to recognise that she was not helping Archie by colluding with the immature behaviour that Archie sometimes demonstrated. She concluded that the situation had largely arisen more from Lottie's need to remain a useful parent than from Archie's need to remain the baby of the family.

A FEW DAYS before the fateful Monday, Lottie had reluctantly entered the uniform department of John Lewis and Archie had stared in dismay at the array of acrylic football shirts and the rugby tops.

"I don't like sport, Mum," he mumbled, while the eager shop assistant disappeared to find a tape measure.

Lottie looked at Archie with what she hoped was reassurance rather than a reflection of her own sense of impending doom.

"Look love, we all had to do sports. It's not fun, God knows, but you'll be fine!" Lottie could hear the insincere undertone in her comment.

Archie clung to her arm, miserably casting a wary eye of doubt over the sombre navy blazers and the stiff tailored trousers. Desperate to engage Archie in the process, Lottie tried to help him focus on the rather more colourful selection of pencil cases and accessories.

ROBBIE HUNG BACK, observing the pair. He was proud to have got them both to the uniform shop where he hoped that they would actually get on and buy the requisite uniform. The last thing that Archie needed was to be going to school in the wrong clothes. It was Robbie's opinion that Archie was potentially a prime target for the bullies, and although he cared about his brother, he also wanted to avoid any reflected embarrassment on his own rather more street cool image — which he liked to think he still had, despite his swift eviction from the school into another secondary, where he was determined to keep a low profile.

He intended to guide his brother through the intricacies of social interaction at senior school, in an attempt to make Archie a survivor of the Scottish comprehensive system, rather than a casualty of his mother's mollycoddling.

Both Archie and his mum glanced across anxiously at him, so he gave them a reassuring nod and pointed in the direction of the trousers with no elasticated waists. His mum grabbed them from the rack and gave him a look of gratitude before subconsciously pulling Archie closer to her.

Robbie shook his head in despair and slunk out of the shop to have a roll-up before the inevitable post-shopping autopsy began on the long car journey home.

LOTTIE COLLECTED HERSELF. She was pretty sure the shop assistant was beginning to lose patience with her. How was she supposed to know Archie's chest size, for God's sake? She ought to have probably known his shoe size however, as she imagined that would be the sort of thing that a yummy mummy would have ingrained in their memory. But between dealing with her chaotic household, which still included a batch of seemingly unrehomeable kittens — mental note to re-advertise the furry nightmares — and her hideous job, she didn't have a lot of time for the finer details of life.

She sighed to no one in particular, as she remembered she'd also promised Alice she'd call in at the registrar's office to see about the process for booking the wedding. Unlikely now, at this late hour. Hopefully a search engine would provide the relevant information.

THE REST OF the weekend passed in a blur, with several unsuccessful attempts to palm the now adolescent kittens off onto the neighbours. For some reason, whenever a prospective kitten mummy came to the house, the aptly named Stripe would corral the troops and put on a phenomenal display of anarchy including curtain acrobatics and blatant furniture spraying.

She was pretty sure he had terrorised them into submission as she found the individual kittens very sweet away from his demonic influence. After smiling politely at the back of the latest empty-handed visitor, she sighed in despair as she looked at Stripe. She would later swear to Alice that he smiled in a smug self-satisfied way before depositing a smelly parcel on her best rug.

Shrieking in utter rage, Lottie launched herself at him, missing his body and landing precariously close to the smelly mound. Apparently unfazed, Stripe strutted forward, swinging his tail high as he paraded out to the kitchen for a pre-dinner snack, or to be more precise, to relieve Odie of his dinner until he had his fill while the anxious Odie waited patiently by his own bowl for permission to eat Stripe's leftovers.

"Things have got to change in this house," growled Lottie as she scrubbed the unforgiving stain on the rug.

THE NEXT MORNING, the late summer sun shone brightly through the bedroom window. Reaching out, Lottie was disappointed to find a cold spot where Alice's warm body should have been. Emotion welled up inside her as the realisation of Archie's first day dawned upon her. With a heavy heart she made her way across the hall to Archie's room which was also mysteriously empty. Wandering down to the darkened end of the landing she knocked tentatively on the man cave door. After no response and a dignified period of waiting, she cracked open the door to discover an empty bed, already made, and curtains open.

"Who's abducted my family?" Lottie mused aloud, as she grabbed her robe and hurried down the stairs towards the kitchen.

The smell of fried bacon rose the length of the staircase to greet her and she smiled with relief as she rounded the corner to be met with the sight of her lovely little family chattering around the breakfast table.

Alice grinned. "Grab a seat, love. I've done us some veggie-bacon and mushrooms."

Not for the first time, Lottie's heart filled with pure love for Alice, who had clearly risen extra early to pre-empt the chaotic preparations for Archie's first day, and the traumatic process of leaving the house for the school bus.

In the corner, she spied his new school bag complete with packed lunch and a full gym bag. At the side were his wallet, his watch and a fully charged mobile phone. Archie was dressed and ready, looking remarkably bright and clearly feeding off the positive energy being exuded by Alice, who was entertaining his chatter and depositing positive affirmations to encourage his belief that new friends would be his for the picking.

When Lottie had made the decision to change Archie to the local high school she knew this would inevitably mean him leaving behind his small and hard-earned friendship group from the primary school he had attended. Wanting to foster in him a more independent spirit, she had made a calculated choice to place him at the local senior school in the hope that he would develop more of a social life in his home area. However, as the start date had beckoned she had become increasingly doubtful that she had done the right thing.

With his new mobile phone, Archie had made valiant efforts to maintain his links with his primary-school friends, but seemingly he had already been forgotten during the lengthy summer break, and his best and closest friend was not responding to his text messages. Lottie felt that this transition was going to be a testing time for them all, but she had tried not to burden Archie with her anxieties.

Nevertheless, as she observed her close-knit clan interacting around the breakfast table Lottie was filled with a sense of immense pride in Alice—that she had both anticipated and managed this difficult morning in her practical and organised way, leaving Lottie with only one task, to wave Archie off at the bus stop. Gulping to stem the emotion once more, she joined them around the table.

Robbie looked up from his plate briefly and, giving her a cheesy grin, he briefly patted her knee. "It'll be okay, Mum. I survived, didn't I?"

She smiled back at him. "You certainly did, and what a lovely person you've turned out to be. You're doing so well in your new school. New beginnings, eh?"

A fleeting look of pleasure crossed his face before he grunted. "Shurrup!" The table erupted into laughter.

A conspiratorial look was exchanged between Archie and Alice, and nodding at him, Alice turned to Lottie. "Babes, I've promised Archie a lift to school today. I know you want him to figure out the bus, but he can do that tomorrow. Okay?"

Lottie looked at Archie, who was struggling to make eye contact with her, and in that second, she realised that Alice had somehow managed to give Archie enough confidence to hit this day head on.

Surprisingly, she felt neither rejected nor disappointed, but instead, felt a sense of peace envelop her. "Sure thing, kiddo, sure thing!"

Fearing Lottie might change her mind, Archie hastily swept up his belongings, and slung the car keys across the table to Alice who caught them deftly. Giving Lottie a wide smile, she followed Archie out the door.

When Alice texted later in the day she told Lottie that Archie had been worried about her coping with the goodbyes, and the fact that she might get upset had been weighing heavily on his shoulders. Lottie was so happy to know he had confided this in Alice, who had subsequently concocted the plan to be up and ready to leave, and that she had thrown in a lift for good measure.

As Lottie plodded through her working day, she still felt a measure of anxiety about how he was getting on. However, a hurried illicit text at lunch allayed her fears.

```
Got new friend, called Lou, she said tea at hers
tomoz, okay?
```

Lottie smiled, and for a moment allowed herself to hope that the transition had been easier than she had feared. Making a friend on his first day was surely a good sign, although no doubt Robbie would pour scorn on his efforts for making friends with a girl.

That evening, Lottie saw a new Archie. Confident and chatty, he filled them in on the delights of the big school, including the unsolicited exercise he had undertaken as they ran to whistles from class to class, and the as yet unidentified dishes in the school bistro. He was filled with excitement about the prospect of visiting Lou's house, which was in the next village, although Lottie was less than delighted to discover that her presence was also required, as Lou's mum wanted to get to know some of the new parents.

THE FOLLOWING DAY, another reportedly successful day in which Archie had his first French lesson, they had a rushed pre-tea snack and Archie and Lottie set out for the quaint village of Rosehearty.

They parked next to Lou's house, and were greeted by a gaggle of excited children. Archie disappeared into the centre of the group and was swept along the path and in through the front door. Alice hung back. Socialising was not one of her strong points and she had hoped that the dawn of the high school era would lessen her obligation to swim in the shark pool of the yummy mummies.

Sighing with resignation, she trudged up the path and rapped loudly on the now closed door. Before she had a chance to withdraw her hand, the door swung enthusiastically open to reveal a buxom woman with wild, red curly hair. Behind her was a tall, handsome man with a handlebar moustache. They both grinned broadly in greeting. Mustering up a smile, Lottie stepped into the crowded hallway where an assortment of women looked up to meet her gaze. Clearly, they were other trapped mothers desperate to further their children's social lives.

Feeling slightly more at ease, she allowed the woman, known as Wynona, to sweep her into the dimly lit living room, where an assortment of nibbles and drink choices were displayed on a heavy oak table. Sitting on the edge of the nearest sofa, eager to make ready an escape, Lottie was spared the embarrassment of starting a conversation by the enthusiastic Wynona, who imparted to her captive audience that hubby, with the porn star moustache, was vacating the building shortly for his bridge club.

"After all, we don't want a man encroaching on our ladies' talk now, do we?"

Lottie glanced at hubby who dramatically raised his equally fulsome black eyebrows in mock horror before grabbing his man bag and vacating the premises.

Lottie stared jealously into the empty space left by hubby. The room fell silent, and she was conscious that the handful of twiglets she had been grazing on were causing her to make an unsociably loud crunching noise.

Wynona's wild eyes swept the room, before settling inevitably on Lottie, who smiled weakly in return, trying to keep the crunching to a minimum.

"So…" Lottie offered feebly, following the protracted silence. Feeling forced into uncomfortable small talk she continued. "How lovely of you to go to so much trouble for us."

Looking around, she caught the eye of another visitor, who nodded mutely holding her twiglets politely in front of her.

Feeling the need to continue to fill the awkward silence, she spoke again. "I'm Lottie, Archie's mum. So lovely to be here."

Wynona nodded excitedly. "Indeed, indeed, so nice to meet the other mums. I was hoping we could get to know one another. You know how hard it is when children move schools." The room muttered a mutual assent to this statement.

Wynona continued on, oblivious to her own overbearing voice. "Bloody marvellous that we can do this, isn't it?"

None of the other women made eye contact with her.

Oblivious to the undertone of apathy in the room, Wynona persisted. "Who watched *Braveheart* last night?"

More nodding.

Lottie found herself nodding along, even though she hadn't watched it at all. After her primary school experiences with the yummy mummies she was not as keen to break from the herd. Anticipating harmonious inclusion by the senior yummy mummies she silently vowed to fit neatly into the background of this group for as long as she could.

Wynona assumed an exaggerated dreamy look and leaning in conspiratorially towards the trapped women. "Mel Gibson! Wouldn't kick *him* out of bed, would you?"

Cackles rippled around the group as the women warmed to the topic of the ripped Mel Gibson and his atrocious attempt at a Scottish accent.

Lottie failed to laugh along and found the eyes of some of the group quickly resting on her. Good God! Surely, they were not asking her. She wouldn't have to out herself already, would she?

Trying not to make direct eye contact with Wynona, she belatedly laughed along with the others, and tried not to offer any direct positive affirmation of her choice of bed mate.

Wynona laughed loudly, downing the remnants of her large glass of red wine as she went for a refill, seemingly confident in her choice of topic. "Well, he'd be my choice anyway, girls."

More laughter as the group slowly relaxed and casually

speculated on their choice of celebrity shag.

Lottie recognised a feeling of impending doom. How did this always happen to her? The dull chatter around her filled her head. Wynona worked the group like an expert, refilling glasses and loitering in places where the conversation was stilted while she appraised her assembled group of new mummy friends. Lottie was already beginning to feel that she was under particular scrutiny.

She was torn.

On the one hand, she desperately wanted to fit into this new group without the past transgressions of her parenting faux pas to haunt her, but on the other hand she couldn't—no, she wouldn't—deny herself the opportunity to be who she was whatever the consequences.

Suddenly she found that the opportunity presented itself. The group silenced as Wynona swept across the room to settle beside her.

"Well, Lottie?" she questioned. "Mel Gibson, or someone else perhaps?"

The silence felt deafening, and all eyes rested curiously on Lottie.

Lottie squirmed with discomfort but taking a deep breath she answered. "Well, I mean, well goodness! What I mean is that I'm on the other boat really, so it would probably be Sue Perkins."

Wynona's eyes narrowed. Lottie was aware that Wynona was deciding whether this was a joke or whether they truly did have a big hairy lesbian in their midst.

"Well!" Wynona let that hang in silence for a moment as she scanned the room for responses from the group.

All remained quiet, although Lottie detected at least one face which registered interested surprise at her brave coming out.

Wynona, keen to maintain the easy conversation that had been developing so well eventually responded. "I have to say that Sue is a dahrrrling! Now then, ladies, who would you fancy if you were picking a woman?"

Lottie cringed. Oh God, please! They were not all going to pretend to have girl crushes to make her feel included, were they? And yes indeed, that's exactly what they did.

There followed a two-minute stretch of increasingly uncomfortable conversation where the women took it in turn to be totally cool with the idea of a crush on a female celebrity.

Lottie tried to smile along as Jo Brand and Germaine Greer were ranked in terms of their fitness—*really*? These were straight women with truly grim taste in women, Lottie was quickly concluding.

The unsavoury discussion was brought to an abrupt end as Archie burst into the living room, looking distraught, followed by a gaggle of giddy girls. Lottie looked him up and down, struggling to identify what was different about him.

His face was creased with stress, and then the smell hit Lottie, as she saw that he was dripping wet from head to toe. Holding out his hands towards Lottie he was struggling to fight back tears.

Lou pushed forward towards the front of the group and crowed loudly. "Archie fell in the pond, eurrghh!"

Between giggles she chanted out. "Pondweed Archie, Pondweed Archie!" A chant which soon turned into a chorus, "kissing the fishes, kissing the fishes!"

Archie hung his head.

Shamefully glad of an excuse to bolt, which momentarily clouded her concern for Archie and his own social ineptness, Lottie swept him towards the door.

"Oh dear, how dreadful. Let's hope the fish are okay. Come on, Archie, let's get you home!"

ON THE DRIVE home, Lottie recovered her motherly concern and commiserated with Archie on his clumsiness, while silently ruminating on her own outing.

She hoped that Archie wouldn't lose all of his social standing following one mishap. She, on the other hand, would no doubt be the topic of many a conversation between now and when they discovered that Archie's other new friend's dad was newly single. She had to bank on the fact that the gossip mill of senior education would not be as brutally efficient as the ruthless fact-keeping memories that the primary school mums had the time to cultivate.

Archie looked at her forlornly, and her self-indulgent ruminations were put aside as she tried to offer him ineffectual platitudes followed by a swift trip home via fast food drive-thru.

While they both morosely contemplated their limp burgers, Lottie decided that it was probably not the appropriate moment to confess to Archie that she may have accidentally damaged his chances of a repeat invitation to his new friend's house, in spite of his own pond escapades.

In reality, she felt very frustrated about her own innate need for truth and authenticity. She was beginning to think that honesty was overrated and that she ought to pay more attention to the bigger picture. After all, what harm was there is being a closet gay? All that she saw at this moment were the advantages. Why make others uncomfortable in her own quest to rectify the balance of her years in the closet?

In so many situations she had faced this dilemma, where people had assumed that she was heterosexual, thus forcing her to either collude or to make some sort of statement. This had been the bane of her life since coming out.

Initially, she had gone all out to try and wear an obviously lesbian wardrobe in order to make her status obvious. However, after a mammoth splurge in the men's department of Debenhams she had reached the sad conclusion that her post-children body was not flattered by the slim-waisted clothing of the average male. Likewise, the high necks of men's T-shirts did nothing to help her manage her obsession with her second chin. Following her failed make-over she had gone with a more obvious embellishment, obtaining a discreet tattoo on her wrist. Yet still, all this time later, it would appear that she was still not an obvious dyke.

Reaching across the table, she patted Archie's hand, as he looked up forlornly, and forced a smile. "Looks like I'll have to find myself some more friends tomorrow, Mum," he said.

Lottie smiled at him. "You and me both, Archie."

Unexpected Departures

SILENTLY CURSING, LOTTIE rubbed her sore knees and readjusted her position. For the past one-and-a-half hours, she had been crawling around her sitting room floor trying to work how three of the kittens, presumably led by Stripe, had found their way into the inside structure of the sofa, and wondering how to retrieve them. She only knew they were in there because she had completed three separate head counts. Missing were two of his more gullible followers who were now making their presence known from the depths of the sofa with a constant round of pitiful mewling. Stripe, on the other hand, was silent. Lottie knew that without his influence, she could easily coax out the other two with the leftovers of Sunday's beef. She wasn't too keen however, on putting her hand into the black abyss where, in the base of the sofa she had eventually discovered the entry point of the trio.

So far she had attempted soft entreaties, cross instructions, and morsels of beef at the entrance point. All to no avail. She knew she was fighting against the clock, as Archie would be home at any minute, and at which point, her attempts to keep the sofa intact would be futile, as he would insist upon immediate disassembling of the furniture to provide a swiftly executed rescue.

Lottie was quite fond of her furniture. Although worn and a bit tatty, it had survived two children and numerous house moves in the early days of her single life, not to mention the fonder memories of her earlier forays into gay dating, where many a virgin fumble had been had late at night on that same sofa. An involuntary smile momentarily passed her lips before she gave herself a stern telling off, and instructions to get back to the task in hand.

Her mission of mercy was disturbed by a loud rapping on the front door. Glad of the distraction, she carefully straightened her aching limbs and hobbled in an ungainly fashion to open the door. A gust of cold autumnal air took her breath away, and she was reminded of the changing weather. On the doorstep stood the postman, and in his outstretched hand he clutched a small parcel, with the unmistakeable handwriting of her absent father. Thanking him, she took the parcel and put it on the side table.

Her father had an untraditional view of the world, and parenthood for that matter. Predominantly because he viewed it from the bottom of a bottle of whisky. Only the finest Scotch whisky of course, she reminded herself with a wry smile. He did, however, have a knack of picking the most exquisite keepsakes on his travels, which she regularly received in the post.

The past month, after his post had finally caught up with her, he had sent his congratulations on their engagement by way of a deer antler that had been inscribed with an ancient wedding poem. Alice baulked at the idea of displaying it in the house, but Lottie had found it thoughtful. It was currently gracing the utility room wall, hopefully serving as a reminder to Boots of what his fate could be if he continued to cause trouble.

Crouching to resume her search, she noticed that the mewling had mysteriously stopped. She dropped fully onto her knees once again, and urgently inserted her hand into the dark hole. Feeling a warm furry bundle, she extricated the first, and then the second of the two kittens. She felt a warm glow that her valiant efforts had paid off. With trepidation, she inserted her hand for the third time, wincing in anticipation of an ungrateful reminder from Stripe that he did not need her feeble rescue attempts. Feeling around in the empty cavity she discovered a small coin and a toothpick, but no Stripe. Sweeping more bravely, she reached deeper into the sofa's interior. Despite her dislike of him, she hoped that Stripe hadn't come to any harm. Feeling the creep of a mild panic, she sat back on her heels to re-evaluate. Maybe he'd found another way out. Her foot cramped, and as she turned to stretch it out, she jumped out of her skin!

Sitting behind her was Stripe, casually grooming his face with one large paw, and standing behind him was Boots.

"How the bloody hell did you get out?" she bawled at the unfazed cat who moved forward slightly, to sit in silent allegiance with his prodigy, Stripe. Together the pair silently eyeballed her. What was it that she saw glinting in their scarily similar gray eyes? It looked like glee, or possibly just a cool disdain. Trying to maintain a semblance of dignity, she stared determinedly back at them, but she couldn't shake the feeling she was staring into the eyes of a feline version of the Kray twins. In perfect unison, both rose to their feet, turned smartly on their paws and swept out of the room, as if her mere presence was a source of utter boredom. Lottie mentally noted that she *must* get around to putting an advert into the paper to rehome the furry nightmares. She knew Archie would protest, but she also knew that the house would be completely destroyed if she did nothing.

Lottie sighed in despair, but her ruminations were interrupted as Archie burst through the door and threw his bag carelessly to the floor.

"Mum, right, you are not going to believe what happened to Jason today! Mum! Are you listening? You can't even make this stuff up!"

At the sound of Archie's voice, Odie bounded into the room, knocking the package off the side table. Lottie suddenly felt an unexplained chill run up and down her spine.

"Mum! What's wrong? You're all pink-looking! You've made a right mess in here!"

Archie scooped up Odie, who had stretched to his full length, trembling with excitement at the return of a saner member of the family. Lunging earnestly at Archie's pink cheeks, Odie managed to get in one or two welcoming licks before he was roughly deposited onto the sofa, as Archie spotted the parcel.

"Oooh, a parcel from Grandad. Cool! Let's open it!"

Lottie smiled, despite the oddity of the usual contents of these parcels and the lack of formal contact with her father, Archie greeted a communication from him with all the innocent enthusiasm that his years commanded. Without waiting for permission, he tore the top layer of the brown paper, but Lottie halted his eager progress swooping the half-opened package from his hands.

"Come on, Archie, you know I always have to see what Grandad has sent us first. It's the rules!"

Archie's face crumpled in disappointment. "I don't understand why, Mum. I know he sends weird stuff but it's always so funny!"

Lottie couldn't help but agree.

Since her father had set off when she was only thirteen, for what turned out to be decades of wandering, she had periodically missed having a more traditional father figure. Despite that, she couldn't help but admire his single-minded, selfish, and yet determined approach to take advantage of life and the open road. His travels were assisted by the purchase of a small motorhome which he had proudly displayed on Facebook. In her younger years she'd had many odd parcels and postcards from various exotic locations. The longest he had been out of contact with her was for three months in the late eighties, when he had abandoned the safety of his motorhome for an adventure aboard a freight ship bound for Russia. Typically, he hadn't fully considered the implications of international politics on his travels, but he had eventually been allowed to return to the UK courtesy of the foreign office who had confiscated his passport for a period of two months in an attempt to curtail his meandering.

Archie implored Lottie to be allowed to open the package, and she eventually relented, handing it to him.

After removing the inner wrapping of the parcel, his face crumpled with disappointment.

"Mum? Why has Grandad sent his watch and his lucky rabbit's foot to us?"

Lottie's knees gave out beneath her, and a wail escaped her lips. Silently, she reached out to take the plastic container into her hands, where she pulled from underneath her father's prized belongings a note. His unmistakeable grandiose scrawl stretched out on the page.

Sensing the gravity of the situation, Archie silently pulled his mum to her feet and guided her towards the only piece of undisturbed furniture, a large and solid wooden rocker.

Her hand shook ever so slightly as she silently read her father's words:

Sweetheart,

If you're now in possession of the rabbit's foot, you'll know that my luck has run out. I always said that when my journey ended I would go out with a bang and not a fizzle. Well, my darling, it seems this is the end of the road for me. I won't bore you with the details, but I've been diagnosed with the Big C and it's seriously curtailed my preferred lifestyle. I don't want to linger on and I don't want long and painful goodbyes. My time is up and that is that, it's simple. I've made my own funeral arrangements, a wicker coffin and a nice pine tree will see me off nicely and it'll all be a done deal by the time you get this box. No lining the pockets of those robbing funeral directors!

Captain Tom from the pub promised a delay on the posting of this as I just don't want you having to deal with all that post death nonsense. He's taken care of everything and you'll be receiving an inheritance of sorts in due course. I sent a letter to your siblings too, so don't worry, you don't have to make that

awful round of phone calls. You'll be upset of
course, but I lived my life to the full and I
have absolutely no regrets. Give my watch to
Robbie and the rabbit's foot to Archie—it really
is lucky you know. Put this letter in the file
and raise a glass of Scotland's finest to me,
and then move on with your life.

Love as always,
Pops xx

The letter slipped from Lottie's hand, and a solitary tear
rolled down her cheek.

"Is he dead?" Archie's tremulous question brought her back
to the present.

She nodded, and Archie reached out to take her hand. Softly
stroking the underside in a childish gesture to comfort her, he
began to cry.

LATER THAT EVENING, after Alice had made tea and Lottie
had commiserated with her siblings and her mother, who was
surprisingly upset, Alice had distracted Archie, while Robbie
dealt with other phone calls.

Finally alone, the pair sat quietly in the kitchen nursing a
glass of Glenfiddich whisky apiece. Lottie's eyes were swollen to
small slits, and a red tinge edged her delicate nose. Alice had
established that Lottie's father had indeed considered everything
in arranging his funeral, as well as the disposal of his few
belongings, nominating old Tom as his next of kin for the
registration of his death.

Although she appreciated her father's attempts to protect her
from the inevitable practicalities of his death, Lottie felt strangely
bereft of anything practical to do. She stroked the rim of her glass
and stared absent-mindedly at the faded floral pattern of the
plastic tablecloth. Alice gently caught her finger tips and
diligently kissed each one in turn. A single tear slipped down
Lottie's swollen cheek. Letting go of Lottie's hand, Alice sighed
gently as she wiped the solitary tear trail away with the tip of a
tissue.

Lottie managed a half smile, grateful for the tenderness of
Alice's obvious loving care in her distress.

"I know this may seem like totally the wrong time, Lots, but
hear me out, would you?"

Lottie caught her breath, but sensitive to the serious tone of Alice's plea, she cleared her throat and tried to give her full attention.

Alice shifted her chair closer to Lottie's in an attempt to remove the visible space between them. She reached around Lottie's waist and scooped towards her, meeting no resistance, until Lottie was sitting gingerly on Alice's knee. Lottie curled up instinctively towards the comfort of her body and rested her hot cheek in the nook of Alice's neck.

"This is what I want to say to you. Just listen, okay?"

Lottie nodded, a tired sign of assent. Assured that she could safely continue, Alice protectively curled her arm around Lottie's waist and caught the edge of Lottie's forearm which she stroked, absent-mindedly.

"Your dad lived his life to the full. He travelled, he drank, and he undoubtedly met a lady or two along the way."

Lottie harrumphed with discomfort at the idea of her father and his possible indiscretions.

Alice continued undeterred. "The point is, Lots, that your dad loved you in his own unique way. He loved your boys and he will be missed, even if he has not always been physically present."

She paused as Lottie looked towards her questioningly.

"You might not be able to appreciate it now, Lottie, but your dad didn't want you to have to deal with all the horror that death brings. He did as much as he possibly could to minimise the impact on you. You can see that, can't you?"

Lottie slowly nodded agreement and Alice continued. "I know you're feeling a little lost, but I think I know what could help you get through this. Let's get on and get the wedding planned. Let's have a positive focus to the future, and then let's raise a glass of the finest whisky to your dad on the day. How about it?"

Lottie's face flooded with fresh tears. "Okay." she said feebly, and Alice stooped to place a tender kiss on her warm forehead.

THE NEXT MORNING, Lottie was still in bed. Alice had slipped away to catch up with work at the surgery and to check on Mr. Dutton's cocker spaniel, who was struggling to recover following his neutering operation. A dull thudding permeated Lottie's semi-conscious state, an after-effect of the crying which she had thought would never end. Odie raised an ear and began a low growl. Lottie rolled, and pulled the duvet up over her head, swatting feebly at the dog who moved to poke a head out of the sheets.

The dull thud took on a more insistent tone, and she heard Robbie emerge from his man cave and take the stairs three at a time. Convinced the dull thudding of the door knocker must be his new FIFA game being delivered, he eagerly swung the door open, only to be greeted by a rugged looking man who proffered a set of car keys.

Confused, Robbie hesitantly reached out and took the keys. The man winked and tipped his plaid cap before disappearing down the path. As he closed the gate, Robbie caught a glimpse of a bright yellow motorhome.

He looked down at the keys in his hand and attached to the ring was a yellow motorhome keyring.

"Mum!" he shouted.

Groaning, Lottie dragged herself out of bed and gingerly made her way down the stairs.

Robbie, dropped the keys onto the kitchen table, shrugged and loped back to his bedroom muttering. "Weirdo...keys...van."

Lottie fingered the keys absent-mindedly, as a wry smile spread slowly across her face.

"Oh, Dad," she sighed.

Picking up the keys, she stepped lightly out of the front door and her smile widened as she was greeted by the fluorescent camper. Emblazoned across its derrière was her father's favourite saying:

```
It doesn't matter if the glass is half empty or
half full. There is clearly room for more
alcohol!
```

Squealing with excitement, she headed towards the van and wrestled with the stiff lock. Clambering aboard, she was greeted with the familiar smell of stale whisky and cigarettes which she closely associated with her father. Stepping over the boxes of clothing and the travel magazines, Lottie caught her breath as she saw the dent in the bed where her father had probably spent his final hours.

Sinking onto the small seating area, Lottie silently surveyed the van.

She picked up a stack of unopened letters which had been rerouted several times around the country.

Amongst the unopened mail, she noticed an envelope addressed to herself and Alice.

Carefully tearing open the thin envelope, she pulled out a single sheet of paper. The handwriting, she noticed, was shaky and she silently cringed, sure that this was indicative of the pain that her father must have experienced before he died.

```
Sweetie,

     Only your old Pops again. Hopefully Captain
Tom delivered the van for you. She's called One
For the Road, look after her! A parting gift for
you and Alice, call it an early wedding present.
Sorry I couldn't be there to give you away at
your wedding, but you know, my girl, it would
only have been a boozier affair with me there. I
loved this van, it took me to places I'd never
have seen otherwise, and I met such a colourful
bunch along the way. By the way, if Captain Tom
is still around, give him a whisky and send him
on his way. He's a lovely fella but tends to
outstay his welcome. I know the van will need a
good clean, but I'm hoping you'll keep the old
girl going and have some adventures of your own.
Marriage is an adventure, full of ups and downs,
but enjoy the quiet times, too. I messed it up
big time with your mum, it's my only regret.
Your time is here now, and Alice will be by your
side. Raise a glass to me, would you? Oh, and I
think there's a mouse somewhere in the top bunk,
best to get rid of that before the boys take a
ride with you!

Lots and lots of love,
Pops xx
```

Lottie chuckled as she recalled her father's tall tales about Captain Tom, named as such because of his successful career as a bank robber. She remembered her father proudly recounting his reign of terror in the southern counties, halted only by having to confess to a robbery in order to avoid being done for a murder which he hadn't committed. After a ten year stretch in prison in Aberdeen, he had retired from the business, but still continued to provide much entertainment to her dad and his drinking cronies.

Lottie smiled as she pulled the worn duvet around her and

inhaled its musty smell. She surveyed the crowded interior of the van, memories of her father flooding her mind.

She remembered trips they had taken in happier times when, as a young girl, her parents had been contented and family holidays had been a time for laughter and fun. Usually they had involved a tent. A large family, their best memories all consisted of camp fires and long games of *Monopoly*. She smiled ruefully. With hindsight, she realised that the trips had probably been hard work for her mum, as she had struggled to cater for the family with primitive cooking equipment and the incessant rain and mosquitos which were familiar visitors to most Scottish campsites. Not to mention her father's frequent disappearing acts to local drinking holes.

Gently pulling the duvet over the conspicuous dip in the old mattress, she swallowed her pain and vowed to make the most of this posthumous gift from her father. She was determined that with Alice and the boys, she would rise to the challenge of a camping adventure next spring as soon as the weather got warmer, and she revelled in the unexpected opportunity that her father had gifted to her.

Best Woman Duties

A FEW DAYS later, and desperate for distraction, Lottie reluctantly went to work. She ran the gauntlet of the call centre, and Alicia threw her a sympathetic glance and patted the desk space next to her as an indication that Lottie should join her. Glad of the friendly gesture, as others avoided eye contact with her, Lottie guessed that her boss Ann had spread the news of her father's death.

As if on cue, Ann appeared in the doorway of her office.

"Lottie, a word please," she said, squeaking a little too perkily.

Lottie reluctantly dragged herself into the shuttered room, where she noticed that the wedding photo of Ann and Greg had disappeared, to be replaced by a larger photo oozing with the blatant sexual vibes of a topless dark-skinned man.

Noticing that Lottie was looking at the picture, Ann became giddy. "Oh, now of course you won't know about my Arzum, will you?"

Without waiting for a response, she grabbed the ornate frame and thrust it into Lottie's face, where her nose met with his very obvious trouser bulge. Lottie tried to avert her eyes, feeling that she may now know too much about the bronzed alpha male, and unpleasant images crowded her mind.

Ann chatted on, distracted from her original intention in summoning Lottie. Deciding that this wasn't going to be a quick word as she'd hoped, Lottie resignedly sat down in the visitor's chair, which was deliberately set lower in order to give Ann height advantage during meetings.

She struggled to focus on Ann's mundane chatter.

"So anyway, it was only my first day in Marmaris and I was just getting a drink from the bar, when Arzum accidentally stood on my foot. I turned around with the intention of giving him a mouthful but, well..." giggling, she turned a shade of pink. "Instead it was me that got the mouthful, if you know what I mean!"

Lottie inhaled in complete trauma. Please, God, don't let her go into the gory details of her sordid encounter!

Leaning in, Ann mouthed incredulously. "Four times! I came four times!"

"Oh." Lottie managed, as she shifted to remove her face from the crotch of Ann's holiday conquest.

Stroking the photo absent-mindedly, Ann appeared lost in her own thoughts.

"When I read the cards, they told me, they really did!" said Ann, referring to her well-known preference for all things mystical.

Lottie was all too aware that a large part of Ann's social life consisted of visiting spiritualists and mediums, whom she considered her colleagues in the world of the psychic, as she also considered herself to be gifted in this area.

Lottie cleared her throat and Ann seemed to become present again.

"Did you want me for something?" Lottie enquired.

"Ah, yes. I just wanted to say I was so sorry to hear about your father. Alicia told me the sad news. Dreadful losing a parent — part of life though, eh?"

Glad that Alicia has pre-empted the inevitable platitudes from her work colleagues by telling Ann, Lottie found comfort in the kindness of her thoughtful friend.

"Err, yes." Lottie replied dutifully.

"Well, anyway, Lottie, I've let that bunch outside know. Nothing worse than having to spread the news yourself. Hope that's okay?"

Lottie nodded.

"Very well. Anyway, work's a good way to lose yourself for a bit, so let's get to it. Those adverts won't frame themselves, will they?" She gave Lottie a patronising pat on the shoulder.

Glad to escape, Lottie nodded in assent and silently reminded herself to try and upsell at least one advert including a white-spaced border in order to keep the psychic cougar off her back.

Slipping into her seat opposite Alicia, she switched on her monitor.

An internal message alert popped up from her friend Virginia.

```
Hey mate, so sorry about your dad. Here if you
need to talk, V xx
```

Alicia pushed a post note under her nose.

```
I'll do the In Memoriam adverts this week xx
```

Lottie shot her a grateful smile.

Leonard gave her an awkward nod as he passed but seemed to have developed some sensitivity in the situation and didn't attempt to engage her in any salacious conversation.

Lottie sank her head into her hands. Everything had been so happy, and now this.

Angrily, she logged onto her computer and took calls on autopilot. She plugged away at her keyboard, racking her brain for how she could turn the clock back to happier times.

Without warning, Lottie felt a warm pair of arms around her neck, holding her in a stiff embrace. A cloud of perfume which she remembered well from the nineties overwhelmed her, and she felt wet kisses on the back of her neck. Struggling to break free and getting tangled in her headset, she turned in irritation to meet the distraught eyes of Linda Lovely, streaks of mascara running down her cheeks.

"My God, Linda! Are you okay?" Lottie voiced genuine concern.

Linda snorted loudly, and Lottie almost gagged as she watched a trail of snot disappear back into her right nostril.

Trying to gather herself, and fanning her face wildly with a cardboard folder, Linda gulped. "Oh, it's just dreadful, Lottie. Just dreadful!"

Lottie nodded sympathetically and pulled up an empty chair onto which Linda collapsed dramatically, continuing to fan frantically. Sniffing loudly, she leaned into Lottie and planted a kiss squarely on the side of her nose, before stroking her face.

Lottie breathed deeply and gently rubbed Linda's knee as sympathetically as she could muster given that it was *her* who had had the loss.

Linda clutched her hand gratefully. "I haven't slept since I heard, Lottie. I mean it's just a *tragedy*. Such loss!"

Lottie stroked her hand kindly. "Oh Linda, I'm so sorry you've taken this so badly, but you know, well my dad was a bit of a drinker. It was fairly inevitable he'd go at some point."

Linda nodded frantically, obviously trying to take comfort from Lottie's words. "Well yes. Of course, he must have died as he lived, a hero."

Hardly, Lottie thought with some sarcasm, but she nodded along hoping to allay this very public display of emotion that she had been so keen to avoid.

Virginia appeared behind Linda, rolling her eyes and mopping invisible sweat from her brow. Lottie took the escape route offered to her.

"Thanks so much for your concern, Linda, but I need to go on my break now. V's here."

Linda swivelled on her chair, eyeing Virginia with mistrust. "Hmm, yes, well it helps to have something to take your mind off things I'm sure. Make sure you have some sugar and get some cake. That will help you keep your strength up."

Lottie was on her feet when suddenly Linda shrieked. "Oh no, oh *NO!*"

Lottie waited.

"The wedding, oh Lottie, the wedding! I expect we'll have to postpone it!"

"*We?*" Virginia mouthed rolling her eyes again.

Lottie drew in a sharp breath, and, struggling to hide her irritation she stated firmly. "Absolutely not, Linda. My dad would not have wanted that. In fact, Alice and I have decided to go ahead and get the arrangements sorted. You have a hen night to organise!"

Virginia and Alicia exchanged a look of horror. The words fell out of Lottie's mouth and a silent scream reverberated around her brain.

No, No, *No!* Don't ask Linda to organise the hen do!

Linda clutched at her ample bosom. "Me? You want *me* to start to arrange the hen do? That means I must be your best woman!"

With renewed sobbing, she threw herself into Lottie's arms

Lottie panicked as the horror of the situation dawned on her. Alice was going to kill her! While she'd never met Linda Lovely, she had heard all about her and Lottie was sure that this was not the sort of hen night that Alice was likely to want.

Linda pushed Lottie to one side, instantly discarded, as she rummaged around to find a notebook, ideas already running through her head.

"Charlotte, leave it with me, leave it all with me. Don't even think about it! Your best woman is on the job!"

Virginia giggled. "That's right, Lots, you're in safe hands now, that's for sure! Come on, that slab of lemon cake won't eat itself."

This was met with a steely glare from Linda, as she cast her final words to Lottie's retreating back, "Waistline! Remember the dress!"

Lottie and Virginia barely made it around the corner of the office before collapsing into hysterical laughter. "*Dress!*" they both screamed simultaneously.

Tears streamed down Lottie's face. "Oh Lord, what have I done?"

The pair giggled their way into a more private corner of the cafeteria. Virginia looked with concern at Lottie and enquired how she was.

Fighting back the real sadness that choked her every time she thought about her dad, she confided in Virginia how difficult the past few days had been as she'd attempted to negotiate with her difficult siblings about the sort of tribute they would like to have for their father. Her mum had eventually declined to return from abroad, telling Lottie that she had tried to move on with her life following her abandonment by her estranged husband. She told Lottie that, while she appreciated the upset her children were experiencing, they were all adults and capable of managing this for themselves.

Lottie was more than a little perturbed by her mother's subsequent cold-hearted approach to the situation, but then she supposed that she hadn't lived with her father as a partner and had not experienced the constant and bitter disappointment which that experience had inevitably brought to her mother. The responses of her brother and sister had been generally impassive. Although each had received their own version of the letter, along with mementos from their father, each had stated a general consensus of opinion that he had given little consideration for their needs as children, and that they felt inclined to treat his departure as unexpected, but not entirely unsurprising, given his chosen lifestyle.

Virginia nodded and listened sympathetically, as Lottie unburdened herself of the unfolding events.

Taking her hand, she counselled her. "Babe, how awful for you. I suppose everyone's had their own experiences of your pop. Why don't you concentrate on what *you* want to do to celebrate his life, and let them do it their way?"

This sensible suggestion from her kind friend immediately resonated with Lottie. After all, who was she to dictate the way other people grieve? Giving up on the idea of a forced family ceremony, she resolved instead to honour her father's memory in a way she knew he would approve—by having a short trip in the campervan, in due course, with her own family.

Willy Hoopla

FROM BEHIND THE heavy purple velour curtain of the department-store changing room, Lottie struggled to remove the red dress that she had been cajoled into trying on by the overexcited Linda Lovely. Against her better judgement, she had been persuaded into a girly shopping trip to find a suitable outfit for her hen night. After a confession to Alice about Linda Lovely's new role, Alice had reassured her that she would not have to go it alone, and a joint hen do was duly confirmed. Despite Alice's reassurances, Lottie was concerned about the expectations of her friends and colleagues, who clearly had no idea what a gay hen do was likely to entail.

At a pre-hen do gathering the previous evening, Lottie and Alice had gathered their friends for what turned out to be several bottles of prosecco, and a lengthy discussion about the type of evening they were hoping to have.

Linda Lovely, the self-appointed officiant of all things wedding could barely contain her excitement as she produced her heart covered notebook and proceeded to trawl through a list of unsuitable venues, which included a spa, and a booze cruise to Amsterdam. Seeing Alice's patience rapidly waning, Lottie had rashly agreed to a follow-up lunch with Linda and the gang to find an outfit, and hopefully steer the evening towards a more realistic version of the event she and Alice had hoped for.

Lottie was quickly beginning to regret the shopping trip though, as detecting a whiff of her own body odour, she hastily rummaged through her bag for her rescue deodorant which she always carried for emergencies such as these. Usually it was only required following a particularly stressful supervision meeting with Ann, or a painful group meeting with Pru, but more recently she had found she was replacing it with some frequency as the impending nuptials approached.

From behind the velour curtain, the noise of her entourage's chatter was increasing to an almost unbearable high-pitched cacophony. She strained to hear the discussion of the hen do conspirators, but she could only make out snatches of the conversation. She was horrified to hear discussion of hen do games and she was sure she heard mention of a stripper. Surely not! Her gentle perspiration was transforming into full-on body odour and she fished out a packet of anti-bacterial wipes stretching to reach the innermost recess of her especially shaved armpits.

Suddenly, a loud ripping sound brought her attention starkly to the seam of the red dress she had poured herself into. With dismay she noted an obvious tear to the seam. Hastily struggling to exit the garment she caught sight of the price tag, £159.99.

"Fuck!" she muttered.

"Everything okay in there, lovey?" the anxious voice of Linda Lovely drifted along to the changing room.

"Oh yes. All tickety-boo, just tickety-boo, Linda," Lottie attempted to inject her voice with the required amount of cheer.

Tickety-fucking-boo? Where did that come from? Lottie fumed as she struggled into the next overly-feminine outfit, and hurriedly replaced the damaged garment on the hanger behind the previous six dresses that had failed to make it into the top two.

Silently, she willed expedition dress to be through, and plotted a swift exit from the shop before the eager shop assistant had time to assess the damage.

Struggling to walk in the fishtail dress that she had carelessly chosen, Lottie swore once again under her breath, as she perfected a shuffle towards her waiting crowd, turning the corner to a collective gasp of delight at her feminine attire, as her excited wedding groupies took it in turns to paw the material, simultaneously spinning her in a circle that nearly knocked her off balance.

Continuing to turn uncomfortably under the glare of this unexpected spotlight, she caught Mel's eye. Noting the look of bemusement that crossed her face, before she caught herself and adopted a dutiful smile. Lottie was fully aware this related to the fact that for the past hour she had been trying on a range of the shop's finest dress. She had been friends with Mel long enough to know that her quizzical expression related to her confusion about Lottie's intention to wear a dress to the hen do.

Mel had long been aware of Lottie's desire to fit in, despite her inevitable discomfort at the thought of a night out with a gaggle of female divas in heels and dresses. This had been the driving factor behind her sudden interest in all things floral. But as their silent interchange played out, Lottie shrugged ruefully at her dear friend and her plea for support was duly acknowledged.

Mel jumped to attention and declared in an authoritative voice. "Enough dresses, Lots. I think we need to revisit this at lunch. Come on, girls, let's hit the pub!"

Grateful for Mel's instant understanding, and suitable distraction technique, Lottie painfully waddled back to the changing room, taking half the time to shed the hideous article before gathering up her less-than-helpful entourage as they headed to the pub for much needed sustenance, during which she hoped to persuade her well-meaning friends into a more realistic venue and hen do outfit. Gap, or possibly just a new pair of Converse had been her original thoughts.

Determined to quash any further discussion about strippers or horrendous *Willy Hoopla* games, she cornered Linda Lovely to ask her advice about possible hairdos for the wedding. Linda, undeterred by Lottie's short hair, and therefore the limited opportunities for embellishments, was easily distracted.

MANY HOURS LATER — it had seemed like a lifetime — the amicable crew parted ways to return back to their individual corners of the Scottish Highlands. Lottie was in a trance-like state as she loitered uncomfortably on the train station platform, juggling her rash purchases with a heavy bag of hen do favours, which included sombrero hats, an acceptable alternative to the penis hats that had been the group's first choice. Her cheeks ached from the fake smile she had adopted throughout the entire proceedings, grateful for the support of her friends, but equally mortified by the horror of the evening that she must now explain to Alice.

A buzz in her pocket alerted her to an incoming message and checking her phone, she noticed a text from Alice who, thankfully, wanted to tell her that she wouldn't be home until the small hours of the morning as Mr. McDonald's herd of Highland cows had been struck down with a mystery virus. Lottie knew from experience that Alice would remain with the animals until she was assured that each and every one was pain free. Her dedication to her profession was one of the many things that Lottie admired about Alice. She was also glad that the boy's trip to their father's that weekend meant that her limited culinary skills would not be required. It would give her time to hide the hideous sombreros until she mustered up the courage to do a sales job on Alice. This was going to be a two-bottle-of-prosecco conversation, she felt. Typing out a quick reply, as she could hear the train approaching, she returned her phone to the limitless depths of her bag and struggled to adjust the heavier of the carrier bags onto one arm as she hurriedly boarded the train.

Finally seated, she took a moment to ensure that her cumbersome purchases were tucked safely out of the way. She fervently hoped for a few moments of silence before a fellow traveller joined her on the adjacent seat. Congratulating herself on her luck at getting a seat on the busy Saturday train, she closed her eyes for a moment and tried to dispel the inevitable images of fishtail dresses from her mind. She soothed her fraught nerves with a renewed focus on the rhythmic rocking of the train as it sailed towards her destination and the comfort of home.

WAKING WITH A start, Lottie realised that she must have drifted off, but for how long? She panicked as she grappled with the contents of her bag to retrieve her phone in order to see the time. As she rummaged endlessly feeling for the comforting shape of her phone, she was somewhat confused by the dimness which surrounded her. Adjusting her sleep-laden eyes, she searched outside for a familiar landmark, but all she saw was her own panicked reflection in the darkness.

With a rising sense of foreboding, she located the phone, 21.38 it reported back to her efficiently.

"Oh hell!" she said aloud, shocked to realise she had now been on the train for nearly three hours. The emotions evoked by the hetero-shopping experience had clearly taken a significant toll on her mentally, and she'd fallen into a deep slumber.

Glancing around, she noticed the only other occupant of the carriage was a fraught mother with her three small offspring. Abandoning her bags, Lottie lurched along the rocking train until she reached them. Clearing her throat to get her fellow passenger's attention, she politely enquired of her. "Excuse me, please could you tell me where we are?"

The woman briefly halted her tirade of wrath towards her sullen elder son to look Lottie up and down with barely disguised derision. "Too much pop at lunchtime, love? We're nearly at Newcastle!"

Lottie fell into the nearest seat noting the lilt of her Newcastle accent. "*Newcastle?*" she repeated pointlessly.

Not bothering to reaffirm the information, the mother hoisted the youngest of her three children onto her lap and attended to the gloop of snot that trailed from his nose across his flushed right cheek.

Lottie looked around. How on earth had she managed to fall

asleep for three hours and end up in bloody Newcastle? Staggering her way towards the front of the train she frantically searched for the conductor. She happened upon him in the final carriage, alone and horizontal, clearly capitalising on the opportunity for a mid-shift snooze.

He snorted loudly, as if sensing her presence and bolted into an upright position. "Yes, pet, yes, just checking the springs in this here seat. There've been complaints. Now you're awake, I'll get your ticket please!"

Assuming an authoritative tone, he thrust his stubby hand towards her demanding she produce her ticket. Fumbling in her pocket for her ticket she feebly produced it.

After close examination, his brow furrowed. "Pet, you're on the wrong train!"

Lottie gritted her teeth. No shit, Sherlock, she fumed inwardly.

Fearing an immediate ejection from the train at a station unknown, she did the only thing she knew how. A pathetic mewling cry escaped her lips, mustering all the misery she could find proved not to be that difficult and a solitary tear slipped seamlessly from her lashes and trailed pitifully down her cheek.

"I know!" she stated the obvious and threw herself on his mercy.

Stirred by the sight of this feeble female, the conductor's tone became less official and he patted her arm anxiously, keen to avoid having a full-blown episode of a crying female on his hands. Despite the absence of an audience, he concluded that they simply did not pay him enough to deal with a traveller who couldn't get on the right train.

After a short and perfunctory discussion, Lottie elicited the facts thus far. She had got on the wrong train in her hurry to reply to Alice's text, she was now a mere twenty minutes from her unintended destination of Newcastle, and she was to be evicted at that station. The placating conductor was keen to assure her, however, that this was in fact the end of the line in any event. A few more tears and the use of the chest clutching feminine wiles elicited that there was in fact a connecting train which would return her to her starting point in precisely three hours and twenty minutes. Resigning herself to the cost of a taxi from the station at the other end, she thanked him profusely and returned to her abandoned bags, silently cursing the waste of her Saturday.

Settling back into her seat, she distracted herself with

Facebook, determined not to fall back to sleep. Soon the train pulled into Newcastle Station and the less ruffled and more alert conductor officiously informed her that she could remain in her seat once she had paid, as this was the service she required on her return journey. Begrudgingly, she fished out her emergency credit card and paid the eighty-nine pounds required to secure her trip home.

When the conductor passed by, he was shoved into the empty seats across from her as a brood of loud, brash middle-aged women descended upon the carriage. Turning with renewed interest, she observed the mayhem that accompanied the noise, but she was soon horrified to discover that a hen party had boarded. Oblivious to anyone blocking their way, they elbowed relentlessly forward and passed Lottie diving onto the four seats and a table at the front of the carriage that they had obviously identified as theirs from the platform. Lottie unconsciously clenched her jaw as she rummaged around frantically for her headphones, intent on blocking out what she knew would be the inevitable shrill tones of the rambunctious women.

The train pulled out of the station, headed in the correct direction this time. The noise reached an intolerable level as the women swayed precariously, attempting to readjust their tight clothing before rustling through countless carrier bags to produce a cheap bottle of red wine. She noticed that between two of the smaller women was a blow-up male doll with an oversized appendage.

Noting her interest, a large woman wearing a hen sash chuckled. "Meet Geoff, love, or as we prefer to call him Geoff Big Bollocks," Grabbling the neck of the doll she created a mock bow before the group descended into raucous laughter.

Smiling weakly, Lottie swiftly retreated behind the headrest as her cheeks flamed red. She was mortified to be caught observing their outing, but could not curb her curiosity about the group, who were clearly hell-bent on creating an authentic heterosexual hen do.

Good God! Why on earth is *that* considered fun?

Gradually, as they headed out into the dark countryside, the train picked up considerable momentum, thankfully headed for home and the respite of the Highlands. Lottie was painfully aware though that the return leg of her journey was likely to be less peaceful than her journey south had been. Turning her thoughts towards her own hen do, only a week away, she decided that evasive action was required in order to reverse the obvious decline of the event into a heterosexual hen do nightmare, much like the one she was now having to share a carriage with.

Deciding it was time for decisive action, she fired a text message to her only hope, Virginia.

> HELP ME. I need you to manage the nightmare my hen do is becoming, Linda Lovely has gone berserk, she's on a heterosexual rampage and is planning all manner of dire party games! Strippers, V, she mentioned bloody strippers. HELP ME!

Satisfied that she could depend on her trusty friend to reverse the nightmare, she slipped her phone back into her bag and settled back into her seat.

Without warning a high-pitched cackle broke her train of thought. "Fuckin' 'ell, pet, why did ya buy the cheap stuff? Vodka comes in all shapes and sizes, bit like ya men!"

Before she could help herself, Lottie was once again peering around the corner of the seat in front, curiosity overriding her instinct to studiously avoid any eye contact with the party of hens. Oblivious to her interest, the four were beside themselves with hysteria, as the ringleader waggled her bottle of inferior beverage at the offending member of her group. Another hen, dressed in a fuchsia pink tutu, at least one size too small with her breasts threatening to escape, wrestled with an equally offensive pink rucksack to reveal an illicit stash of alcohol which she ceremoniously plonked onto the table. The table roared with approval as they crowded round the offensive bag frantically scavenging inside to reveal the contents.

Satisfied with the additional refreshments, they ceremoniously raised their pink-tinted plastic champagne glasses chanting loudly. "Up yours, and he will be!" they called, before taking a generous slug of the lukewarm liquid.

Out of the corner of her eye, Lottie spotted the conductor reluctantly making his way towards them, and he requested their tickets sheepishly.

A unanimous roar sent him bowling backward as the sniggering brood grappled with his money belt. "You've got a big one! What ya got in there then, big boy?"

They howled with laughter as his face coloured puce with embarrassment. Muttering his excuses, he skilfully evaded the wandering hands, nodding stiffly at Lottie before he swiftly exited the carriage.

Lottie slumped miserably back into her seat. Her mind raced with the endless possibilities of her own hen do if this is what women considered to be a good night out. Checking her phone for something to do, she noticed a reply from Virginia, hitting the open button she was met with a solitary emoji, a smiley winking face.

Bugger! Clearly Virginia was not planning to be her saviour after all.

"Nearly-Weds Quiz! Fucking amazing, come on girls, let's play!" For a moment the group fell blissfully silent as they concentrated on sharing out the pack of cards that had appeared from the gaudy rucksack.

Taking on the role of hen do officiant, the slightest of the group greedily grabbed back the cards from the others. "No cheating, you fuckers!" More laughter ensued, and Lottie cringed with embarrassment.

Clearing her throat, she addressed her first question to the hen. "Right, pet, these were all asked of your Damon before we came out tonight! If ya get three right we'll let you have a quick fumble with old Geoff Big Bollocks."

The hen giggled making lewd gestures with Geoff Big Bullocks' oversized appendage while the others cackled in encouragement.

"Question one," she announced, calling them to order. "Did he say you had any sex toys you like to use together?"

Before the hen could answer, her seat companion piped up. "Aye, pet, he did, but the last time they plugged it in it made so much noise the neighbours thought they'd bought a cement mixer!"

The group fell about, clearly finding that answer more entertaining that anything the hen was likely to say. Unable to speak as spittle flew from her mouth, the hen waved her hands in protest.

Lottie pressed her fingers into her ears before more unwelcome information filtered into her brain which would, she knew, conjure up images that she would struggle to forget.

Despite pressing hard, she could still vaguely make out the chesty wheezing of the company. "Question two. Where is the weirdest place you and he have got jiggy with it?"

At the mention of sex, the group simultaneously raised their fleshy hips imitating a grotesque rhythmic grinding before the motion of the train threw them sideways, collapsing in a heap on one another's laps.

More laughter and the hen shyly volunteered an answer. "Well, we're both proud members of the mile-high club."

Winking salaciously, the others cooed with approval.

"Gotta do summat, pet, when you're on a long haul." Winking, she sat once again to a round of applause from her coven.

"Arggghh!" Lottie thought. Never again would she think of British Airways in the same way!

She could take no more, and, rummaging beneath the seat, she grasped the handles of her bags and dashed towards a carriage farther back. Catching her swift exit, the voices of the group drifted towards her as she hammered at the exit button.

"Hey, just because she did it, don't mean you can't, pet!" As the carriage door whooshed shut, the laughter erupted once again.

As she settled into her hiding place, she fought the bile that rose in her throat. The thought of enduring such an awful night as she had just witnessed was simply out of the question! Locating her phone, she dialled Mel, but it rang with no answer. She sent a desperate text.

```
Mel, mate, you're the only one that can help me.
I can't face the idea of this bloody hen do and
I have no idea how I'm going to get out of it.
You've got to help me, please!
```

Rubbing her forehead, she took several deep breaths before she was overcome with a steely determination, and logging into Facebook she boldly announced:

```
Hen do—revised arrangements. It will take place
at ours, BBQ and NO party games thank you.
```

Feeling relieved that she had finally grasped her own destiny, Lottie settled into her seat to endure the rest of the very long journey home.

The Non-Hen Do

THE FOLLOWING MORNING, secure in the knowledge that the sombreros were safely tucked under the bed, Lottie went down to greet Alice, who was already up and making coffee in the kitchen.

Smiling, Alice slid her a mug of steaming coffee across the work surface. "So, you had an eventful evening, then."

Lottie shrugged, sipping gingerly on her hot brew.

Pulling two chairs to the side of the table, she guided Lottie into the nearest of the two and held her hand firmly.

"Now, Lots, let's get this in perspective. I know you don't like being centre of attention, but your friends have really embraced the idea of this hen do and you don't want to disappoint them do you?"

Realising that Alice required a response, Lottie shrugged half-heartedly before replying. "It's easy for you to say, babe. You have *normal* friends!"

Alice chuckled, it was true that her two best friends were remarkably normal in comparison with Lottie's colourful group of misfits. Choosing not to take her up on this comparison of the attributes of her friends, she steered the conversation in a more purposeful direction.

"The thing is, Lottie, your friends are going to have a do for us, regardless of your need to micromanage every angle of it! Why not just relax and let them get on with it? How bad can it possibly be?"

Lottie looked at Alice with suspicion. It was true that she didn't like the idea of her friends having sole control concerning their pre-wedding celebrations.

"Just relax?" she repeated slowly, as if saying it out loud would make it a more accessible concept. "Just relax," Alice repeated firmly.

Handing Lottie her phone, already logged into Facebook, she had typed a post which was awaiting Lottie's approval to post:

Dear friends, after my hen do meltdown, Alice and I would like to invite you all to join us at the Rainbow Bar in Aberdeen on Saturday at nine for dancing, laughter and fun! No penis favours allowed! Thank you.

Reluctantly Lottie's index finger hovered above the send button. With a deep resigned sigh, she posted the message, and silently finished her coffee.

THE REST OF the week passed in a blur. Despite her promise to Alice that she would just relax, Lottie pursued her mission to ensure that the evening would be tasteful and blow-up doll free.

During coffee in the break room on Friday afternoon, Lottie coerced Virginia into a firm agreement that she would police the not-so-secret arrangements that Linda Lovely had thrown herself into so wholeheartedly. Virginia remained perplexed as to why Lottie had developed such a hang-up about the goings-on of a hetero hen do.

"Surely you must have had a hen do at your first wedding, Lottie?" she enquired tentatively.

Lottie scowled in response. "If you class a night in a pizza joint where I had to make a pastry willy which ended up with the chef's floury handprint emblazoned on my arse, then yes, I had a hen do," she muttered mutinously.

"Oh!" replied Virginia, for once unable to offer any assurance.

"*Oh!* Indeed!" repeated Lottie not sure how she could convey to Virginia in one short coffee break how utterly mortified she had been on that particular occasion.

Virginia smiled at the thought of Lottie making a mighty pastry erection, and a tiny chuckle escaped her.

Lottie slapped her arm. "For God's sake, V, get that Lovely woman under control. She's becoming a total Bridezilla!"

"Of course, leave it with me and I'll have a word," Virginia said solemnly

And as if summoned by their mutual telepathy, a breathless Linda appeared behind them.

Lottie clenched her teeth before turning to give her a forced smile.

"Linda, I didn't think you were due a break yet. Actually, V was just about to come and find you."

Linda's face furrowed into a frown, and Lottie couldn't help but notice that she clutched the ever-present wedding-arrangers accessory, the heart covered notebook, close to her chest.

Lottie nodded meaningfully at Virginia, who was refusing to

make eye contact with her—although Lottie didn't miss the supressed grin.

"Yes, that's right, Linda. Come and take a seat. Just a few things to go through for the hen do!"

Linda perched anxiously on the hard arm of Virginia's chair, and V patted the seat beside her.

Why did the damn woman always have to invade people's personal space? Lottie knew that she had unleashed a demon the day she had accidentally appointed Linda as her wedding planner and now she was going to be left to tactfully mop up the carnage. Lottie patted Virginia on the shoulder in a no messing around manner, and swiftly exited the canteen, for once looking forward to the mundane task of *In Memoriam* adverts.

Lottie was finishing up an entry for a lonely-hearts advert, popular in Saturday's edition, when Linda appeared at her side. Whatever Virginia had said had clearly had the desired effect as Linda radiated contentment.

Instantly warming to her, Lottie gave her a grateful smile. "I know we've put a lot on you, Linda, and it really is so sweet of you to spend your time organising our evening. I promise there's at least one sex-on-the-beach cocktail in it for you!"

Linda beamed in receipt of the praise and winked back at her before moving in for a smothering hug, which left Lottie wondering which enormous breast had been crushed against her left cheek.

Almost breathless with joy, Linda gushed forth a torrent of gratitude. "Oh, it's suuuccch a *pleasure!*" she purred. "I promise, not a willy in sight and Willy Hoopla is soo last year anyway! Tasteful is the word, I promise, T-A-S-T-E-F-U-L!" She spelled it out, as if for emphasis as she squeezed the secret notebook to her ample bosom.

However, Linda visibly shrivelled as she caught the eye of Ann who was mouthing silently at her. "Sixteen calls waiting!" She pointedly directed Linda's attention to the mounting tower of lights blinking frantically on the wall.

Alicia, who was sitting opposite Lottie gave her a concerned look. "Lottie, you do know that woman wouldn't know tasteful if she had an unlimited credit facility at Laura Ashley, don't you?"

Lottie sighed with resignation.

"What can I do, Alicia? The woman is on a mission, and Alice told me that I should relax and go with the flow."

Alicia smiled in appreciation of Alice's ever-optimistic advice. "Well, I suppose she's right. After all what could possibly be *that* bad?"

Lottie scowled in return. "What indeed?" she mumbled sarcastically before losing herself in an unusual situations vacant advert for a free-thinking individual, must be vegan.

THE DAY OF the non-hen do arrived, and Lottie applied hair dye. Determined to look her best that night, she didn't want Alice to regret combining their hen dos. After dispatching the boys to their father's house for the weekend, Lottie set about analysing the contents of her wardrobe.

A small glimmer of doubt slipped into her thoughts as she momentarily wondered whether she'd done the right thing in avoiding the purchase of a new outfit. Abandoning her task, she sat idly on the bed while the hair dye took, wondering what Alice would wear — something simple and classy she concluded glumly.

Sitting up straight, she readjusted her left breast which was trying to escape the bra she now knew to be too small. She glanced across at Alice's compact wardrobe and tentatively pulled open the firmly closed door.

An *oohh* escaped her pursued lips as she appraised the contents. So much choice! She casually fingered a delicate cotton top, black with a shimmer of silver dancing around the collar. Glancing furtively over her shoulder, half expecting Alice to appear and admonish her for her snooping, she snuck the top from its safe position in the wardrobe and tucked it neatly into the chaos of her own. Well, if she doesn't want to wear it then what would be the harm?

Lottie hurried to the bathroom realising the black slime skidding towards her chest was a reminder that her dye had gone well past its allotted cooking time of thirty minutes.

Rushing to remove the pungent gloop, she mentally put together her outfit. Casual Levis, the new Converse trainers that she'd added to her emergency credit card, and of course the now perfect top — hopefully on loan from her beloved.

Eager to put it on in the hope that Alice would agree to the loan, she dropped her towel and rummaged for a clean pair of knickers before sliding into the outfit, careful not to let it touch her still wet hair.

Pausing to admire her reflection in the full-length mirror she caught sight of her newly dyed hair. Gasping in horror, she clutched at the frazzled ginger strands which protruded provocatively from above her ears.

"No. No. *No!*" she screeched, stumbling towards the mirror. A closer view did little to soothe her angst. She had been so engrossed in snooping, that she had managed to infuse her newly cut hair with a golden ginger hue.

Slumping onto the bed, she sighed. "Why is this *such* hard work?"

"What is such hard work?" came a voice from behind the door and Alice appeared looking delightful in a red T-shirt and low-ride hipster jeans.

Lottie sighed loudly, feeling the inevitable pre-going-out meltdown approaching.

Alice smiled. "You look fabulous." She said — without conviction — Lottie thought.

Lottie responded with a steely silence as Alice collapsed on the bed beside her.

"Well, *Annie, the Musical.* We're going to have a fine old time regardless!" she stated with a sure determination.

Suddenly, she pulled Lottie roughly towards her and muttered throatily. "You haven't got time to worry about your hair, there's a pre-hen do tradition that we've only just got time to complete before we need to catch that train."

Gently caressing her lips against Lottie's, she cupped her nipple before tenderly addressing its needs.

After a welcome distraction, Lottie — feeling much more positive — hurried to apply her usual sweep of make-up and the two caught the later train to Aberdeen.

FOLLOWING A BRISK walk from the station, Lottie held her breath as she entered the Rainbow Bar. The premises were dimly lit, and she adjusted her eyes to the low light, grateful for the lack of any mirrors, which could draw attention to her hair disaster. A squeal alerted them to the presence of Linda, proudly sporting a T-shirt commanding everyone to *Keep Calm and Love a Lesbian.* Minus her notebook, she rushed them efficiently into the bosom of their waiting entourage, all of whom blew on whistles, clearly mistaking the hen do for the pride parade. Linda bustled forward officiously waving two additional T-shirts which she thrust into their unsuspecting hands. Shaking open the first of the gaudy pink T-shirts, Lottie noted the logo — *She's with me!* Alice chuckled and they both decided to embrace the gesture hastily pulling on the garments.

When Alice went to the bar under the supervision of Virginia—who smiled resignedly at Lottie and studiously avoided being within speaking distance—Lottie took a moment to take in the scene before her. Her best efforts to play down the event and the banning of all things penis had clearly led the group in a different direction, as adorning the head of each party goer was a pert pair of tits.

Alicia met her, grinning from ear to ear. "Hey, Hen, check out the titty hats! Well, you did say no to the male genitalia!"

Lottie hugged her. God love these crazy people and their complete inability to do anything by halves, she thought.

Mel approached her, clearly already having sampled the delights of the cocktail menu. Roughly sloshing a glass of something welcome into Lottie's outstretched hand, she tapped at the bottom of the glass, indicating the need for Lottie to catch up. Welcoming the warm glow associated with the frosty beverage, Lottie downed the cocktail and found herself slipping into the inevitable pink sash entitled, *Gay Hen.* Glancing over her shoulder, she briefly caught sight of Alice, guarded by Linda as her own sash was secured against her T-shirt.

Catching her eye, Alice silently mouthed, "See? Fun!" before disappearing into the dance floor area, where she had spied her decidedly normal friends.

Turning her attention back to her group, Lottie allowed herself to relax a little. It wasn't quite as bad as she'd imagined, and a tingle of anticipation of the fun of the night to come tickled its way up her spine.

SEVERAL MOJITOS LATER, Lottie found herself on the dance floor feeling more than a little relaxed and was delighted to catch sight of baby-dykes, Davina and Trina, as they ran towards her, dressed identically in black logo emblazoned T-shirts and jeans. Lottie shrieked with alcohol-fuelled delight and planted a kiss on the cheek of Trina. Hugging Davina, she came face-to-face with a disapproving Pru.

Unlike the majority of her lesbian crew, Pru was wearing a shapeless navy linen smock. Her hands were clasped anxiously towards her chest as she studiously tried to avoid bodily contact with the crowd who was surging enthusiastically towards her, to the tune of "True Blue." Just behind her, the mousy Mim gave a timid wave and Lottie smiled in return, noting the duffle bag hooked over Mim's bony shoulder.

Gratitude flooded Lottie for a second time, as she couldn't believe that Pru and Mim had come to her non-hen do! Pru being so clearly out of her comfort zone, Lottie made a mental pact to ensure that she had a good time. Mutinously, Pru muttered about sexual looseness before she was swept to the centre of the dance floor by the baby-dykes. Lost in the darkness at the centre of the group, as she allowed herself a moment to readjust her view, Lottie caught sight of Pru's giant arm waving to the beat of the music.

Alice slid her arm around Lottie's waist and spun her away from the spectacle of Pru and into a lingering kiss. Whispering in her ear something Lottie couldn't quite make out, she hooked her thumb through the belt loop of Lottie's jeans and steered her towards the ladies' room.

With the door shut, the throb of the music persisted, but both were lost in the moment as Lottie fumbled for Alice's zipper. Their lips pressed together, Lottie could taste the bitterness of Alice's indulgence, Jack Daniels. Not a Scottish tipple but definitely something they had indulged in on their earlier dates, when Jack had provided Lottie with the courage she was lacking in order to progress their relationship to a sexual level.

Giddy with the kiss and the gentle caress, Lottie felt a hot rush to her head and realised she'd accidentally activated the hand dryer which was uncomfortably hot to the back of her neck. Giggling, Alice spun her, placing her against the cool tile of the washroom. Sliding her hand into the warmest part of Lottie, Alice was breathless as Lottie cupped her chin before hungrily kissing her in return.

A sharp rapping on the door interrupted their moment. Alice paused, her hand still in the warmth of Lottie's deepest recesses and called out throatily. "Be out in a minute!"

Lottie giggled, the rush of the alcohol fuelling her own inebriation. Alice held a finger to her lips, quietening her. The rapping continued more insistently.

Sighing, Lottie readjusted her trousers and Alice hurried to straighten her T-shirt before boldly opening the door to challenge the intruder.

"*Surprise!*" shouted a chorus of voices. A woman wearing only a showgirl thong and a workman's tool belt containing a variety of lesbian paraphernalia, including a giant fake dildo and a spanking paddle, shimmied provocatively towards them.

Lottie's eyes widened in horror as the stripper, aptly named Trixie, entered the bathroom to perform what turned out to be a very sensual routine. Alice, on the other hand, fuelled by their tantalising encounter, hand on hip, appraised the sight of the nubile female with a more welcoming approach. Amused by her fiancée's lack of embarrassment, Lottie couldn't help but be enthralled as the woman sashayed around her future wife, egged on by the raucous crowd of onlookers. Alice needed no encouragement to enter into the spirit of things and was soon wielding the spanking paddle towards the waiting naked buttocks of the flexible Trixie.

Virginia pushed her way to the front to get a better look before being dragged back into the crowd by her exasperated partner, Jess. Lottie looked at Alicia who was leading the whoops of delight, as she mouthed at her. "Only fifty quid. Bargain!"

Flushed from the encounter, Alice and Lottie eventually stumbled back along the corridor giving up on the idea of an illicit encounter, for now, anyway.

As they reached the end of the corridor, Lottie caught sight of Mim secreted in a dimly lit corner surrounded by a group of scantily-clad males who were clutching what looked like ten-pound notes. Spotting Lottie, she thrust a package into the outstretched hands of the nearest male before melting into the shadows.

Alice leaned in and whispered to her. "Mim is never one to miss a business opportunity! Forget it, Lots, it's not our problem tonight." Clutching her hand, she pulled Lottie back towards the dance floor where their friends were waiting.

Lottie struggled to see any members of their group. Pushing her way through the scantily-clad men and the assortment of dykes, she finally reached the front of the crowd.

In the inner circle Lottie met with a sight that she could barely believe. Struggling to catch up with her, Alice arrived at her side and voiced the thought that was struggling to make its way out of her mind,

"Holy Shit!"

They looked at one another in disbelief and slowly Lottie's gaze returned to the sight before her. Trixie the stripper was unrecognisable, wearing the same shapeless smock that had previously done a good job of covering Pru's hefty frame.

Pru, now stripped naked with the exception of a gray hammock-like bra, which was fighting a losing battle to contain the mountain of flesh, was wobbling to the tune of Prince's "Purple Rain", her hands perched provocatively on her swaying hips. Lottie was powerless to stop her eyes wandering down the gelatinous shape towards her groin, where Pru was sporting a sparkly thong—presumably the previous property of the less than demure Trixie. Pru shimmied, her hips out of time to the music, her inner thighs rubbing furiously together working some seconds behind her buttocks which swung to curve her body.

Beside her the baby-dykes clapped in unison, their eyes sparkling with sheer delight at the spectacle Pru was providing.

Casting her eye around the inner circle, she caught sight of an anxious-looking Mim. How did that woman seem to be everywhere? A loud whoop from Mel brought her attention back to the dilemma before her.

Alice leaned in. "Spiked, Lots! Her drink has got to have been spiked!"

Galvanised into action as the reality of the situation hit her, Lottie dived forward, and grabbing a nearby rainbow flag she dived onto Prudence intent on protecting her modesty.

A groan went up from the crowd and Lottie noticed a man discretely switching off his mobile phone camera and tucking it safely back into his top pocket. Lottie did not have time to process the implications of photographic evidence as she hustled the reluctant Pru towards the foyer.

"Time to go home everyone, time to go home!"

The male scrabbled to keep up with them. "Can I get a name, love? YouTube sensation this one is, for sure!"

Pru shrieked with drug-induced delight. "The name's Pru, my dear, do have a look at my blog!"

Alice clamped her hand firmly over Pru's gaping mouth and, hastily redressing her in her smock and a coat, produced by Mim, they hustled her out of the club and headed for the station.

Suits You Sir!

A GROAN FROM under the duvet confirmed to Lottie that Alice was suffering more than she was after their eventful night out. Smiling, she recalled Alice's unexpected enthusiasm for the stripper routine and she couldn't help but think that there were some aspects of Alice that she did not always fully understand. Generally the quieter of the two, Alice appeared to have revelled in her excitement at being a hen and had wholeheartedly embraced the evening arranged by their friends.

Rolling, she reached for her phone and logged onto Facebook, where a variety of pictures had already made their way onto people's timelines with comments such as: *Top night.* Lottie was satisfied that everyone had enjoyed the evening. She jumped as the phone rang, and she quickly answered, creeping out of the bedroom to avoid waking Alice.

"Hello?" she whispered.

A high-pitched squealing pierced her eardrums, followed by snuffling, and then the sound of someone blowing their nose.

"Hello?" she asked again, struggling to identify the unexpected caller.

"Charlotte!" This was followed by a pitiful mewling sound.

"Pru?" Lottie replied.

More snuffling followed.

Finally, the caller identified herself. "Yes, it's me, Charlotte. What shall I do?"

Struggling to find a context for the conversation, Lottie waited for further qualifying information.

Finally, Pru pulled herself together and recounted her tale of woe. Alice's suspicion that her non-alcoholic drink had been spiked had been correct. This had led to a total loss of inhibition, culminating in a video of Pru's raucous activities being posted on YouTube.

Struggling to contain her amusement, Lottie attempted to placate the distraught Pru, promising that she would contact the website and have it removed.

As soon as the call ended, Lottie logged on to watch the offending video. While feeling sorry for Pru, she was glad that, for once, she wasn't the subject of internet humiliation.

After locating the clip, titled *Big Momma Gives It Large in Gay Club*, Lottie was fully awake and highly amused. She decided she wouldn't contact the help desk until Mel had time to view the clip, as a few more minutes surely wouldn't matter. Lottie abandoned her phone and headed for the kitchen, where she made some fresh coffee for Alice, intent on reviving her fiancée to begin their busy day.

THE REMOTE PART of Scotland where they had made their home had some limitations. Although gay marriage had been embraced by the citizens of Scotland, the church had some way to go to catch up with the more liberal views of the country.

Shortly after their engagement, Lottie and Alice had quietly booked a registrar from Banff for their wedding, which was to be held in Pennan Village Hall, with its spectacular beach location. The finer details, including outfits, along with the food and entertainment had yet to be decided, and that was to be the focus of what remained of their Sunday.

Determined to make the most of their child-free weekend, they had planned a full day of wedding prep. However, before they headed out on their trip, Lottie had the unfortunate task of trying to dispatch the kittens to the owners of a variety of enquiries she had received following the advert that she had placed the previous week. She sat patiently on the sofa as a steady procession of visitors came to appraise their potential new pets. In anticipation of some resistance, she had waited until Archie was with his dad, knowing he'd be furious on his return, but she felt it would be easier to face the fall-out after the event.

Taking her rehoming duties seriously, she had a few questions for the intended adopters. The whole process proved to be remarkably unproblematic with the exception of Stripe who appeared to have anticipated her evil plan, and remained missing in action for the duration of the viewings.

After the final visitors left, she had completed an unsuccessful sweep of the house but failed to locate him. With a sigh she resigned herself to being defeated, but not altogether surprised, by his deliberate intention to remain and torment her.

Putting aside her search for the elusive Stripe, she mustered Alice, reminding her that they only had three weeks to go until their big day. Their first stop was to be a visit to a local wedding dress shop. There were only two in Fraserburgh, but Lottie was determined to wear a wedding dress. Although not a fan of dresses, she had baulked in horror at the poor selection of mother-of-the-bride type female suits available on the internet.

Arriving at the *Beautiful Babe Bridal Boutique,* Lottie bustled towards the front counter while giving Alice a meaningful look, which communicated her desire for Alice to hold all negative opinions to herself. At the counter she came face-to-face with a heavily made-up and beaming shop assistant called Libby, who was eagerly awaiting her first customer of the day.

"Hi, I have an appointment to try on some dresses," she informed the youthful Barbie doll. Libby glanced past Lottie towards Alice, who stopped behind Lottie to loiter uncomfortably, hands thrust deep into her pockets.

Although she had chosen not to speak or make eye contact with the assistant, it was very evident that Alice was not embracing the idea of hours trapped in a shop full of overly-feminine taffeta gowns.

However, determined not to let Alice's lack of enthusiasm dampen this experience for her, Lottie decided that a distraction was in order. "Are there any women's suits that my partner can look at while I try on some dresses?"

Peering over Lottie's shoulder, Libby eyed Alice with curiosity. A silent moment passed as the shop assistant appraised the situation.

Lottie felt increasingly uncomfortable, recognising Alice's steely glare as a sign that she did not wish to be overly involved in the process. Looking between them suspiciously, the shop assistant had determined the status of their relationship, and her disapproval was clearly evident in her furrowed brow.

"Suits?" she questioned.

Alice remained determinedly rooted to the spot refusing to make eye contact with either of them, and a haze of anger simmered around her.

Lottie could feel disapproval in the air, which only served to increase her level of general anxiety.

Seeing her commissioned sale slipping away, however, the shop assistant revived her fake smile and pointed assertively in the direction of the stairs. "Men's suits are upstairs, love."

Lottie drew in a sharp breath and chanced a glance at Alice who looked crestfallen, and their eyes met briefly, with Lottie registering the pain of rejection etched across Alice's delicate features.

Before Alice had a chance to respond, Lottie leaned towards the startled assistant and hissed at her. "She's not a fucking man!

She's a very beautiful woman. What the fuck is wrong with you?"

The woman stuttered an incomprehensible reply, clearly at a loss as to what she had said to evoke such a venomous response.

Without waiting for an apology, Lottie grabbed Alice roughly and pulled her into an embrace. Lottie's face set with steely rage. "We are lesbians and we're getting married, whether you lot like it or not! By the way, your shop is shit!" And as if to confirm her assessment, she snatched up a turquoise taffeta off-the-shoulder number, and threw it dramatically onto the floor, before steering Alice towards the door.

Outside, Lottie leaned against the doorway, suddenly overwhelmed and shaking. She wasn't sure whether anger or upset was her primary emotion.

Alice was beaming, her previously sour mood had evaporated. "My hero! Lottie, that was amazing. Men's suits, for God's sake. What a bloody joke!"

Pleased that Alice had roused from her apathetic state, Lottie grinned coyly in response. "All in a day's work for my beautiful fiancée! Stuff this, Alice. Let's get the cake sorted and get the rest on the internet!"

Grabbing Alice's hand firmly, she headed for the bakery, determined to sort out at least one of the preparations on what was proving to be a long and exhausting list.

After an uneventful conversation with their local baker, Lottie and Alice retreated to the safety of home, and peacefully decided on a variety of items to add the finishing touches for the wedding reception.

Lottie concluded that the internet was clearly far more evolved than their local shopkeepers, and they had even found the number of a local tailor who had confirmed via e-mail that he would be more than happy to do a rushed job on a couple of matching outfits for their special day.

Satisfied with their efforts, Lottie rang to update her mum, while Alice busied herself with the Sunday roast and the smell of crisped potatoes and a slowly roasted juicy lamb joint filled their cosy living room.

Wedding Eve

THE EVE OF the wedding arrived, and Lottie opened the front door to a hyperventilating Linda Lovely, who was buried beneath a mound of rainbow bunting and two parcels, which Lottie hoped were their wedding outfits. Not waiting for an invitation Linda collapsed onto the sofa breathless and squealing with delight under the weight of the parcels.

"Well, my lovely ladies, tomorrow is the day!"

Lottie nervously returned her smile, her eyes drawn to another colourful T-shirt. Slightly too small, it hugged Linda's unforgiving curves. Peering for a closer look she noted the inevitable motto, *Marriage is about love not gender!* Meanwhile, Linda, oblivious to the names on the front of the parcels, ripped the first one open, and squealing followed as she fingered the material of the tastefully crafted, last-minute suits that had been express-mailed to them.

"Oh look! Just look. These are delicious!" she cooed, her face flushed pink.

Lottie was fairly sure that there was a blood pressure issue that she should be concerned about and, anxious to calm the Bridezilla before she had a stroke, she gently retrieved the suit and hung it on the back of the door for closer examination.

Gently fingering the cuff of the jacket, Lottie felt a surge of excitement.

"I'm getting *married* tomorrow!" she whispered to no one in particular.

Joining her from behind, Alice gently kissed the nape of her neck. "I'm getting married to my best friend tomorrow, too," she affirmed, causing Lottie to giggle.

Another knock at the door announced the arrival of an excited Pru, who immediately launched into a vivid description of her media fame since the infamous YouTube video.

Lottie, having recovered from the guilt she had felt about forgetting to contact the help desk about removing the post, couldn't help but feel amused that Pru had chosen to view her media success as something positive, ignoring any derogatory commentary that had followed on Facebook and beneath the video clip.

Breathless with excitement as she recounted the response of

her public. "I simply can't even go to Waitrose anymore for my chai tea without being accosted by the locals. I tell you, Charlotte, I've had so many hits on my website as the paps have tracked me down. It will do my business profile the world of good!"

Lottie smiled, but secretly doubted that Pru's debauched act with a not-so-famous stripper was likely to do her credibility as a therapist any good, but she chose not to challenge her on it. The woman was clearly deluded with a sense of her own importance.

Alice appeared from the utility room where she had been tending to Boots, who was still licking his wounds after his recent encounter with Alice's surgical skills, after she had finally persuaded Lottie to allow her to neuter him. Since the op, Boots had indeed seemed slightly less psychotic.

Stripe had remained in hiding until Archie had returned home from his weekend visit to his dad, whereupon he miraculously reappeared, sticking determinedly to Archie. Intuition seemed to be his friend, and he somehow seemed to know that soft-hearted Archie was his only chance of escaping rehoming. It had taken Archie some days before he was able to forgive the pair for the disappearance of his cat children, and he had belligerently carried Stripe around the house with him until Lottie had relented and agreed they could keep him.

"I really think the signs are good," Alice mumbled to Lottie as she passed, studiously avoiding eye contact with the ever-eager Linda whose eyes glistened with excitement at the thought of adding Alice to her newfound collection of gay friends.

Lottie cautiously ventured into the utility room, where Boots met her gaze and gave a meek pitiful mewl. Encouraged by his attempts to communicate with her, she tentatively reached out and Boots rose to greet her hand, vigorously rubbing against it. Lottie felt a warmth towards him and reached to stroke his underbelly. He rolled to allow her access and she squealed with delight at the apparent reformation of his character.

The front door slammed, and Lottie's mother appeared dragging behind her a suitcase that represented the essentials that she needed for her week-long stay to babysit the boys, while Lottie and Alice disappeared for a honeymoon in Venice. A short, but important, break for the pair, who had been determined to go somewhere neither had been before, and to discover it together.

THE REST OF the day seemed to pass in a blur of last-minute arrangements, and the trying-on of outfits. Family members came and went as they gathered for the wedding, and Lottie's phone chimed regularly with well-wisher messages. Linda Lovely and Virginia had been tasked with the decoration of the village hall where the ceremony and reception would take place, and the hastily constructed guest list had proved to be a successful mix of friends and family, eager to attend what was, for most, the first same-sex union they had ever experienced.

Robbie appeared in the doorway anxiously clutching the ring cushion.

"Mum, I don't know whether to put the rings on this thing now, or take them down in the box. What would happen if I lost them? You do have spares, don't you?" His face furrowed with worry.

Jumping up from the sofa, Lottie gave him a heartfelt hug.

"Keep them safe in your pocket, and put them onto the cushion when you get down there. Gran will help. It'll be fine, promise!"

His frown dissolved into a grateful smile, and clearly assured that he was capable of great responsibility, he resorted to a grunt in response before disappearing back upstairs to his man cave. Hot on his heels was his now-permanent girlfriend, Annabel, who shot her an apologetic smile.

Lottie had warmed to the girl during the past few months deciding she was a genuine and kind-hearted soul who seemed to have a very good effect on her sometimes-wayward son. She worried about the amount of time they were spending in his bedroom and Alice teased her about the number of impromptu visits she made to the said bedroom to deliver drinks and biscuits, while firmly wedging the door open as she left.

Elspeth appeared in the doorway. Lottie smiled, genuinely pleased that her mum had made the return trip to be there on their special day.

"Thanks, Mum," she said simply, her mum giving her a coy wink in reply. Elspeth had never been one for outbursts of emotion, and the fact that her mother had travelled so far was all the affirmation Lottie required that she loved her and supported her in getting married.

Breaking the moment, John, Lottie's brother, joined them in the kitchen. Lesley loitered behind him, and Lottie caught her disdainful appraisal of the wedding suits. Choosing to ignore her, Lottie rushed forward towards John, planting a kiss firmly on his bristly cheek.

"Kids, Uncle John and Auntie Lesley are here!"

Archie thundered down the stairs to greet his uncle with a round of high fives and rough-man wrestling. Robbie appeared at the bottom of the stairs shortly afterward, and the pair hugged. John had provided a much-needed male presence in the boy's lives, and Lottie was thankful that the calm and placid nature of her brother provided them with an excellent example of what she would consider to be a good man. Lesley still loitered uncomfortably in the doorway and, feeling sorry for her, Lottie moved towards her and the pair exchanged an awkward hug.

"So, Lottie, tomorrow's the big day," said Lesley, as she shuffled from foot to foot.

Smiling, Lottie responded. "Yes, I can't believe I'm getting married. It's so exciting!"

Lesley looked momentarily perplexed. "Married?" she queried. "I didn't think we were going to the church!"

Lottie's facial muscles tensed. Why did this bloody woman continue to make an issue of everything relating to her sexuality?

Taking a breath, she explained patiently. "Yes, married, Lesley. You don't have to go to church to be married. It's a civil ceremony rather than a religious one, but it means the same thing really."

Lesley frowned, but knew better than to express her confusion.

Archie appeared at her side. "Come on, Auntie Lesley. I want to show you my Lego Death Star. It took me three weeks to build it!"

As they passed, it was not lost on Lottie that Lesley rolled her eyes at John, who gave her a warning glare before turning back to talk to Elspeth. Lottie sighed. Thank God that friends outweighed family at this wedding. Hopefully, someone would educate Lesley about the new laws for gay marriage and save her the laborious task. She made a mental note to text her sister Amanda after she arrived tomorrow, and ask her to keep Lesley away from the more radical attendees, especially Pru.

Dusk settled on the small village, and the family gathered around the kitchen table with a Chinese takeaway. An easy silence ensued, interspersed with commentary on their final preparations and responsibilities.

Archie took the opportunity to hold centre stage, announcing with some gravity that he had a surprise for the pre-nuptial couple. Lottie and Alice waited patiently as he disappeared to his room, reappearing with a disgruntled Odie, who was sporting a rainbow bow tie. The group laughed raucously, more at the discomfort of Odie, than at his new attire.

Archie laughed too, announcing his delight. "A rainbow tie for the wedding. He's going to wear this when I take him into the hall."

Despite her reservations about whether it would stay that long on the wriggling creature, Lottie congratulated Archie on managing to add the finishing touch to their wedding party. Full of pride, Archie removed himself and Odie to the living room, where he proceeded to prep him on walking with decorum for their audience.

A short time later, when everyone else had gone to bed and they had finished tidying up, Alice held out her hand to Lottie.

"Bed?" she enquired.

"Bed!" Lottie agreed, although whether she would be able to sleep, was a different matter entirely.

Happy Ever After

LOTTIE AWOKE TO see a naked Alice attempting to tease up the sash window, which subsequently revealed the sounds of the seagulls, and the waves drawing in and out on the small beach below. Despite the time of year, the sun shone and Lottie could smell the salty air as the breeze filled the room. She glanced at the clock and was shocked to see that it was almost ten. They'd slept in despite her fear about not getting any sleep.

Slinging on a shirt, Alice leaned through the window to get a peek at the village hall farther down the road, and squealing with delight, she insisted Lottie join her for the view. Along the narrow street was rainbow bunting leading down towards the hall, which was just in sight from the window.

Breathing deeply, Lottie savoured the coolness of the sea air before shrieking when she saw what Alice had noticed. "Oh my God! I can't believe they've done all that! The bunting Alice, and look at the beach. It looks amazing!"

Peering against the sun, they drank in the view of the scene that had been lovingly created by their friends the evening before, after they both had been banished inside the cottage with Lottie's family. On the lower beach, just outside the hall, their friends had erected an open-sided gazebo which was decorated with lanterns, and entwined around the supporting posts were strings of red and cream roses.

Alice's grin was immense and her eyes sparkled with excitement as she clutched Lottie's hand, and they leaned farther through the window to drink in the view.

The chatter from below indicated that their wedding party was up and breakfasting, so they threw on their casuals before rushing downstairs to enjoy every moment of their long-anticipated day. The delicious smell of warming pastries greeted them, and a cheer went up from the waiting party as they appeared.

Lottie's mum was busying herself preparing endless cups of tea, as Robbie and Archie, oblivious to their arrival quietly bickered about who was assuming responsibility for Odie. Linda Lovely hovered anxiously at the edge of the scene, clutching an official clipboard which she periodically glanced at as she muttered last-minute amendments to nobody in particular. In the living room hovered Lottie's sister, Amanda, who was anxiously signalling for Lottie to join her. Reminded that she needed to ask Amanda to monitor Lesley's interactions with the guests, she hurried to greet her.

Weaving her way past those assembled in the kitchen, she smiled warmly at Linda. In the hallway, Amanda immediately set upon Lottie, babbling about Tony and his new look. Looking over her shoulder into the sitting room, Lottie took a sharp intake of breath. In the chair sat Tony, Amanda's husband — at least she thought that's who she was looking at.

Her brother-in-law grinned back at her. The first thing that struck Lottie was the flamboyant floral shirt and rainbow bow tie, not unlike the one that Odie was currently sporting. Working her way up, she noted that the previously traditional Christian boy haircut had been transformed into a perfectly coiffured gay-man's hair, styled to within an inch of its life. She also noticed that he had a diamond stud in his right ear and, wait...was that a tattoo peeking above the collar of his shirt?

Hastily, Amanda tugged her to one side whispering furiously. "I think he's having a mid-life crisis, Lots. I mean he looks...well I don't know — "

Lottie laughed. "Gay?" she offered.

Amanda snorted with derision. "Goodness me. Of course not! Just a little over-dressed. It is a gay wedding, after all!"

Lottie experienced an unsettling flashback of the dating profile picture of Tony that she had not yet discussed with her sister. While she had felt it was somewhat cowardly not to face that conversation, after discussing it with Alice, she had decided that it wasn't her place to meddle in her sister's relationship. She knew that it was unlikely her sister would accept or understand the issues with Tony, and she didn't want to hurt her unnecessarily. In the end, Alice had been the voice of reason assuring her that if, as Lottie suspected, Tony was on the turn, sooner or later the unfortunate news would reach the ears of Amanda and Lottie's job should be to support her sister at that time.

Nevertheless, a sliver of guilt gnawed away at her, and keen to placate her overwrought sister and avoid any pre-wedding drama she patted her sister's arm reassuringly.

"Yes, just dressed for the occasion, I expect," she reassured her, before reminding her to keep an eye on Lesley, and moving quickly on to greet Virginia and Jess.

After a warm embrace from Jess, Virginia pulled her to one

side. "Okay, mate?" she looked Lottie square in the eyes.

Lottie smiled in return, always glad of the seemingly never-ending support of her lovely friend.

"Yes!" she replied emphatically. "You know, V, I really thought I'd be terrified, but all I feel is excited! I feel like everything is bright and clear and I'm absolutely certain that this is the best decision I'm ever going to make in my life!"

Virginia beamed at her. "Proud of you, mate, so proud!"

They were interrupted by Linda Lovely, who was tapping furiously on her clipboard. Efficiently, she dispatched all but the wedding party from the cottage and a temporary peace descended. Mel loitered nervously in the doorway, clutching what Lottie could only assume was her wedding speech. Taking a moment away from the furious instructions of Linda, she passed Mel a glass of prosecco.

"Dutch courage?" she offered.

Mel snatched the glass and greedily drained the contents. "Bloody hell, Lottie. I'm terrified! I didn't realise there would be so many people, and that bloody Pru has been Facebook-messaging me all morning saying she's looking forward to a catch up. I swear, Lottie, if that woman makes a pass at me I'm on the next plane to Australia!"

Lottie chuckled at the image of Pru chasing Mel around their wedding reception. Linda appeared at her side, snorting nervously and reminded Lottie that it was time to get ready. She dispatched Mel through the front door before scooping up Odie to straighten the bow tie he was frantically trying to dislodge.

Finding one another in the bedroom, Lottie and Alice chuckled about Tony's choice of clothing. Alice shook her head with bemusement, "Let's hope he doesn't get frisky with the waiters today! The sooner it's just the two of us the better!"

Lottie couldn't agree more.

Much as she was looking forward to the ceremony, they had deliberately kept the reception small, and planned on finishing at five so that they could spend some time with the boys before they headed to the airport.

"*Venice!*" they both squealed. The beauty and romance of Venice would undoubtedly provide them with a sanctuary for a few days, to recover from the events leading up to the wedding and the day itself.

Without any sense of urgency, they showered and readied themselves, marvelling at the different cuts of their suits, which, despite some similarities gave them each a definitive look, thus avoiding Lottie's horror of looking like two identical butch dykes.

Tenderly, Alice tucked Lottie's short hair behind her ears, as Lottie peered anxiously into the mirror for a closer look.

"Not bad," she muttered, before turning her attention to Alice, who was struggling to attach her corsage.

Alice's face assumed a serious look and she gently clasped Lottie's hands, stilling them.

Lottie felt vaguely anxious, but Alice kissed the furrow of her brow. "Silly worry wart! It's nothing bad."

Reaching into the inner pocket of her jacket, she pulled out a single sheet of paper.

"I know we'd agreed to do the traditional vows, but I changed my mind and I've written something I'd like to say."

Without saying any more, she handed the paper to Lottie, who sank onto the bed and turned her attention to the crisp sheet of paper:

```
Lottie,
you are my best friend and my soulmate,
I'll always be by your side,
Let    nothing    come    between    us,    neither
stubbornness nor pride.
I promise that my love for you will grow
stronger every day,
And all that I ask of you in return is that you
love me in the same way.
```

Lottie's eyes filled with tears.

Alice smiled.

"Perfect." Lottie stated quietly.

Satisfied, Alice returned the paper to the safety of her top pocket and took Lottie's hand to go downstairs for the final time as singletons.

Turning the corner of the stairs, a silent ensemble greeted them. Lottie's heart swelled with pride as she saw her boys dressed in their morning suits, both with a single red rose tucked neatly into their buttonholes. Robbie patted his pocket confidently, indicating the safety of the rings and Archie furiously tugged on the lead of the hyperactive Odie who was clearly anticipating a long romp on the beach.

Clasping Alice's hand, Lottie smiled.

"Ready everyone?"

"*Ready!*" the group answered in unison.

Turning to Alice, Lottie smiled. "Ready?" she asked.

Alice beamed in response. "Ready for the rest of my life to be married to you. Let's go!"

LOTTIE AND Alice took their time making the short walk down to the village hall, drinking in the unseasonally warm day and the clear skies. The seagulls serenaded them with a chorus of good cheer as they circled above and the sea lapped the harbour as they made their way down to the lower beach and the village hall.

The haunting Celtic tune played by their bagpiper drifted to greet them. Lottie's heart lurched as the sound of the pipes always evoked in her a deep emotion and reinforced that she was Scottish to the core. The wedding party hurried ahead of them to enter the hall before the doors were closed, encasing the guests in the hall, giving Lottie time to adjust her suit jacket as the bagpiper adjusted his pipes and played "The Flower of Scotland". The girls loitered a moment to enjoy the music.

Alice pulled Lottie towards her, kissing her tenderly on the cheek. "You're my flower of Scotland," she whispered huskily.

Lottie returned the kiss and whispered against Alice's lips. "Soon to be wives!"

The bagpiper finished, and inside the hall Lottie could hear Ellie Goulding's, "How Long Will I Love You", and the resounding "ooos" and "ahhs" from their captive audience.

Archie and Robbie reappeared, Archie's eyes bright with excitement.

"Mum, am I walking with you?" he asked, suddenly older in his demeanour.

Nodding, Lottie casually linked arms with him as Robbie more formally offered the crook of his arm to Alice, who took it, giving him a squeeze.

They started to move forward. The baby-dykes surged past them muttering apologetically about a flat tyre, although judging by their dishevelled appearances Lottie wryly concluded they had made a detour into the sand dunes.

Linda Lovely lowered her clipboard and smiled broadly at the couple, her eyes shining bright with tears. She signalled officially for the doors of the hall to be opened, and the music flooded the terrace.

As Lottie and Alice walked into the entrance hall, the room collectively turned to take them in.

Lottie felt overwhelmed with the love in the room as she

tried to take in the happy faces that turned to greet them. Alice gasped as she noticed her parents in the front row. Lottie only recognised them from photographs, and she knew that Alice did not have a close relationship with them. When they were planning the wedding Lottie had tried, without success, to get Alice to contact her parents and Alice had agreed she would once the wedding was finished, but she did not want to risk the chance that her parents would not be receptive to her wedding plans and spoil anything. Alice's dad, a portly man and her mother an older and equally beautiful version of Alice gave her an anxious smile. Alice's eyes filled with tears and she waved at them, momentarily losing her cool as she turned to Lottie. "My mum and dad!"

Lottie turned and beamed in return.

With great ceremony, Archie led Lottie along the makeshift aisle scattered with more red rose petals. Lottie smiled at as many people as she could, noting that most of their guests were filming on their mobile phones. Lottie's attention was caught by Ann, who was frantically pointing to the alpha male beside her, shirt unbuttoned to the waist with a mat of curly dark hair exploding from the crevice.

"My new man!" she mouthed. Lottie smiled politely and made a mental note not to get trapped by Ann later on.

Feeling suddenly scared, she glanced behind and managed to catch Alice's eye, full of love. Overcome with emotion, a tear slid gently down her cheek.

Turning once again, she felt confident as she walked, taking in the stunning floral displays of cream and red. As she reached the top, she beamed at Mel, who stood fidgeting anxiously in her role as the best woman.

Alice arrived at her side and they both stood before the celebrant. Robbie ceremoniously handed the arm of Alice to Lottie, who gratefully received it.

The ceremony was later referred to by their friends as the best wedding they had ever attended. Lottie and Alice both affirmed their vows before the kindly celebrant, to cheers from the gathered crowd. Linda had abandoned her clipboard and taken on the responsibility for instigating appropriate cheers throughout the ceremony, which helped to lighten the atmosphere. Lottie noted that Linda seemed to have grown in confidence and come into her own, as a result of this wedding planner experience.

They exchanged their rings, then Lottie and Alice joined hands and raised them to the room to whoops and cheers from the onlookers. Robbie wiped a few tears, anxious to maintain his manly façade, but Archie cried unashamedly, still having childhood on his side.

LATER THAT AFTERNOON, the couple once again took centre stage as they chose to overlook the obvious mistake in the announcement by the hired help, as Mr. and Mrs. Grant-Blair.

Mel anxiously prepared to deliver her best woman speech. Lottie had been intrigued to know what she had managed to include, after she had given her a list of subjects to avoid, including any mention of Lottie's façade as a heterosexual.

Pru appeared at Lottie's side. "Lovely ceremony, dear, you do make a spectacularly handsome couple, I must say. Now you've resolved your issues, I think you'll do very well, sweetie."

Lottie gave her a forced smile and bit her lip, refraining from voicing the thoughts she had about Pru and her almost certain narcissistic personality disorder.

Grabbing a nearby chair, Pru inappropriately placed herself on the top table, presumably to get a prime view of the object of her desire, Mel.

Clearing her throat Mel eyed the crowd nervously, choosing to ignore the sudden arrival of Pru.

"To all of Lottie's and Alice's friends and family—Hello! I was surprised when Lottie asked me to do a speech. I don't know if she mistook me for somebody that was good at this sort of thing."

There was a ripple of laughter around the room. Mel took a deep breath and continued.

"I have a sneaking suspicion she wanted me to say a quick hello, do some comedy dancing, and my walking down to the cellar routine. I'm not going to do those things. What I want to say instead is how special marriage is. It's the ultimate declaration of love. A good marriage gives you confidence and a strength that's greater the sum of its parts.

It's a wonderful thing.

In this country we have only just caught up with the idea that everybody should be able to do it. Everybody that is lucky enough to find that special someone they want to spend the rest of their lives with.

And love. What is love? Someone once said that it is passion, respect, and admiration. If you have two, you have enough. If you have all three you don't have to die to go to heaven. Lottie and Alice are definitely in heaven."

Spontaneous applause erupted from the assembled guests at this point, and Lottie and Alice exchanged a loving look.

"I want to say a bit more about love. When I asked Alice for her thoughts in preparation for this speech, she sent me this text — 'How do I feel about Lottie? She is sweet, sensitive, loving and generous. She always gives one hundred percent to me, her family and her job. I quite simply love and adore her. She is funny, super intelligent, and stubbornly proud. She is fiercely protective of those she loves.'"

There was a heartfelt round of applause at this point, before Mel continued.

"Some of you may not know Lottie all that well so here is my quick guide to Lottie Grant-Blair.
She is an absolute delight. She is fantastic at what she does. She inspires me, and she is the life and soul of her workplace
She has that rare quality of someone who can walk into a room and change the atmosphere — she can make everyone feel ten-times better than they did before.
She loves the fact that Alice has a sausage dog, and is the best vet in the Highlands.
I have not known Alice for long, but I do know that she has made Lottie the happiest woman in the world. She is the final piece that makes the Grant-Blair family complete.
Ladies and gentlemen, I give you Lottie and Alice!"

Lottie wiped the tears away, noting Mel's pride that she had pulled it off without a hitch. She blew her a thankful kiss.
Pru was on her feet, tears streaming down her face as she roared, emphatically turning to the crowd demanding they clap louder. Mel quickly found her seat next to the safety of Elspeth.
Alice rose and tapped her glass, and the room quietened. Lottie was surprised that Alice had decided to make an impromptu speech. Although confident in her professional capacity, Alice usually shied away from public attention.
"Hi everybody," she began, and as Lottie noted a tremor in

Alice's voice, her heart filled with love. She was aware of the huge applause and much whooping, spurring Alice on.

"I didn't plan to make a big speech, but I couldn't let this day pass without saying a few words.

"Firstly, and most importantly, thank you all from the bottom of our hearts for coming today. When I look around this room, I see the most important people in our lives, and this day would not have been the same without each and every one of you. Thank you to Robbie and Archie for the part they have played in this special day. With every day that passes, I have the privilege of being part of this incredible family and getting to know these two young men as they grow older. I never imagined that I would be part of a family with children, in fact I would say that I never considered that children would ever play a part in my life."

There were more cheers and laughter from the crowd at this point, and Alice reached down to clasp Lottie's hand as she noted a solitary tear trickling down Lottie's cheek.

"I am so incredibly proud to be able to call myself part of this family. When I met Lottie, I was instantly entranced. She was bubbly, funny and kind, and I know that I have met my soulmate. I admire who she is and the incredibly brave path she has chosen in her life."

She turned to face Lottie

"And now you're my wife, I intend to spend the rest of my life making you happy. Finally, I know there is one important person who is missing today. Lottie's dad. I don't want to make her cry, but I did want to acknowledge that his presence here today is missed. Therefore, I would like to ask you all to join me in one final toast."

The room quietened and took on a more sombre tone as all the guests stood with their glasses raised.

"To Graham, missed by your family today but not forgotten. Your memory is treasured. Cheers!"

The crowd returned their glasses to the tables, before an impromptu round of applause broke out and the guests turned to chatter amongst themselves.

Turning to face Alice, Lottie saw the love she felt reflected back at her in equal measure. "Babe, that was beautiful. Thank you."

Lottie choked back her tears and Alice tenderly kissed the back of her hand.

"Can we have a moment outside?" Alice asked, and without waiting for a reply she gently pulled Lottie away from the crowd and out onto the relative calm of the beach, under the shelter of the gazebo.

The lanterns twinkled as the sun lowered in the sky. Turning towards the open sea, they both breathed in deeply, trying to take in the magic of the early evening.

Lottie turned to face Alice. "I'm so proud of you, Alice. Look at this day, it's been absolutely perfect!"

Alice smiled. "I can't quite take it all in. It seems to have gone so fast, but I feel like I'll remember every detail forever!"

Lottie kissed her deeply, their tongues entwined in a lingering embrace.

Pulling away and slightly breathless, Alice paused, and Lottie noted a trace of worry etched across her features,

"Babe, I have one more thing that I've been meaning to talk to you about," Alice ventured.

Raising an eyebrow quizzically, Lottie waited.

"I know it's our wedding day, and it feels like this is the beginning of our journey. I meant what I said about feeling privileged to be part of your family, I really never thought that having kids was important. But, Lottie, after living with you and the boys I can't imagine life without their boisterous chaos!"

Lottie chuckled. "I know. I was worried when you first moved in, about how it would work out. I mean, you went from a seaside sanctuary to an episode of *Dawson's Creek!*"

Alice giggled. "I can't deny it was a bit of a shock, babe! But you know those boys are really just an extension of you. I see you in Robbie's stubborn pride, and in Archie's sensitive and caring nature. It has made me rethink what family is and what it means to me."

Lottie raised an eyebrow. "I feel like this is building up to something."

Alice smiled tremulously.

Clearing her throat, she spoke quietly. "So, Mrs. Grant-Blair, bit of a curveball I suppose, but I wondered if you'd just consider something for me?"

Waiting patiently, Lottie nodded for her to continue.

"I want a baby. I want to have our baby."

Lottie froze.

"Seriously?" she questioned.

Surprisingly, she did not feel as shocked as she thought she might have been at such an unexpected request.

Alice leaned forward and breathed against her lips. "Really," she affirmed.

"I didn't expect this. I mean how? Who? Oh God. I'm forty!"

Alice placed a finger gently against her lips. "Let's not talk about it again for a while, I just wanted to plant the idea and let it sit. See how we both feel."

Lottie smiled and lay her cheek against Alice's. "Well, you certainly know how to take a girl by surprise!" she said, chuckling.

Alice fell silent as they turned towards the sea to watch the sun set meet the horizon.

The noise of merriment from the hall drifted out into the evening, and Lottie was left with her internal dialogue. A baby, I mean, God. A baby!

Their peace was shattered by the dulcet tones of Pru, accompanied by Mim who seemed to be struggling with a cat carrier with a single *Congratulations* balloon trailing pitifully behind it.

As Pru loomed into view she bellowed out. "Darlings, darlings. Oh, have I got a gift for you!"

Alice turned, taking in the cat carrier, and shot a glance at Lottie who was frozen to the spot.

Ignoring the silence, Pru snatched the carrier from Mim and thrust it forcefully in the direction of Lottie, who had no choice but to reluctantly accept it.

Alice raised an eyebrow at Pru, and seemed about to decline the gift, but Pru launched into a rambled explanation.

"Darlings, now I know that you didn't want gifts, but I simply couldn't bear to leave such a fabulous occasion unmarked. Sappho has been pining terribly for your moggy. She's clearly distraught and refusing to eat! Since you have a vet in the family now, it would only seem right that I put aside my own feelings to ensure she is back where she belongs!"

Signalling the finality of the arrangement, she firmly crossed her arms, ignoring Alice, and challenging Lottie with a stern gaze.

Lottie wilted under the intense scrutiny. "Thank you", she said, simultaneously being elbowed sharply in the ribs by Alice.

"Right. That's settled then!" Pru boomed enthusiastically.

Behind her, Mim gave an apologetic shrug before ambling in the direction of the hall, no doubt to seek solace in the free alcohol.

Pru followed in hot pursuit, and Lottie heard her smug comment. "See, Miriam dear, I told you it was the best solution. I can't have the responsibility of an animal when I have such pressing business demands."

As if in agreement, Lottie heard Sappho purring with pleasure from deep inside the carrier. Turning to Alice she grinned. "Our family seems to have grown already. Maybe it's a sign."

Alice chuckled. "It certainly looks like it."

Pulling Lottie closer, Alice kissed her lovingly.

About the Author

Originally from Edinburgh in Scotland, Lisa Young now lives near Sherwood Forest in England. She has always been a keen observer of human nature and personal relationships. With a witty and mischievous sense of humour, Lisa generally sees the funny side of life. She loves to travel and can often be found planning her next adventure. She also likes nothing more than jumping into her campervan with her wife, sons and miniature dachshund and heading off on a road trip.

After a traditional marriage and two children, Lisa entered her thirties as a more authentic version of herself. She accepted her sexuality as a lesbian and embarked upon a new and exciting stage of her life which eventually led her to meet her wife, Lucy. As an out and proud lesbian, she met many extraordinary people and experienced both the joys and the complexities of dating as a single gay parent. Her experiences led her to create a hilarious fictional world of lesbian dating in her first novel *Out and Proud*. While her human characters are fictional, the names of the animal characters have been changed to protect their identities. Lisa was inspired to write her first book by her wife who told her, 'You've lived it, now you just need to write it,' and Lisa is currently writing the sequel novel.

OTHER REGAL CREST PUBLICATIONS

Brenda Adcock	Soiled Dove	978-1-935053-35-4
Brenda Adcock	The Sea Hawk	978-1-935053-10-1
Brenda Adcock	The Other Mrs. Champion	978-1-935053-46-0
Brenda Adcock	Picking Up the Pieces	978-1-61929-120-1
Brenda Adcock	The Game of Denial	978-1-61929-130-0
Brenda Adcock	In the Midnight Hour	978-1-61929-188-1
Brenda Adcock	Untouchable	978-1-61929-210-9
Brenda Adcock	The Heart of the Mountain	978-1-61929-330-4
Brenda Adcock	Gift of the Redeemer	978-1-61929-360-1
Brenda Adcock	Unresolved Conflicts	978-1-61929-374-8
K. Aten	The Fletcher	978-1-61929-356-4
K. Aten	Rules of the Road	978-1-61919-366-3
K. Aten	The Archer	978-1-61929-370-0
K. Aten	Waking the Dreamer	978-1-61929-382-3
Georgia Beers	Thy Neighbor's Wife	1-932300-15-5
Georgia Beers	Turning the Page	978-1-932300-71-0
Lynnette Beers	Just Beyond the Shining River	978-1-61929-352-6
Sharon G. Clark	A Majestic Affair	978-1-61929-177-5
Tonie Chacon	Struck! A Titanic Love Story	978-1-61929-226-0
Cooper and Novan	Madam President	978-1-61929-316-8
Cooper and Novan	First Lady	978-1-61929-318-2
Sky Croft	Amazonia	978-1-61929-067-9
Sky Croft	Amazonia: An Impossible Choice	978-1-61929-179-9
Sky Croft	Mountain Rescue: The Ascent	978-1-61929-099-0
Sky Croft	Mountain Rescue: On the Edge	978-1-61929-205-5
Cronin and Foster	Blue Collar Lesbian Erotica	978-1-935053-01-9
Cronin and Foster	Women in Uniform	978-1-935053-31-6
Cronin and Foster	Women in Sports	978-1-61929-278-9
Jane DiLucchio	A Change of Heart	978-1-61929-324-3
Anna Furtado	The Heart's Desire	978-1-935053-81-1
Anna Furtado	The Heart's Strength	978-1-935053-82-8
Anna Furtado	The Heart's Longing	978-1-935053-83-5
Anna Furtado	Tremble and Burn	978-1-61929-354-0
Melissa Good	Eye of the Storm	1-932300-13-9
Melissa Good	Hurricane Watch	978-1-935053-00-2
Melissa Good	Moving Target	978-1-61929-150-8
Melissa Good	Red Sky At Morning	978-1-932300-80-2
Melissa Good	Storm Surge: Book One	978-1-935053-28-6
Melissa Good	Storm Surge: Book Two	978-1-935053-39-2
Melissa Good	Stormy Waters	978-1-61929-082-2
Melissa Good	Thicker Than Water	1-932300-24-4
Melissa Good	Terrors of the High Seas	1-932300-45-7
Melissa Good	Tropical Storm	978-1-932300-60-4
Melissa Good	Tropical Convergence	978-1-935053-18-7
Melissa Good	Winds of Change Book One	978-1-61929-194-2
Melissa Good	Winds of Change Book Two	978-1-61929-232-1

Melissa Good	Southern Stars	978-1-61929-348-9
Jeanine Hoffman	Lights & Sirens	978-1-61929-115-7
Jeanine Hoffman	Strength in Numbers	978-1-61929-109-6
Jeanine Hoffman	Back Swing	978-1-61929-137-9
Jennifer Jackson	It's Elementary	978-1-61929-085-3
Jennifer Jackson	It's Elementary, Too	978-1-61929-217-8
Jennifer Jackson	Memory Hunters	978-1-61929-294-9
K. E. Lane	And, Playing the Role of Herself	978-1-932300-72-7
Kate McLachlan	Christmas Crush	978-1-61929-195-9
Kate McLachlan	Hearts, Dead and Alive	978-1-61929-017-4
Kate McLachlan	Murder and the Hurdy Gurdy Girl	978-1-61929-125-6
Kate McLachlan	Rescue At Inspiration Point	978-1-61929-005-1
Kate McLachlan	Return Of An Impetuous Pilot	978-1-61929-152-2
Kate McLachlan	Rip Van Dyke	978-1-935053-29-3
Kate McLachlan	Ten Little Lesbians	978-1-61929-236-9
Kate McLachlan	Alias Mrs. Jones	978-1-61929-282-6
Lynne Norris	One Promise	978-1-932300-92-5
Lynne Norris	Sanctuary	978-1-61929-248-2
Lynne Norris	The Light of Day	978-1-61929-338-0
Paula Offutt	Butch Girls Can Fix Anything	978-1-932300-74-1
Kelly Sinclair	Getting Back	978-1-61929-242-0
Kelly Sinclair	Accidental Rebels	978-1-61929-260-4
Schramm and Dunne	Love Is In the Air	978-1-61929-362-8
Surtees and Dunne	True Colours	978-1-61929-021-1
Surtees and Dunne	Many Roads to Travel	978-1-61929-022-8
Rae Theodore	Leaving Normal: Adventures in Gender	
		978-1-61929-320-5
Rae Theodore	My Mother Says Drums Are for Boys: True	
	Stories for Gender Rebels	978-1-61929-378-6
Barbara Valletto	Pulse Points	978-1-61929-254-3
Barbara Valletto	Everlong	978-1-61929-266-6
Barbara Valletto	Limbo	978-1-61929-358-8
Barbara Valletto	Diver Blues	978-1-61929-384-7

Be sure to check out our other imprints,
Blue Beacon Books, Mystic Books, Quest Books,
Silver Dragon Books, Troubadour Books,
and Young Adult Books.

VISIT US ONLINE AT
www.regalcrest.biz

At the Regal Crest Website You'll Find

- The latest news about forthcoming titles and new releases

- Our complete backlist of romance, mystery, thriller and adventure titles

- Information about your favorite authors

- Media tearsheets to print and take with you when you shop

Regal Crest print titles are available from all progressive booksellers including numerous sources online. Our distributors are Bella Distribution and Ingram.

CPSIA information can be obtained
at www.ICGtesting.com
Printed in the USA
BVHW040919151118
533210BV00013B/291/P

9 781619 293922